PACIFIC BEAT has received outstanding reviews in the United States:

'A gifted writer, Parker draws characters so real you could touch them. His sense of atmosphere, setting and mood is hypnotic and his plotting is superb. The narrative hurtles along . . . smart and compelling.'
L.A. Style

'After a gripping opening, the story bolts off, hair in flames. Parker is a powerhouse writer.'
New York Times Book Review

'Parker is not the first to explore the peculiar psyche of Orange County, he is simply the best. He evokes the ambiance of this trashed but still beguiling Eden with both affection and sorrow . . . constantly surprising, richly rewarding.'
San Diego Union

'Parker's mystery adventures are vastly more sophisticated than traditional whodunits; he provides in-depth looks at human nature and the everyday miseries that plague people. A masterful job . . . one of the best writers around.'
Sacramento Bee

'Grief so well described that it sets up disturbing resonances in the reader is rare in most crime fiction; in *Pacific Beat* the grief felt by a murdered woman's husband and brother is almost palpable.'
Los Angeles Times

'Beautifully plotted . . . so filled with events and emotions that the reader is left in a swirl of plot so complex as to be mind-boggling. Yet in reality it is the simple and basic story of love and betrayal and death.'
Indianapolis News

'*Pacific Beat* keeps Parker ahead of the pack of contemporary crime writers – and right on the heels of MacDonald.'
Orlando Sentinel

'Generous detail, heartfelt characterisation and impressive language – an outstanding, memorable and magnetic work. This exciting, multi-dimensional plot should grab even the most demanding reader.'
Library Journal

Also by T. Jefferson Parker

Laguna Heat
Little Saigon

PACIFIC BEAT

T. Jefferson Parker

HarperCollins*Publishers*

This novel is a work of fiction. All of the events, characters, names, and places depicted in this novel are entirely fictitious or are used fictitiously. No representation that any statement made in this novel is true or that any incident in this novel actually occurred is intended or should be inferred by the reader.

HarperCollins*Publishers*
77–85 Fulham Palace Road
Hammersmith, London W6 8JB

Published by HarperCollins*Publishers* 1992

9 8 7 6 5 4 3 2 1

First published in the USA by
St Martin's Press 1991

A catalogue record for this book is
available from the British Library

ISBN 0 00 223869 1
ISBN 0 00 223961 2 (Pbk)

Photoset in Linotron Trump Medieval by
Falcon Typographic Art Ltd., Edinburgh & London
Printed in Great Britain by
HarperCollinsManufacturing Glasgow

To Catherine Anne
With all the love that heaven will allow

ACKNOWLEDGEMENTS

I would like to thank the following people for their generosity and their help. This book couldn't have been written without them . . . Gail and Betty Bagley, Tom Bagley and Vilma Dunn, Sioux Herlihy, Peggy Darnell, Dorothy Glover, Lynn Cooper, Jeanne Sandifer, Julie Sedevic and Dana Blakemore. Special thanks, again, to Donald A. Stanwood.

1

The main thing here is the Pacific. In the long run, the land and the people on it amount to only that. In the short run, a lot can happen.

The Franciscans ruined the Indians, the Mexicans bounced the Spanish, the Anglos booted the Mexicans and named the town Newport Beach. Dredgers deepened the harbor, and the people lived off the sea. There was a commercial fleet, a good cannery, and men and women to work them. They were sturdy, independent people, uneducated but not stupid. Then the tuna disappeared, the nets rotted, and the fishermen succumbed to drink and lassitude. Two wars came and went. Tourists descended, John Wayne moved in, and property values went off the charts. Now there are more Porsches in Newport Beach than in the fatherland, and more cosmetic surgeons than in Beverly Hills. It is everything that Southern California is, in italics. There are 66,453 people here, and as in any other town, most of them are good.

Jim Weir grew up on the Balboa Peninsula of Newport, in a bayfront home that, in one form or another, had been in his family for ninety years. The first Weir male to make it to the new world had fallen off the *Mayflower* at what is now Provincetown and drowned. Descendants of his pregnant wife later came west during the gold rush. Jim's great grandfather worked with the Newport Harbor tuna fleet and died in comfort, if such a thing is really possible. His grandfather fished the waters when they were still abundant. Success had gone skinny by the time it trickled down to Jim's mother, Virginia, who, with an air of stubborn efficiency, ran the café at Poon's Locker. Weir's father – Poon himself – died ten years ago of a stroke. His older brother was shot in the heart by a sniper at Nhuan Duc. His sister, Ann, operated a little day-care center two blocks from the home that the Weir kids grew up in, and slung cocktails at night.

1

Jim was a salvager by trade, a diver. He had worked ten years for the Sheriff's Department: one at the jail, two on the streets, five with the Harbor Patrol, two with Investigations. Then he quit to do local salvage work, and find an English pirate ship called the *Black Pearl*, which was sunk by Spanish warships off Mexico in 1781. So far as Jim knew, he hadn't even come close. He had lived most of his adult life aboard *Lady Luck*, in slip B-420 of Newport Harbor.

From his father, he had inherited a deep brow and dark hair, a humorless face, a frame that carried weight without announcing it, and an outward calm that could be mistaken for dullness. He had his mother's pale blue eyes, big hands that had always looked ten years older than the rest of him, and a temper that lived uneasily beneath the calm. He was reserved in the odd way that born Californians can be – a kind of knowing reticence that amuses Easterners, and has little to do with beach beer commercials or the common parodies of cool. To be cool is to be ready. Jim was thirty-seven, strongly built, never married, and occasionally employed. In the ways that matter, he was still looking for his first big score.

He stood on the ferry as it slid across the bay from Balboa Island to the peninsula. Lights wobbled on the black water and the bay rang with the pinging lanyards of sailboats. A May breeze came straight onshore, pressing its cool hands against Jim's face. The Newport Beach police helicopter droned above, then banked away, trolling for crime by spotlight. Jim looked across to the houses clustered on the other side and almost smiled to himself: the old neighborhood. Awful good, he thought, to be home again.

Weir had spent the last six months in Mexico diving for the *Black Pearl*, and his last thirty-four days as a special guest of Mexican police in Zihuatanejo, Mexico. He had scratched the cell wall with his thumbnail each dawn when the roosters outside woke him in the stinking darkness. Jim had lost fifteen pounds, two thousand in cash, some very good dive and salvage gear, and his home, *Lady Luck*. The charges were drug-related, false, and, for reasons that Weir was not told – dropped. The *policia* clerks released him with his wrist-watch, the clothes he was arrested in, and bus fare to San Diego. To the Zihuat cops, zero tolerance was a venerable tradition.

The ferry groaned, slowed, then settled against the ramp. Jim stepped off, his legs unsteady: Beans and bad water take their toll on muscle tone. He moved down the sidewalk and wound through the tourists, breathing deeply the salt air, the fumes of cars idling in the ferry line, the smell of beached seaweed. The Fun Zone cast pink lights onto the sidewalk and someone screamed from atop the Ferris wheel. The tourist girls looked pretty as ever. Were they all getting younger or what? He listened to the sound of his boots on the cement, felt the jarring of his weakened legs with each step, and again he almost smiled: Mom will be at the Whale's Tale, having a glass of wine, and Ann will be there serving it to her. Raymond's probably on patrol, working the night shift. Home, man, *home*.

He was right. His sister, clad in a dumb sailorette outfit that showed off her legs, was standing beside a window booth, yakking it up with Virginia. His mother was huddled in the pale yellow windbreaker that matched her hair. Ann had her back to him. Jim walked up quickly, wrapped his hands around her waist, buried his nose in her pretty blond waves, and snorted like a hog. She elbowed him sharply, turned, and threw her arms around him. He hugged her and looked down at Virginia, who sipped her wine and offered him a rare smile.

Ann spun him around and pushed him into Virginia's booth. 'Two months and not even a postcard? Did you find it? Why didn't you write? God, you're skinny. You all right? Does Ray know you're back?'

'Yes, no, jail, yes, no. Boy, I'm hungry.'

'Jail? My God, Jim.' Ann felt his forehead like the mother she would never be. Jim could see the three dark spots in the blue of her left eye, which he had always thought of as islands in a sea. She was two years older than he, but looked five younger.

Virginia placed one of her big gnarled hands against Jim's ribs. 'What happened, son?'

'First can I have some food?'

Ann's jaw dropped in mock affront. 'I spend six months worried sick about you, and you want *some food*. Here, eat this.' She dangled the navy blue napkin in front of him.

'Frisky tonight, aren't we?'

'Oh gee, am I really? Then let me fulfill my life's work and locate you *some food*.'

'You look good, Annie. Your skin is rosy.' Jim noted without

3

comment that she had lost some weight, that the fret lines between her eyes had deepened.

'It's just the Mop 'n Glow I use. But thank you ever so much. Excuse me, irritation calls from the corner four-top.'

Jim ate some bread and clam chowder, more bread, a swordfish dinner, cheesecake for dessert, and drank most of a liter of house red. He recounted his Mexican misadventure in installment, whenever Ann could come by the table. He left out the beating he received on the night he was arrested, because it had hurt too much then to talk about now. Weir long ago had discovered that words make some things worse, that silence confuses the devil, that dumping misfortunes on loved ones is akin to using the pot without shutting the bathroom door first. To Jim, the true heartbreak in Mexico was not in failing to find the *Black Pearl*, or the beating, or the rank sickness in the Zihuat jail, but the fact that his boat – his *home*, and everything on it – was gone. Only now, back stateside, did the loss seem actual. Until now, fear had hogged the emotional road, but Jim was starting to just get pissed. Fuentes was right: A gringo in Mexico is euthanasia. By the time Jim finished his story, he had avenged himself in a dozen half-plotted, violent imaginings, but he was so tired he could hardly keep his eyes open.

'You need some sleep, son. Stay with me in the big house. Your bed's still made up and I ran your truck once a week like you wanted. Becky would like a call.'

Ann bent over and hugged him. 'You stay right where you are until my surprise gets here. And guess what? Ray and I are having a party on Friday. Be nice and I'll invite you.'

Jim asked about the occasion, but Ann was vague and coy, as she often was. A cup of coffee later, Jim looked up to see Ann's husband, his oldest and finest friend, coming toward the table. Newport Beach Police Lieutenant Raymond Cruz walked across the floor with his usual graceful slowness, his gun, stick, radio, and assorted equipment neat around his waist, as systems-heavy as any cop on the beat. Jim felt a surge of happiness for which he wasn't prepared. Ray smiled widely, threw open his arms – left hand low and right hand high – and caught Jim in a bear hug. Weir could feel the strength in Ray's hands as they slapped against his back. It was an embrace of thankfulness. Raymond broke away first, and regarded Weir. 'You look busted,' he said.

4

Jim nodded. 'You were right. They took it all.'

A darkness passed through his eyes: Raymond's first instinct would be to return there and take it all right back. He kissed Ann, bent down to peck Virginia, then turned again to Jim with a look of incomprehension. 'How many times did I try to tell you?'

'Too many. I don't want to hear it again.'

'You don't want to listen, you don't want to hear. My friend, dumb as a stick. How can it be so goddamned good to see you?' For a moment he stood there, reading Weir's face with his bright, clear stare. Then he looked at Ann, who simply, for a moment, beamed.

'Tell him,' she said.

'You tell him, Ann.'

She stepped forward, reached down, and placed Jim's hand against her stomach. 'How's Uncle Jim sound?'

For just a moment, Weir was speechless. Ann could not conceive. Armies of doctors had told her that, and twenty years of marriage had proven them right. And here, suddenly, what could not happen had happened – the simplicity of miracle showed plainly on her face.

Then she was racing along with the details, using words that once had curdled her with jealousy: seven months to term, a December baby, sick this morning, got to get the house ready, still haven't picked names.

Jim saw that she already had entered that world where no man could follow, the parallel universe of motherhood. He had never seen such a thorough joy in her. Even Virginia had a sort of giddiness. Raymond's posture had changed – head a little higher, neck a little straighter – and there was a new roundness to his trim Latin features.

'Annie,' said Jim, 'you'll be the best – uh – second best mom in the world. It was worth getting skunked in Mexico to come home and hear this.' For as long as he could remember in his adult life, Ann had wanted a child. She had kept the faith.

Ann smiled freshly, as if realizing all over again the blessing that had befallen her. She caught herself, reigned in her joy and proposed breakfast in the morning at the big house, where Jim could 'tell us what really happened' down in Mexico. This decided, Raymond kissed her lightly again, then checked his watch. 'Back to the mean streets of Newport,' he said. 'Glad you're here, Jim. See you tomorrow.'

He walked across the floor with a final turn back, a smile that was aimed at Jim but strayed quickly to his wife.

Five minutes later, Weir felt the exhaustion hit him. He downed another half glass of wine and stood. 'Don't anybody wake me up before noon.'

He labored wearily down the stairs and into the moist peninsula darkness. The fog was gathering low in the sky and the spring chill still clung to his bones.

But Weir didn't go to his mother's house. Instead, he walked right past it, along the little bayfront homes and alleys that had comprised the geography of his youth. The neighborhood was quiet. Squat cottages conferred beneath overgrown hedges of oleander and bougainvillea; tiny yards sat with an air of preferred neglect. Half a block down was Poon's Locker – the family business that had brought in enough money for Poon and Virginia to raise three kids. It sat solid and darkened, and Jim stopped for a moment to look through one of the double O's of the neon sign that had hung in the window since 1963. He could see in bare outline the chairs and tables of the coffee shop, the postcard rack by the door – Wet Your Line at Poon's Balboa! – the trophy fish hanging on the walls, the counter and cash register. With a little effort, he could have conjured Jake, running through the café on some obsessive mission, followed by the curses of Poon.

Half a block farther, he came to Ann's Kids, the day-care center run by his sister – in lieu of her own family, Jim had long ago concluded. Would she close it by December? It was a small old house with a six-foot chain-link fence around the grounds to keep the tykes in. The yard was concrete and Jim could see the trikes and building blocks stowed neatly beside the front door. It had the look of something soon to become history.

Then past Ann and Raymond's house – a dinky two-bedroom bungalow with a wooden porch. The veranda was strung over with fishnetting festooned with starfish, abalone shells, sand dollars and cork floats. From the sidewalk, the objects seemed to hang midair, unattached. Ann, he thought, the collector of small treasures.

6

He walked another three houses down, to where a tall hedge of white oleander formed a wall around the lot behind it. He stood for a minute, took a deep breath, and found the gate hidden in the foliage. He reached over the top, muted the brass bell with his hand, then slowly pushed it open. He stopped just inside. The yard was small and neatly kept, the air touched with the sweetness of the orange tree that blossomed near its center. Spring annuals nodded lazily from their pots. The walkway stones were even and swept. A cottage sat at the far end, lit from within. The wooden door was open but the screen door was shut and Jim could see her sitting in the dining room, back to him, her head tilting against her left hand, and her right holding a pencil to a notepad. Her light brown curls caught the light when she turned and looked in his direction, but the rest of her face remained in shadow. Jim became the oleander. He watched her stand and walk across the living room toward him, a pretty, full-bodied woman in a green silk robe. She stood at the screen door, hands on her hips, looking out. Weir's desire was to step forward and say something, but he had no idea what it should be, and his legs refused to entertain the notion. From deep inside he breathed a sigh of relief, a sigh that he had not been able to muster for the six months he was in Mexico, a sigh that he had yearned for on each of the thirty-four days he had spent imagining this woman from his cell in the Zihuat jail. Then the porch light went out and the wooden door closed, and Jim could hear the dead bolt sliding into place.

The first call woke him up at one in the morning. Jim lay in his old room, tossing in the penumbra of half sleep, sweating and clammy, his stomach in knots. For a moment, he couldn't figure out where he was. It was Ray.

'Jim, you and Ann catching up?'

'No.'

'You leave before she got off?'

'Yeah. Ten or so. What's wrong?'

'She's not home. She's always home when I get here. I went by the restaurant again and they said she left at ten-thirty — half an hour early. She's not here. So I thought —'

'Maybe she's at the Locker, maybe she took a walk,' grumbled Jim, his stomach in revolt. Raymond was always worried too much about something. He seemed to need it.

'A two-hour walk around the peninsula in that outfit they make her wear? The fog's in, too. I'll try the Locker.'

'I don't know, Ray.' What Weir did know is that the first time Becky Flynn had not come home to him, she was out with another man. She had actually gone on, after the breakup, to marry this third party, but Weir could never figure out whether that was a consolation or not. Jim said nothing, silently cursing himself for projecting his own romantic disappointments onto his sister and friend.

But there was a moment of silence when he sensed that Raymond was doing it, too. 'Well, she's never done this before.'

'Try the Locker, Ray.' Jim had always thought Raymond tried to keep too tight a leash on things, Annie included. It was typically cop, and understandable.

'Sorry. Get some sleep.'

'Night, Ray.'

Raymond called back an hour later, at 2:05 A.M. 'Jim, she's still not here. Not at the Locker, either. Her car's gone. You sure she's not with Virginia or something?'

Weir had been dreaming of his Zihuatanejo jail cell. He was so deep into it, he could smell the rotting walls, feel the roaches scratching across his feet. 'Lemme check downstairs.'

Ann's old room was empty. So was the living room, the den, Jake's old room. Virginia slept heavily in the master, a rectangle of soft light from the streetlamp lying upon the floor. For a brief moment, he thought back to the old days, when Jake and his father were alive and the house always seemed so busy and disheveled and stuffed with life.

He even looked in the garage, but all he saw were his pickup truck, Virginia's old VW, her collection of clutter. His stomach rumbled as he walked back upstairs to his room. 'No. Not here.'

'It's after two, Jim.'

'You call patrol?'

'Yes, nothing. I might cruise myself.'

'Just stay by the phone. She knows where you are, Ray; she'll call.'

'I got a bad feeling.'

The same feeling lapped at Weir, then retreated. 'Don't feed it. She'll be back.'

'Sorry.'

Weir couldn't sleep. At 3:25, the phone rang again. 'Still not here, Jim.'

'I'll be over in five minutes.'

Jim dressed in the darkness and went downstairs. His mother was sitting in her favorite living room chair, both arms extended along the rests, her back straight, head erect. She looked like Lincoln. She asked Jim what was wrong and Weir told her Ann wasn't home yet.

'Call the Whale's Tale and the Locker,' she said.

'Ray did.'

'Try Sherry, from the restaurant.'

'She'd call if she was with a girlfriend.'

'Then call the watch commander.'

'He did that, too.'

Virginia was quiet a moment. 'I don't like this. It's something your father would have done. Annie got more of Poon than you or Jake did, so if I taught her one thing, it was how to take care of herself.'

'That doesn't make her home, Mom.'

'Go ahead. I'll try Becky's.'

Jim closed the door quietly behind him and walked north along the bayfront. He was passing Ann's Kids when he saw that the door was cracked open. Weir stopped and looked at his watch: it was 3:37 A.M., Tuesday, May 16. He tried the gate, which was locked, then climbed the fence and landed heavily on the other side. The chain link chimed briefly, then settled. Six steps to the door, boot heels on concrete, no lights on. He poked the door with his finger and it swung easily on quiet hinges.

Weir stepped into the house and flipped on a light. This was the playroom, with clean hardwood floors and all manner of toys – plastic buckets and shovels, dolls and dollhouses, big blocks with letters on them – arranged along one wall. A rocking horse waited on its springs, frozen in gallop. A low case filled with picture books stood along another wall. There was a trash basket filled with tops, yo-yos and jump ropes, and a larger one that contained those big red balls that smell of rubber and ping beautifully when you bounce them.

The second room was for quiet time and videos. The kitchen was clean. Jim nudged open the door to Ann's office with his toe: desk, three folding chairs, a typewriter, telephone, answering machine.

9

An empty flower vase, half-filled with water, sat beside the phone. He smelled it – the water was fresh.

Looking out a window to the backyard, he saw the dark outlines of a playhouse, a rabbit cage, a sandbox.

He switched off the lights, locked the front door, and pulled it shut behind him. Climbing back over the fence, he wondered why the door had been left open and why there was a flower vase on Ann's desk half-filled with clean water, but no flowers.

Four houses down the sidewalk, he went through a wrought-iron gate, up a short walkway, then onto a wooden deck that gave humidly beneath his feet. Ray opened the door before he knocked.

'The preschool door was open, Ray.'

'I know. I went there first, looked around, left it the way it was. Did you lock it?'

Jim nodded.

Raymond looked at him sharply. His forehead was shiny with sweat and the hair around his ears looked damp. 'I hope you didn't contaminate it.'

Jim understood now just how panicked Raymond really was. 'It's not a crime scene.'

'Something's wrong. I can feel it. When you're married for twenty years and something's wrong, you know.'

Jim stood in the living room while Ray poured coffee. The house was a small two-bedroom, with low ceilings and knotty pine walls that seemed dark as walnut. They'd been renting it for ten years, and it was a step up from their old apartment. They both wanted to stay in the neighborhood, and rent wasn't cheap anymore. The second room was the study, where Raymond labored over his books. Jim could see in the dim lamplight thick volumes stacked on a table, a legal pad lying beside them, a dozen pencil tops emerging from a green coffee can. Ray had been going to law school part-time since Jim had quit the Sheriff's, two years back. He had told Weir that compared to studying law, the streets were a vacation – he was more comfortable with crooks than books. To Jim, Ann and Ray seemed like a lot of other people from the neighborhood: blue-collar, hardworking, and not much to show for it. Ray's JD was his ticket on the upward express. Virginia paid the tuition.

Weir understood Raymond's struggle to break out – his own ticket was in his hand. The fact that he had quit a detective's job

10

to hunt treasure was something that everyone in the neighborhood seemed to approve, but Weir had always sensed a bit of contempt mixed with it, the insinuation – trailing along just behind the good wishes – that he had sold out. In one sense, he knew that he had, but it wasn't the money he wanted, it was the liberty. No more cops, no time clocks, no oppressive county bureaucrats, no endless hours waiting in courthouse halls to put away the same people for the same dreary, vicious, stupid crimes. There had to be more than that.

Raymond understood. Raymond always had, although this was the least of what bound Weir to him. Deeper than this yearning for something more were layers of friendship that had endured nearly thirty years, trust that only time can build, years of competition and loyalty, years of honest confession and minor deceit, years of being boys together and men apart, years of Ann as the shared hypotenuse of their lives. Jim had long understood – with awe – that if Raymond had to, he would offer his life for him. Weir had first attributed it to the partnership in a job that can get people killed; later, to something sacrificial in the very blood that coursed through Raymond Cruz's veins. Finally, he had seen it for what it was: a simple product of love. Weir believed that if the moment came to offer the same gift, he would be able to give it in return, knowing, too, that it is not a question that can be answered ahead of time.

The phone rang in the kitchen. Jim studied Ray's face as he picked it up. Raymond stared at Weir and didn't say a word until he put the handset back down. He drew a deep breath. 'They found Ann.'

2

Fog powdered the windows of Raymond's car as he drove down Pacific Coast Highway toward the bridge. The pavement shone and tiny specks of moisture arced in the headlights. The Mississippi paddleboat *Reuben E. Lee* sat at dock, strings of lights sketching its profile against the black water of the bay. A halogen-baked construction site pressed the traffic into one lane.

Raymond did not say a word. Jim glanced at him several times, noting the clammy face, moist, unblinking eyes. Jim had seen enough expressions like that to recognize it as the mask of tragedy. A coolness spread into his palms.

Raymond turned onto Dover, took Westcliff to Westwind to Morning Star Lane. The Back Bay, Jim thought: nobody out of their million-dollar homes this late, a habitat solely for drunks and fishermen. The estuary was a shallow incursion of the sea running a mile inland between two bluffs that lay roughly a mile apart. The brackish flats had once been tended to produce salt. This minor utility had been abandoned decades ago, leaving the Back Bay to joggers, nervous seabirds, fish running in and out with the tide, and people like Virginia battling developers over the future of it all. For Weir, it had always been a place of strangeness – neither sea nor land, neither saltwater nor fresh, neither liquid nor solid, neither beautiful nor ugly.

'Okay, Ray. What's going on?'

Raymond turned to him and his eyes said it all. Jim could smell Ann's hair, feel her elbow going into his side just – he checked his watch – six hours ago. In his mind, a sense of unreality began blurring the edges of his thoughts. The hardest thing for him to do when he'd learned about Jake was to keep his mind clear. It was a feeling he hated more than any other, strong and incessant, a heroin of the soul. The fog coiled, struck, blew past.

Two squad cars were already parked at the dead end of Morning

Star Lane. The lights of one flashed obscenely. The door of the other was open and an officer sat half in, half out, talking on the radio. Jim looked up to the big houses, saw an upstairs window yellow with light, saw the perfect silhouettes – Mr and Mrs Citizen, good people, frightened, side by side – staring out.

The officer in the car stood quickly when he saw Raymond, replaced the handset, then led them down a narrow trail in the embankment. The ice plant on either side of the path glistened; the water of the bay wavered to shore in rapid black ripples; the fog slid by in patches that burst upward and vanished with each gust of breeze.

'She's over here,' said the officer gently.

They walked fifty yards east, across the weedy, sandy patch that fronted the inlet. Jim felt the damp soil giving under his boots, the slip and slide of *rosea* and fescue. Far ahead, two more shapes moved slowly behind two triangles of light. Weir's stomach squeezed something vile into his throat.

The officer leading them – his name was Bristol – moved to the shoreline, and stopped a few yards short of the water. His light beam ran the length of a dark green blanket covering a body on the ground. Nothing had been roped off yet. 'Fisherman brought her to shore – called us at three-fifty. He told us what he knew and we cut him loose. I recognized her. I called as soon as I could, sir.'

Jim and Raymond stepped toward the blanket together, knelt down, and, each taking a corner, lifted it away. Ann's face was pale and peaceful, her blond hair falling back into the damp earth. Her eyes were dull and seemed focused on something very large, right in front of her. She was wearing a short red skirt that clung heavily to her legs, a long-sleeved white blouse, and one espadrille – on the left foot – that matched the skirt. Her arms lay comfortably at her sides, palms up, fingers gently curled. Her legs were slightly apart, toes pointing off in almost opposite directions. A bouquet of purple roses was stuffed down the waist of her skirt, stems lost inside, drowned blossoms sagging in heavy unison against her ribs. From beneath the hem protruded another stem, and Jim could tell from its angle where the blossom was lodged. Her white blouse was soaked in pale red, and stuck closely to her body. There were so many thin angular cuts in it that Jim's breath caught in his throat and he tipped buttfirst onto the ground and closed his eyes.

This was not Ann. Ann was never meant to be a thing lying on the

13

earth. He could hear the water lapping at the beach, and Raymond's quick, shallow breathing. When he opened his eyes again, Ray was on his knees, cradling Ann's head in his arms, his cheek against hers, rocking her slowly and in silence. Jim saw the rose blossoms jiggling against her breast. Officer Bristol loitered deferentially in the background. The distant flashlight beams still worked patiently toward him. From Raymond now came the low, haunted sounds of agony. He looked up once at Jim, his face little more than shadow and tears.

Weir slid his hand under Ann's curled fingers and held on to her for dear life.

Jim stood with Officer Bristol, ten yards away from Ann and Raymond. He could not remember the specifics of how he got there. 'Tell me what you know,' he said in a voice he hardly heard.

Bristol droned away as if on a long-distance line – got a call from Dispatch at ten 'til four. Local fisherman saw her floating fifty yards off. He was out with his wife and son for the day, trying to make the isthmus at Catalina by sunup. He used a gaff to get her in to shore, then he motored over to the bridge, walked to the pay phone at the Mobil station, and called us. Took a statement, but the guy's wife got sick a couple of times, so we let them go. What he knows is what we know. We haven't tried the neighborhood yet. No disturbance calls.

Bristol looked toward Raymond and Ann. 'I'm awful sorry, Mr Weir.'

'Did the gaff do any of this?' *I have to ask these things, Annie.*

'He said he snagged her cuff, brought her alongside his boat easy as he could. No.'

'Was she facedown?' *It's important we know, Annie.*

'Yes, sir. He tried to move her as little as possible.'

'You guys touch her?' *They shouldn't have touched you, sweet sister.*

'I checked her artery, then put on the blanket.'

'What about the other shoe?' *You don't mind, do you, Ann?*

'We're looking, sir. I know you were a Sheriff's investigator a while back, working the harbor here. How fast would a body float this time of day?'

Weir listened to his own answer: depends where it went in . . .

14

close to shore, with an ebb like this, two hundred feet an hour
. . . farther out, faster. *They killed her. Someone killed my sister,
Ann. Close your eyes, wipe it away like a dream. You are still in
Mexico. You are hallucinating with fever. Begin this night again.*

'Would she come to shore if she was dumped out far?'

'Not this soon.'

'So we should be looking east of here for the crime scene?'

Weir listened for his answer, but his body simply walked off
and stood closer to Ann. She looked so desecrated, so invaded,
so unquestionably without life.

'Sir . . . if he killed her out here, it's not likely he'd take her up
bay to put her in, is it?'

'Shut the fuck up.'

Dwight Innelman and Roger Deak, two NBPD crime-scene inves-
tigators, emerged from the fog ten minutes later. Innelman was
a tall, lanky man of fifty whom Weir knew from the Sheriff's
Department years ago. Deak was short and thick, and looked about
twenty-two at most. He had a burr haircut and carried a heavy case
in each hand. They prodded Raymond away from Ann and went to
work with cameras and video.

Jim stood beside his brother-in-law down by the shore. Raymond
shook violently, and in the first faint light of morning Jim could
see that his face was white. His breath came fast, sputtering on
the inhale. Jim knew the signs.

'Let's go back to the car and sit down, Ray.'

'I'll stay here.'

'We're going back to the car.'

Raymond made it three steps before his knees buckled and he
crumpled down and sat in the dirt with his legs out like an infant.
His face was ice. Jim got a blanket from Bristol and told him to
call the paramedics. Raymond was slipping into shock by the time
Weir got back to him. All he could do was lay him out, cover him,
and try to talk him through it.

Jim told him about Zihuatanejo, the dreamy blue water and white
sand, about languid descents to eighty feet, the first perilous giggles
of rapture of the deep, about the dives that didn't yield even a shred
of the *Black Pearl*, the setup with the drugs, his days in jail. Weir
felt himself slipping away to Mexico, because being here was a hell
he never knew existed on earth, until now.

Raymond's teeth chattered and his body twitched intermittently,

15

as if electrified. His eyes were wide and unblinking. Jim talked on, a port of words in this storm, gazing all the while across the beach toward Ann and the strobe flashes that blipped her pale body in and out of focus like some cheap disco gimmick. For a moment, Weir had the sensation of standing alone on the bow of a ship, steering a course from the blackness of one shore to the blackness of another. *I promise you, Ann, in the name of this moment, that I will find him.* It was the most dismal commitment of his life, and Weir knew it.

By the time the medics finally got there and took Raymond away, the fog had battled the sunlight to a gray standoff. Jim sat on the beach with his arms crossed over his knees and watched Ann Cruz, age thirty-nine, borne upon a stretcher by two men she had never met, one red shoe peeking from beneath the blanket, heading for the first of several checkpoints she would need to pass before crossing the last border into her grave.

Back at Raymond's car, he got the tire iron out of the trunk, then walked a hundred yards down the beach and found something vertical. It started out as a NO DIVING sign, but when Jim was too tired and his hands too blistered and bloody to hit it anymore, it was basically just scrap metal and splintered wood. He screamed his curses to the yawning sky, aiming straight for the face of God. He screamed things that actually scared him.

Then he went back to Raymond's car and threw the iron in. He walked to the coroner's van. 'I'm riding with her,' he said.

The driver said sure.

3

Raymond was already in the chief's office when Weir walked in at two in the afternoon, three days later. The chief's secretary shut the door behind him. Raymond, unshaven and still pale as the walls, looked up to Jim and said nothing.

Sitting slightly off to the side of the big metal desk was a man that Weir had never seen before. His legs were crossed primly, his back erect, his dark straight hair gelled away from his forehead to reveal a sharp widow's peak. His nose was a larger version of the peak: abrupt, pointed, assertive. His suit was proudly European. He looked at Jim through rimless round spectacles, then stood.

Brian Dennison, the interim Newport Beach police chief, stood, too, offered Jim his hand and said, 'I'm sorry. I'm so deeply sorry, Jim.'

Jim had hardly slept or eaten; he had not, in fact, truly done anything since seeing Ann's still body on the dark earth of the bay. He had simply gone through motions: answering questions from a series of cops, bumming a ride back to Ray's car, telling Virginia what had happened, holding her rigid body close in a long embrace that he wished would impart comfort but he knew didn't. It was impossible to get away from himself. He could not adjust to this stark new order of things.

The big house had served as a fulcrum for family sorrow in the days following. Virginia's brother had stopped by for an afternoon and spent two nights; Poon's sister had done likewise; a large contingent of Cruzes had materialized and spent their nights in sleeping bags strewn about the Eight Peso Cantina – Raymond's parents' bar – which they had closed for mourning. Funeral arrangements were made, pending the autopsy. The house filled with floral arrangements and the individual scents of family, which for Weir formed an invisible, suffocating cage. Just as he was about to break – break into what, he wasn't sure – Virginia mobilized and threw

17

everyone out, gathered up most of the flowers and tossed them into the dumpster behind Poon's Locker, then retreated into the grim efficiency that was her nature. Jim spent some long hours with her, just sitting in the living room, wordless passages of time unfolding with a paralyzing slowness. Virginia would seem ready to speak, then change her mind and descend again into herself to do private battle with her demons. Weir had executed his responsibilities with what dispatch he could muster. In his moments alone, often as he lay in bed and waited for sleep to release him, he shed tears that did less to reduce the mass of his grief than to reveal fresh exposures. At these times, he felt as if his body had been turned inside out, and that every nerve and organ was exposed to the abrasions of the air, the bed, the terrible rawness of a world without comfort. Twice, Raymond had begged Jim to take him down into the sea, and twice they had suited up at Diver's Cove, lumbered through the shorebreak, and floated out to the rocks, where they finally descended into a world of silence and oblivious sea creatures that somehow helped to underscore the breadth of life that, with or without Ann, would go on.

'Thanks,' was all Jim said to Brian Dennison.

Dennison was a barrel-chested man with a strangely animated face and an attempted sense of decorum. He'd put on some weight since Jim had last seen him. He introduced Widow's Peak – Lt Mike Paris. Paris was Community Relations officer, a job, Weir knew, only for the lame or the administration-bound. Paris nodded and shook Jim's hand with the intimacy of welcoming someone to a secret, exclusive club. 'You have the sympathies of this department.'

Weir sat down next to Raymond and looked at him again, a glance from one private hell to another.

Dennison strolled behind his desk, sat down, looked at each of the three men before him, then stood and went to the window. He cradled an elbow on his chest, resting his chin in the upraised hand, then turned to Jim. 'We've got . . .' he said, but didn't finish the sentence. He exhaled audibly, then looked out the window again, regrouping.

Jim occasionally had run across Brian Dennison during his ten years with the Sheriff's, mostly at parties and law-enforcement symposia. He was a smoothly aggressive type, who could bang heads on the street and kiss ass at the station with equal aplomb. He had always seemed to Weir to be the archetypal Newport

18

Beach cop. Dennison was popular among the movers and shakers because his department patrolled their neighborhoods with a visible ferocity. The everyday folk believed that Chief Dennison – like his predecessor – was arrogant and heavy-handed, and there was a long list of brutality and harassment suits to support their view. Most of the trouble happened on the peninsula – Jim's neighborhood – where the blue-collar people blow off steam and the tourists can behave like swine.

Dennison's official title was Interim Police Chief because the former chief had died suddenly of a heart attack seven months ago – a few weeks before Jim left for Mexico. Weir had followed the stories in the papers: Dennison was moved up from captain on a temporary basis, awaiting a final decision by the city council. But with the mayor's seat up for grabs in next month's election, the appointment of a new chief had been postponed when Dennison – suddenly and without the usual rumor and speculation – announced his candidacy for mayor.

Watching with concern as this unfolded in the papers, Weir was impressed with Dennison's sense of running to daylight. He had gone from obscurity to interim chief virtually overnight, then parlayed the momentum into his political debut – all with a smoothness that made the transition look natural. Weir had seen a huge blowup of Dennison's face on the back of a transit district bus on the way to the station, and in some indescribable way, it looked perfect there.

Weir noted a large GROW, DON'T SLOW! poster on the chief's wall, and easily figured why a cop/mayor would throw in with the land developers: bigger tax base, fatter budgets, expanded power. Likely, they were financing his campaign.

This was Virginia's latest cause, he thought, Proposition A – another slow-growth measure that she and like-minded citizens had shoehorned onto the coming June ballot. Jim wondered whether Ann's death would bring Virginia's activism to a halt. For a moment, he could see her face when he told her.

He tried to rally his thoughts back into the room. He needed a handle. His gaze fell on the MAYOR BRIAN DENNISON poster and for a moment he was held by the big black pupils of the eyes. Apply yourself, he thought: Remain present.

He tried to picture Dennison's opponent, attorney Becky Flynn, a local beauty who'd grown up in the same neighborhood that Jim had. Jim had followed her career, mostly in the papers, since quitting the Sheriff's two years ago to find the *Black Pearl*. That was when he had quit Becky, too, and she him. Her occasional calls since then had the tone of discovery motions. He imagined her without effort now, standing in a green robe in the porch light of her bungalow. Becky had been, to date, the love of Jim Weir's life.

The interim chief looked briefly at his GROW, DON'T SLOW! poster. Dennison's lively eyebrows always seemed to be compensating for the calm of his pale, unhurried eyes. They arched up now in a blend of concern and helplessness. 'Jim, we've got a . . . a very uh, interesting situation here. I've talked with Mike and Raymond about it, and we agreed to give something a try. Something that we've, uh, never tried before. Never *had* to try before . . .'

Weir waited, noting how hard Dennison was trying to talk like a politician.

'Jim, we have a witness.'

Weir's sense of abstraction was replaced by a pristine clarity. He straightened in his chair.

'Kind of. His name is Malachi Ruff. Ring a bell?'

'One of the bay bums.'

'That's right. Mackie was sleeping down in Galaxy Park that night – a couple hundred yards east of where we found . . . Ann.'

'What did he see?'

Dennison walked slowly to the coffee machine. 'Some of this, Jim?'

'What did he see?'

Dennison stirred in some creamer with a red plastic stick, laying out Malachi Ruff's story. Ruff was sleeping and he was drunk. Mackie, of course, is always drunk unless he's in the tank. He woke up when he heard a woman scream. He looked over the bushes he was in, couldn't see anything because of the fog. Mackie figured he was dreaming. He lay back down. Then he heard footsteps down by the water – that was about a hundred feet away – so he got up from the bushes again and looked. The footsteps were of someone running, running steadily, like a jogger might. He still couldn't see very well because of the fog, but he got a glimpse of a man running toward the street. Then he heard a car door open and shut. The engine started, and a second later – says Mackie – a car rolls down Galaxy, going toward Pacific Coast Highway.

Jim watched Dennison sip his coffee, look at Paris, then go back

20

to his desk. He straightened something in front of him and looked at Paris again.

'Mackie said it was a cop car,' said the chief. 'One of ours — white, four-door, emblem on the side.'

Raymond stared at something on his thumbnail. Weir saw that Dennison's thick, heavy face had reddened. Paris sat immobile, knees crossed.

Not a good plank in a new mayor's platform, Weir concluded. He said nothing.

Dennison sat down and looked at Raymond. Jim saw that some transfer had been made. Raymond spoke next, his voice soft, with little inflection. 'You know and we know that Mackie Ruff is about an unreliable a witness as we could find. But for right now, he's what we have. We can't function as a department if a Newport Beach cop on patrol three nights ago killed Ann. We think Mackie got it wrong. But nobody here takes a statement like his lightly, even if it's from a drunk.'

Mike Paris collected a glance from Dennison, uncrossed his legs, and looked at Weir. 'At the same time,' said Paris, 'we're kind of stuck, Jim. We don't want a word of this out, and we don't want Internal Affairs on it unless we've got more than a drunk's word. The press, the suspicion – morale would go to hell. If one of our men did it, then we'll take him down. Until then, we don't want the press or the public or anybody else speculating. It's my job to keep things going smoothly on the outside, *and* on the inside. Our going-in position is that Mackie Ruff is full of shit, and we don't want to turn this place upside down if we can help it.'

Raymond stood up and went to the window. 'We could use someone on the outside, someone who knows the ropes, can work with evidence, and has some halfway plausible reason to be hanging around, checking facts. I thought of you.'

'And I think it's a good suggestion,' said Dennison. 'You've got the tools, two years with the Sheriff dicks, and you can ask questions about the death of your sister without drawing too much suspicion.'

The death of your sister. The words struck Jim oddly, as if Ann had gone from flesh and blood to a case number in less than a heartbeat. The fact of the matter was that she had. Something cold stirred inside him, then sat up alertly on its haunches and

21

waited. 'I can't get much that would stand in court,' he said. 'Not as a civvy, I can't.'

'If you find anything that will get us *near* a courtroom, this department will be all over it,' said Paris.

'That's the whole issue,' said Dennison. 'The second you find something wrong, we take over. You'd walk point for a few days — that's all.'

Weir looked at Raymond, slouching against the window.

'We need you, Jim,' he said.

Weir said nothing. If a Newport cop had killed Ann, Weir knew he'd have a war on his hands. If not, he would still make a lot of trouble for himself, fast. But when it came right down to it, there was really no choice. 'I'm on,' he said.

Dennison nodded, staring at Jim with his placid gray eyes. 'There are three things we need to get clear on before you start. One, not a word from you to anyone about who you're looking at, what you're looking for. If rumors start, we'll leave you hanging in the wind. Two, we'll pay you a hundred an hour under the table — no records, no IRS, nobody knows you're on the roll. Three . . . Cruz, you want to cover this?'

Raymond sat down next to Jim again and leaned forward in his chair. 'It isn't lost on me or Brian that we're just as much suspects in this case as any other cop on the force. We expect you to be looking at us. We suggest you start with the chief and me, since we're the ones you'll be reporting to and —'

'We don't suggest it,' said Paris, more to Dennison than Jim. 'We demand it.'

'We demand it,' echoed the chief. 'We've got to start clean, Jim. Clean . . . from the top down. When you're satisfied that it wasn't me driving Mackie Ruff's cop car that night, and it wasn't Raymond, then I'm your contact here in the department. In my absence, report to Mike here. Until then, we don't know you. I've talked with Ken Robbins at the Crime Lab. He'll be available to you for all the forensics backup you'll need. That's Robbins, personally. His people won't know what you're doing. Of course, my men are investigating the murder while we sit here. Innelman and Deak. I personally woke up Dwight's wife when I called that morning, and he was sawing logs beside her. He drives an unmarked, anyway. So Dwight's clean — we know that.'

'Who took Ruff's statement?'

22

'Innelman. I've encouraged him to ignore it as the alcoholic bullshit that it probably is. And I've ordered him to keep it quiet. Dwight's a quick study.'

Weir looked again at Raymond, who stared out the window now with dark, unfocused eyes. 'Ray, you taking some time off?'

Raymond nodded slightly.

'Three weeks,' said Dennison. 'And he's not touching this case. There are regulations about that – good ones.'

Interim Chief Dennison closed the bulging file that was in front of him and tapped it with a thick forefinger. 'Ruff's statement, Innelman's crime-scene report, and some photographs of . . . Ann. More to the point, the personnel schedules for my department for the last three weeks. There were thirty-two officers on the street the night that Ann was killed – Robbins says time of death was between midnight and one A.M. So we've got two shifts to account for – night and graveyard. We had twenty-four patrol cars out – eight partners, sixteen solos.'

'Night shift ends at midnight?'

'It's staggered. You've got photocopies of the time cards so you'll know who came and went and when they did it. There's also a transcript of Dispatch and a copy of the tape – we record everything now because the public is so damned eager to sue. The tapes help us cover our butts.'

'Is the transcript clocked?'

'Fifteen-minute intervals, marked by Carol Clark in red pencil. She came on at four P.M., worked a twelve-hour.' Dennison leaned forward and studied Weir. He tapped the files again. '*This* is your job, Jim. Your job is not to solve the case. Your job is to clear my men. If you pick up a scent, it's all mine. You answer to me. You remain silent. You are alone.'

The chief's phone rang. He picked it up, listened, and thanked somebody. 'That was Robbins. He's finished the autopsy and he's ready to talk when you are, Jim.'

Weir stood.

'I may as well tell you right now that I had a squad car out myself that night,' said Dennison. His face flushed to a deeper red again, which made his pale gray eyes seem all the cooler. 'My old Jag wouldn't start, so I took home one of the fleet cars with a bad radio. Dobson in Maintenance would tell you the same thing, so I'll save you the trouble. Here.'

23

Dennison placed the thick file in a new briefcase and snapped it shut. There was a MAYOR BRIAN DENNISON sticker on the lid, and a GROW, DON'T SLOW! button beside it.

Weir took it. 'How much did you drive the squad car that night?'

'Just home. Then back to here. Check the odometer against Dobson's log. I'll have my wife call you – I was with her all night.'

'Paris, where were you three nights back?' asked Jim.

'Off shift,' he answered, moving toward the door. 'I haven't driven a beat since eighty-five – wrenched my back in a pursuit.'

Weir studied Paris's carnivorous face, a series of sharp angles all aiming down.

'Have you found Ann's car yet?'

Dennison shook his head. 'No, but the Harbor Patrol divers found the murder weapon Tuesday afternoon – standard kitchen knife with a six-inch blade. And Innelman found a piece of gold jewelry at the crime scene. It's the back of an earring, maybe a tie tack. We're tracing it through the local jewelers, but it's going to be tough. Everything is in the reports I gave you. You've got what we've got, Weir. No secrets.'

Weir left and Raymond followed him out. The station seemed taut with some energy that wasn't there before. Jim noted the pivoting shoulders, the lapsed conversations, the eyes that followed them down the hallways and out the front door.

They walked out to the parking lot. The haze had burned off and left a cool, muted afternoon. Weir looked at all the GROW, DON'T SLOW! and MAYOR BRIAN DENNISON stickers that the PD people had stuck to their bumpers. He wondered whether Becky had a chance.

And he realized fully now why Dennison had recruited him to investigate his own department: Opponent Becky Flynn now had a friend, an old lover, in fact, paid to assure her that nothing of the sort was taking place.

Raymond wiped his eyes and put on a pair of sunglasses. They walked through the parking lot in silence, finally stopping at Raymond's ancient station wagon. He and Ann had bought it almost twenty years ago, for the family they were going to have.

'What's the story on Paris?' Jim asked.

'Just a flack, but Dennison relies on him a lot. We call him Parrot because he can make his voice sound like anybody's. Does

24

these great imitations of Brian when he's not around. He's all right.'

Ray had the key aimed toward the lock, but he couldn't get it in. Finally, it found its mark and the door opened with a grating, metallic groan.

Raymond turned to Weir, took a deep breath, and stood straight. He braced on the door to keep himself up. His eyes were invisible behind the dark lenses. 'Jim, I want to tell you something. Sometime not too long from now, we're going to find the guy who did it. And I want you to know right now that I'm going to kill him. That's how it's going to go down. You have any problem with that?'

Weir's answer surprised him, not because of its black implications, but because it gave him, for the first time since that moment on the bay when he saw the blanket, a glimmer of something that he could substitute for hope.

'Save a heartbeat for me,' he said.

Raymond nodded. 'We have to dive again, Jim. Get down there deep and wash all this away.'

'Sure, Ray. Whatever you want.'

4

Ken Robbins, head of Forensic Science Services for the County of Orange, met Weir in the parking lot of the coroner's building. Robbins was a sturdy man in his early fifties, with gray hair that grew long around his collar and the weathered tan eyes of a sailor. Weir had gotten along with him well in his days with the Sheriff's. Robbins seemed to lack ambition, and because of it he tended his duties with a scrupulous devotion rarely found in public servants. Ken Robbins was always focused. He was carrying a briefcase, which he set on his lap as he sat down beside Weir in the truck.

'I'd ask you in, but tongues would flap.'

'This is better.'

'You don't want to view her, do you?'

View her. 'No.'

'Good to see you again, Jim. You lost some weight.'

'What do you have for me, Ken?'

Robbins took out a file and set it on top of his briefcase as Jim guided the truck out of the lot and down Civic Center Drive.

'Okay. Glen Yee did the work; he's my best man. Some of what we have is preliminary, some of it's hard. Yee got her after the other lab work – hair and fiber, latents, blood and semen.'

Weir's stomach sank. 'Was she raped?'

'I'll get to that. First, time of death between midnight and one A.M. Yee's firm on that because we got her six hours later. Food in her system, blood loss, lividity, rigor mortis, the usual. She was stabbed with a sharp knife, thin, single-edged, nonserrated, with a six-inch blade and no hilt. It's called the Kentucky Homestead, made in Japan, and there's a picture of it in the file here. Any one of thirteen wounds were fatal – they were done before the others. The first three happened when she was standing – the other twenty-four when she was down. No sign of resistance, so apparently our man got tired

26

or scared – what have you. Twenty-seven penetrations in all. Now there wasn't so much as a cut on either of her arms or hands, so we'd have to say she lost consciousness almost immediately, before she could defend herself. No bruising that would indicate a struggle before the knife hit her. Eight of the thirteen fatals penetrated the heart; the others hit the aorta or the pulmonary artery or both. He was forceful, Jim. Very.'

Weir rolled down his window and let the air hit his face.

'I'm sorry.'

'Keep going.'

Robbins flipped a page and folded it under. 'Semen inside the vagina and minor bruising of the mons and symphysis suggest that she was raped before she died. We found some abrasion of the vaginal canal, but not a lot, so she lubricated quickly. We found semen in the uterus, as well as on the labia and underwear – trace only, there. If she'd been found on dry land, we could guess how much time elapsed between the rape and death, but the seawater could have rinsed off a great deal of fluid, so we're kind of stuck. We think between five minutes and half an hour. At least five minutes, though – we're sure on that. The roses don't tell us much. We're tracking variety and supplier for Innelman. Ten in the waist-band of her skirt, one inserted with some force into the vaginal canal ... after death, we assumed. The other one probably floated away, or else he saved it.'

The road went blurry in Weir's eyes; he turned on the air conditioner full blast and directed the stream onto his face. He was now on some side street in the barrio – no idea which one, and it truly didn't matter.

'Pull over, Jim.'

'I think I will.'

He found a shady spot under a big olive tree. The curb was littered with the purple stains of crushed fruit. He breathed deeply and unwound his fingers from the steering wheel. Robbins offered him a cigarette, which he took. They both sat back and smoked. Weir watched the plume hesitate at the window, then rush out and up.

'What I'm about to tell you now isn't going to make you feel better, Jim. She was pregnant.'

'I know.' Weir drew the smoke, felt the rush in his head, the warmth spreading down to his feet. He also knew something that

27

Robbins wouldn't understand, that even he, as a man, couldn't fully comprehend – that Ann had wanted a child more than anything in the world.

'Seven weeks along, Jim. God, this is tough to do to you.'

Jim stared out the windshield and saw nothing. He could feel his heart pounding away in his ears, and his hands had begun to tremble. 'Keep going, Ken. I'd like to get this over with.'

'Want to just read the report?'

'I said keep going.'

'Okay, the perp. He's a type-B secretor, which means –'

'I know what it means.'

'Right-handed. From the angles of penetration, Yee figures five foot ten to six feet tall, if they were both standing on level ground. The first three penetrations were done when she was upright, like I said before. Yee's good at his angles and estimates. We took a hair off her blouse – it was worked into the fabric. Two inches long, dark-brown, wavy. Prelim is male Caucasian, thirty-five to forty-five years. Latents didn't get much – the seawater saw to that. We took partial prints from the upper arms and face, nothing we can send through Sacramento. We combed her for trace and found some possibilities, but running through the samples will take some time.' Robbins was silent for a long while. 'It's also going to take some time to run the semen through the DNA lab. We've never tried it after seawater contamination. I wouldn't hold my breath. That's it, Jim.'

Weir stared out the window and finished the cigarette. A little girl in a pink dress with white ruffles kicked a ball down the sidewalk. Jim watched her black shoes pick their way through the olive stains. 'Play it back for me, Ken. Put the pieces together.'

Robbins drummed his fingers on the briefcase. 'I see it like this. First, what do we know? That she was raped, struck twenty-seven times with a knife, that eleven roses were . . . arranged on her person, that she was left floating in the Back Bay. All that and *no signs of a struggle* except the bruising of the mons area. We know she was killed a hundred yards up the bay from where they found her – a dark night, a remote region, not the kind of place she'd just happen to go to for no reason. Reason, then? He had a gun on her, maybe the knife. She was frightened, couldn't resist until it was too late. But she managed to stand up after the rape, because that's what the penetration angles tell us. The first stab could have killed her, any of the three while she was still upright. After she was down, he just kept at it.'

The scene played through Jim's head with obscene clarity.

'What do you think?'

'Go on.'

'So, he pulled the gun, or showed the knife early, forced her into his car. Or maybe he was smoother than that. There's a thousand ways to get a woman into an auto. I worked a case last year where a guy used his own baby daughter to lure a woman in – said he couldn't figure out why the kid was crying. He raped her in the backseat. We matched seat belt material with what we took from under her fingernails. Anyway, Ann let herself be taken out to the bay, maybe even let herself be . . . presented with a bouquet of roses. He's a sicko and she knows it by now. She plays along, trying not to make him furious.'

'There's no evidence at all of a gun.'

'He raped her and she didn't so much as get a fingernail into him. He threatened her with a gun, maybe the knife. Maybe with just his words, but he threatened her with something *to which rape was a preferable alternative.* She had her clothes on when they found her. They weren't torn, they weren't even radically disarranged. The skirt was short enough he could have just pulled it up. Her underpants were on. What's that tell us? That he let her put them back on after he was finished. That was part of the deal: You lie back, let me do my thing, and you walk. Considering the knife – or the gun – Ann weighed the offer and took it. No resistance, even though the genital bruising indicates some pretty rough treatment. She took it, on the belief she'd be okay. She got up, put herself back together, and he killed her. Now sure, he could have put her clothes back on after he killed her, but why bother?'

Jim's hands trembled. He laced his fingers together to stop it. He looked down to see them locked contritely in place, but still twitching.

'Account for the five minutes between the rape and the time she died.'

'It was *at least* five minutes. And remember, she was still lying down. Okay, try this: She thought he'd left. She lay there, heard him leave, *thought* she heard him leave. She was stunned, starting to go into shock. She lay there a long time – or what seemed like a long time to her – then she put her clothes back on. She stood up, she started to walk, but he wasn't gone. He was waiting, and he got her before she could make a move.'

Weir watched the scene again in vivid detail. His hands were clenched now, and his ears rung with a wavering intensity, as if a siren was approaching fast. When he blinked his eyes to banish the vision, the barrio street asserted itself before him with strident, mocking clarity. He started up the truck again and pulled back onto the street.

'Who's working this for Brian?'

'Dwight Innelman and Roger Deak.'

'Dwight's good.'

Weir navigated back to the coroner's building in silence. They got caught behind a transit district bus with a picture of Brian Dennison's face on the back. The exhaust had left the interim chief tainted with black. Ken Robbins slipped his papers into a folder and set the folder on the seat beside Weir. 'I probably don't have to say this, but I will anyway. Twenty-seven wounds. Our man was in a rage. But he was cool enough to bring along a dozen purple roses.'

Weir considered the empty flower vase on Ann's desk at the day-care center. 'Maybe she was carrying them when he took her. Maybe he didn't bring them at all.'

'It's possible.'

'Maybe he sent them to her earlier.'

'Wouldn't that be nice. I imagine the Newport Beach Police thought of the same thing. The local florists could tell you if he was that stupid.'

Robbins got out of the truck and shut the door. 'Let me know what else I can do. I'll have Yee's finals ready for you by this time tomorrow. I'm sorry. How'd it go in Mexico?'

'Better than this.'

Weir stopped at a bar three blocks away, downed two shots of scotch and a water back. From a telephone over by the shuffleboard table, he called Raymond's house and got no answer. He tried the Eight Peso Cantina on Balboa and found Raymond's mother, Irena. Irena and Ray's father, Ernesto, had owned the Eight Peso — a neighborhood cantina that offered good food and cheap drinks — for forty years. She told him between sobs that Ray had gone to

30

the hospital. 'He just fainted. It's all too much for him,' she kept repeating. Ernesto – Nesto, to family and friends – had gone to stay with him, but Irena was keeping the bar open for business.

'Here's your mother, Jim. *Vaya con Dios.*'

Virginia's voice was firm but faint.

Jim told her he needed her help and she said nothing. Virginia's complicity was understood.

'Go home, sit down at the kitchen table, get out the phone book. Call every florist in Newport Beach and find out who either sold a dozen purple roses to Ann, or had them delivered to Ann's Kids. If you strike out, try Laguna, Corona del Mar, Costa Mesa. Try every number in the book. Don't stop until you know.'

'He sent her those roses? The ones on her desk at work?'

'It's an outside shot. This is our secret, Mom. Just ours for now, understand?'

'The police should have thought of this.'

'They have. I just want you to get the answers before they do.'

Virginia said she'd be starting her calls as soon as she got home.

Jim told her to remember what he had said early that morning, that they would get through this, that there would be an end to the way it felt. He hadn't known then whether he believed it, and he didn't know now.

For a moment, there was nothing but silence between them, a silence that bred in Jim terrible visions of the days to come.

'I love you, Mom.'

'I love you, too, Jim. And anyone who thinks I'll quit working for Slow Growth because of this has got another goddamned think coming.'

Virginia hung up, her sense of multiple missions declared to Jim by the loud crack of the phone hitting its cradle.

Weir called Hoag Hospital. A nurse told him that Lt Cruz was apparently exhausted and had not been eating. He was sedated now and sleeping soundly.

5

A Newport Beach cop car followed him down Pacific Coast Highway for a mile or two. Jim studied the two officers in his rearview. They were young, groomed, alert. When the unit swept past him, the cop on the passenger's side looked up and regarded Jim blankly from behind his shades. Kids, thought Weir, like Ray and I were once.

He parked on Morning Star Lane, walked past the park, down to the bay, and looked east. The sky, heavying with a marine layer, was an unemphatic white. The tide was on the flood now, higher than when Jim had seen it last, and the water broke into wedges of gray polished by the May breeze. A big Glastron motored slowly down the bay, making a white cut in the surface that healed as the boat passed.

Looking to the east, Jim could see the curve of bay, the narrow beach, the patches of ice plant and grasses that grew thicker toward the cliffs from which the big houses looked down. Beyond the water lay the mud flats, black and odorous, dotted with white seabirds.

He thought back to his days on Harbor Patrol, the placid mornings, the thick salt air, the partnership of Ray, the feeling of liberty that they both had, zipping around the water in their own boat, gainfully employed to catch bad guys. Two kids from the neighborhood never had it so good. Jim had gone to dicks – better pay, a bump-up; Raymond joined the NBPD for his sergeant's stripes.

He stopped for a moment at the place he had seen Ann last, unremarkable now except for an excess of footprints and a smooth body-length patch of earth where she had lain. Somewhere overhead a jet droned invisibly. In a world lacking absolutes, he thought, only death is nonnegotiable. The horror is the dreary efficiency of it all. It seemed less a part of the grand eternal cycle than a concept developed by CPAs. Still, there was the sadness growing inside him and it felt as if when the sadness got big enough, his body would just cave in around it and there wouldn't be anything left. And with the sadness came the guilt, a deep and fundamental conviction that there was something he could have done, would have done, should have done. Vengeance seemed the obvious antidote. *Ann had been pregnant.*

He continued along the shore, his knees less reliable with each step, his ankles feeling brittle and ready to turn, his elbows and hands aching like those of an eighty-year-old predicting rain. He wished he had a coat. He stopped, took a deep breath, squeezed his hands into fists to get the blood moving again. For a brief moment, he hovered outside himself, looking down, and what he saw was a thin old man with pale skin and whispy white hair, standing alone, bent like a cane on the shore of a vast uncertain marsh, a man impermanent as the birds flitting overhead or the breeze that brushed across his sunken white cheeks.

The crime scene was undelineated, but he found the location by Innelman's report, and by the browned, bloodstained earth. A couple of neighborhood kids stood by glumly; two more skidded around a trail on a pair of MX bikes. Lovers, arm-in-arm, watched from the shoreline with an air of forbidden curiosity, as if death were a black-tie party to which they had not been invited.

Jim read Dwight Innelman's crime-scene report as he stood upon the unhallowed ground. It read like Ken Robbins's summation: Ann being forced down to this midnight shore, the rape, the waiting, the final attack. No defense marks on Ann. No sign of struggle. Neighbors saw nothing; heard nothing. Door-to-doors got zip. A kitchen knife. The back of a tie tack or earring. Eleven roses, arranged. He pictured Ann, alive and beaming, at Virginia's booth the night before.

Why no fight? Ann was five foot ten, 130 pounds. Good shape from work. Strong and capable. Did she offer herself as a sacrifice for what she carried inside, for her life? What he came up with in regards to Ann – what he had seen in her for thirty-plus years – was that she was the gentlest of all souls, and that she was capable of doing just that: offering her body to save her life. And the life of her unborn child, certainly.

Jim looked across the bay to where the other shore diminished in the haze. A sea gull winged by with a cry and the hiss of feathers on air. It was so close that Weir could hear the gristle working in its joints. In the west, the sun was starting its last rally of the day: a surge of doomed orange splendor before evening.

He stood, asking himself the most basic question of all: Why? In the simplest of terms, what was the motive? And as he had so many times in the last three days, Jim could offer no answer. She had no money. She had no power on earth to promote or hinder, really. She had none but the most casual access to the channels of power. She had no large ambitions that might lead her to blackmail, betray, leverage, connive, manipulate. She was a symbol of no cause, a proponent of no revolution. Ann was just a woman getting by, he thought. *Why?* Was it all done for the few minutes that her anguish could become someone else's pleasure? Or *had* she had a more far-reaching agenda, did the branches of her life spread into places he had simply never known? Could someone have struck at Virginia through Ann? At Becky, at Raymond, at himself? Weir knew that he had snubbed the life – and therefore the men – of law enforcement when he quit, but how could that account for this monstrous revenge by a Newport Beach or any other cop? Nothing fit.

What he felt most strongly right now – besides the grief, guilt, and anger that continued to multiply silently inside him – was that Robbins and Innelman were trying to make something fit that wouldn't. A vague, shapeless idea coalesced inside him, too unformed yet to hold, vaporous enough to hide itself in the looming geography of sadness. But the longer he watched the gray water of the bay, the more embodied and specific the notion became. It formed, wavered, darted away. Then it was back again, quick as a hummingbird, taunting. Weir nailed it.

Ann knew him, he thought. She came down here without a struggle because she trusted him. All the crime stats on this planet would bear out that probability.

Weir's mind rewound quickly: Ann's friends, coworkers, acquaintances, relatives – any male she'd trust enough to follow down here on a fog-heavy night. The list was short and obvious: Raymond, Nesto, Jim himself, a couple of Poon's rickety old friends who'd doted on her almost as much as Poon had. Ann wouldn't just hustle down here with anyone. Ann was private. Ann was wary. On the obvious level, she knew everyone, from the clerks at Balboa Grocery to the boys who ran the ferry – she'd lived here for thirty-nine years, gone to high school and two years of junior college, had two jobs –

both of which brought the public to her. She was bright, friendly, likable, pretty. Jim thought back to a surprise party Raymond had thrown for her last year. A couple of hundred people had packed into the Eight Peso to celebrate, half of them male, many of them knowing her well enough to offer a kiss, a present, ask for a dance. Would she follow one down here to the Back Bay on a fog-heavy night? No. Not unless they were lovers. Would she take a man on the side? It didn't seem like Ann, but neither did the lifeless form lying upon the damp earth that morning.

She didn't even have a coat.

She changed her clothes after work, Jim thought, but she didn't put on a coat. No coat because she wasn't planning on going out. Maybe coming down here was the last thing on her mind. Maybe he had the knife to her throat, under her beautiful long hair. Maybe a gun to her back, like Robbins had said.

He turned to the picture of the murder weapon – an unremarkable kitchen knife with a wooden handle and a gently curving one-sided blade. The handle was in good condition and had the words KENTUCKY HOMESTEAD branded into it, along with a little logo of a kettle in a fireplace. JAPAN was etched onto the steel, just above the handle. The darkened juncture between blade and wood could have been blood, sludge, stain – or any combination. He closed the file.

As Jim climbed the embankment toward Morning Star Lane, an obvious possibility presented itself: There was so little evidence left because someone had cleaned it up and taken it away.

Like a cop would.

The cop that Mackie Ruff had said he saw.

That's what he was doing during those minutes when Ann lay on the ground, full of someone's brutal seed, staring up at the fog and praying that he would leave, just leave us, just walk into the night forever, and let me keep alive inside me the one miracle I thought I never could have.

He was cleaning things up.

35

6

Jim stood on the sidewalk outside Becky Flynn's bayfront cottage and gazed through the oleander that walled her property from the rest of the world. He passed through the gate, bell chiming, a certain pressure gathering in his head. Moving toward Becky's house was for Weir like walking into yesterday, only knowing how the days ahead would end. Each step echoed with the thousand memories of others so much like it, of the thousand peninsula nights they'd spent here in the varying stages of love, disillusion, abandonment. His stomach fluttered as he climbed onto the porch and looked through the screen door.

She was sitting on the couch, her head cocked to one side to hold the telephone, a yellow legal pad propped on her crossed knees. Becky was always making notes on something. He watched her nod in profile, bring a yellow pencil to her mouth, and touch the eraser to her lips. She had cut her hair into a loose fall of light brown curls that ended abruptly above her shoulders. Becky's hair had always been a primary vanity – the longer the better – but this new do spoke of adjusted priorities. We're getting older, thought Weir, his fist poised to knock. He watched her for another surreptitious moment, beholding the perpendicular curves of thigh and calf as she raised her bare feet to the coffee table and wrote something on the pad. She nodded, took a deep breath, and hung up. For a second, she stared off into space, smile cracks forming at the edge of her lips.

She got up, came to the door, and swung it open.

She met him inside with a measuring look that turned into a hug. The top of her head smelled the way it had for the three decades Jim had known her. Over her shoulder, he looked at the old place for the first time in – what, he wondered – almost two years? There were some new things: a Pegge Hopper print on the tongue-and-groove wall above the hearth, a big gray torchiere in the far corner, a Persian rug on the hardwood floor before the fireplace, a new coat of paint.

The rest was the same, though, right down to the heavy old dining set that took up too much space at the far end of the room, the deep soft couch, the curtains that Becky had made all those years ago of chintz now faded by sun, the cut flowers she bought each Friday from the stand down by Poon's Locker. There was a FLYNN FOR MAYOR banner – green on white – tacked across one wall, a smaller SLOW THE GROWTH poster on another, boxes of campaign fliers and mailing envelopes on the floor by the fireplace.

Becky herself had added a few things, too: Her skin was paler, her hips and breasts a little larger, and there was a deepening network of lines at the corners of her dark brown eyes. Mileage was implied, not all of it smooth. All in all, to Weir, she just looked beautiful. He had held her image all those hours in the Zihuat jail, comforted by memory but tormented by her distance and the fact that they had messed it up so badly.

'God, Jim. I don't know what to say to you.'

'No.'

'I've been so worried about you. *God*, I'm sorry.' She held him again and sighed – a declared need.

They stood in silence for a moment, then Becky turned and walked toward the kitchen. Weir followed – a seemingly ancient habit – took down two heavy glasses and filled them with ice. Becky poured in some good gin, a dribble of vermouth, shaved off a lemon peel, and swept one around each rim before dropping them in. Through her kitchen window, Jim could see the fog floating down like a lowered blanket. His hands were shaking again as he picked up the drink. He felt as if his heart were made of wood, beating slowly and begrudgingly toward the moment when it could just stop.

'It's good to see you,' she said. 'I left messages.'

'Thanks. This has been bad.'

They settled into the couch, the standard positions, Weir's feet already yearning for the boots to be off, to be warming from the fire. The answering machine picked up an incoming call: a Proposition A proofreader at the print shop had just discovered fliers with the word *public* misspelled as *pubic*.

'I saw her early that night at the Whale,' said Jim. 'Ray came by and Mom was there. She looked good and strong – a little thin, maybe.'

'I hadn't talked to her for a few days.'

'How had she been, Beck?'

'I've been asking myself that question ever since I heard. It's not as easy to answer as I thought it would be. Okay, Ann and I have been friends for what, thirty-plus years? We did everything from roller-skate together in pigtails to borrow each other's doll clothes, to share our diaries, to take the same classes, have crushes on the same boys, to . . . everything. We were girls, then we were women, and we went through all of it together. Except for the few months she spent in France – what, fifteen years old or whatever it was – we've been like this.' Becky twisted her fingers in the wish-me-luck sign and stared from behind it into Jim's face. 'But back in November, something started to change. It was just before you left for Mexico.'

'I didn't see it.'

Weir heard Becky's silence accuse him: If you'd been paying attention to your family instead of getting ready to chase rainbows, *you might have.*

'It was subtle, Jim. I thought it was something just between us, so I didn't really worry too much. Now, well, after what happened, everything has its own terrible resonance.' She drank, then set the glass down on the coffee table. 'Ann was pulling back. She was putting something between herself and me and it bugged me.'

'What was it about her?'

'Smiles, mostly. Sometimes she was so . . . polite. It was like the smile was there to deflect me. She'd be so sunny, so comprehensively positive, so . . . fucking vague.'

'About what?'

'Everything. I'd call and ask her how she was and it sounded like a state-of-the person address, something she'd planned out and rehearsed. You know Ann. You could always rely on Ann for straight answers, straight talk. If Ann thought what you were doing was wrong, she'd say so. If she didn't feel good that day, you'd hear about it. She was never evasive. But back in January, that's what I felt. I ran into her at the market late one night – eleven say – and she's picking up her groceries for the week. We're standing in front of the soup and she actually stared through me for a second, then, she clicked in – big smile, this strained grimace she's trying to pass off as a smile. I ask what's wrong and she says, "Not a thing! I'm just tired out a bit tonight; that's what I get for shopping without my makeup on!" She pulls off a can of something and the whole stack falls over, all these red cans banging down to the floor. So I

38

play along like I believe her, but I make a note of it. I called her a couple of nights later, and she sounded so giddy, so up. I swear to God, Jim, I wondered for a second if she was into the blow or something. We made a lunch date for the next Sunday and she seemed . . . not there. She held up her end of the conversation but she really didn't bring anything to it. She left most of her food. Her mind was somewhere else.'

'You call her on it?'

'Of course I did. Annie laughed it off, turned it back around on me, like I was projecting my own usual neurotic character onto her. I almost bought it; I'm *always* ready to buy that one. We'd just gotten Prop A on the ballot, there was the march in Laguna Canyon to organize, I was trying to get my candidate's apps finished up. So, well, you had your treasure and I had mine. But it just wasn't her. I saw her a lot this winter, ran into her here and there, went by the Whale and had dinner in her station. Sometimes she seemed just like Ann. The other times – and there were several of them – she was somewhere else.'

Jim groped back to November to corroborate Becky's story, but he couldn't. Ann had seemed like Ann. He had been lost in getting ready for the *Black Pearl* off of Zihuat: dive gear and compressor, the air lance and water dredge, the winches and cables, the grid stakes and surface buoys, everything from a rebuild on the engine to spare regulator gaskets. I missed it, he thought, plain and simple.

'Did you talk to anyone about her? Ray, Mom?'

Becky shook her head. 'With Ann, I always went straight to the source. Like I said, I thought this was all just between her and me. Friends fall out, waver, get back together. Sometimes you have to hold a match to the bridge just to remind yourself how strong and needed it is.'

They exchanged glances, mutual acknowledgement that such matches were held – all too often and by both parties – to their own bridge, but the result was not a warming reminder of value, but fire itself.

Becky drained her glass. 'What can you share with me?'

'What do you want?'

'I got a copy of Bristol's report, so I know the basics.'

'Small town.'

'It wasn't hard – a former public defender has her networks.'

39

'I can't add much. I saw where they brought her up, and I was at the crime scene this evening.'

'Innelman and Deak?'

Jim nodded. 'Innelman's a good man. I don't know about Deak.'

'He's young and cocky, but he's thorough, too.'

'If you've seen the report, you know as much as I do.'

'Do I?' Becky looked at him sharply, then smiled. 'Dennison must be twitching. If things played out just right, this could sway the election. Now he'll really avoid a debate.'

Becky squinted her dark brown eyes, and offered up a satisfied little smile. It was a look far less impish than cunning. Weir had always hated it.

'What did Dennison want to see you and Ray about today?' she asked.

Jim made up a story about him getting the dive job for another search of the bay. It was fairly solid for a quick lie, something Poon would have been proud of.

'That's Sheriff's jurisdiction.'

'That's what I tried to tell Brian. Anyway, Harbor Patrol divers found a kitchen knife just a hundred feet from where Ann died. Six-inch blade, no hilt, unexceptional.'

'Then why would Brian want you to dive again?'

'He's just being careful.'

'Make on the knife?'

'I didn't see one,' he lied again.

'You're getting rusty, Weir. And your hands are shaking.'

'I know.'

The telephone rang again, this time an invitation for Becky to speak to the Newport Beach Chapter of Women in Business. Becky made a note on the yellow pad. 'They'll try to skewer me. Know something? I liked life better when it was simple.'

Jim was quiet for a moment. Becky's last statement had the ring of a can of worms about to be opened. Maybe that's what we needed all along, he thought – get the bad things out so we could figure out what to do with them. One of Becky's primary faults – which she was always the first to confess – was her penchant for doing a dozen things at once, but not necessarily right. He tried not to sound accusatory. 'Well, looks like you have plenty of campaign work.'

She looked at him, then away. 'It seems . . . appropriate. I decided not too long ago that liking your life isn't everything. You've got to bring something to the party, make a difference . . . maybe that sounds naïve. But I had the feeling I had to contribute rather than just take. Anyway, I was always impatient when I was with you, toward the end. Working as a PD got old fast. I'm just that way – I like to move on. Greener pastures maybe, I don't know.'

'Like you said, we all have our own treasures.'

She shot him a hard glance. 'You weren't just looking for treasure, you were looking for a way out . . . of everything.'

Same old scratchy record, he thought. Becky had never understood why he quit the Sheriff's. To an ambitious young woman dedicated to the grindstone, his jump from full-time employment into the speculative waters of salvage and treasure hunting was the very pinnacle of whimsy, reeking of adolescence and insolvency. Becky's family had been poor – not dirt poor, but lower-middle-class poor – always on the edge of a utility shutoff, a car repo, an insurance cancellation. Becky's first deal with herself as an adult was to keep that from happening to her. The more Jim had talked about things like his freedom and his time, the tighter-mouthed Becky had become. She had made him doubt himself, when doubt was a luxury he couldn't afford. To Becky, doubt was something you live with every day, something you listen to with respect – the point scout of conscience. Her marriage to a hotshot Newport lawyer had lasted less than a year. Becky, he had always thought, was a more complicated animal.

'I was looking for the same thing you were,' he said finally. 'You were wrong to think any different, and you still are. No matter how hard you try, you'll never know me better than I do, Becky.'

She studied him, retreating invisibly. Her eyes said, I don't know about that, but her words were, 'I guess we've been through all this before.'

'I thought about you a lot in Mexico.' He placed his shaking hands on his knees and looked into the fireplace.

'I thought about you, too.'

'Did you come up with any answers?'

Becky's hand found the back of his neck and her fingers twisted a lock of his hair. A warming surge came up through him.

'No answers. Just questions. Sometimes I think it's all behind us, then I think about something and it feels like it never ended. It's like looking back on a battlefield, wondering if you've got the balls to jump in again. Come to think of it, I did come up with one

41

answer. The answer is, I want someone who's going to stay, stick it out.'

Jim nodded, realizing how little the description fit him.

'Tell me about Mexico,' she said.

He did, from the promising blue-water dives to the frustration of trying to cover so much bottom alone, to the surprise of being found with marijuana that wasn't his, stuffed conspicuously in the engine compartment of *Lady Luck*, to his thirty-four days of hell in the Zihuatanejo jail, then his sudden and unexplained release.

For a while, they talked about Becky's run for mayor of Newport Beach, the practice, the Slow Growth proposition on the coming June ballot. It was a walk through. Becky sighed, took a deep drink, and stared into the black fireplace.

Weir stood, took another look at the big FLYNN FOR MAYOR banner on the far wall.

She walked him to the door, the polished hardwood floor creaking in the same places it always had. 'I want to leave you with something, though. I saw Ann about five-thirty that . . . last day. I was walking down the bayfront, taking a break from the mailers, and she drove through the alley. She was going to work. Why did she drive it when she could walk?'

Weir had been wondering the same thing himself. He could think of only one earthly reason for Ann to get in her old car and drive the three blocks to work, then spend ten minutes looking for a parking space when it would take two minutes to just walk. She was wearing street clothes when they found her. Provocative street clothes. Had she changed at work? In the car? Somewhere else?

'Because she wasn't going home after work,' he said.

'I wouldn't think so.'

Into the air around Weir settled the fact that Becky had done just this thing to him once, years ago, the first official pivot point upon which their relationship began its long and anguished descent. 'Did she ever say anything about another man?'

'No, that's not something I think Ann would talk about. She had her private side – the Weir trademark. It's possible. She was attractive, alive . . . oh, you know, all that kind of thing.' Becky wiped away a tear, glaring with a certain fierceness out the window toward the buildings of Newport Center on the mainland.

Weir leaned against the doorjamb. Things kept welling up inside him. There didn't seem to be any end to them. For a blessed, frightening moment, he felt stripped of pretense. 'I don't know what to do, Becky.'

She held him for a long while, then straightened him by the shoulders and wiped some hair off his forehead. 'Fight, Jim. Stay and fight it out. Be kind to your heart.'

Jim stepped onto the porch and let the screen door bounce shut behind him. It was strange to him how quickly the old antagonisms could reappear, along with the feeling that he'd love to take Becky in his arms again and press his face against the soft, fragrant plane of her neck and lose himself in her.

Walking down her steps, he had the feeling again of being isolated on the bow of some great ship, wind on his face, gliding from one dark shore to another in search of something he was yet to identify. He was tiring, even in his own visions, of being alone.

Raymond's room at Hoag Hospital had a view of north Newport and a glimpse of the Pacific. Weir found him deeply asleep, with his hands crossed over his stomach and his mouth slightly open. He had on a light blue smock that tied in the back and a plastic wristband with his name and some numbers on it. There were flowers on the counter and bed stand, and taped to the walls a collection of get-well cards made of construction paper and crayons by his young cousins.

Weir pulled up a chair and poured Ray some water from a blue pitcher. For a while, he looked out to the dull gray horizon and the glimmering sea. As Jim watched his friend sleep, the idea hit him that Raymond might not make it through this. Ray was strong, but he wasn't flexible. He was married to routine, laws, procedures, clear delineations of right and wrong. They kept him ordered, and Jim understood why. Weir had noticed in his training at the Sheriff Academy that, among others, a certain type was drawn to law enforcement – people who needed to belong to something, to be told who they were. Rather than slog their ways through life, trying to figure things on their own, these few needed to have the questions answered for them, needed the clear definitions set out by the uniform they would wear, the gun they would carry, the code – California Penal – by which they would live. And although Jim never considered Raymond to be one of those people, he had often wondered whether Ray didn't adhere too closely to the job

43

he had taken, didn't see things in the simple black and white picture suggested by the words *guilt* and *innocence*. That was fine. The trouble is, what happens when life betrays you and the law can't help? What happens when the foundations fall away? In the absence of belief, what rushes in to replace it? Jim said a brief prayer for Raymond, that he would have enough strength to build a new belief, and enough love to build a new strength.

He went to the nurse's station and managed to find someone not too busy to talk. She told him what they'd already told him – that Raymond had apparently neither eaten nor slept in three days, and that he had finally just passed out. He was taking food now, and sleeping the rest of the time. None of this was uncommon to the grieving, she said. He'd be out soon. 'I'm so sorry about your sister.'

7

Jim Weir, hunched down in his jacket against the fog, walked south along the bayfront toward Ann's house. It was just before nine o'clock. His joints felt old again and his fingers were clenched tight on the handle of Brian Dennison's briefcase. He had not been in Ann's house since that night, and he felt some duty to enter it, to show her it held more for him than horror, that in his memory Ann was more than her end. Besides, he wanted to be alone. He entered with an extra key that Ray had given him, and quietly closed the door.

Walking slowly through the house, Jim noted that Innelman and Deak had been here. There were traces of black dusting powder on the inside doorknob, on both white bathroom drinking cups. The impound list on the counter said that three wineglasses sitting here were now in Evidence at the County Crime Lab. Three glasses, he thought: three drinkers? He saw that Ann's address book, which always hung by a ribbon beside the kitchen phone, had been carted off to Evidence, too. Likewise, the message tape from the answering machine. There was a sprinkle of safecracker gray on the floor in front of the refrigerator, where they'd dusted the black plastic handle and door. He followed their thinking: Ann had come home, changed, been confronted here and forced to drive. Not likely, he thought. It didn't feel right.

Two drawers in Ann's bedroom chest were partially open, as was the closet door. He stood there in her room for a moment, a room redolent with the smell of her perfumes and lotions, feeling confronted by her presence, half-expecting her to speak. Such a trampling of you, he thought. I'm sorry. He shivered inside the jacket.

More fingerprint powder beside the table lamp in Raymond's study, cabinets ajar, a Polaroid film envelope lying on top in the wastebasket. Straws, he thought: Ann never came back here. She

45

got in her car and drove to wherever it was she was planning to go. Dennison is desperate for a break. How many times had Raymond stood amidst such a scene, he wondered. Did he dream that someday such props of tragedy would be his own?

He went back to the kitchen, took Malachi Ruff's interview from the briefcase, and smoothed it out before him on the wobbly kitchen dinette. The questioning had been done by Innelman at eight the morning of Tuesday, May 16. It was written in the usual police English, and contained nothing of importance that Dennison hadn't already told him. Basically, a drunk named Mackie Ruff had heard a scream, seen someone run along the bay, seen a cop car speed away, then fallen back asleep. Dense fog, dark, much booze inside him. Innelman noted on the report that 'Ruff has an outspoken dislike of law enforcement' and that 'Witness Ruff was intoxicated at time of alleged incident. Because of dense fog and considerable alcohol, Ruff could not determine age, race, dress, or attitude of possible suspect. Suspect disappeared northbound. Approximately thirty seconds later, Ruff heard a car door open and shut, then an engine start. He reportedly walked back up to Galaxy Drive to observe a white four-door car in motion southbound. Ruff states "it was a cop car." Upon further inquiry, Ruff elaborated that the "emblem" on the car's side indicated it was a police patrol unit. Ruff was not close enough to determine any details concerning this alleged "emblem."'

Innelman noted, too, that Ruff had no permanent address but could sometimes be found at Frankie's Place, the Porthole, or the Eight Peso Cantina, all located near the ferry landing on the Balboa Peninsula.

Weir remembered finding Mackie Ruff knee-deep in the chilly water of the Back Bay one winter, dragging a shopping cart behind him. The cart contained an old car tire and a massive tangle of fishing line. Mackie said he was after lobster. Jim had aimed him back toward dry land after Ray gave him five bucks for some food. How trustworthy was Ruff as a witness? Jim noted, too, that Ruff had been placed in custody but not charged. Of course, he thought: If the DA needed him, why bust him, and why admit he was drunk?

Weir smiled humorlessly, set aside the interview, and brought out the chief's personnel information, the Dispatch tape and transcript, and a small cassette player that Dennison had been thoughtful enough to include.

First task, he thought, is to consider the interim police chief, and Sergeant Cruz.

Dennison was fifty pounds heavier than the 175 pounds estimated by both Robbins and Innelman. He had an O positive blood type; Ann's killer was B. Dennison had short reddish-brown curly hair; the hair found on Ann's blouse was straight, medium brown, almost two inches long – male Caucasian between thirty-five and forty-five. Dennison was fifty-one. Brian had told him this morning that he was asleep beside his wife between midnight and 1:00 A.M., and Marlene Dennison had vouched for him. Above it he wrote, HOUR IN QUESTION, and underlined it twice.

Raymond's stats were even more contradictory to evidence: type A blood; wavy black Latino hair. Raymond was left-handed. He weighed ten pounds less than the Crime Lab estimates, and Weir knew from buying him a pair of swim fins one Christmas that Ray wore shoes a full size smaller than their man did. He could remember with perfect clarity telling the Dive Shop owner that he wanted a pair of black rubber Scuba-Pros for a man's eight and a half. Funny, he thought, how some things stick in your mind. Becky had stood beside him and quipped something about the Fellini film. Eight and a fucking half, he thought, pushing the Dispatch tape into the player. Pretend for a minute that Ray's physicals matched up. Let's see if he has an alibi. He ran the tape forward toward midnight, then slowed it down, found his place on the transcript to read along, and listened to the entire hour in question.

Raymond communicated twelve times with Dispatch. He was patrolling the Corona del Mar beat, which left him almost three fog-clogged miles from the peninsula where Ann was likely picked up. One shortcut – the ferry that shuttles between Balboa Island and the old neighborhood – closed down at midnight. Raymond took three interviews between midnight and one; wrote two traffic citations – both for speeding in Corona del Mar – and made no arrests. The Activity Log and Citation Book carbons enclosed by Dennison showed that Ray had written the tickets at 12:10 and 12:50. He had done field interviews at midnight, 12:20 and 12:35. Jim checked the photocopy of Raymond's time card. He'd clocked back in at the station at 1:00 A.M., exactly on time. Just like Raymond, he thought: on the dot, and by the book. And no more than six consecutive minutes unaccounted for at a time, either by voice or on paper.

47

Hard to believe, he thought, leafing through the file, that Ray is a fifteen-year veteran already. Raymond's career flew before him: eight commendations from two different chiefs; six citations from the city for outstanding performance; others from Lions, Kiwanis, the Chamber of Commerce, the Latino Studies Department at Cal State, Fullerton. He had been named Officer of the Year three times. He had gotten a special Certificate of Meritorious Conduct for collaring a burglar in the home of a ninety-two-year-old former city councilwoman, and a special Community Service Award for helping deliver a baby in his patrol car. He had resuscitated a waterlogged boy on the Twelfth Street beach one summer evening, performing CPR until paramedics arrived through the peninsula traffic. The kid pulled through. Weir could still remember the headlines. As he read on in the file, he realized how well Raymond had done, for an unentitled kid from the neighborhood – taking a bachelor's degree in sociology before choosing law enforcement, finishing high in his classes at the Sheriff Academy, making sergeant at thirty, and lieutenant at thirty-five. He had enrolled in law school just after getting the promotion – the same year Weir quit the Sheriff's to seek his fortune – and now had just two more semesters to go. We all have our treasures, he could hear Becky say.

Now Raymond was adrift, he thought, untethered and on his own. If he meant what he said about executing Ann's killer, then he was risking more than his career – he was risking his life. Maybe mine, too, thought Jim, if the man we're after is a cop.

The last page of Raymond's file offered an interesting fact, of which Jim knew nothing. The ACLU had moved to bring a class-action suit against the Newport Beach PD in the summer of 1988, alleging that minorities were either not hired often enough or not promoted high enough. But Ray had refused to cooperate, and actually had spoken out against it in an interdepartmental letter to the then-chief, Lawrence Hiller. A letter back from Hiller, included here in Ray's file, stated, 'We commend Lt Cruz's discreet handling of these potentially disruptive matters, and consider it a substantial recommendation toward the lieutenant's eventual promotion to captain.' The suit was dropped. Ray, thought Weir, was a stand-up guy. He had bigger fish to fry: law school, graduation, the bar exam, practice. Raymond, true to form, wanted to prosecute someday.

And who, really, would be better at it? Raymond Cruz had lived

48

in Newport Beach longer than anyone else on the force, and his great-great-great-grandfather had been a cop before the word *cop* was invented. Ray's family, generations ago, had owned Rancho Boca de la Mar, seven thousand acres that included what would become Newport Beach, long before land became real estate. The patriarch, Francisco Cruz, had ruled over the rancho in its glory days of the *vaqueros*. And Francisco Cruz, as Raymond had told Jim so many times in his childhood, had been a Justice of the Plains, as appointed by the Mexican governor. *Justice of the Plains:* The phrase had rolled with pride off of Raymond's youthful tongue.

Weir remembered the tragic story now as he sat in Ann's small kitchen and felt layers of irony forming. He had first heard it from Raymond himself, in the fourth grade. Francisco Cruz was married to Lisbeth, a beautiful woman of German-Irish blood, who was kidnapped for ransom by the bandit Joaquin La Perla in a daring daylight raid on the rancho. Joaquin was nicknamed La Perla for the pearl-handled revolvers he wore, which, if Weir remembered correctly, were displayed at local fairs for years to come when Joaquin was finally caught and hanged. In Raymond's fourth-grade version of the story, Francisco had tracked La Perla and shot him down like a dog in the dirt, rescued his wife, and rode home to Rancho Boca de la Mar to celebrate with the largest fiesta in the history of the territory. Weir remembered the toy revolvers that Raymond had brought in as props for his story, complete with the white plastic handles. What actually had happened, however, was that Francisco's men had abandoned him in the eleventh hour and Cruz had continued after La Perla alone. He finally found the outlaw in what is now Silverado Canyon, where La Perla shot him full of holes and hung his body from an oak tree that is still standing today. Lisbeth was never found. Weir could remember that some heartless fourth-grader had pointed out the discrepancy between Ray's story and the version in a book of Orange County history, which he brought to class the next day as evidence. Raymond had stated flatly that the book's author was a liar and probably wasn't even there when it happened, then had withdrawn into brooding quiet that had lasted for days.

Now this, thought Jim. History might not repeat itself, but its echoes come sounding off the walls. He pondered the fate of the Cruz family. In the last 120 years, they had gone from being major landholders to renters of little houses and apartments, employees, proprietors of small businesses. Francisco's debt-riddled rancho was eventually sold off by his sons. Now, every inch of it belonged to someone else – even the Eight Peso Cantina was on leased land now held by the PacifiCo Development Group. Irena and Nesto had named it the Eight Peso because that was about how much money Nesto had waiting for him when he came back from Guadalcanal in 1946. His father had invested Nesto's service checks on a new idea – an automated car wash – which had gone belly-up earlier the same year.

It struck Jim that Raymond had never bemoaned the downward legacy left to him, never developed the sour pride of the fallen aristocrat, never considered himself entitled because of blood or race. Quietly, in his own way, Ray had been trying to turn it around. If he executes this guy, Weir thought, he'd be killing a part of himself, too. If he doesn't, Ray might join Francisco at the gates of heaven with similar stories to tell.

Next, he divided the time cards for the thirty-two officers on night and graveyard shifts – some of which overlapped one hour for obvious reasons – into partners and solos. The partners he set aside. That left eight solo officers out on each shift. Next, he checked their personnel files for blood type, and came up with five type B's. Four were right-handed, but two of these clocked out on the early stagger, at 12:02 and 12:18, respectively.

He wrote down the two remaining names on his legal sheet: Philip Kearns and Dale Blodgett.

According to Kearns's application and performance reviews, he was thirty-four years old, a bachelor. He'd made sergeant at thirty-two. Good, if not outstanding record. Helped deliver a baby in his squad car while partnered with Raymond Cruz, summer of '87. Yellow-slipped in September of the same year for parking his patrol car in a woman's driveway and leaving it unattended for twenty minutes – an irate neighbor had complained about the radio noise. An evaluation by Captain Chris Saunders lauded Kearns's 'easy disposition with the public' and 'low-key approach to law enforcement.' Kearns had been on the Police Pistol Team, Distinguished Marksman, ever since he was first hired.

Jim wondered whether Ann knew Kearns well enough to get into his car.

The transcript from Dispatch showed that Kearns stopped for coffee at a doughnut shop on Balboa between 11:15 P.M. and 11:35. So, thought Weir, he was patrolling the peninsula, where Ann lived and worked, where Ann was last seen. There was no communication between Kearns and Dispatch from 12:30 to 12:50. His Activity Log and Citation Book showed nothing, either. Twenty minutes, thought Weir, smack dab in the middle of the hour in question. On his legal pad, he wrote, KEARNS UNACCOUNTED FOR 20 MINUTES BETWEEN MIDNIGHT AND ONE. He studied the personnel file of Sgt Philip Kearns: a slender, small-featured face, wispy mustache, lively eyes, handsome in the way that cops are handsome. Medium brown hair, thinning and worn long, combed back from his forehead. Would it match the hair on Ann's blouse? Jim could feel his hands warming, a ripple of adrenaline easing through his body.

He sat back in the uncomfortable dinette chair and looked around the Cruz kitchen. Neat but not too neat: lived in. A cat clock hung from the wall behind the fridge, with eyes and a tail that moved with each tick and tock. Ann was a cat person. Ann was also a sweats-and-socks person, around the house. Why had she driven to work, then changed into something minimal and flattering? BECAUSE YOU WEREN'T COMING HOME, Weir wrote. Why no coat? BECAUSE YOU WEREN'T PLANNING ON BEING OUTSIDE. WHERE WERE YOU GOING, SWEET SISTER, WHERE DID YOU CHANGE YOUR CLOTHES?

He called the Whale's Tale and asked for Sherry. Sherry was Ann's favorite compatriot at work, a woman with an easy sense of humor and the hard legs of a professional waitress. She came on the line a little breathlessly, and when she was done talking, confirmed that Ann left the restaurant in her uniform, not street clothes.

Weir thanked her and hung up. Did Annie change in her car? How come the cops hadn't found it yet?

He picked up Dale Blodgett's file. Blodgett was a sergeant now, like Kearns. He was forty-eight years old, and his personnel mug shot showed a face that looked heavy, humorless, tough. Married, three kids, an average record. His evaluations always stressed the same thing: 'Blodgett shows little interest in promotion or future administration. Prefers his beat, works well alone. A capable officer. Recommend step increase commensurate with experience.'

There was one interesting addendum. Blodgett and Raymond

51

Cruz were called onto the chief's carpet two years ago for a fight in the locker room. The gist was that Blodgett and Ray had exchanged racial insults, then started swinging before three fellow cops broke it up. Warnings were issued. A final note added that a 'quantity of canned refried Mexican-style beans' was found by Raymond in his locker one night after shift, packed into his street shoes. He had accused Blodgett, who denied. The matter was not referred to again in Blodgett's file.

He closed it and ran the Dispatch tape through the hour in question one more time. He listened to Raymond's nearly constant communications from Unit 8, to Kearns's less frequent messages from Unit 12, to Dale Blodgett's clipped dispatches from Unit 6. Weir followed on the transcript. Blodgett signed off at 12:10 and didn't come back on until almost 1:00 A.M. He told Carol Clark he was stopping for coffee – but failed to give his location. Fifty minutes to drink a cup of coffee? Jim checked Blodgett's time card, but the blunt sergeant who'd filled Ray's shoes with frijoles never bothered to clock in. He wrote on the pad, BLODGETT HOSTILE TO RAY – 50 MINUTES OUT OF CONTACT – NO PROOF OF CLOCKING OUT – HOW LATE BACK TO STATION?

Weir crossed his arms and stared at the swinging plastic tail of Ann's cat clock. Malachi Ruff may have seen a cop car at the Back Bay that night, but Dennison wasn't in it. Neither was Ray Cruz. But Philip Kearns and Dale Blodgett had, between them, over an hour of time unaccounted for during the hour in question, when Ann was being tormented in the darkness by the wild tobacco plant.

At midnight, Jim was standing on the Balboa Pier, watching the black Pacific heave against the pilings. Lamps cast dismal triangles of light against the darkness. The fog came off the water from the west, like some overweight and earthbound cloud. The hour in question seemed close around him now, pressing in from all directions, hurling possibilities. Can anybody else hear them? It was this time, he thought, exactly three nights ago, when Ann took her final steps along the shore of the Black Bay.

Weir could see her as she moved down the trail through the ice plant, see the way she leaned back for balance, the way the red espadrilles threatened to buckle, the way she lifted her elbows up and out to steady herself, the strain of her calves, the shine – even down there in the foggy night – of her long golden hair. And the man behind her? Weir saw nothing more than a shadow, a shape in the darkness discernible only as a greater darkness. Together, he and Ann moved east along the shoreline, vanishing one unhurried step at a time into their own very private destiny.

The air around Jim hummed, charged by the dark energies of everything that had happened. Two kids on skateboards rolled by. A Japanese man added one more twisting mackerel to his bucket. The fog held the moon in a white web and wouldn't let it out. Jim turned back toward town, lowered his head, and wept.

He sat again at the kitchen table, watched the pivoting tail of Ann's cat clock. A gnawing late-night hunger came over him and he went to the fridge for something. He poured some milk and checked the leftovers – most of them probably going bad, he thought. There were drumsticks in a plastic bag, some stir-fried rice in a bowl, a collection of foil-wrapped surprises on the condiment shelf. One had anchovies he had to throw out. Another had a fat brownie that he ate while he stood there. The last contained three glass test tubes, each half-filled with clear fluid, each with a cork in the end. The first thing Weir thought was something to do with a pregnancy test, but why here?

He held them in his hand and read the handwritten labels: PCH BRIDGE 4/12; B. ISLAND 4/28; and BACK BAY 5/7. The writing was Virginia's.

What?

He set them on the kitchen counter and looked at them for a short while, noting the slight sediment collected in the bottom curve of each tube. He uncorked one and smelled it, then touched a little on his finger and tasted it. Seawater, no doubt. Checking the impound list for anything that might explain these things, Weir found nothing.

Why?

Samples from the bay. Brine. Hidden in with things that are bound to get thrown out.

He wrapped them in the foil, put the package back, and went into the living room, where he lay down on the couch. The cat clock

53

ticked from the kitchen; electricity buzzed through the power lines outside; the bay lapped lazily at the shore.

He fell asleep there, surrounded by the same walls that had held Ann's life, and dreamed deep in the night of a man's fingers holding a purple rose up to her smiling, radiant face.

8

At six the next morning, Jim let himself and Interim Chief Dennison in the back door of Poon's Locker. Virginia had closed the place for a few days. The blinds were drawn against a sunrise throttled in fog. He looked out across the bay, but he couldn't see the other side. The mast of a big yacht found a hole in the gloom, through which it passed like a disembodied remnant from another age. Jim poured water into the coffeemaker.

'You were faster than I thought you'd be,' said Dennison. His eyebrows raised with curiosity, but the rest of his face braced for something he clearly didn't want to hear. He had the look of a tax sneak about to open a letter from the IRS.

'I'm motivated. I saw Ray last night. He's going to be okay – out today, hopefully.'

'How is your mother taking it?'

'She's crushed, Brian. Have a seat.'

Dennison took a blue plastic chair off a table and sat. The coffee machine hissed and gurgled. Jim looked out to the sidewalk and thought about how many times as a teenager he had stood right here, brewing up coffee for the breakfast crowd, bursting with eagerness to get out of the café and aboard one of Poon's charter boats heading out to sea. Ann always had table work: refilling salt and pepper, setting out the creamers and napkin dispensers. Jake, the firstborn, helped Poon with the boats. Virginia presided over the kitchen and walk-in, heated up the grill, brought out the eggs and bread, separated the bacon slabs ahead of time, because when the rush came nobody had a minute to waste. Poon would traipse through the café three or four times each morning, going between the coffeepot and the boats, hurling orders, bemoaning the weather no matter how good it was, cursing the landlubbers from whom he made his living. He and Virginia would scream at each other like old Italians. Jim remembered looking through these windows

55

at Jake aboard one of the charter craft, naked to the waist, his body browned by sun, devotedly checking oil level or battery charge or lining up the game-fish rods in the racks behind the cabins. Jake was four years older. Jake could do everything. He was the best there was.

'I used to come down here and charter out your dad's boats,' said Brian.

'Mom sold them off a while back, except for *Sweetheart Deal*.'

'Yeah, well I've certainly noticed that one.'

The fact of the matter, thought Weir, was that Annie had bawled relentlessly when Virginia got ready to auction off *Sweetheart Deal*, the last of the charter fleet. The little thirty-footer was always Ann's favorite, moored just fifty feet offshore of the big house, kept neat as a museum piece by Poon. In the ten years since his death, the boat had been taken out only once that Jim knew of, by Ann. It had peeled, slouched, been nested in by birds, and was now moored outside Poon's Locker, testimony to his absence. Every year, the city sent a Notice of Dereliction to Virginia, and every year Ann would do some cosmetic cleanup on *Sweetheart Deal*, then let her sit unattended and unused for another season.

Jim set down coffee for Dennison and himself, then pulled a chair from the table and sat. If Brian wants *Sweetheart Deal* out of Newport Harbor, he thought, he'll have to talk to Virginia himself.

Dennison lifted his cup and peered over the lip at Weir, eyebrows on full alert. 'What do you have?'

'Kearns and Blodgett. The physicals match up pretty well, and both of them took some time off between midnight and coming back in.'

'How much time?'

'Kearns, twenty minutes – a coffee break, he says. Blodgett, almost the whole hour. Fifty minutes, no contact.'

'Fifty fucking minutes? Which beats?'

'Kearns had the peninsula, where Ann was working. Blodgett was on north end.'

Dennison leaned back and crossed his arms. His pale gray eyes had gone hard and his eyebrows had cut the comedy routine. There was in Brian Dennison, as in most of those in law enforcement, a mandatory capacity to perform violence. He looked at this moment more like a tough cop than a mayor.

56

Dennison's head jerked when the back door slammed open behind them. Virginia marched in, wrapped in her yellow wind-breaker against the morning cool. She glanced at Dennison, then at Jim, then stared at Brian in unmasked disbelief.

'Good morning, Mrs Weir,' he said quietly.

'What exactly is good about it?'

'That's just an expression. I'm awfully sorry about Ann.'

'Well, yes . . . so am I, Brian. It's been very hard.'

When Virginia turned her pale blue sun-worn eyes on Jim, they said, What the hell are you doing with this fascist mayoral candidate *in my café*? That established, Virginia announced that Jim had an urgent call.

'Who is it?'

'I don't think that should be public knowledge.'

Brian shrugged and started to stand, but Jim held his mother's arm and took her back toward the walk-in. Out of earshot, Jim raised a finger to Virginia and shook his head. He explained that Chief Dennison was there to talk about Ann, to find her killer. Politics, mayoral races, and neighborhood rivalries would have to be set aside. She met his look head-on, her 'you're talking to a rock' expression. Jim knew that in some ways, he truly was. The way around Virginia was submission: If she thought you deserved help, she was usually willing to give it. As would anyone who had spent a lifetime with the vagaries of someone like Poon, she enjoyed feeling kind when she was sure it wouldn't cost her much.

'Gold,' she said. 'Dr Robert Gold. Said it's important. He's holding for you.'

'I'll call him back.'

'I remember that name.'

'One of my teachers at State, Mom.'

'Maybe he knows something.'

'Tell him I'll call back in a few minutes. Take a number. Can do?'

Virginia's hard stare broke down and she looked at the floor. 'What I can't do is make any progress with the flowers. The Sunday . . . before Ann . . . was Mother's Day – busiest day of the year. I finally got through the Newport Beach listings. Nobody sold Annie any roses, or delivered any to her.'

'Keep on it. What are those test tubes doing in Ann's refrigerator? They've got your writing on them.'

She crossed her arms, shot a look toward the dining room, and lowered her voice. 'We'll have time for that, later. Get back to your *friend* now.'

'Believe it or not, he'd like to help.'

Virginia regrouped her forces. 'I do not want that man in my café. He's a stooge for C. David Cantrell of PacifiCo, and he stands for everything I oppose. He won't even debate Becky in public. From now on, you meet him somewhere else.'

'He wants answers as much as we do.'

'Don't you believe it. Call Gold. He says it's important. When you're done with that self-serving oaf in there, I can tell you about the tubes.'

Virginia cast a contemptuous look toward the dining room, then headed out the service door. The back of her yellow jacket had a jumping marlin on it, with the words NEWPORT BEACH LADY ANGLERS below in red embroidery. Virginia was president, ten years running.

Back in the dining room, Dennison had both hands around his coffee cup, and a worried look on his face. His urge to violence must have crawled back down its hole. 'You didn't tell her what —'

'Of course I didn't. Don't worry, Brian.'

'That woman scares the hell out of me.'

'She has that effect on people.'

Dennison chuckled, himself again, eyebrows raised in hyperbolic doubt. 'What scares me most is that she thinks she's the only one with the interests of this city at heart. She thinks that people like Dave Cantrell and I are trying to change it, but believe me, the real threat comes from somewhere else.'

Jim waited for the revelation.

But Dennison must have thought better of it. He settled back into his chair with a sigh that said, If these people could only share my burdens.

Jim waited again, wondering whether silence would bring the interim chief to his point. What Dennison said next surprised him.

'I hope Virginia knows she can come to me anytime. I know she thinks my Toxic Waste unit is a joke.'

'She's never said that to me,' said Jim. What Virginia had said was that Dennison cared more about getting a new chopper into the city sky than he did about keeping the harbor clean. He had

58

seen correspondence from the EPA on Virginia's desk. Was she making an end run?

'The last thing we need is the feds running all over this town, Jim. I hope Virginia is smart enough to see the danger in that. We need to be taking care of Newport Beach, ourselves. We ... the people who live here.'

So there it is, thought Weir: another reason why Dennison hired me for this. I can talk to Virginia on his behalf because I am her son. That, while I dissuade Becky from learning that the cops are looking at the cops, because I am her friend, ex-companion, ex-lover. Dennison looked less antic to him now, wholly disingenuous. The idea crossed Jim's mind that he himself had inherited his mother's thirst for conspiracy.

'I'm sure she'd agree.'

'She won't sit still long enough to listen.'

Weir understood the corollary: Bring Virginia to the bargaining table.

Dennison studied him for a moment, apparently convinced that he had been effective. 'Okay, Blodgett and Kearns on patrol, time not accounted for with Dispatch. What else?'

'Blodgett and Ray had some run-ins. The race stuff.'

'That was two years ago.'

'It's something to consider.'

Dennison nodded silently, staring out the window. Weir followed his line of vision to the bay, where the morning light had risen an octave against the fog. The look on Dennison's face told Weir that the chief already regretted letting his files go. 'Kearns and Blodgett,' he said quietly. 'What else do you need from me?'

'Whatever you've got.'

'I've got nothing you don't know, and you still have an open line to Robbins. Use it.'

'I'd consider a polygraph if I were you. Do both shifts, every man on patrol. Have the operator angle the questions toward something else – drugs or sexual favors – anything. Ask your men to take it, but don't insist. What we need is an explanation of what Kearns and Blodgett were doing. If they talk, fine. If not, we'll have to wonder why.'

'No. The union would have my ass. That's exactly the kind of thing I don't want to do. That's exactly why I brought you on.'

Dennison leveled his pale eyes on Jim, then jumped again as

Virginia barged in from the back door. 'He called again,' she said. 'Says it's important.'

'I'll call him back in five minutes.'

'He's waiting for you.'

'*I'll call him, Mom.*'

The door slammed shut.

'I want you to talk to Kearns and Blodgett. If their answers don't add up, I'll refer the whole thing to Internal Affairs. I'd rather not do that, but I will. Don't mention the Dispatch tape, or I'm dead in the water.'

Weir thought. 'Can you get me into the station locker room when no one else is there?'

Dennison's eyes came to life, a glimmer of curiosity. 'The hair on Ann's blouse?'

Jim nodded.

Dennison pondered for a moment, shaking his head. 'Too risky. Try talking to them first. Check their alibis for the downtime. We'll get hair samples if our options come down to that.'

Jim thought it through. What he needed was more leverage. 'Kearns and Blodgett don't know what Mackie saw, do they?'

'Not exactly. That report is for me and Paris and a couple of captains. And you.'

'I might embellish. Keep the interview under wraps if you can.'

'I am. If the stories around the station get a little wilder, I'll know where they came from.' Dennison handed him an envelope. 'Here's for yesterday, today, and three more. After that, we'll talk. Four grand, Jim. Silence. Don't hang me out to dry on this.'

Jim pocketed the money. A hundred an hour, he thought, to find who killed Ann. He felt dirty.

'We got Ann's car. Officers spotted it about two hours ago. Innelman worked the area, and we took it to impound.'

Jim's heart sped up for a moment, then settled. 'Where was it?'

'A mile from here, down by the Wedge.'

'And?'

'Window was pried open, so we figure he might have been waiting inside when she left work. It was just parked on a side street like a thousand others. Innelman said it was crawling with prints – hopefully not all hers. I happen to think she had somewhere to go that night – otherwise, she'd have walked to work, right? So, where?'

'Neither of us would be sitting here if I knew the answer to that.

60

What about that piece of jewelry that Deak found – prints, make, anything?'

'A couple of jewelers told Innelman it's probably the back of a tie tack. A custom piece – irregular and expensive. Twenty-four-carat stuff.'

They stood and shook hands. 'The world's a funny place, Jim. You're investigating my own goddamned police force and I'm making a speech at noon to the Kiwanis, about what a good mayor I'd make.'

'I'm sure you would.'

'I'd expect your vote to go to Becky.'

'We go back a ways.'

'She's a good lawyer,' said Dennison. He turned to leave, then hesitated, looking toward the back door. 'You know, Jim, you could do me a favor. It's obvious your mother doesn't like me and she's doing what she can for Becky in this campaign. That's okay; that's what makes this country great. But tell her something for me. Tell her if she's got worries about the water in our bay, she can come to me. There's no reason to run to the EPA or the state. If she's onto something, I'd like to know about it. I care about this city, too, in spite of what she says.'

'What is it you think she's found?'

Dennison shrugged. 'She sure as hell won't tell me. Maybe you can find out.'

Jim got Dr Robert Gold's number and took it upstairs to his old room. Gold was a soft-spoken man who even fifteen years ago when Jim took his classes in criminal psychology seemed aged and eroded by his study of violent crime. He was a statistician at heart, a collector of data, a theorist who based his ideas on a combination of immutable facts and unpredictable behavior. Jim did a rough calculation: Gold must be pushing eighty years old now.

Mrs Gold said her husband would be right with Jim, but Weir waited at least two minutes.

'Many years, Jim,' he said in greeting. His voice was overloud, that of a man who no longer hears well.

'Too many, Doctor.'

'Can you speak up? I'm sorry you had to wait. I'm stuck in a wheelchair now and it can take incredible amounts of time to roll

61

across a room. That's because my right arm doesn't work anymore and neither does my right leg. So the effect, of course, is pretty slow going. Stroke, summer of 'eighty-nine.'

'I'm sorry, Doctor.'

'What?'

'*I said I'm sorry, Doctor.*'

'Well, thank you, but eighty-four years old is eighty-four years old. At least the right side of my brain still works.'

'Have you retired?'

'Oh, yes, ten years back. Now I spend my time with the aviary, and reading the journals. It's too hard to write anymore, so I read for . . . well, pleasure wouldn't quite be the right word, would it?'

Gold's booming laugh came over the line. Weir thought he detected something desperate in it. The idea crossed his mind that Dr Gold was easing around the last great bend. At least he's doing it with a sense of humor, thought Weir. There seemed to be too much sadness in the world.

'What do you have for me, Doctor?'

Gold cleared his throat. 'Jim, I have to say first of all how sorry I am about your sister. I feel badly for you, and for Raymond, too.'

'We're going to be okay, Doctor.'

'I'm sorry, I couldn't quite make out —'

'*We'll be okay.*'

The line was suddenly quiet. Jim could hear Gold's breathing. Ten seconds went by.

'I'm back,' said Gold, very quietly now. 'I'm sorry. Every now and then a tiny seizure, a little focal seizure, but I can't clear my head for a moment. Give me just another few seconds . . . is it Jim?'

'Yes, Doctor, it's Jim Weir.'

'Oh my, this is . . . just hold on now. Wait.'

A minute later, Gold spoke again. The strength had returned to his voice, but Jim now understood how much energy the doctor used in just talking.

'Now, Jim. The reason I called is because I was going through the Sex Offender Registration files for the last three months. I review them quarterly, just to glean the numbers for my recidivism model. Does the name Horton Goins mean anything to you?'

'No.'

'Well, he raped and stabbed a young woman in Ohio nine years ago. She didn't die, but she's been in and out of hospitals ever

62

since, terribly disturbed, schizophrenic. There's no way you would know of him. It didn't make the papers out here. But he was interesting to me for many reasons. He was only fifteen years old. He was raised in foster homes. He had a troubled boyhood, and an oddly variable IQ. He also had a perfectly readable schizophrenic metabolism.'

'Readable?'

'Positron emission tomography – the so-called PET scan. Dr Field at UC Irvine was kind enough to let me work over his shoulder a bit on Mr Goins. We flew him in from Dayton, very hush-hush, state police and Mr Goins's keeper from the hospital in tow. You can imagine the strings we had to pull. But what a subject! We could see the hyperstimulated thalamic stem — bright yellow and red, and the corresponding frontal activity that is usually suppressed in normal people. Goins's PET scan was a virtual road map of schizophrenia – tracked chemically. *National Geographic* included a picture of his brain in its January 'eighty-seven issue on imaging technology. At any rate, I used Goins as a case study for class, and his . . . proclivities stuck in my mind. Jim, can you share with me the blood type on the suspect?'

'Type B positive.'

'Interesting. Goins is, also. The particulars of his episode are very similar to what I understand about Ann. He took his victim to a swampy area not far from town. It was late at night. He'd been watching her for a matter of weeks, it was discovered in the competency hearings. She was a waitress. Goins was committed to state hospital as a mentally disordered juvenile sex offender. They kept him almost nine years, performing the standard drug and psychotherapies, apparently to great effect. The PET that Dr Fields did helped them prescribe even more helpfully – it's not like they use these people as guinea pigs, then dump them.'

'No.' Jim could hear Gold catching his breath.

'This January, they remanded Horton to his parents – legal guardians, that is. It was the same old story. The state couldn't keep him, his doctor approved a release, and the DA's hands were tied because Horton had been in custody of one kind or another for almost nine years. In late January, Horton Goins and his foster parents moved to Costa Mesa. That's what – two miles from where Ann was found?'

Jim felt his throat thicken, a coolness spread into his feet. 'Do you have an address?'

'Emmett and Edith Goins, courtesy of Pacific Bell.' He gave Jim the street address and phone number.

'According to your models, Dr Gold, would Goins be likely to repeat?'

'Oh my, please wait . . .'

The line went quiet again. Jim could hear the doctor's steady breathing. Gold's seizure lasted half a minute.

'Hello?' His voice was very faint now.

'Hello, Doctor . . . it's Jim Weir.'

'It's so hard . . . so hard to come out from behind this cloud. And the seizure medications they give me – Dilantin, Tegretol, then more stuff to keep the others from eating away my stomach. It's like . . . watching myself in a dream. Where were we?'

'I'd asked you if Horton Goins was likely to repeat.'

'It would be irresponsible to answer that question directly. So many factors, so many unknowns. But, well Jim, I *did* call you, didn't I?'

'Thank you, Doctor. Is there anything I can do for you?'

'Well . . .' Gold's voice was reedy and thin now, as if the breath upon the cords was not enough to play them. 'You know, Jim . . . just a few months ago I would have asked that if you apprehend Goins, you would put in a good word for me. Arrange an interview. But now . . . but now . . . I think I just want to rest. I have my birds.'

'God bless you, Dr Gold.'

9

Emmett and Edith Goins lived on the east side of Costa Mesa, on Heather Street. It was a neighborhood of apartments built in the fifties: uniform rectangles, flat roofs, cement stairways with iron banisters leading to the upper units. The Goinses' complex was called Island Gardens, and looked the same as the others around it except for one large bird of paradise plant and a six-foot-high stone head that stood off from the walkway. The statue was Polynesian in attitude, and covered with graffiti. The sign that stood behind this 'island garden' was so faded by sunlight that Weir could hardly read it.

The Goinses lived downstairs, in 1-C. Jim walked past three reeking dumpsters busy with cats, past the stairs, down a walkway choked with weeds and dog turds, along the open windows of downstairs units, from which came the sounds of television and the smells of breakfast. The screens were dotted with flies that shone in the dull morning sun.

He knocked and stepped back. A game show sounded through the window – horrible laughter followed by carnivalesque music, then applause.

'Who is it?' A woman's voice, low and rough.

'My name is Jim Weir.'

'We don't want none.'

'I came to see Horton.'

'He's not here.'

'May I talk to you for just a moment, please?'

Then the door opened about six inches and a pale, soft, red-haired woman looked up at him. She was wearing a blue terry robe with cigarette ash on the lapel. Her eyes were brown in the middle and bloodshot everywhere else.

Edith Goins's eyes went down him, and back up – brown, red, brown again. 'You the police?'

'No. But I'd like to ask some questions.'

'Another doctor?'

'No ma'am, just a regular guy.'

'Nobody regular's interested in Horton.'

'May I come in?'

Edith Goins shut the door in Jim's face. He heard voices, questions, a hopeful agreement. She opened the door a moment later and turned back inside. Jim followed. She was short, heavy, rounded. 'This is Emmett,' she said. 'Em, this is Mr Weird.'

Jim didn't see him at first. He was locked in shadow in the corner of the room, wrapped in a black robe with a big silver anchor emblazoned over one breast. His head was narrow, his hair cut short, his ears nearly flush with his skull. He wore a thin, almost prissy mustache. His face was red in the TV light, then it shifted – to great applause – to blue. He looked up at Jim and offered his hand. 'Horton isn't here,' he said finally.

Jim shook his hand, then sat at the far end of the couch from Edith. He set down his briefcase. 'Thanks for having me in. Nice little apartment you have here.'

'Ought to be for eight-fifty a month,' said Emmett. 'And if they pass this Slow Growth deal, then they're going to stop the construction and rent's going to go even higher.'

Jim glanced at the TV, where some frantic young couple made fools of themselves for an Amana range. 'I had a talk with Dr Robert Gold earlier. He's a man who keeps track of people when they get out of hospitals. He told me that you and Horton moved here to Costa Mesa just this January.'

'January twenty-eighth,' said Edith. 'Why are you so interested in Horton? The woman that got kilt?'

The question threw Weir off balance. This was going to be a strange ride. 'Yes. A young woman. Five nights ago, down in the Back Bay in Newport, a couple of miles from here. We were . . . very close. Was Horton at home that night?'

Edith and Emmett exchanged blatantly furtive looks. Emmett nodded to his wife.

'That was Monday,' she said. 'Horton was out Monday night. Horton comes and goes as he pleases these days, even though his release people told him to stay put here.'

Jim nodded, waiting for more. The game show droned on stupidly. Weir sensed that big things were not being said here, things that

66

might lay groundwork. 'Would you mind, at all, telling me about Horton? I'm not a cop or a doctor. I've got no official standing. I just lost someone close and I'm doing what I can to help out.'

Emmett looked at Edith, then nodded again, but neither spoke. Their continuing silence implied that what was about to be revealed here was of such size and scope, it would dominate the entire moral landscape, but there was nothing theatrical in their faces. Edith brought a bottle of bourbon from beside the couch and poured a small shot into a coffee cup, Weir understanding now that he had provided a service – his presence was an excuse to drink. She swished it around for a moment, then drained it. 'Horton ain't ours. We got him from the agency when he was four.'

'He wasn't four, he was almost six,' said Emmett. When Emmett looked at Jim straight on, one eye wandered and one stayed on target with sharp black intensity. 'The agency lied about that, and plenty of the other, too.'

'We didn't know four from six anyhow,' said Edith. 'On accounta not being able to have our own. See, Emmett was in a bad –'

''Nuff a that, Edith.'

'. . . So we got one from the agency.'

'What agency was that?'

'Hardin County Adoption Agency. Hardin County being in Ohio.'

'Ah,' said Jim. He suddenly felt badly for these people. They seemed like lightning rods for calamity, and he'd only known them for five minutes. He recognized in them, too, the overwhelming desire to divulge, so common to children, adulterers, and drunks.

Edith poured another bourbon and studied it with a measured, rational air. 'We were happy to get him. See, you usually got to wait a long spell, but Horton, we got him quick. They just made us sign a bunch of papers and out we went.'

'The fact they let us have him so easy should have told us something was up, but it didn't,' said Emmett.

Edith shrugged. 'We got a little brown cowboy shirt for him to wear out, some cowboy pants, too. I remember walkin' with him between us out to the Buick, feeling like I finally had my family. I think that walk from the agency door to the Buick was the first and last time in my life I was happy. It was exactly twenty-four steps. I still remember that, for some reason.'

'Don't get sloppy, Edith,' said her husband.

'I count steps sometimes, too,' said Jim.

Emboldened, Edith sipped again and continued. 'Funny the things you remember when you're happy. So we got Horton home and he was silent. He didn't look at us or say a thing for five days. He ate a lot. We were told about the 'justment period, how the child had to grow into your life and feel secure before he could be happy. The agency told us to try a pet. We got him two hamsters, but they disappeared, and Horton didn't know where. Later, we got him a dog, and he liked the dog a bunch. Dog ran off after a couple of weeks, though. Month later, some of the farm dogs dug up Horton's dog and the hamsters outta the swamp down by the bridge, came parading around the yard with them. Horton didn't seem too surprised.'

A long silence followed. Emmett stared at the TV. 'I talked to the agency about him. They said it was normal and that Horton didn't have any history of bad behavior, so we had to be patient. The thing that got us the most was he'd never say nothing. One day, Horton stood up on his chair in the middle of dinner and pissed on the ham. I used a belt on him good, but he bit my leg so deep, it took eighteen stitches and a tetanus shot. It healed black for some reason.'

'That's when we put Horton in the car and drove him back to the agency,' said Edith. 'They couldn't figure out why Horton was being so naughty, and they told us his record before was good. They tried to make it sound like we were doing something wrong and maybe we weren't fit to have him. We said we'd try more lovin' and understanding, on accounta that's what a child needs, they said. We felt bad.'

'I didn't,' said Emmett. 'I knew right then from the look on that lady's face, she was lying about him. I remember on the way back from the agency, Horton was sitting in the backseat of the Buick, burning a firefly in one of them cigarette lighters the old 'sixty-fours had in the rear.'

The silence got long again. 'Pretty bad kid,' said Jim to fill it.

Edith nodded. 'So we had a private investigator get the records from the agency. It was just like we thought. He'd burnt down his own house when he was four. He was really six when we got him, like I said, they tried to fool us. That's why they let him go so fast. He was a lemon. So we tried to take him back, but they wouldn't take him. Finally, he stuck a dead water moccasin down Pammy Fritzie's underwear, and we turned him over to the Juvenile Authority. He was seven by then. They kept him two years. They did a lot of tests and told us they thought it might be a chemical problem. Maybe that was the second happiest time of my life, when we got rid of Horton then.'

Emmett held out his coffee cup and his wife poured in some bourbon. 'A few months after Horton was at the Juvenile Authority, he started sending us letters. They were done in real nice writing, and the spelling was good. He had a real good vocabulary for a seven-year-old. He was smart. He wrote us about how sorry he was for what he'd done, and how much he missed the farm. I'll tell you, we sat there at the kitchen table and cried because he sounded so full of sorrow and because we'd held a lot of love inside us just waitin' for a reason to let it out, but we never had no reason. It was like Horton in the letter was the son we always wanted.'

'So,' said Edith, 'we made the petition and got him back.'

Emmett sighed and looked at Jim. His face went blue again in the TV screen's light. 'As I look back on my life, Mr Weird, I can honestly say that was the dumbest fuckin' thing I ever did.'

'Me, too,' Edith added solemnly. 'Horton was fine for a few years after that. That was, say from nine years old to twelve. He spent a lot of time out in the fields and the swamps, catching snakes and critters and bringing them home. He did his chores, earned some money, and bought books on animals. At school, well, Horton didn't make many friends. He got beat up a lot because he wasn't big and he was one of those kids – you know how they pick out one to badger all the time? They singled out Horton and made him kind of miserable. But, gosh, his grades! When Horton went into seventh level – that's age thirteen about – he got all A's and only one D. The D was in speech. He just couldn't get up in front of everyone and talk.'

Weir was quiet as an invisible ripple of memory issued through the room. He understood that what he'd just heard represented the apex of happiness in the Goins family unit. 'So I guess the Juvenile Authority did him some good.'

Edith nodded and drank again. 'When Horton came back to us, he had learned self-control. He was very polite. He was quiet. He liked to move things into his room so he wouldn't have to come out much. He wanted to eat in there, but we never allowed that. But you know, Horton never once told us he loved us. He never

69

once remembered a birthday or made us anything for Christmas. He lived in some kind of other place. There was the Horton that nodded politely and did the dishes. Then there was the Horton that lived in his room for hours at a time, or spent whole days out in the fields or in the swamp. There was two Hortons. I'm convinced of that.'

The Goinses went quiet again, each lost to a separate remembrance. Edith's head turned toward Jim. 'You have kids?'

'No, ma'am.'

'Then you probably think we're a couple of dumb farmers, but we're not. We've got love in our hearts – or at least we did a long time back – and we tried our best to find something to attach it to. There was nothing in the world we wanted more than to get through to that boy. After the first year, we started thinking it was us, and the more bad he did, the more we thought it was our fault. By the time we put him in the Juvenile Authority, we were just about crazy ourselves. We offered Horton our love. Nobody can say we didn't. We stood by him. We still do.'

Emmett held out his cup for more. He looked at Jim, and in the TV light his eyes took on a cathode glow of surprising tenderness. 'From age twelve to age fifteen, Horton was kind of distant. Still polite to us, never argued. For a brief time, he had a girlfriend, a girl his age who lived two farms over. Her name was Lucy Galen and we saw them together a few times, walking home from school. You could tell from the angle of Horton's head, the way he looked at her, how ... fascinated he was with this girl. He'd go to the fountain where she worked. We never knew exactly what happened, but Lucy's parents called us one night and told us to keep Horton away from her or they'd call the police. Something about him and their daughter behind the smoke shed. So we forbid him to see her, and so far as we know, he didn't. Horton spent more time in his room after that, quiet.'

Emmett turned off the TV with a remote. The apartment got suddenly darker and smaller, as if crouched in anticipation. 'In May of that year, when Horton was fifteen, they found Lucy out in the swamp, stabbed bad and raped. They put Horton in jail but decided he was too crazy to help defend himself. They committed him. Lucy didn't die, but she never got well, either, from what we heard. Nine years of hospital came after that, for Horton. They finally took a picture of what was making him crazy, and gave him a bunch of

70

good drugs. He was getting better before that, but the new drugs cured him. January last, they let him out to us. Cured.'

Jim observed a moment of silence, for Lucy and Horton, but mostly for Emmett and Edith Goins. The apartment seemed to vibrate with their pain. 'And you moved here to California?'

'Yes.'

'Why?'

They exchanged looks again, looks of utter resignation. 'Horton asked us to,' said his mother. 'And besides, we were ready. Em couldn't find any work in Ohio – we'd moved to Lima by then – so we thought California would be a good new start.'

'Did Horton say why he wanted to come here?'

Edith sipped again from her cup. 'No. But he told us that California was rich in opportunity for Emmett, was a place we all could start over, and the weather was nice. He spent a lot of time doing research, and he decided Costa Mesa was the best place we could be. Close enough to the beach for good breezes, and close enough to the freeways for work. Horton got a job at a PhotoStop, soon as we moved out. See, during his stay in the state hospital, he got interested in photography. Took some real nice pictures of the other patients, though I must admit they're some pretty scary people.'

'Which PhotoStop?'

'Right out here on Harbor Boulevard. To be honest, Horton must have lied just a tad on his application.'

'How has he been since he got out?'

Emmett set down his coffee mug. 'This part might be hard for you to believe, Mr Weird, because it was hard for us to believe. Horton is a changed man.'

'How so?'

'He's clean and neat. He smiles upon occasion. He enjoys his work and takes it – well, *took* it – very seriously. He saw all the people around here so trim and suntanned, and he began doing exercises in his room. With his first few paychecks, he bought clothes. He likes the colors you got out here – the Hawaiian shirts and the baggy pants with the tight cuffs and those big jogging shoes that look so complicated. He puts Wildroot or something on his hair to hold it in place.'

Edith lit a cigarette and blew the smoke out her nose. 'But you know, it's not just his appearance or how he acts. We learned the hard way how a person can act one way and be another. It's in the way he looks at us, at the world. There's a light in his eyes now. There's a . . . joy in them.'

Jim watched the smoke ease across the room, window-bound. 'You say he quit his job?'

Emmett and Edith looked at each other again and shook their heads. Edith sighed out a lungful of smoke. 'Starting out in early February – just a couple of weeks after we got here – Horton spent less and less time here. He told us he was working overtime, but we'd drive by to see and there'd be someone else in his booth. The terms of his release specifically say he's gotta live with us, so we told him to stick close. He smiled and hugged us both – they seem to do that a lot in California – and said everything was "cool" and not to worry. Well, two months ago today, Horton moved out. He took most of his things, his cameras and clothes, and he just disappeared. He never showed up at work, they said. He comes back here twice a week and spends the night – so's not to violate the release. He calls every few days to say he's fine, and we've gotten three postcards. But he won't say where he is. Once a month, he's got a review-board meeting, and he always shows up for it. Rest of the time, 'cept for a couple of nights, he's gone. He took our Chevy and left us the truck. He's actually pretty good about changing oil – did it before we left Ohio and when we got here.'

'Where do you think he went?'

'I honestly got no idea.'

Edith and Emmett looked at him now, the ball clearly in his court. Edith sat forward. 'What exactly is motivating you at this point, Mr Weird?'

'The woman who was killed was my sister, Ann.'

'Oh, my,' said Edith, her grief calling for another drink, which she poured with care.

Emmett sat forward, too, elbows on his robed knees. 'Mr Weird, we've been honest with you up to now, because we've found after all we've been through with Horton, that honesty is the easiest thing to do. We don't feel we got anything to hide. We answered your questions even though you're a stranger, and we'll answer more if you got them. We've spent most of our lives answering questions about Horton. But I'll tell you right now that Horton didn't do it. He's a new man. I'd bet everything I have on it.'

72

'I'm sure you're right, Mr Goins.'

'If you were sure I was right, you wouldn't be here, would you?'

Jim nodded.

'Thing is,' said Edith. 'We believe in him.'

But you really don't believe in him, thought Jim, no matter how bad you want to. Can I? 'May I see his room?'

Again the Goinses looked at each other. They regarded Jim now, shrugging at precisely the same moment. 'Not much to see,' said Emmett. 'But you're welcome. We've got not one thing to hide, and neither does Horton.' He stood, tightened his robe sash with a martial tug, then led Weir down a short hallway toward Horton's room.

It was the second on the right. Emmett swung open the door and followed Jim inside. It was small, with clean white walls, a twin bed, a desk with a blank blotter on it, sliding closets opposite the bed, and thin green shag carpet. To one wall was tacked a poster of a sunset over a swaying wheat field, with Thoreau's 'different drummer' quotation in fancy gold script at the bottom. On another were two promotional posters for a Japanese camera maker, featuring leggy blondes in swimsuits, draped with photographic gear. Between them was a colored picture of a human brain. The various parts of the organ were different colors, ranging from pale yellow to hot red. 'That's a PET picture of Horton's brain,' said Emmett. 'They do them to see the parts that make them crazy. Horton's is that little red area way down in the middle. Over the last couple of years, it got smaller and smaller from the drugs.' A folded tripod leaned in one corner.

'Is he still on medication?'

'You bet he is. Costs us nine hundred a month, no generics. He's real good about taking it – has a little electronic pillbox that beeps when it's time for something.'

Jim nodded, his nerves jumping, a feeling growing inside him that he'd like to trash this place and see what he could find.

'Not much to see,' said Emmett. 'Even when he was here a lot, the room was always neat. They taught him that in the hospital.'

'May I open some drawers? Look in the closet?'

'Help yourself.'

'I was wondering, too, do you have a recent picture of him?'

'Let me see what I've got,' said Emmett, heading for the door.

Weir slid open the closet door and looked inside: a few shirts and coats on hangers, pants folded and stacked on an upper shelf, cardboard boxes stacked at the far end. He pulled open the top one and saw the neat collection of photography magazines, proof sheets, developing gear. He removed one of the proofs and angled it toward the faint window light. Group shots in an institutional setting, dazed, scarcely attentive faces. Horton's fellows in the state hospital, thought Weir. The last row were closeups of a man's hand holding what looked like a crayon to a sheet of unmarked paper. It was a handsome hand – deeply lined, well proportioned, capable. Weir checked the date on the top magazine: June '89. He could hear Emmett come into the room behind him.

'Got a couple here,' he said.

Jim left the closet door open, but backed out and accepted two snapshots from the hand of Emmett Goins. He could smell the bourbon on Emmett's breath. 'Just a month ago, these,' he said.

They were both pictures of Horton and Edith. Horton looked surprisingly good: wide-set, placid blue eyes, a high forehead, wavy dark brown hair, a strong but slender jawline tapering to a firm chin. His smile – a little crooked, a little shrewd – revealed large white teeth. There was something ulterior about that smile, though Jim couldn't put his finger on it, something . . . employable. Looks like any other twenty-four year old Southern Californian, he thought. For just one fraction of a moment, Weir sensed recognition, but his mind, flying backward through the years, found nowhere to land.

'Take one if you want,' said Emmett.

'Thank you, I would.'

Jim slid open the top desk drawer: two loupes, a roll of masking tape, pencils and pens. The side drawers were nearly empty, just a few loose snapshots and some boxes of slides.

'Horton's got pictures of everything. Most of 'em, he took with him.'

'Mr Goins, do you have any idea where he is? Any clue at all?'

'Well, somewhere not too far is my guess.'

'No address?'

'All's he ever said is it's cheap. You can read the postcard he sent us if you want to.'

They went back to the living room, where Edith had turned on a soap. She brought down the volume and looked at Weir expectantly. 'Not much to see, is there?'

'No, not really.'

Emmett pulled something off of the refrigerator and handed it to Jim. The writing was small and neat, done in a well-sharpened pencil. The postmark was April 26.

Dear Mom & Dad,
  Things are fine here in my 'hideaway' and the purpose of my life is becoming clear to me. I'll be back in a few days to visit, and we'll be together. My permanent address is still at your place — so don't let Dr Wick forget it! The Chevy is fine and I'm living off savings.

Love, Joseph

'Joseph?'

Edith explained. 'Horton changed his name. The courts wouldn't allow it because of his record, but he calls himself that, anyway. We can't get used to it.'

When Jim flipped over the card, the blood rushed into his face. It was the old standard from Poon's Locker, a shot of the shop with the words *Wet Your Line at Poon's Balboa!* written across it.

'You know where Balboa is, Mr Weird?'

'I grew up there.' His heart was throbbing hard now.

'We're sorry about your sister,' said Edith, 'but we know that Horton's innocent, so we don't mind talking.'

'Can you tell me what kind of car he has?'

'It's an 'eighty-seven Caprice. White, four doors, blue interior.'

Weir decided to let Dennison's men get the license-plate numbers — along with the postcard from Poon's Locker, and a hair sample to check against the one found on Ann's blouse. Who knows what else they'd find.

'Thank you very much, again. Both of you. You don't have to mention this visit to Horton. No reason to get him upset.'

'Good luck. We got nothing to hide, and neither does Horton anymore.'

'I can see that now.'

'Good luck on your sister. Judging from you, she must have been a nice girl.'

'She was great.'

Jim skidded to a stop at the first pay phone he could find. He dialed Dennison's direct number and the secretary told him Brian would be right with him. Weir stood, engulfed by the hazy smog on Harbor Boulevard, his stomach fluttering with eagerness. When Brian came on, Weir flew through the story – Dr Gold, Horton Goins in Hardin County, the sudden unexplained move to Southern California, Edith and Emmett, the postcard. 'The girl that Goins did in Ohio was a waitress, too. He befriended her, got her trust, and took her out to a swamp.'

'Good Christ in heaven, Weir.'

'That's exactly what I thought.'

'Okay, I'm sending Innelman and Deak over there as soon as I can – they can ask a few questions, then pop the shit out of the place. Any chance Goins would show up and try to cart anything off?'

'Not with me watching the door.'

'Good. What's your call on ... what we talked about this morning?'

'I think Blodgett and Kearns have some questions to answer. Horton Goins wasn't driving any cop car out at the Back Bay.'

Dennison was silent for a moment. 'It's your show with them, not mine. Blodgett's off shift for the next few nights – might be a good time to find him home.'

'What did you get from Annie's car?'

'A whole lot of hair and fingerprints – all hers. Robbins is working it over again right now.'

Weir hung up, his heart still beating fast. He spent the next forty-five minutes parked outside the Island Garden apartments, alert for a white '87 Chevy Caprice. It never showed, but a new one did. Dwight Innelman and Roger Deak climbed out, followed, to his astonishment, by Interim Chief Brian Dennison and Mike Paris.

Jim smiled to himself as he started up the truck. Arresting a mentally disordered sex offender would be good for Brian. Good for the city. Good for the news media. Good for a campaign, too: Who wouldn't want this crime-stopper to serve as mayor for their town? He watched Dennison bend down and check his hair in the side mirror of the cop car before leading his detectives toward the apartment.

10

Two blocks south of the ferry landing on Balboa is the Weir family home. The first house was built by Jim's great-grandfather in 1891, on a site obtained by a hundred-year lease from what is now the PacifiCo Development Group. The original structure was destroyed by flood. Jim's grandfather rebuilt in 1922, but the Pacific claimed both the home and the man in the now-infamous storm of 1939. Poon built a third house just after the war. It is a weathered, fading two-story Cape Cod-style home with a wall around it, and the wall is engulfed in bougainvillea. You have to know what you're looking for to find the gate.

Jim passed through, shut it behind him quietly. The courtyard was overgrown with foliage that cut off the outside sounds, and the pavers were ankle-high in bougainvillea bracts, dry and light as paper. The fountain was clogged and inoperable. Jim reflected that his mother was a capable businesswoman, but when Poon died ten years ago, the house had begun a nosedive that really never stopped. Virginia had done little to check its decline. There was in her, Jim had come to understand, a genuine and simple need to keep at least something the way it used to be. With the death of Ann, he now realized, this house – and he himself – were the sole fixed bodies in Virginia's diminishing galaxy. And he knew that if PacifiCo and the development cartel of Orange County sunk the Slow Growth Initiative and allowed the Balboa Redevelopment Project, this house, and Poon's Locker, and Becky's place, and Raymond's and Ann's Kids, and the Eight Peso Cantina and scores of other low-rent domiciles and mom-'n'-pop businesses like them would slide helplessly into the churning maw of progress. Weir understood the vehemence with which Virginia and others like her opposed the neighborhood's proposed date with 'redevelopment.' Selfish and provincial as it sometimes seemed, they were, in some respects, fighting for their lives. The thought lay heavy inside Jim as he walked through the door.

Virginia was sitting in the living room, erect in an old swivel chair, with four rickety card tables set up in front of her. It was Virginia's 'office.' The tables were piled high with Slow Growth fliers and envelopes to be addressed, circulars for Becky Flynn as mayor of Newport, invitations to the Wrecking Ball, Coastal Commission tomes, Environmental Impact Reports, State of California Codes, coffee cups, legal pads, green and white pencils that read SAVE THE PENINSULA – FLYNN FOR MAYOR on them. Pinned to the wall in front of her was a list of phone numbers almost two feet long – the volunteer army that she liked to call the Newport Irregulars. Virginia's back was to him and her head was cocked at an extreme angle to hold the telephone in the crook of her neck. She was stuffing envelopes as she talked. *'I don't care what the* Times *says, we had close to seven thousand people at that protest march. They can't even get my newspaper onto the porch, and you expect them to count seven thousand people . . . then split the difference and call it six thousand, I don't care!'*

She pivoted suddenly to face Jim, her elbows out, envelope passing between her mouth and the telephone, then into the ready-to-mail box. 'The governor's on the other line; I'll call you back.' She hung up and shook her head at Jim. Her pale blue eyes had an exhausted, dull sheen to them. 'I tried every florist in Newport, Laguna, and Costa Mesa. Nothing. Then I went alphabetically and made it to the El Modena listings before it got too late and they started to close. There's a hundred and forty-six in the county and I've got a hundred and twenty-eight left. Where have you been?'

'Ann's. Around.'

Virginia studied him with suspicion. 'What was that meeting with Brian Dennison about?'

Jim explained that he was helping in the investigation of Ann – unofficially, tangentially, as a citizen and a brother. Virginia accepted it but suggested there might be, in fact, some plot at hand to penetrate the Flynn for Mayor and Slow Growth camps. Weir decided to let her entertain her conspiracy theories: Virginia was happiest when she was most paranoid. As far as he knew, the *L.A. Times* had never had any problem delivering a paper to the Weir household.

'Anyway,' she said. 'I want to talk to you about Annie and tell you how it should be handled. I don't think Brian Dennison's force is doing anything correctly.'

Jim took a chair beside his mother, who immediately pushed in front of him a stack of Flynn for Mayor brochures and a pile of envelopes. He looked at Becky's face on the front, a hyperglossy mug shot that made her look older and more reliable than Becky truly was. He wondered how many times he'd kissed that mouth, lost his fingers in those wonderful brown curls. Some memories never go away, especially when you cling to them like a life preserver for thirty-four fever-ridden days in a stinking Mexican jail. Maybe that's what they're for, he thought.

'I hear you finally dropped in on Becky,' said Virginia.

Jim nodded. Maybe that was one of the reasons we fell apart, he thought, because every time we held hands or had a fight, everybody in the whole neighborhood knew. Years ago, Weir had entertained the thought, rarely shared, of trying something genuinely storybook with Becky. The phrase *go off somewhere together* had, at times, an almost electrically urgent ring to it. But Becky was deep into the Public Defender's Office, and he was mired in his forty hours a week of playing sheriff. Plus, Becky had no sentimental streak that Weir had ever been able to find. Becky, for instance, had found a revival house rerun of Zeffirelli's *Romeo and Juliet* to be comic, although after Weir took her to see it, she'd made almost frighteningly emotional love to him that night aboard *Lady Luck*. Who could figure it?

'It was good to see her,' he said.

'Give her a chance,' said Virginia, case closed.

They looked at each other for a long moment, and Weir could see the injury in his mother's cool blue eyes. There comes a time when a son can look at his aging mother and see the girl she used to be, the girl who accepted the awesome responsibility of motherhood, the girl who sacrificed her youth and her heart and her lithe young body to give him – this wailing, insatiable, unformed long shot – life. Was there any way to understand the bigness of it? Jim stood up and wrapped his arms around her. As he hugged her and ran his hands over her taut bony back, he looked around the old living room and sensed the memories – the afterimages and aftershocks of events now decades old but somehow still present. 'Thank you,' he said.

Her hands pressed into his back. 'For what?'

'Everything.'

'Well . . .'

'I'm starting to understand some of what you did.'

Her voice was hesitant now. 'Now don't start feeling sorry for me. Because I'd start feeling sorry for myself, and I'd go to pieces, and going to pieces is a luxury I can't afford.'

A luxury she can't afford, he thought. So Weir. He broke away and gave her a smile as he sat down beside her. It was the kind of smile that suggests whatever silly thing just happened, the wearer is now back in control. Virginia had one, too. Another Weir trademark.

'Couple of real stoics, aren't we?' he asked.

'I've made a career of it,' she said. 'Well . . . now, I . . .' Then all of a sudden Virginia's face decomposed and she wiped at a big tear that ran across her hand and off a knuckle and landed audibly upon the old wooden chair. 'Goddamn it, Jim,' she whispered.

'I know.' This has been a long time coming, he thought.

'Poon and Jake and now Ann. How much of this is a woman supposed to take? I . . .' She was sobbing now, her big gnarled hands trying impossibly to wipe away the tears. '. . . I miss her and I think about her every second and she's . . . *gone*. I mean even when your father had his heart attack, we knew it was coming, and even when Jake, in the war, that's something you can understand . . . but Annie out in the cold, down by that horrible muddy swamp, and this . . . this *animal* uses a *kitchen knife* on her, all those times . . . oh my God, it just changes the way I feel about everything. It's not enough, Jim, the way I tried to live wasn't enough, thinking that if you didn't cheat and took care of your own that when it was . . . all said and done there'd be more good than bad and you could take a little comfort from the fact that there really was some kind of . . . oh . . . *justice* . . . .' She wiped the sleeve of her yellow windbreaker across her face, but the tears kept coming. She inhaled in jerking little gusts but nothing seemed to come back out. 'Was it my fault?'

The girl, thought Jim. 'No, Mom. Everything you did was right.'

She was shaking her head now, miles of regret in every wide, despondent arc. '*Then why?*'

'Maybe only God in heaven knows.'

Her pale blue eyes focused on him through the tears. 'I have a new theory about God in heaven. My theory is he's not much help to us down here. When I say my prayers, I don't ask forgiveness anymore. I don't ask for mercy. I don't ask for peace. What I ask

81

for is that I be treated with a little respect. That's all. Just a little respect.'

The phone rang. To Jim's astonishment, Virginia lifted the receiver and spoke her name into the mouthpiece with some semblance of control. She nodded, and looked at Jim with an expression of near-disbelief. 'I understand your confusion, Mrs Simpson, and I'll put it in a nutshell for you. The Slow Growth Proposition will make it possible for the people of this county to exercise some control over a development industry that wants to drain the last penny of profit from the land before they pack up their bags and go do it somewhere else. Slow Growth is your chance to slow them down. It's your chance to save what little is left of what made this a beautiful place to be. It's that simple.'

She listened and looked at Jim again. 'No, Mrs Simpson, in spite of what that commercial said on TV last night, the Slow Growth Proposition will not kill our economy and make our traffic worse. It is not something proposed by rich Yuppies living in beachfront condos. It is not only for the south county, at the expense of the north. Those are lies told by developers who actually believe people are dumb enough to believe them. The lies were invented by a consultant in Los Angeles by the name of Harvey Keep, who is paid large amounts of money to invent such things. If you don't understand that, Mrs Simpson, I can't help you. Tickets to the Wrecking Ball are fifty dollars. It's a fund-raiser and, believe me, we need the funds. It's Tuesday.'

In the moment of silence that followed, Jim watched his mother – the girl his mother once had been – pull a handful of tissue from a box and dry her face. 'The battle keeps me sane,' she said.

'Everyone needs one.'

'Now . . . let me tell you about Annie.'

'First of all, she thought that someone was watching her.'

'When did she tell you this?'

'Twice. The first time was months ago – late February, say. You know how Ann liked to walk the peninsula, late at night sometimes, just walk around and look at things? Well, she'd stopped by the Locker before going to the preschool. I remember clearly, she got a cup of coffee, poured in some milk, and told me how nice the sky was the night before, how many and clear the stars were. It was right after a storm, and the wind was coming out of the east, dry and colder than hell. And she told me that when she was walking around the neighborhood, she felt as if someone was behind her, but when she turned around to look, there was nothing.'

Jim considered. It was not like Ann to imagine things, or to say something was happening before she was sure it really was. Ann would not say someone was walking behind her unless she believed there was.

'When was the second time, Mom?'

'It was three weeks ago. I'd taken off around two to go help her with snack time. When I walked up, she was standing in the yard area, surrounded by all the kids. She stood still while the breeze whipped around her, looking out toward the water. She was kind of white. She looked like she was in a trance or something, until I came up and she broke into a smile. And she said, "Mom, it's the strangest thing, but I feel like someone's watching me." She hadn't seen anything or heard anything – just a feeling this time. I wouldn't even think much of it, but Annie's not the type to make up those kinds of things. *I'm* the paranoid in this family. Besides . . . the same thing happened to me.'

'The following?'

Virginia nodded. A whisp of yellow hair, much the same color as her jacket with the marlin on the back, unwound and settled across her face. She blew on it, then positioned it behind an ear with her fingers. 'I walk from here to the Locker every morning, right? There's thirty feet of alley I go through, to the back door. Three mornings in the last two months, I saw someone standing at the corner, watching me head for the café. It's still dark that early, so I couldn't see much. At first, I thought it was Mackie Ruff or someone like him. He had the shape and the stillness of a waiting man. Then, two weeks ago, I went out with the Lady Anglers on twilight boat. We were all on board, weighing anchor, and I looked back toward the Locker and there he was. Same shape. Same attitude. It was him.'

'Did you recognize him?'

Virginia shook her head, then leveled her sun-paled blue eyes at Jim. 'My belief is he's one of Dennison's men.'

'What makes you think that?'

'Stay here.' Virginia rose and disappeared into the kitchen. He heard the outside door slam, then silence. She's going to the

83

Locker, he thought. A few minutes later, she was back, with a heavy cardboard crate in her hands, one of the wax-sealed ones the frozen burgers arrived in.

Virginia set in on the floor, took a seat again, and pulled off the top. Inside were rows of test tubes, all labeled in her handwriting, each poked into foam to keep it upright. 'This is your bay,' she said. 'Someone's been dumping in the ocean and the stuff's coming in on the tides. I've got samples here for three months running – starting back in late February.'

'When Ann thought she was followed.'

'Exactly.'

'What is it?'

'Seawater, with a twist – 1,1,1-trichloroethane. It's a solvent that kills things when you dump it in the sea. I've collected all these myself. Annie helped with a few. Most of them are in the Locker walk-in, but I've got some here at home, and Annie had three, too. We spread them out so they couldn't all be taken at once.'

'By one of Dennison's men?'

'That is correct. By whoever was following your sister and me. Let me tell you what's going on here, Jim. This city is about to have the most important election in its history. The outcome will affect us more profoundly than that of any vote we've ever had. On one side are people who want to sell and exploit every last inch of what's here; on the other are people who think that what's precious should be protected. Brian Dennison's run at mayor is being financed by the developers – mainly by C. David Cantrell of PacifiCo. It is no secret; you can read about it in the papers. Well, one of the things Cantrell wants to do is 'redevelop' this whole peninsula. It goes way beyond our neighborhood. The city can acquire property from anyone who won't sell – from me, for instance, or Becky – by exercising their right of eminent domain. Dennison, as mayor, would exercise it. According to State Health and Safety Code, he's required to close access to any public beaches when the toxic levels of TCE hit fifty parts per million. If the beaches close and stay closed long enough, people will be ready to give up and leave. This ocean here is everybody's livelihood – directly or indirectly. My personal belief is that Dennison wants to let the levels rise until the city has to close the beaches, which will shut down this whole peninsula. Mayor Brian would tell the world what a polluted sinkhole it's become. He'll get council to condemn the structures. When that happens, Dave Cantrell's redevelopment plan is going to look awfully good to the city council, especially with the value of the land way down. Basically, they're shitting in our bay so they can buy it up cheap.'

Weir tried to grasp the magnitude of Virginia's latest conspiracy theory. It was one in a long line that stretched back as far as he could remember. His favorite had always been the idea that the Beatles' music was being used by Moscow to undermine the youth of America. There had been a booklet entitled *Communism, Hypnotism and the Beatles*, which Virginia had bought and distributed among peninsula parents back in the early sixties. There was also fluoridation of drinking water, LSD as government-supplied, and something about UNICEF as a way of draining U.S. dollars into the Communist bloc. These beliefs had left Jim, even as a boy, more worried about the theories than the conspiracies.

'So Dennison is using his men to shadow you, and Ann? To worry you about taking the samples.'

'Exactly. Maybe even to get the samples themselves, or tamper with them. You see, he can't let the bay pollution become a campaign issue until it's gotten bad enough to do him any good — otherwise he'd have to stand up and do something about it.'

Jim remembered Brian's unease about the feds. 'And he's afraid you're going to blow the whistle early.'

'Yes.'

'Why haven't you?'

Virginia placed the top back on the box. 'All we have is trace. So far. Eight parts per million under the Coast Highway Bridge on May 3 — that was the highest.'

Jim sighed and shook his head. 'God, Mom. You've got a pollution theory and no pollution. And cops running around after you to keep you from collecting evidence you've already got that doesn't show anything.'

She looked at him and waited, clearly an admission that there was more here than met Jim's eye. His mother had always been fond of watching Jim swim upstream into her silences. It took him a minute, then it was clear.

'Dennison doesn't know you've only found trace. He thinks you've got more than you do.'

She nodded.

85

'How's he know all this in the first place?'

'I've got one friend on his department – the Toxic Waste officer. He's a good man, and he's ... well, intimated that I've been collecting data.'

'All this to get Dennison distracted from the election.'

Virginia's pale eyes took on the clarity of anger. 'All this *to save the city I live in.*'

Weir knew better than to argue. He stood, glanced down at the picture of Becky Flynn on the pamphlets, then went to the window and looked out at the descending evening. 'Who's the cop you're so friendly with?'

'Sgt Dale Blodgett.'

Jim considered this, let the implications roll around inside his head, let them come to rest with as little interference as he could allow. There was the obvious. 'Did he know Ann? Blodgett, I mean.'

Virginia tracked his movement back toward the table. 'We made a few sample runs together. The three of us spent some time patrolling the bay in his boat. *Why?*'

'I'm just curious, Mom. That's all.'

Virginia's silence accused him. Weir let it wash off him, as he had done so many times in his life. The thing about his mother was that she was losing people to care about, and replacing them with people to hate. Poon had always been such a goofball, he thought: How did they ever stand each other? It seemed important now to get back on track.

'I wonder why she didn't tell Raymond – about being followed.'

Virginia shook her head, clueless, then sighed very deeply. 'I don't think that she and Ray had been talking much, Jim. Annie was far too private to confide something like that to me, but I think there may have been some ... strain. This is interesting: I saw a light on at Ann's Kids one night when I couldn't sleep. This was back in early April. It was midnight – after Annie was done with work but before Ray would be home. So I walked over to the school, and there was Ann in her office, writing in this book. It was a leather-bound journal, good paper, blank pages. She seemed embarrassed, asked me not to tell Ray she was spending precious time keeping a diary. And I remember thinking, What business is it of Ray's what my daughter writes?'

Jim remembered no diary in Ann's house, nothing on the impound

86

list to account for it in Evidence. Check with Innelman he thought, and check the office of Ann's Kids.

'Of course,' said Virginia, 'Ann always did like to write things down.'

'Yeah, I remember that.' Jim remembered a favorite Ann writing, a short story called 'The Fists of Muhammad,' in which a teenage girl dreams of having hands like Muhammad Ali's in order to beat up on her obnoxious younger – but stronger – brother. She'd typed it up on Virginia's old Royal and left it tacked to the door of his room. Ann. 'Becky told me that Ann didn't seem right lately.'

Virginia took a deep breath and looked down at her big rough hands. 'Jim, I really don't know if she was happy anymore. This was a bad winter, but you wouldn't know because you were gone. Cold enough to freeze my hot-water pipes – the old ones that run over the roof – wind all day, just couldn't thaw out. You know how Annie and Ray's house is – just a shell with carpet inside. I got them a good electric blanket and one of those electric heaters that cost a thousand dollars a day to run. Anyway, Ann was down, withdrawn, smiling all the time when she didn't mean it. You know Annie – she was tough to read, but if you knew the way she was, you could see the falseness in her. Then, the end of April, she was coming out of it. We got freak weather then – eighty degrees, dry and clear. I thought maybe she was just thawing out with the sun. She was okay for about a week. She looked great, put on a little weight, rosy in the face. Pregnant, right? Just absolutely alive with promise. Then, second or third week of April, she went back down, worse than before. And she tried to hide it even harder . . . pure Weir. It lasted until about a week ago. She went up again, like nothing was ever wrong.'

Virginia was quiet for a while. As the silence stretched on, Weir could feel the ghosts of Poon and Jake and now Ann lurking about them, easing around the air, trying to get through and mutter the truth to them. The curtains swayed, and a shadow did or did not pass across the reflective surface of the sliding glass door. 'Did you see her that day, Mom? Before you went to the Whale for wine?'

Virginia nodded. 'I went by the preschool at two, to help with the milk and snacks. Scotty handles the café when I'm out. She wasn't all the way there, Jim. Little things, like she gave milk to Danny, but Danny's allergic to milk and always has orange juice. She caught herself, but I thought she was going to break into tears

87

over it. She dropped a plate of crackers and almost cried. Something was wrong, but she wouldn't say what. She said hormones. God.'

'Did you go into her office?'

'Yes.'

'That's when you saw the roses on her desk?'

Virginia nodded. 'Purple ones. Lovely. Come clean with the roses, Jim. What's the connection?'

'There were eleven roses . . . at the scene. On Annie's body.'

'Oh, Christ.'

Jim tried to graph Ann's ups and downs over the last months, the months he was away. So much of the picture was missing. 'When Annie was having a bad time this winter, did you ask her about it?'

'Of course I did. She admitted to me that things were getting to her. You have to understand how hard she and Ray worked. Look at Annie's life: up at seven to get breakfast for Ray, then be off for the preschool. Home at four to do the house, do her errands, then off at six-thirty for the cocktail rush at the Whale. Back home again at eleven to get something ready for Ray to eat when he came home. Wait up for him, go to sleep at midnight or one, unless Ray was studying for an hour or so, which he usually did. Look at Ray's life. Up at seven, study a while, drive up to morning class, home early afternoon for a nap, then go to work at five. He doesn't get home before midnight, sometimes one in the morning. I never saw two people work harder in my whole life. I think they got so used to the treadmill, they wouldn't know what to do if they got off it. Sometimes when I looked at them, I had the feeling that the only thing holding them together was the struggle. Like if they slowed down to smell the roses – there are those roses again – they'd just blow away in the breeze.'

'Is that what Annie told you?'

'That's what she said. I waited around the Whale one night to walk her home. Terrible rainstorm, cold, arctic air. We went into her place for some tea, and we huddled in our coats and waited for those dumb wall furnaces to kick in. We stayed up a while and talked. She told me the whole thing might be worth it if she had a family around her. She wanted a child so badly, but the uterus . . . and she told me she wished she could point to one thing and say, 'It's all worth it because of this.' She just looked so lost, wrapped in that big parka of hers. Thirty-nine years old and working two jobs to provide for a family she thought she'd never have. I don't want to cry again.'

'Mom, do you think she'd see another man?'

Virginia looked at him a little vehemently, shaking her head. 'She might. There was enough Poon in her. Do you?'

Jim thought for a moment, though he'd been wondering about this question since Raymond's first call that night, saying that Ann wasn't home. The truth of the matter, he thought, was that Ann would never tell him if she was. Not just because of Ray, but because of Ann herself. How well had he really known her? There had always been an unspoken agreement between them not to drag each other through every pit. That would be demeaning. There was the unspoken assumption that they didn't mess each other up with things that were beneath a certain level of dignity neither had defined but each recognized. There was always the formality of borders, of belief in the idea that good fences make good siblings. Weir thought now: What shit.

'I really don't know,' he said finally. 'I wish I did.'

Virginia looked at him. 'I know. It's okay, Jim.'

'Have any of Ray's friends from the department been around the last few months?'

'You mean around the café?'

'I mean around Ray and Ann.'

Virginia thought for a moment, shifted slowly in her chair. 'Last month, a Saturday night, Annie and Ray and a young man – I think his name was Kearns – came by to say hello. Kearns is one of Ray's friends from the cops. They were all dressed up, hitting the local bars. When they left, Ann had each one by the arm, in the middle of them, you know. It reminded me of when the men came home from the war. Why?'

'I'm trying to get a feel for whom she was seeing.'

'I sure as hell didn't say she was seeing him.'

'Blodgett, maybe?'

Virginia's gaze was fierce and cold. 'Just on our runs out to the bay. I can categorically tell you that there was nothing between Annie and him. Nothing.'

'Anyone else? Any men you haven't seen around before?'

'No.'

'How about him?'

Jim pulled out the snapshot of Horton and Edith Goins. Virginia

89

studied the picture at length, first at arm's length, then up close. 'No. But he looks ... I can't say familiar, but he looks like he might be familiar.'

Virginia continued her reconaissance of the snapshot. She held it up at different angles to the light. 'Who is he?'

'He's a released sex offender. He did something like what happened to Annie, back in Ohio, years ago.'

'Is that his mother?'

Jim nodded. 'He sent her a postcard from the Locker, Mom – the "Wet Your Line" ones.'

'I've seen him!' Virginia's wide eyes went from Jim, to the photo, then back to Jim. 'He's come in three or four times. He wears these bright Hawaiian shirts and loud pants. He *looked* like someone from Ohio trying to fit in here. I'm positive it's him. He should be arrested immediately.'

'The police are taking some evidence from his parents' apartment. I think they'll bring him in for questioning. Soon.'

Virginia looked at the picture again. 'I'm sure I've seen him, at the Locker. I'll testify to that, under oath.'

'First things first, Mom. I don't have to tell you what to do, if you see him again.'

'You sure as hell don't. I'll hold him at gunpoint with Poon's forty-five.'

'Call me, would be good enough. Or Brian Dennison.'

Virginia was about to say something about Dennison but stopped short. She started stuffing Flynn for Mayor circulars, with a vengeance.

'When was the last time Dale Blodgett saw Ann, as far as you know?'

'I'll tell you about Dale Blodgett. He's a cop. He's a quiet man, doesn't say much. I kind of like him. He's the only cop with the guts to speak out for Becky and for Slow Growth. He's the only cop Newport Beach has who works Toxic Waste, and he has to do that as overtime. But he wasn't *seeing* Ann. I'm amazed Dennison hasn't fired him or something.'

'Besides Kearns, have any other cops been hanging around with Ray and Annie?'

'How come you're so interested in Ray's cop friends?'

'I'm thinking they might be willing to put in some volunteer time, for Ann,' he lied.

90

'I think they should be considered suspects. Annie was fully aware of the TCE dumping.'

'There hasn't *been* any dumping, Mom. You said that yourself. Trace only.'

Virginia looked at him with her customary deep suspicion. Wouldn't she like to know what Mackie Ruff saw, he thought. The telephone rang again. Weir kissed Virginia's cheek and went upstairs to get Dale Blodgett's address from his file.

When the phone was free, he called Dennison to see whether a personal journal belonging to Ann had been booked in by Innelman. None had. He called Blodgett to see whether tonight would be a good time to talk, but the line was busy.

Jim wrote down the address on a slip of paper, put it into his pocket, and slipped back downstairs. While Virginia stuffed mailers in the living room, he found the extra key she kept for the pre-school.

Jim was surprised to see a faint light on inside Ann's Kids. The chain-link gate was open and someone sat at Ann's desk. Jim could see the motionless profile enhanced by the soft fluorescence of a reading lamp.

His pulse quickened as he pushed open the gate, crossed the little play yard, and climbed the porch steps. In the front room, he stopped for a moment. Whoever was sitting in Ann's office neither spoke nor moved.

Jim took two steps down the short hallway, then followed the light. At the doorway, he leaned forward and looked in.

'Don't go for a career in burglary,' said Raymond, seated at Ann's desk. 'Let me guess. Virginia told you about the diary, and you wanted one more look at a flower vase that had fresh water but no flowers in it.'

Jim went in, studying Raymond's face, his nerves settling. The lamplight bounced off a blotter, illuminating Ray from below. His eyes were black but clear, and Jim could see in them the unmistakable influence of pain. In another time, Jim thought, Ray would have stood up and bear-hugged him. In another time, he thought, we wouldn't even be here. 'You okay?'

'Thanks for the calls and visit. Guess I slept right through it. I needed some sleep.'

'How are you feeling now?'

'I'll get there,' Ray said. 'You?'

'I'll get there, too.'

Raymond took a deep breath and leaned forward. 'Innelman came and got the vase for prints, but all Robbins could find were Ann's and a few tyke-sized smudges. I've looked through here three times for her journal. It's not at home. It's not here. It's starting to piss me off.'

Weir looked down at a half-eaten sandwich and a carton of milk that sat on the desk in the pale light.

'Get this,' said Raymond, tapping the desk blotter. 'Upper-right corner here – "Rita," "Renata," "Renée." Ann liked these *R* names for girls. I was holding out for Mary. Typical Catholic.'

Their eyes met, then darted away from each other like aquarium fish. Jim wondered at the terrible capriciousness of life, the way it dangled so much possibility, then yanked it away. Life was a little of heaven, a little of hell, and a whole lot of neither.

'I wish for just ten minutes I could forget,' said Ray. 'Just ten minutes of being . . . well, being not this.'

'Let's walk the neighborhood.'

Ray clicked off the light. 'Sure.'

They headed north up the bayfront, past Becky's, toward the yacht club. The little docks and private piers jutted out to their right, lost in fog. No sky was visible above them, just the pale marine layer that seemed both lazy and eternal. It was the kind of afternoon not content to surrender to evening. Weir was easily drawn back in time to the long summers when he and Ray ran amok here – skateboards and fishing poles, mud fights and running dives, sandbagging the Locker during the storm of '68, the occasional blessed trip out to sea with Poon and Jake. They say we have our memories, thought Jim, but really our memories have us.

Raymond walked along, a half step behind him, in that slow, even gait he'd had since boyhood. 'What do you think of the Lakers?' he asked suddenly.

Jim understood that for the next few minutes at least, Ray was going to be in the world without Ann. It was a shakedown cruise. 'Detroit's too tough. Portland is, too.'

Ray dribbled an imaginary ball past Weir, stopped, sprang, and sent off a fadeaway jumper. 'They need a guard who's a little reckless. A guy who can make things happen. How about me?'

'You're too short, too old, and too slow.'

Jim looked at Raymond now, but what he saw was Raymond at the age of sixteen, on the basketball court at Newport Harbor High. He wasn't tall then, and he still hadn't lost all of his baby fat. Raymond wasn't fast. But his results were astonishing, especially on defense. An opposing guard would bring the ball down court, angle left or right to set up a play, make his first pass, and . . . there would be Raymond, easing across the court in seeming slow motion, gathering the pass midair into an outstretched hand and turning toward his own basket. If there was a loose ball, Raymond would come up with it. He couldn't jump, but he knew *when* to jump. His passing was so cunning and anticipatory that he'd bounce beautiful leads off the heads of teammates too slow to realize an assist was coming their way. Raymond seemed to play the game in some time zone of the near future, while everyone else scrambled helplessly in the contested present.

Ray sank another jump shot. 'Maybe I'll play the Italian league. They love Americans over there.'

'That doesn't make you any taller, younger, or faster, Ray. I think you're better off as a cop.'

Jim took an imaginary pass; bounced it back. He watched Raymond out ahead of him a step and thought again how Ray's anticipation spilled over into his work as a cop. Jim remembered the dozens of times he and Ray worked Sheriff patrol together, when Ray would just seem to *know*. They might answer two different alarm calls in the same hour. On one, Ray would sigh, get out of the unit, saunter up to a door, let himself in, and turn off the nerve-jangling security system. On the next, he would study the building from behind the windshield of their car, get this bright, eager look in his eyes, suggest that Jim take one entrance, then slip around to the other. Sooner or later – usually sooner – Ray would come marching out with some hapless junkie handcuffed to himself, or some terrified kid just then finding out that crime doesn't pay. Ray would smile like a fisherman with a great catch.

Anticipation, thought Weir. Ray always had called it just luck.

'Or maybe Mexico,' said Raymond. 'Forget basketball. Go to a village, become a fisherman, marry a Mexican girl who'll have ten of my babies.' Ray stopped, touched his toes, straightened, and took a deep breath. 'It's weird, Jim – you spend your life on the treadmill and when it shuts down and you can do anything you want, all you can come up with are dumb clichés. I really want to live in a Mexican village, don't I? With the pigs and chickens running loose and everybody sitting around a TV in the cantina watching soccer and "Starsky y Hutch" in Spanish.'

'I can think of worse things.'

'You know why that scene appeals to you? Because you're basically lazy. Who else would quit the Sheriff's on his way up to section head, so he could boat around the Pacific and look for other people's treasure?'

'If I listened to you and Becky, I'd be sitting in some county cubicle nine to five, trying to catch bad guys I don't care about. I'd still be drinking a sixer a night to put an edge on the boredom. No thanks.'

'True. You'd be an actual adult.'

'I felt pretty adult – my ass in jail.'

'Maybe I'm dumb, but I'd rather be putting dopes in jail than sitting in one myself.'

'I'll opt for neither. How's that?'

Raymond smiled. 'Good for you, James. I give you shit but you know I'm pulling for you. Just remember that sometimes you have to stay and fight it out.'

'Noted.'

'Becky missed you a lot, I think.'

'I missed her, too. It surprised me.'

Raymond looked at Jim, a little knowingly. Ray had always billed himself as a step ahead in matters of the heart. It was also a back-handed compliment to Jim, with Ray being married to his sister. And Jim had always envied them a little. He had found himself, long ago, aspiring to the simplicity of Ray and Ann, but there was something in the marriage contract that on the most basic of levels scared the hell out of him. His deepest instincts told him that nothing between two people is ever really simple at all, especially if one of them is a Weir. Fact of the matter, he thought, is that people change. Is that good or bad?

A mullet splashed somewhere beside them, invisible but disclosed by its graceless plop.

Raymond waited a few steps ahead now, frozen, looking over the seawall to the narrow strip of sand below. Jim caught up and followed his gaze. A pure white heron stood not ten feet away, its tapered head housing an intense brown eye that beheld them

94

without moving. A breeze touched its feathers. It stepped toward the bay with one stilt leg, its neck essing out, then freezing. The perfect eye locked onto them again.

'I didn't do it,' said Raymond.

'What, Ray?'

'Didn't think about Ann for ten minutes.'

Weir knew how much his sister had loved the herons. She had caught up with one as a girl, suffering a punctured shoulder for her trouble, later making a necklace from the feather she'd retained in her pudgy girl's hand.

'Annie,' said Ray.

'I know.'

'Everywhere I look, man. She's everywhere I go.'

11

A late-evening breeze picked up, pushing flat-bottomed clouds west along the horizon while a pale white sun dropped into the Pacific. A palm tree rattled silver as Jim parked under it, across from Dale Blodgett's house in north Newport. He was on the upper peninsula, Sixtieth Street, not far from where the mouth of the Santa Ana River forms the northern limit of the city. He'd passed three NBPD units on the short way here, wondering how the crooks had a chance in this town. Whoever took Ann had made it look easy.

Jim cut his lights and compared the mug shot of Blodgett with the face of the man who now bent in his driveway, lowering a trailored thirty-foot Chris-Craft into place behind a new Ford pickup. It was Blodgett, his face lit theatrically by the utility light that hung from the fore gunwale of the boat. The Chris-Craft, *Duty Free*, was set up as a sportfisher, Jim saw – a live-bait tank, two fighting chairs, a harpoon plank extending from the bow. Sixty thousand dollars' worth of toys, he thought. Not bad for a police sergeant with a family who likes to work alone.

Jim got out, walked across the street, and started up the driveway. He'd gone only two steps when the air filled with a huffing sound undercut by a metallic whine, and a shining black shape shot toward him from his right. Weir hunched down and brought up his hands as the whine spun higher and the shape hurtled faster.

Blodgett's voice was so loud, Weir could feel it hit his chest. 'KNIGHT . . . DOWN.'

The dark rocket dropped as if shot. It lay growling up at Weir, a hypnotic collage of fangs, lips, furious eyes, flattened ears.

Jim's heart was in his throat. Only now did he sense the weakness in his legs, feel the cool surge of panic breaking into his face.

Dale Blodgett looked at him from under the utility light. He was a tall, heavy man with a strong neck and a flat-top haircut grown long at the sides in the manner of fifties tough guys. His face was a veteran: A thin scar ran perpendicular to his lower lip; a fighter's mass of tissue clung to each brow. The left eyelid was heavier than the right, giving him an expression somewhere between sleepiness and sly humor. He had a barrel chest and a wide belly that didn't look soft. 'Do you have some business here, son?'

'I'm Jim Weir. Ann Cruz's brother.'

'Knight,' he said warmly. *Friend.*

The change was instant: Knight's muscles loosened, his tail thumped the cement, the snarling mouth closed, and Knight looked at Weir, then to his master, ashamed.

'Good boy,' said Blodgett. 'Good Knight. Your nuts back in place, Jim?'

'It might be a few minutes.'

'Had a guy faint one time. The chain only reaches ten feet, though; he'd have choked himself silly if you'd have stayed where you are.'

'I'll remember that.'

'I've been broken into three times here on the peninsula. I think some of the locals know I'm a cop, make a game out of it. I've been broken into exactly zero times since Knight became my burglar alarm.' Blodgett smiled, a tight little smile that revealed large crooked teeth. The heavy left eye seemed to glitter, almost gaily.

Jim moved in a widish arc around Knight, who gazed up at him with subdued but very apparent interest. Something in Knight's face admitted that friend or not, he'd have a nice time tearing Weir's throat out. Jim had never been a huge fan of the Doberman.

Blodgett came forward and they shook hands. 'I'm sorry about Ann. I didn't know her very well, but I really did like her.'

'Thank you. She was a fine woman.'

Blodgett gave him a cop-to-cop look, a mixture of genuine sympathy with an undercurrent of disgust in it. These swine, it said, it's them and us. 'I've got some coffee in the thermos.'

'Sure.'

'What can I help you with?'

'I'm doing what I can on my own, following up. It might be as much for myself as it is for Ann, or Ray.'

Blodgett nodded and handed Weir the steaming plastic cup. 'I'm not a friend of Ray Cruz's, but my heart goes straight out to him. I understand what you mean.' Blodgett waited, looking at Weir appraisingly, his left eye recessed, unrevealing.

'Can we talk here?'

'I don't see why not.'

'There's some suspicion a cop might have done it.'

Blodgett nodded. 'I read Ruff's statement. Everybody did, even though the chief tried to sit on it. You can't very well hide something like that from a whole police department.'

'No,' said Weir. 'If it leaked as far as me, I'm sure you guys were on to it before. What do you think?'

Blodgett shook his head and leaned up against the boat. 'I can't put any faith in it. Mackie's always given us a hard time. He's always too drunk to see straight. We all got a laugh out of that 'statement,' to tell you the truth.'

'What if he was right?'

Blodgett looked at Knight, who looked at Weir. 'Then it's one helluva dark day for the Newport cops.'

'Not as dark as it was for Ann.'

'No, you're right about that. Jim, I hope you didn't come here expecting me to talk about the men I work with. That's not something I'd do, not with you, not with anyone on the outside.' The heavy left eye seemed almost to be laughing.

'Maybe we could just stay hypothetical a minute.'

'We never left hypothetical, Mr Weir.'

'Okay, try this: Say someone on the force was hired to kill Ann. She knew too much about something – toxic dumping in the bay. Big money passed hands; a bad cop took it. Say Mackie Ruff saw exactly what he says he did. Say you're me. How would you smoke him out?'

Blodgett considered, staring at Jim. Then he shook his head, turned to the trailer hitch, and bent down to hook up the cable fittings. 'You'd have to know who was on, first. Then you'd have to know who was solo. There's no evidence of two perps, right?'

'That's right.'

'So, you find the solos whose physicals match up with the Crime Lab evidence. If Robbins has anything good from the scene, you could make a move – if it matched up.'

'If there wasn't enough?'

Blodgett completed the connection and straightened up. 'Then you as hypothetical investigator ought to figure you don't have a hypothetical case.'

98

'But remember, if it was a cop, he'd clean up the scene. He'd know what to do, how to sanitize it.'

Blodgett smiled again – big uneven teeth, left eye merrily inscrutable behind the heavy lid. He shook out a cigarette and lit it. 'Nobody can clean up everything.'

'Say he left enough to limit the field. Two solos who might have done it – according to the evidence.'

'Then you get the Dispatch tape, check the Citation Books and Activity Logs – see who was where, when.'

'And you find that each one had, say, half an hour unaccounted for, when she was killed.'

Blodgett's expression flattened. The left eye was nearly closed, and the other fastened a suspicious beam on Jim's face. Breeze hissed through the fronds of the palm tree by the driveway. 'There are a couple of things you're saying here, Weir, that I don't like the sound of very much. One is that Dennison, or maybe your friend Raymond, was stupid enough to let go of the Dispatch tape and the Crime Lab reports. The other is, you've done all your hypothetical detective work, and landed on me.'

'Maybe I landed on a couple of people that aren't you. Maybe that's why I came to you first.'

'You ready to name names?'

'I could.'

Blodgett approached Weir now, a wide-stepping, arms-at-the-side movement. He was smooth for being heavy. His battered face, this close under the utility light, was even more battle-hardened. The kind of man, thought Weir, who was far more menacing at fifty than he probably was at twenty. Jim relaxed himself and felt the adrenaline mounting inside. Blodgett's thick forefinger tapped lightly against his chest. 'Don't do that. Don't say a name to me. If you've really come that far, go straight to Dennison, or the DA, or the grand jury. I don't want to know. I've worked with some of those guys for sixteen years, and nobody standing in my driveway is going to finger one of them to me. We stand together, Weir; it's them and us. Right now, you're them.' He stepped back. 'Still hypothetical?'

'Always was.'

A strange smile crossed Blodgett's face, neither mirthful nor unforgiving. He sighed heavily. 'I'll give you something straight now, because I like your mother and I liked Ann, and you seem all right yourself. The night that Ann was killed, I was having coffee on PCH, at the café just south of the bridge. The fog was thick and the night was slow. The two other north-end units were there, too – Sims and Lansing, Blakemore and Nolan. At midnight, a patrol car came off the bridge, heading south, toward the Back Bay. Whoever it was was way out of beat, because we were the whole north end – Lansing, Sims, Blake, Noley, and me. I couldn't see it very well because of the fog, but it looked like one of ours.'

'Midnight exactly?'

'Midnight exactly. It might have been a security unit, that's possible. It could have been a car from another department, for that matter. But it was coming off the peninsula, where Ann worked, and heading for the bay, where she died. It wasn't moving fast and it wasn't moving slow; it just kept with the traffic. That isn't make-believe, Weir – it's fact. And it's all I'm going to say to you. I already don't feel good about it.'

'Thank you.' Jim set the coffee cup on the Ford's bed.

'Don't come around here anymore. It's nothing personal.'

'I understand you and Mom and Annie cruised the bay a few times. Toxic Waste patrol.'

'That's right.'

'Did she ever tell you she was being followed?'

Blodgett stared at Weir for a long moment. 'No. I didn't know her very well. Out on patrol, we'd talk about the tides and the fish and who'd be a big enough asshole to dump into the bay. Nothing about being followed.'

'Did you find something out there that would make someone need to shut Annie up?'

Blodgett looked at Weir, running a hand over the heavy muscles in his arm. 'I don't think so. We've gotten some trace solvent. But Ann wasn't the only one who knew. There's Virginia and me and Dennison.'

'Mom thinks Dennison was scared about the patrol – what you might come up with.'

'And he'd use a cop to snuff her? What about everyone else? Ann was the least involved.'

'And the most vulnerable.'

'Doesn't wash with me. I'll let you know if something does.'

'Thanks again, Sergeant. See ya, Knight.'

The dog stared at him.

'Good luck,' said Blodgett.

Jim cruised the upper peninsula, looping in a wide pattern back toward Blodgett's. The duplexes huddled close against the chilly night and the waves slapped crisply on the beach. Through the alleys, he could see the sand, paired crescents of shadow and pale light disappearing into darkness toward the water. The parked cars glistened with condensation, windshields clouded. He came toward Blodgett's place from the opposite direction, parked five houses down, and cut his lights. Sunk down in the seat, he could see the glow of the utility light and the outline of the boat between the upper curve of his steering wheel and the dash.

An hour and a half later, Blodgett's driveway went dark. Twenty minutes after that, the red back-up lights of the trailer glowed through the fog and the rig backed gently into the street. Blodgett cut the turn perfectly, easing the truck into a pivot that left it pointed away from Jim, heading toward Ocean Boulevard. Weir started up the engine and moved tentatively, duplicating the right turn with plenty of night between them.

Weir hoped that the Chris-Craft was big enough to cut Blodgett's vision down to the sideview mirrors. Blodgett backtracked Pacific Coast Highway, cut across on Superior, and headed up into the industrial zone that separates Newport from Costa Mesa. Weir let a couple of cars between them. Following the sportfisher was like following a white elephant. The body and tranny shops slipped by, the custom-paint places, the machine shops and boat yards – chain link, modular buildings, trailers, security lights, watchdogs.

Blodgett turned left on Placentia, then right on Halyard. Jim drove past, then doubled back in time to see the boat disappearing through a chain-link gate topped with three strands of barbed wire. Two men slid the gate shut as the trailer wobbled past, then retreated to the dark confines. Weir parked past the entrance, across the way.

The compound was surrounded by the chain link and barbed wire. Behind it were a low one-story building with small windows, two modular 'offices' that looked new, and a large lot filled with pump

101

trucks, generators, drilling rigs, small Cats, mobile heavy-duty auxiliary pumps, and a few pickups. A plain black and white sign atop the one-story building read CHEVERTON SEWER & SEPTIC – EST 1959. There was a new Corvette parked outside one of the offices. Weir lost sight of Blodgett's boat as it moved past the heavy equipment and the fog closed in behind.

Ten minutes turned into twenty, then thirty. Jim listened to the radio again. Five minutes later, the two men opened the gate again and out came Blodgett's rig. The trailer sat a little heavier on its springs, thought Weir, but it was hard to be sure. The deck of the boat was covered with a blue tarp. Tall shapes suggested themselves beneath the canvas. When Blodgett had made a ponderous left turn back onto Placentia, Jim started up and followed.

They left the industrial zone, followed Newport Boulevard west, then negotiated the loop-around bridge that left them southbound on Coast Highway. The same bridge that Blodgett's phantom cop car used, thought Weir, the same bridge that Ann and her man had taken that night. The lights of the restaurants smeared by in the fog; the traffic signal ahead pleaded a faint and stranded yellow. There were four cars ahead of him. Blodgett has his hands full with the rig and the fog, he thought, as the boat lurched ahead, moving south still, toward the Back Bay.

Down Pacific Coast Highway now, past the yacht brokers and coffee shops, the restaurants and clubs, onto the Bay Bridge, to Jim's right the static glitter of houselights in the fog, to his left the water of the bay widening, deepening, spreading darkly toward the eastern reaches where it doubles in salinity, seeps into the mud that never dries, stagnates around grasses for which it provides no nourishment, advances with mullet and catfish that prowl the uneasy bottom for food, moving farther east into a final exhausted eddy that leaves it flat and spent, prey to hours of unhurried sun.

At Jamboree, Blodgett's boat turned left, then again at Back Bay Drive, continuing past the Newporter resort and golf course. Jim followed another quarter mile east, headlights off now, along the dark estuary, until the truck angled to its left, stopped while Blodgett unlocked a chain-link gate, then climbed back in and guided his rig into a wide turnaround that ended in a dock.

Weir pulled off the road, climbed the minor elevation of a hillock,

102

and parked. Through the fog, Blodgett's boat formed visibly, then vanished. Jim could hear doors opening and closing, scraps of voices blown to him in the breeze. So, he picked up a fishing buddy at Cheverton Sewer & Septic, he thought, ready for a night run off the twelve-mile bank? Weir got out, shut his door quietly, and moved toward an untended row of oleander that sheltered the dock entry from the road. Squatting amid the poisonous foliage, he could see the truck backing *Duty Free* onto the ramp, Blodgett driving and his buddy – a short man in a flannel shirt and a baseball cap – already aboard. A moment later, the ship was afloat, its propeller pulling it back into the bay. Blodgett left the truck on the ramp, climbed onto the dock, and ran out to the end. *Duty Free* glided in to pick him up, accelerating noisily. Within seconds, she had entered the fog, leaving for Weir only the departing growl of an overworked, poorly maintained engine.

Jim walked down to Blodgett's truck, boot heels sliding in the sand, and climbed the fence. Blodgett is the kind of guy, he thought, who's got a burglar alarm on everything. Jim peered through Knight's smudges on the passenger-side window: an empty cup of coffee on the dash, a few compact discs scattered on the seat, a police radio fastened beneath the CD player. For a moment, he stood on the dock and looked toward the other side, but the fog choked off his eyesight at a hundred yards. Half a mile across, he thought, is where Ann went in. The water lapped against the pilings and a low-flying seabird hissed past invisibly above him.

Forty minutes later – it was 11.55 – *Duty Free* appeared mid-bay, engine clanking horribly, trailing smoke that mingled quickly in the fog. She labored into dock. Then, the reverse of what happened before: Blodgett off at dock's end, Baseball Cap and Knight bringing the boat in close and finally running her up onto the trailer while Blodgett, knee-deep in water, helped to guide her on. Within five minutes, they were back in the truck and the stern of *Duty Free* was clearing the bay. Whatever was under the tarp was still there now. Jim watched the water steaming off the taillights as Blodgett followed the loop that would bring him to the gate, then back to the road. Weir let his truck roll down the hill, shifted to second, popped the clutch, and rumbled along the road well ahead of *Duty Free*.

He pulled off on a utility road by the golf course and waited. Two minutes later, Blodgett drove by, faster now, the boat swaying heavily upon its trailer. So, Weir thought, a sportfisher with no fishing rods, no tackle, no landing net, no game bags, no gaff. Two fishermen without a fish. A trip that took two hours to get ready for, and forty minutes to complete. If they weren't after fish, what were they after?

He watched the trailer moving along the bayfront, heading for Jamboree Road.

12

While Jim Weir watched the red taillights vanish in the fog, Joseph Goins was sitting in his tiny motel kitchenette, listening to the hideous rock and roll that pounded through the wall from the unit next to his. He set his mind against the noise, then went to the small gas-leaking oven and removed the journal from the upper rack. It was after midnight now: time for Ann. He looked up at her faces, presiding from the walls around him. With great pain and pleasure, he began reading, at the beginning, where he liked to start.

MARCH 24

What happened last night changes everything, and I have to write this down, I *must* write this down. Maybe it's because I can't tell these things to anyone, that I need to tell them to myself. Dear One, you will never see this, but this is for you. Now that I know you are here and will someday be with me, everything has changed.

It started – started again, I should say – at a party on this huge, elegant motor yacht called *Lady of the Bay*. It was January tenth. It was a fund-raising party for Brian Dennison, who was running for mayor of Newport. I took the job to get out of the Whale's Tale, and believe me – you would have, too. Ten years of that place is enough. Plus, I knew the tips would be good and the night would be lovely if the storm didn't hit early. I was right. It was ferociously cold, with the paper lanterns strung above the deck swaying furiously in the wind. I could feel that wind right up to the crotch of my panty hose, blowing up under that little skirt. I am thirty-nine years old. Thirty-nine years old,

married and childless, with legs still worth showing
off – the sum total of my accomplishments to date.
It is almost the end of the century, and I am just
beginning to realize that more of my life is behind me
than ahead. Dear One, if you ever have these thoughts
at my age, I pray you will understand how much can
happen, how much can still lie ahead!

Yes, thought Joseph Goins, you did have legs worth showing off,
but you accomplished much more than that, dear Ann. More than
you will ever know.

I got there late, just before *Lady of the Bay* shoved
off, because I had a huge load of laundry to do before
Ray went to school in the morning. The ship was
already full. All of the Power Crowd was there,
because they all wanted Brian to be mayor. Brian was
a Power Crowd Wanna Be. He was wearing a dark
blue suit that must have cost him a grand at least,
but the lapels pooched out because his chest was too
big and his shirt looked like it was choking him. His
eyebrows were bouncing around on his face like field
mice. The congressman was there, Cox, just back
from Eastern Europe. And Eleanor, the outgoing mayor,
hobbling around with those terrible varicose veins
she tries to hold in with the ortho stockings. Poor
woman. Then all the usual Power faces, Bren from the
Irvine Company, James Roosevelt, the catsup people
– the Heinzes – who had the Dalai Lama when he
won the Nobel Prize, Argyros, the airline owner, the
Segerstroms, the Tappans, Kathryn Thompson, even
Pilar Wayne and Buddy Ebsen. The Watergate guy was
there – John Dean, and so was Mr Blackwell with a
new face-lift, and Buzz and Lois Aldrin, and I couldn't
believe it, Charlton Heston. Why would Moses care
who's the mayor of Newport Beach, anyway? These
people will be dead and gone by the time you are my
age, Dear One, but know that these were the movers
and shakers in our little city back then. They were the
people who made things happen, for better and worse. I
wish you could know all this. I know you never will.

106

I worked the crowd, hauling around a silver platter of appetizers for their Power Crowd Mouths. I didn't mind them. The difference between the powerful and the rest of us is that we work for them, but they make most of the money. Raymond would disagree; he says that the richest man still quivers before the Law, that the Law is the real power and money only makes people feel safe. Buddy Ebsen and I had a little chat — he's such a nice old guy. I imagine you've seen him in reruns. Then I decided to go abovedecks and brave the elements to do my job. There was only one group of people there, too cold and windy, but the stars looked like they were about ten feet away and the lights of the houses twinkled like jewels and the leftover Christmas bulbs blipped red and green in the wind. And all the halyards and lanyards chimed away against the masts; it was like music when the wind blew in the harbor then. Is it still, now?

I went over to the group with my tray. It was only four guys. On the left was Harley Wright, the supervisor, smoking a cigar as usual. Next to him was Brian Dennison. Then Francis Messenger, the oil millionaire, and beside him — a man I had known for twenty-five years — David Cantrell. I hadn't seen him since he moved back to Newport, five years ago. I knew I'd run into him sooner or later, but honestly, I had no idea how it would feel or what I would say. Right then, I just felt nervous.

Harley said to me, 'What a sight you are on a cold winter's night.'

'A sight on any night, Ann,' said Francis, smiling and taking a shrimp off my tray.

'If you gentlemen had any sense, you'd be belowdecks,' I said.

Dennison asked me if I'd quit the Whale, and I told him this was just a free-lance job for a change of pace.

David looked at me very warmly and said, 'Hello, Ann.'

I said hello Mr Cantrell. How strange the words sounded, *Mr Cantrell*. He looked pale and tired, but he

107

also had that air of being ready to spring, of something coiled.

Dennison asked me if Becky Flynn had sent me to spy on his fund-raiser. Becky is my best friend, and she was running against him for mayor. It was meant as a joke, but Dennison was always half-serious and suspicious as hell – a true cop.

What appetizers you eat won't make or break the June election, I said. He really is vain.

She's a formidable opponent, he said, his eyebrows dancing up and down.

I said, 'She's a good friend, too.'

Supervisor Wright exhaled hugely from his cigar. The wind seemed to be drawing the smoke from his mouth. He is a powerful man who wears his power casually. Too casually, if you listened to people like my mother. Well, he said, if Becky wins, she ought to make you her flack. You'd be great at it, Ann.

'Two jobs is enough for me,' I said. I looked at each of them in turn, but couldn't wait to get to *Mr Cantrell*. He's one of the few Power Crowders who really came from among us; most of the others are tourists who stayed. Of all the boys I'd known since high school, he had changed the least on the outside, in spite of the fact that he owned half the county and was worth about $3 billion, *way* ahead of Donald Trump, if you believed the papers. By the time you have grown up, Dear One, the world will probably have forgotten Donald Trump and C. David Cantrell. Back then, they were coastal versions of each other. Trump liked being rich and famous; Cantrell liked being rich and mysterious. And there he was, looking at me with this expression of utter blankness.

I smiled at each of them, offered the tray once more, then turned and leaned against the wind on my way to the stairs. Inside, I felt as uneasy as the ocean around us.

Five minutes later, I was serving some Power Crowd Wives and I got The Feeling. The Feeling is when you know something that there's no reason to, but you

108

know, anyway. My father, Poon, taught me about it.
The photographer was pulling my sleeve to get me
away from the Wives – how they love to have their
pictures taken – and I just kept moving away from
them, through the crowd, past the bar and the piano
and the Victorian sofas, past Mr Blackwell consoling
Dori DeWeiss because she'd worn the same dress
(beautiful) as Flo Baldwin and oh what a chuckle *that*
was getting – to the stairway, and climbed back up
again. Of course, everybody was gone by then, but
. . . well what can I say? I knew he'd be there. He was
mostly in the shadow of the bridge deck, just a splash
of white shirt against a tuxedo coat, the black triangles
of his bow tie, and a bunch of dark hair lifted by
the wind.

He asked me how I was and I said fine, last I
checked.

There was a moment of silence while the lanterns
rocked and the laughter and music came from
below. The wind was just about freezing. He kept
looking at me from the darkness. Finally he said, 'I
was wondering when I'd see you. Five years back
in Newport now, and I haven't gone to the Whale's
Tale once.'

I asked him where he'd been, even though I already
knew. It's demeaning to tell someone you've followed
him in the newspapers and magazines, especially
someone with whom you have . . . well, I'll come to
that, Dear One.

He said Montana, where he owned a ranch.

I said he owned half the state, from what I heard.

'People say I own half of Orange County, too, but
that's not even close to true.'

'I think it's good you're back,' I said. After
everything we went through, I couldn't believe,
standing there looking at him, how good it was to see
him again. David Cantrell has an unhappy face, though
he's quick enough with that smile to look boyish in
the papers. He has the look of a future sour old man.
He did even in college. I don't think he's ever been

109

surprised by the darkness of human nature – maybe
that's why he does so well. But you could see it in
his face.

He told me I looked wonderful.

I told him he looked all right himself. 'But you're
pale. Don't you Power Crowders ever get outside?'

Not enough, I guess, he said apologetically.

I've often wondered why the same men who will kill
each other over the silliest things stand there dumb
and oaflike when a woman gives them a little needle.

What he said to me next hit me hard, much harder
than any gust of wind.

He said that he still thought about me. He said it
like he was surprised, like he'd thought of me in spite
of himself. Know what I think? I think that women
deceive men, but men deceive themselves.

'Well, I've thought about you, too,' I said. How can
you have been pregnant by a man, for chrissakes, and
not think of him? Think about him a lot – the same
way you think about something that's gone forever
and not coming back, like your father maybe, or your
first dog.

He said it was nice to get my letter.

'When was that?' I asked him. 'Eight years ago?'

We were out past the jetties now, rocking steadily on
that wild sea. I thought of the *Titanic*.

'Nine,' said David, then asked me if I still ran the
preschool.

I said yes and asked if he was going to be sending
us a toddler soon. I will admit to knowing the answer
ahead of time.

He said his wife, Christine, could not conceive. 'I
won't adopt,' he said, in much the same tone of voice
that Raymond used when he pronounced his feelings
on adoption.

I told him I was sorry.

'How about you?'

David knew about my trip to New York that summer
long ago, because he was the reason for it. But I had
never told him all the details of the aftermath, the

110

terrible hemorrhage and the infection that set in later. Between the two, I was made infertile.

I told him New York had taken care of that.

God, Ann, he said, I had no idea.

'It's all over and done with. You just move on to what you have left, that's all. I've never been one to dwell.'

Ho-ho.

He nodded. Nothing makes a man strong like a woman who is, some genetic obligation to outdo you. But I could tell he was very shaken, and his next questions came out in a disturbed jumble – are you healthy . . . are you happy . . . do you have a good life. . . .

I told him I had a great life and wouldn't trade it for anything in the world.

I don't know why I lied.

But I do, thought Joseph Goins. He stared for a long moment at a knothole in the pine paneling of his kitchen. He could smell the oven gas, faintly. The rock and roll next door was over, and the sounds of the cars on the boulevard rushed in to claim the silence. Reading Ann's journal always made him think how wise a woman can think she is, how . . . in control. They just keep insisting there's something good in the world, bubbling happily about this and that, right up to the time it ends for them. That's why you love them so much, he thought, because they won't give in to the dark currents, even when the water rises up to their lovely smooth throats. Look what happened to Cricket at the hospital, that nervous, beautiful, chubby girl who came to the fifth floor – the infamous fifth floor – and bestowed upon all of us her presence. What a mouth, what a smile – I could see the glow around her as she walked by, past the bars and the double-paned reinforced steel-meshed *safety* glass and the nets and the fabric of drugs that was always pulled across my eyes like a curtain across a window. One week was all she lasted before Papini handled her in her own office – Papini, a trusty, medicated into oblivion, but he cut through it all for a few prodding moments up against her – and she fled. For those few days, though, the confidence she had, the grace. The knowledge that *Lima State Hospital was a better place because she believed it could be a better*

111

place. Look what happened when your world ran into Papini's. And look what happened to you, sweet Ann, when your world took you to the Back Bay.

You lied, Ann, thought Joseph Goins, so that you could hope.

It was enough to make him sick. He turned back to the journal.

And how about your life, I asked him.

The same, he said, wouldn't trade it. He smiled. David always knew when I was lying, but he was generous enough to play along. 'What I think is, we work like slaves to keep from admitting that we really are.'

I said amen to that.

He asked about Ray.

'He's fine. He's a wonderful husband.' It made him sound icky, not what I'd intended at all.

David said that Brian Dennison thought a lot of Ray.

'Made lieutenant at thirty-five,' I said proudly.

The difference between Raymond making lieutenant young and David Cantrell owning half of the universe was never a difference that meant much to me. It still doesn't. But somehow, the sheer size of it loomed there a moment around us. It was kind of an acknowledgment that the two of them – the two of us – were simply components of two different worlds. I was never able to understand how David could maintain all this humility and ambition at the same time. There may be some arrogance roosting inside his seeming good nature, but I didn't see it that night, and I've never seen it since. As a college boy, he was actually shy – even with me – seven years younger, just a high school sophomore. Still, I believe that there are borders to defend in life, so I defended away.

'Don't be so humble,' I said. 'You're not that great.' I stole the line from Indira Gandhi, I think, always a favorite.

He laughed and said it was nice to see me.

I said it was nice to see him.

112

He turned and walked past me with a nod, the kind of nod I imagined him giving some corporate doofus in a hallway of the PacifiCo Tower. That nod was an insult. What I yapped at him next was supposed to be a rebuttal, the kind of glib remark that tells someone you could care less about them. But the second I said it, I realized it was really a much more simple message. And I can say now, Dear One, that it contained your very beginnings. 'Well, be sure and write,' I said.

He stopped and looked at me with what I can only call flattered surprise. And I heard then what he had heard, and suddenly it didn't sound like such a bad idea at all. It sounded like a wonderful thing. It sounded like opening a small window to the sun on a hot and stifling day.

'I'd love to,' he said.

'That would be box two-two-one-two, Newport,' I said, my heart pounding. 'No sense in pulling the lion's tail.'

He looked surprised again, feigning an innocence about human nature I know he never had.

'Send mine to Dave Smith, at Cheverton Sewer and Septic in Newport. I've got lions, too. They wear pinstripes.'

I laughed and so did he. There were a million things I could have said, about writing 'secret' letters to a sewer place, but for once I held my tongue. My head was spinning like the lanterns on the wire. God, I thought – what if Ray found out? What if Mom found out? As if Dave Cantrell hasn't put us all through enough.

I saw him a few more times that night, always with Christine, who is an attractive woman, if a little self-conscious. Our eyes kept bouncing off each other's like billiard balls. The Power Crowders made Buddy get up and dance while someone played piano. There he was, Jed Clampett, eighty-plus, limber and graceful and casting his tall, lanky shadow up against the teakwood ceiling while the ship rocked and the lanterns swayed, and I thought, *Buddy, you're a beautiful man*. Across

the room, through the gowns and the tuxedos, beyond
Buddy and his devoted dancing shadow, I caught David
looking at me.

Dennison raised $85,000 for his campaign that
night, but the Power Crowd buzz was that most of it
would go to the No On Proposition A Committee, of
which Brian was, of course, treasurer. GROW, DON'T
SLOW! was their motto, because most of the Power
Crowders were businessmen of one kind or another,
and businessmen are always happy for new people to
sell things to.

I made three hundred in tips.

More than that, I made the realization that
everything in my life was about to change. In fact, it
already had.

I haven't kept a journal since I was ten, but I feel
I've got to get this down now. Too much confusion.
Too much deceit. Too much betrayal. Can we do
bad things for good reasons? I wish I had someone to
talk to. I can talk to my Dear One, warm and snug
inside me.

Goins marked his place in the journal with a postcard from Poon's
Balboa. Time to write Mom and Dad again, he thought. In some
kind of incomprehensible way, he missed them.

He stood up, a little dizzy, overwhelmed by thoughts. There was
a time in his life when he felt great emotions. It was so difficult to
tell sometimes if they were his own or someone else's. Goins had
read an interview with a popular songwriter once, who said that
songs were already in the air and he just listened and wrote them
down. Joseph knew exactly what that meant. But now, since the
hospital and the picture of what was wrong with his brain, and the
medications they gave him, he no longer felt so strongly. Instead,
the emotions – the *feelings* – were always dim, as if hovering
around him in a haze. If he concentrated on them, they would
finally coalesce, and never – at least not yet – were they terrible,
like they used to be.

What he now felt was confusion. He had left Ohio for Ann, and
it was over. Nothing had ended as he planned it, though there
were moments of brightness, times of serendipity. He looked at the

images of Ann around his cramped dungeon of a kitchenette, drawn into their illusory life almost as strongly as he'd been drawn to her in taking them, and with the feeling that if he could only go back in time to one of those moments he captured her with his camera, he could do something to set Ann's course – and his – toward a safer, more forgiving shore.

The timer on Joseph's pill container beeped. He moved toward the kitchenette counter, exactly one step away from the little table, and looked down at the bottles of pills arranged there. These were the forces, he understood, that kept him as he was. Without them would be the feelings, the urges, the dark and irresistible imperatives. It had been so long since he had lived without psychoactive interference, he had to close his eyes and concentrate for a moment just to get a taste of the way things used to be. A bright blue bolt of light cracked through the darkness in him, and a warm surge followed it through his body. The big difference was clarity. Without the drugs, he'd had clarity. Feelings and clarity. Now, only dullness.

Joseph stood there, eyelids tight and trembling, trying to think his way out of the confusion of what had happened and into a place where objects were clearly defined, where effect followed cause and cause was understandable. I've made such a mess of it, he thought. And now what? If only he could think clearly about what must be done next, he could implement. Through the unfocused surges of color and feeling that began to heave behind his eyelids now, Joseph heard only one thought, again and again, faintly but almost clearly: *You should turn yourself in. Tell them everything you did.*

Beyond that was only chaos. He opened his eyes and looked again at the pill bottles arranged on the counter like the buildings of a little city. If I stay, he thought, I need the old clarity back, I need to have the old feelings. *No.*

But to go away now was to leave his life unfinished. There was an obligation here, a commitment to Ann and to himself. He knew that to stay was peril – the police would be all over the place, smelling him out. Yes, to stay, he would need the old portfolio of skills and instinct. *No.*

He'd been faithful to the medication for years, almost obsessively faithful to it since his release, and what had it gotten him? What had it gotten Ann? *No.*

115

Joseph turned on the faucet, twisted off the bottle caps – child-proof, so amusing – and counted out his midnight dosage. They scraped his throat as they went down, bringing with them the promise of a haze that would substitute for sanity. Why have I never had them, he wondered – feelings, dependable emotions – good and true and mine alone?

13

Sergeant Philip Kearns's home was a small upstairs apartment on Newport Island, a tiny piece of land accessible only by a bridge so narrow, it would admit just one car at a time. Around the island stood a forest of masts, bobbing patternlessly in the stiff morning breeze. Each waterfront home had a dock and a yacht of varying size, the vessels tethered to the islet like a litter of pups to a mother.

Jim parked on the boulevard and walked across. A Newport cop car slid by, both officers eyeing Jim with long, hard stares as he crossed the bridge. He wondered whether Virginia's theory could be true. That was the trouble with paranoia, though: It was contagious. The morning sun gave the harbor a low-gloss finish. Coming off the small bridge, Weir surprised a couple of ducks, which squawked, then waddled huffily into the water, where they paddled away, glancing back at him as perfect ripples advanced from their breasts.

Kearns had been easy enough on the phone. He had invited Weir over at seven, in a tone of voice that suggested neither suspicion nor submissiveness. He answered the door wearing a black silk robe and a pair of Japanese sandals. Kearns was taller than Weir had expected, slender for a cop. His sandy brown hair was receding from a suntanned forehead, and tussled from sleep. Lighter than the hair on Ann's blouse, Jim thought — but how much? What struck Weir was his skin: smooth, unwrinkled, unblemished. His handshake was firm. 'Getting a late start,' he said.

'Thanks for meeting.'

'Have a seat, I'll get some coffee.'

Kearns's apartment was almost all glass, which gave him views past city hall toward Balboa, up Newport Boulevard, of the huddled duplexes on the upper peninsula and the ocean beyond them. The west wall was mirrored to expand the room, which couldn't have been more than twelve by twelve. Weir looked down a very short

117

hallway that ended at a closed door. The kitchen in which Kearns was now pouring coffee had the small versions of everything – refrigerator, oven and two-burner stove, a microwave and wineglass rack tucked under the cabinets to save space. It looked like a ship's galley. The living room furnishings were masculine: black leather and metal, minimal, expensive. The place smelled of cologne and talc. The ultimate bachelor-on-a-budget pad, thought Weir. Not bad. Through the window behind Kearns, Weir could see a sea gull perched on orange feet atop a yacht mast.

Kearns's coffee made Virginia's taste like sludge. 'I'm sorry,' he said. 'For you, for Ray, most of all for Annie. I knew her pretty well and I liked her more than I knew her.'

Annie, thought Weir. Ray called her that, Mom did, I did. 'When was the last time you saw her?'

Kearns reclined comfortably into his leather couch, glanced quickly at Jim, then sipped his coffee. 'Let's get a few things out in the open, okay? There's talk around the station that Dennison put you up to this, because of Mackie Ruff's statement about the cop car. He's using you because you're unofficial and deniable, and because Ann was your sister. Is that about right?'

Weir nodded. So much for deep cover. 'It was more Ray's doing. The idea was that I could waste my time checking out Ruff's lead while everybody else does something more constructive.'

Kearns looked at him impassively. If he didn't buy the version, he was gracious enough to hide it. 'Jim, I'll tell you what I did that night, or any other night. But don't ask me about the men. I won't talk about anyone but myself.'

'Agreed.'

The phone rang, a muted chirp. Kearns raised a finger to Jim, then produced a slim receiver from somewhere in the couch and put it to his ear.

Weir gazed out the windows toward Balboa while Kearns purred on quietly with a lot of 'yeah, babes' and 'love toos.' Kearns looked over the receiver at Jim with a smirk on his unblemished face and an actual twinkle in his eye. 'Call me later, then,' he said, and hung up. 'Sorry.'

'Sounded important.'

'Well, some more than others. You married?'

'Almost, once.'

'I was. Talk about human sacrifice. The day I walked out of that

118

condo in El Toro and into this place alone – it was like getting out of the big house. There's nothing wrong with a man living alone, as long as he can get himself taken care of once in a while. I don't see how Ray and Annie did it.'

Annie. 'You pretty tight with them?'

Kearns leaned forward and cupped his coffee in both hands. 'Well, it was getting that way. Raymond thinks I'm . . . how should I say it . . . wasting myself. We were partners for six months and he kind of took me under his wing. I learned a lot from him. There was an assumption on Ray's part that he had something I didn't. I think the idea was to show me that two people could get along and be happy. So he and Ann and I did some things. Ray's so domestic, and Ann was, too. But it was, well . . . it was interesting.'

'How so?'

'I think Ann was faking it.' Kearns looked at Weir over his coffee cup. Beneath the high, smooth forehead, his eyes were cool and clear. 'Ray adored her, that was obvious. And Ann played along. But I sensed something false about her, something offered for show. I was the juvenile delinquent, remember.'

Jim heard the toilet flush from behind the hallway door, then the sounds of someone moving about. 'What was it that didn't ring true?'

'She looked like an animal in a cage. You could almost see her pacing. Sure, she'd tease Ray when he teased her, she'd squeeze his nose if he pinched her cheek, she'd let him kiss and make up after they bitched at each other for a few weird seconds. But she was always reacting. He was always reaching in for her and she was always backing up. When Annie and I were alone – like if Ray went to the head, or had to make a call – she'd be completely different. With Ray gone, she had slow hungry eyes, not hungry for me, I mean, but hungry for what was going on around her. You could see her unplug from Ray and plug into the world. She relaxed. It was like she was offstage. She'd sneak one of my cigarettes before he got back. They actually had a fight about that one night at Dillman's when Ray caught her. Two people married for twenty years and they fight about a cigarette. She shocked me once. We were sitting in the Studio Café, the three of us, and Raymond goes back to the car because he forgot his wallet. I'm watching the waitress lean over to lay down a plate on another table. Short skirt, perfect ass. I know Annie's watching, too. Then she says, "Frontward or backward if

119

you had your way, Phil?" She's smiling at me like Ann could, real wicked, and real innocent at the same time. I said, "Just like you see it." And Ann says, "She would, too." So I asked her why and she says, "Because that way you could be anybody in the world." Two minutes later, Raymond's back and we're talking about the preschool again, or some shit. It was strange.'

The story collided with what Jim believed of his sister, but who can really know, he thought. Poon was the philanderer – untrustworthy, shameless, indiscriminate. Virginia, on the other hand, forsook these things, as avowed. Poon led secret lives. Virginia suffered them. Poon had actually encouraged duplicity in Jim . . . did he promote it to Ann, too? She was always daddy's girl. Mother's daughter, but daddy's girl. Weir's next question sounded strange to him. 'Do you think Ann had it in her to see someone else?'

'I think she did, and I think she was. I worked the peninsula all of February, half of March. Couple of times, I was cruising past the Whale when she got off. She was heading down Balboa in her car, away from home.'

Where they found her car, thought Weir. 'Still in uniform?'

'I couldn't tell.'

'Did you ever tail her?'

'Not once. Not my business.'

'Did you tell Ray?'

'Never. That's *definitely* not my business.'

'Have you told him since?'

'I haven't seen him. He's still in the hospital, isn't he?'

'He got out yesterday. They made him sleep and eat a lot.'

The phone rang again and Kearns answered it. Chuckles, a whisper that Weir couldn't make out, then some innuendo about what's good for the goose being good for the gander. Kearns said noon would be fine and hung up. He looked at Jim, then out the window. 'Anyway, I told you I'd talk about myself and here I am telling you about your own sister and your friend. I've said enough about that, I think.'

'Did Ray ever seem to think she was seeing someone?'

'Not that he let on to me. Ray was trusting. He was also pretty distracted, with school and all. You can go right to the source on that one.'

'I have,' said Jim. 'And he didn't.'

The door at the end of the small hallway suddenly opened and

120

a woman came from the bedroom, wrapped in a bright green robe. She was slender and barefoot, fortyish, Weir thought, and her auburn hair hung around her face in tangles. She squinted as she came in, and headed for the coffeepot.

'Morning, beautiful,' said Phil. 'This is Jim Weir. Jim, Carol Clark.'

The dispatcher, he thought. Cozy. He said good morning. She eyed him sleepily.

'Coffee's almost gone,' she said.

'Make some more,' said Kearns.

'You need a bigger pot.'

'Get me one for Christmas.'

'Jerk,' she said sleepily, and not without tenderness, her face breaking into a yawn that she covered up with a small, smooth fist.

To Jim's astonishment, the sound of a flushing toilet issued again from the bedroom, and a moment later another woman came traipsing down the hall and into the living room. She looked half Carol's age, maybe younger. She was short and pale, with long strawberry blond hair that ended just above the shoulders of a white terry robe that had an Everlast label on the breast. 'Bachelorette Number Two,' she mumbled. 'Crystal.'

'Hi, Wonderful,' said Kearns, smiling mightily at Weir. 'This is Jim.'

She looked at Jim without apparent interest, then walked over and sat down beside him. 'Make this guy quit doing this to us. He's sick and spoiled and there's never enough coffee for three.' Crystal's chest was pale and freckled where it disappeared into her robe. She examined a fingernail, then brought it to her mouth. In profile, she was a girl. 'Can you do that for me?' she asked Weir, still biting on the nail.

'You don't exactly look captive.'

'I'm a prisoner of his mind.'

'Door's open.'

Kearns was smiling still, immensely impressed with himself. 'Okay. You're free, Crystal. You may return to your former life of boredom and neglect in beautiful downtown Barstow. Go on, get outta here.'

She grunted, went into the kitchen, and started grinding more coffee. Carol headed back to the bedroom and shut the door. Crystal stepped outside to a small sun deck and plunked herself down on a chaise while the coffee brewed.

'Remember one thing,' said Kearns. 'Every time you see a beautiful woman, there's a man in her life that's sick of her. I read that somewhere.'

'Is that what you thought when you met Ann?'

Kearns smiled slightly. 'No. One thing I learned real early was that Ray wasn't anywhere near sick of Ann. Like I said, that's why they made us a threesome, to show me that two people could be happy with each other.'

'Did she ever come on to you?'

Kearns shook his head and looked out at Crystal on the sun deck. She had her pale little legs stretched out to catch the minimal sun, and the boxing robe pulled up close around her neck to cut the spring chill. 'Crystal's from Barstow, by way of Oklahoma. She tries to get every ray of California sun she can. Sweet kid. No. Annie never came on to me. And since you're going to ask it next, no, I never came on to her. But I will tell you I appreciated her as a beautiful, mysterious woman, and I think she appreciated me back. We recognized something very important about each other, something that only the people who have it themselves can see.'

'What's that, Phil?'

Kearns turned thoughtful now, sipped his coffee with a furrowed brow and glanced again out at Crystal. 'The capacity to go through with things.'

Jim followed Kearns's gaze out to the girl. The sea gull on the mast appeared from his angle to be sitting on Crystal's head.

'The capacity to go through with things, and all the dangers that come with it, especially if someone's married,' said Kearns.

'And you two recognized it in each other, but it was never acknowledged?'

'It was acknowledged the first time I laid eyes on her. That was our connection. We saw beneath the surfaces, straight to the ulterior. Annie was one big ulterior, waiting to happen. I guess I don't have to explain to you how ulterior *I* am.'

Weir heard Carol Clark thumping around in the bedroom. 'What was it that kept you and Annie from consummating all this humid mystery?'

'Ray Cruz,' said Kearns. 'Pure and simple. No woman is worth destroying a friendship over. Not one. Not even two.'

122

Weir wondered whether it might have been Ann who kept up that end of the bargain, and Kearns who wanted to challenge it. Still, it was difficult to imagine Kearns taking her – or anyone else – seriously enough to commit murder. 'There's an hour I want to talk to you about, when you were on patrol. Monday night, the night Ann died.'

Kearns looked at Jim, his self-satisfaction turning to interest and concern. 'I was working the peninsula.'

'I know that. I also know you were off radio for twenty minutes, between twelve-thirty and twelve-fifty. That's too long for coffee and too late for dinner.'

Disappointment registered in Kearns's eyes. 'And just enough time to kill Ann?'

'That's an awful long jump you just made.'

'I make long jumps, Weir, because it saves time. I hit a lull a little after twelve – nothing happened. No calls to answer, no tickets to write, no disturbances to check out. Things usually kick in about twelve-thirty when the first shift of drunks is on its way home.'

'Where were you?'

'I looped down to the Wedge, parked for a few minutes, looked for drinkers on the beach. Then I headed back, checked out the sidestreets, cruised a place on L Street that's been hit twice the last month. Nothing cooking.'

'You see any other units?'

'Seeing anything was tough that night. No, no other units. There were three others on my beat, but I didn't see them.'

Weir considered. 'Blodgett says he saw a patrol car out of area that night, coming off the bridge and heading south, toward the Back Bay. Midnight, on the dot.'

'No. I'd have had to be out of area myself to see that. Like I said, I was on the peninsula, all night except the runs I made in to the tank. Two to be exact – a drunk in public and a B and E.'

'You didn't see Ann that night?'

'No.' Kearns's gaze lowered to the floor and stayed there for a long beat. Then he looked back out at Crystal. 'I'll miss her.'

Carol came from the bedroom again, dressed in jeans and a light sweater and a pair of low pumps. Her purse was slung over a shoulder. She set down her coffee cup, walked over to Kearns, and kissed the top of his head. 'Later, Phil.'

'Bye.'

'See you when I see you. Nice to meet you, Jim.'

Weir nodded and watched her go through the door, appear on the other side of the glass, whack her purse against the legs of dozing Crystal, whose head lifted sleepily, and disappear down the stairs.

'So,' said Kearns. 'I hope you've gotten what you wanted from me. Now I'll give something that might help. Consider it a gift to Annie.'

'Shoot.'

'I've got days off, right, so I've spent a little time on my own down on the Back Bay. Dennison encouraged anybody who wants to work some "overtime" for Ray. No pay involved, by the way – just volunteer. Yesterday I spent the afternoon going back to the houses with a view of Galaxy, past Morning Star, where this guy might have parked. Of course, we'd talked to everybody before – or thought we had – but I kicked up this old lady whose husband didn't want her to talk. He was the king, you know, she couldn't say anything he wouldn't contradict. So I sent him out of the room for a ticket he'd gotten – some story about a parking pass that wasn't expired – so I could talk to his wife. It turns out she heard a car pull up and park about midnight. It woke her; she had to use the head, so she took a leak and on the way back looked outside. What she sees is a white four-door parked along the curb. She doesn't know the make or model but she does notice two things. Whoever is driving it doesn't get out – he just sits there behind the wheel. And two, the car's got a big dark patch of something on the driver's side door. Sounded like primer to me, maybe some body work that didn't get finished. Definitely not a cop car, she said.'

Weir pondered this. To someone who saw it moving, the primer patch could have looked like the city of Newport emblem.

'Now get this, early this morning, patrol found a car registered to Emmett Goins parked down at the end of the peninsula, by the Wedge. It's a white 'eighty-seven Chevy with a big patch of primer showing on the driver's door. It's got a chrome luggage rack on top. His son, Horton, had taken it. Horton's a serious nut case from Ohio, a big fat prior like what happened to Ann – just arrived here in sunny Southern Cal.'

'No Goins in the car?'

'No Goins. Innelman and Deak were working it, as of three A.M.'

'Can you tell me what they got out of Goins's apartment?'

124

Kearns smiled wryly and sat back. 'Nobody could figure out how Brian got on to Goins in the first place. Was it you?'

Jim nodded.

'Well, whatever he got from the apartment, he's sitting on it, so it must be hot. Hot enough for this, anyway.' Kearns tossed Weir the morning *Times* from the couch. Front page Orange County section ran the headline:

MESA SEX OFFENDER SOUGHT IN
BACK BAY KILLING—
COMMITTED 9 YEARS AGO
FOR SIMILAR CRIME

Horton Goins, a 24-year old convicted sex offender who moved to Costa Mesa just four months ago, is being sought for questioning in the brutal stabbing death of Ann Cruz at the Back Bay last Tuesday. . .

Jim sped through the article, wondering why Dennison hadn't tipped him. Had Brian tossed the cop theory, or was he blowing smoke to cover it? A snapshot of Horton and Edith ran beside the article, a good-looking, solitary young man standing with his soft, bloodshot-eyed mother.

'Nice work on the car.'

'It's a start. We'll hand out fliers of that snapshot this afternoon, down by the Wedge. Chances are, if he ditched the car there, he's nowhere nearby. But it's worth a try.'

Jim stood up and looked again at the dozing Crystal. There was something sublime about a sleeping woman.

'So,' said Kearns, 'you've got a drunk who saw a cop car and a sleepy old lady who saw primer. Who do you pick?'

'I don't pick,' said Weir. 'Not yet.'

'I'm going with the lady.'

'Maybe Mackie Ruff's recall will be better, now that his brain's dried out.'

'I wouldn't count on it.'

'You guys still have him?'

Kearns smiled and nodded. 'Rumors of press interest in a "secret witness," so Brian's trying to keep Ruff out of circulation for a while. Paris was going nuts. Goins will change all that, I'd guess.'

125

'I'd guess.' Jim rose to leave, shook Kearns's hand, and looked once more around the little apartment. 'Thanks.'

'Give my best to Ray. He ought to get back to work, try to have a schedule, something like normal.'

'I think you're right.'

On his way past the sun deck, Weir glanced at Crystal. Her freckled nose was clearly visible, just beneath the line of shadow cast by the rooftop. 'See ya, handsome,' she said.

'Hope so, beautiful.' He saw in her – now that Kearns had pointed it out – a definite capacity to go through with things. He wondered what she saw in him. Where did Kearns find these women, anyway?

He walked across the bridge and toward his truck. Carol Clark sat in a sporty red convertible, smoking a cigarette and signaling him over with a slender finger. She started the engine as he approached. 'Kneel down here so I don't have to yell,' she said.

He knelt beside the car, bracing his hands against the body. He could see himself, reflected and disproportional, in her dark glasses.

'You've heard the Dispatch tape?'

'That's right.'

'There's no pause button on the tape recorder, but I can use the other dispatch station when I want to. The recorder's only set up on the active one, right? Tuesday morning, I called Phil four times between twelve-thirty and twelve-fifty, on the dead station.' She blew a plume of smoke over Jim's shoulder.

'I guess I wonder why.'

'You should. Slow night, no action. I buzzed Phil for a little chitchat. Everybody's in on our . . . situation, but it's not the kind of thing you want recorded. Follow?'

'So far.'

'Well, Prince Philip didn't answer. He wasn't in the car for twenty minutes. That doesn't exactly match what he told you in there. Small apartment, thin walls.'

'Hazard a guess where he was?'

'You hazard it. We're talking about murder, and men I know.'

'You think Kearns is . . . uh, capable of going through with something like that?'

'He's capable of getting women to do things they never even dreamed they'd do. I'm not a bimbo, contrary to what you might

126

conclude from that embarrassing little situation in there. I'm not sure how he reacts when he doesn't get his way. Never seen him not get it.' She put the car in gear and inched forward. 'Forget all this. I don't exist.'

'Got ya.'

She looked at him from behind the dark lenses. 'You know what the reason is, what the thing behind this is? Boredom. Boredom and narcissism.'

'I guess you've found the antidote.'

'You think of a better one, you can call me.'

Capacity to go through with things, thought Weir: Mix it with boredom and narcissism and you get two women and one man in a glass house on the water in Newport Beach. Maybe the sun here just burns people dumb after a while. Maybe a six-month summer does something to the groin. Maybe people are just bored and in love with themselves and they're going to spend every drop of what they've got right here and now because they can't spend it in the grave. Doesn't anyone worry anymore?

14

Jim and Raymond sprung Mackie Duff from the holding tank at nine that morning, with instructions from Dennison to take him out the back door. While Raymond signed the paperwork, Jim leaned against the wall and waited. A fat plainclothes that Jim vaguely remembered from his sheriff days – Tillis, he thought – walked by and looked wordlessly at him, then a glum young officer in a uniform who smiled and said, 'Eat shit and die' quietly enough for only Jim to hear. His nameplate said Hoch. Two cadets glowered at him on their way past: One turned back to fix him with a look of adamant disgust.

Mackie was a short, wiry man in his mid-sixties, with a violently red face and the palest of blue, booze-bleached eyes. He wanted to wait until noon for lunch, but they promised him something better. He smelled sharply of old sweat.

'I could use a drink,' said Ruff as they walked down the steps of the station. His pants were too long, even though the cuffs were rolled up at least four times, and the stiff, filthy material scuffed as he walked.

'Maybe after breakfast,' said Ray.

'I'm hungry, boys. How about the Balboa Bay Club?'

'You need a tie,' said Jim.

'Only wore a tie twice in my life – when I got married and when I buried her. How's your dad?'

'He died back in 'eighty-one.'

'I'm sorry. Nobody told me.'

Raymond glanced over at Jim. Ruff had snored in the back of the chapel during Poon's memorial service a decade ago.

'Jake?'

'For chrissakes, Mackie, he died in the war. You cried like a baby at the funeral.'

'Shit,' he said. 'I guess I'm getting old.'

128

'You've been drunk for forty years,' said Raymond.

'Never hurt my career,' he said.

'You never had one,' said Ray.

'I worked for Poon Weir ten years,' he said hotly.

It was true, thought Jim: Mackie had swept the sidewalk and crushed empty boxes for the dumpster in return for breakfast and winter nights inside. He could still remember the sight of Ruff, spindly and unbalanced, trying to stomp the stiff cardboard boxes flat while he swayed and pitched like a deckhand in a storm.

'Nice of you boys to come get me,' he said. They had stopped at Jim's truck.

'We've got some questions,' said Ray. 'And you're going to give us some answers to go with breakfast. Fair?'

They ate at the Porthole, one of the few peninsula bars left that was too bleak for tourists and college kids. The Porthole opened at ten for people who liked to get an early start. There were blowfish lanterns hung from knotted ropes, a sparsely populated aquarium behind the bar, and an anthology of small sea creatures lacquered into the countertop. Mackie fitted himself to a bar stool with the ease of a lid going onto a jar, then rubbed an orange starfish with his thumb. 'That's my lucky star,' he said. 'If I rub it, somebody always buys me a drink.'

Jim and Raymond sat on either side of him. Mackie exchanged pleasantries with the bartender, Jangle, a thin, sun-darkened man with skin like jerky. Against all odds, he wore a bow tie. Jangle set up Mackie with a shot of Wild Turkey and a Bud. Jim and Ray got coffee. Eggs and bacon were on their way.

'Tell us about Monday night again,' said Raymond. 'Don't make anything up. Don't leave anything out.' He produced a pen and a small notebook from his coat pocket.

Mackie looked appraisingly at Jim, then at Ray. 'Monday night,' he said, 'was a night like many others.'

Stretching out the drink ticket, thought Jim: This might be a long breakfast. But Raymond always had a way with drunks.

Ray leaned into Ruff's face with an earnest expression. 'Hey, Mackie? Cut the shit. You don't talk sense, you don't drink. Got it?'

'And, in some ways it was quite different.'

'Ante up, Ruff. You either saw a cop car or you didn't.'

Ruff glugged down some beer, then lifted the shot glass to his

129

mouth with a trembling hand. Down went the booze. 'It was hard to see because of the fog. I was sleeping and I heard the girl scream. Who was this girl, anyway? What's the big deal?'

Jim explained that the woman was his sister, Ray's wife, Poon's daughter.

Mackie seemed first bewildered, then fixed. 'The one that used to read a book while she roller-skated?'

Jim nodded.

'I'm sorry. How's Poon taking it?'

'He's handling it in his own quiet way.'

'What did you say he was doing these days?'

Jim sighed. 'He's in real estate. Has been for ten years.'

Ruff nodded, then reissued the same story he'd told Innelman.

'How'd you know he was a cop?' asked Ray.

'Because he got into a cop car and drove away. You guys don't rent those things out, do you?'

'No, we don't, Mackie,' said Ray. 'That's a stupid question for you to ask. Now, you followed him to the car?'

'Not exactly. I listened after he ran by and heard the engine start up. So I walked up toward the road and saw the car.'

'What did it look like?'

'You ought to know, you drive 'em.'

'Describe the car, Mackie.'

'White with a big dark sticker on the side, and a bunch of lights on top. You guys got to admit, a cop car is a cop car.'

'Could you see the . . . sticker?'

'I just told you I did.'

'What did it say?'

'Beats me. It was foggy.' Mackie drank deeply and shook his head. 'That little Ann was a cutie.' For a moment, a look of deep loss etched itself into Ruff's face. He shook his head again and looked down, as if contemplating a huge regret.

And with that movement, Jim guessed that Ruff knew something he wasn't telling. Raymond caught it, too, looking over Mackie's shoulder to behold Jim with a wide, open expression.

'Mackie,' said Jim. 'If you couldn't read it, how'd you know it said Newport Beach?'

Ruff's faced reddened and his eyes went narrow. 'I never said what it said. *You* guys said I said what it said. It was a cop car. It coulda been a Detroit cop car, for all I know. I've seen Sheriff cars down there, I've seen PacifiCo security cars down there, I've seen Highway Patrol cars down there. Take your pick.'

'Was it a black and white or just white?'

'Just white.'

Raymond pushed Ruff's beer closer to him. 'Mackie, when you saw the guy run, what color was the uniform? This can really help us.'

Ruff looked at Weir with an expression of complete annoyance. He sighed into his beer, drained it, and ordered another. He pushed the empty shot glass up behind the beer bottle as an afterthought. 'What is it with you guys? Don't you listen? I didn't talk about any uniform because I didn't see any uniform. The guy was wearing regular clothes, some jacket that flew up while he ran and a pair of plain old pants. Hope they fit better than these damned things,' he said, looking down at his filthy trousers.

How had Innelman missed this? Jim thought. He caught Raymond's glance behind Ruff's shoulder again, then put the photograph of Horton Goins on the bar. Mackie picked it up, shook his head, and put it down. 'I couldn't see that good. Pants and a coat. Coulda been a chick, for all I know.'

'Is that what you told Innelman?'

'I didn't tell him nothin'. Didn't like his attitude.'

Raymond smiled at Ruff and clapped a hand on his shoulder. 'You're doing great, Mackie. I'm proud of you.'

Mackie turned to Weir, and for a moment another look of great sadness came to his face. 'Annie,' he said. 'Little Annie Weir.'

Jangle brought the breakfast. Ruff finished his in two minutes, then ordered a bag of peanuts, two pickled eggs, a candy bar, three packs of smokes, and another beer.

'Feel like I'm on a game show,' he said.

'You think this is a game,' said Ray, 'I'm going to kick your stinking ass all the way back to jail.'

Mackie looked at Jim with an expression of appeal. Jim shrugged. 'The woman who died down there, Ray loved her a lot. He's got a short fuse these days.'

Ruff's mouth hung open as he turned to Raymond. 'Sorry, Lieutenant.'

'Don't be sorry. Be helpful.'

Mackie was nodding. He wiped his face rather formally with the napkin, tossed it onto his plate, then unscrewed himself from the

131

stool and stood. 'If you guys could give me a ride home, I think I got something to help.'

'I think you do, too,' said Ray.

Ruff's 'home' was a precarious collection of cardboard and scrap wood that was tucked into the far recess beneath the Coast Highway Bridge. Cars thundered by, a few feet overhead. The earth was damp and oily and packed, and the 'walls' slouched at perilous angles, held in place by old tires, rocks, a five-gallon canister full of dirt, and the remains of a shopping cart. A collection of fishing rods leaned against the cement pylon of the bridge, no doubt scavenged by Mackie from forgetful fishermen on the bay. Ditto a red fuel tank, a diver's mask and snorkel, a pair of good thermoses, and assorted bathing and wet suits.

Jim squatted on his haunches in front of Ruff. Raymond leaned against a pylon. Each passing car on Coast Highway sent a taut vibration into the ground, up the heels of Jim's boots, straight into his ears. From this shaded lair, the bay looked glaringly bright. The bridge cast a thick angular shadow against the embankment, which seemed to divide Ruff's dark world from the one just beyond it in the light. Weir watched Mackie lower himself into a reclaimed beach chair whose bottom was ready to tear out.

Ruff pursed his lips. 'I got a legal question for you. Suppose a man knew something he didn't tell the cops at first? How long in jail?'

'That depends on what it is, and how long he waits, and why.'

'I didn't say it was me. I said "suppose."'

'I didn't say it was you, either,' said Weir. 'But, just say for instance it was you, nobody would get too alarmed. You're the kind of guy who's been around the Bay a long time. You know everybody. You're a solid citizen. When a guy like you offers something, everybody's happy.'

Two Newport uniforms appeared above them, gazing over the bridge railing. They climbed over and slid down the embankment, straight into Mackie's living room. It was only then that they recognized Raymond. 'Checking out a complaint,' said the older one, Oswitz.

'We're on it,' said Raymond.

'Who's he?' Oswitz asked, indicating Jim.

132

'George Bush. What the fuck do you care?'

The younger cop, Hoch – Weir recognized him as the 'Eat shit and die' guy from the station – never stopped staring at him.

'We've got this wrapped,' said Ray.

The two officers nodded with strange mixtures of arrogance and duty, then headed back up to the highway.

Mackie, smiling dreamily, reached inside a filthy tire and removed from its recessed curve a bottle of Thunderbird. There was actually some left. He unscrewed the top and tilted back the bottle. He offered it to Jim, then to Raymond, with the smug optimism of a drunk who knows he won't have to share. 'See, too many cops in this town. That one on the left took me in once for minding my own business. We stopped at the big sliding door where they have to call in through that speaker box, and he told me it was my last chance to eat and I'd better order up some food real quick. 'Talk right into the speaker box,' he says. He ordered a burger to fool me. 'Cept some other Newport cop already pulled that one on me and got a big laugh from his partner, so I told him if the food was so good, he could have it himself. I said, 'Well, sir, I'll have a martini up with a twist.' Now that detective I talked to, in and out . . .?'

'Innelman?'

'Yeah. He rubbed me the wrong way. His whole attitude was I was a useless bum who doesn't even know what he sees. He treated me like I was having visions or something. I've been down here for forty years off and on, even when I had Lynette . . . and I've been rousted and busted and booked and beat up and pushed around and taken in and let out and . . . hell, I've been through more cops in my life than's good for anybody. So, I know who I am. I know where I stand. Some cops, they're okay, like you guys. Some are just assholes, like what's his name. Guys like that don't get anything from me.'

Raymond pushed off and came forward, lifted Mackie by the front of his shirt, clear off the ground, and pressed him against the big Coast Highway pylon. Weir noted the sureness with which Raymond pinned him there, so he wouldn't fall.

'You ought to talk to him,' said Jim. Mackie's feet were dangling in midair. The angle of the embankment was steep: A fall would be wicked. Mackie glanced down, then at Jim.

133

'I think he's ready to talk, Ray. Let him go and let's see.'

Rather than dropping him, Raymond set Mackie back on his feet and straightened his shirt for him.

Ruff raised his hands as if calling for a time-out, then squatted in the dirt and unlaced his right shoe. When he took it off, Weir saw that Mackie's filthy brown sock didn't go past his ankle: It was a sock dickey. Ruff's foot was a translucent white. Mackie gathered up the flimsy canvas tennis shoe and started prying around under the rubber patch that covered the toes. He lifted the rubber, held up the shoe toward the light of the bay, and looked in. 'Got it,' he said. A moment later, he had worked it out, cupped it in his fist, and held his hand out to Jim. 'Found it down by where she screamed before the cops came. They treated me so bad when they woke me up, I figured they could just do without this. That was before I knew it was Annie Weir. *Swear.*'

Jim felt the small, smooth object drop into his hand. He stepped out of the shadow and into the hazy sunshine. The surface against his thumb felt hard, specific. Something sharp prodded his palm. He looked down at a clear, marquis-cut diamond – half an inch long, a quarter wide – with a small bezel around its perimeter and a bent gold post protruding dead center from its back. The surface was smeared with blood.

'We got the tie tack,' he said.

'Something that big's got to be fake,' said Mackie. 'But I still coulda got twenty for it.'

Raymond reached into his coat and pulled his wallet. He slid out some bills and handed them to Ruff.

'Thanks, Lieutenant.'

Ray said nothing as he walked by Mackie, but he trailed a hand against the man's shoulder. He stood beside Weir and looked down at the mounted stone. 'How many cops you know wear half-carat diamonds to hold their ties?'

'None, offhand. But I know what kind of guy wears this. The same kind of guy who lives in a glass house on an island and answers his door in a black silk robe. Same kind of guy who left twenty minutes dangling between midnight and one.'

'Kearns was in uniform.'

'He changed into street clothes, then changed back. It would take about six minutes.'

Raymond looked at Weir, then started off toward the truck.

Mackie tossed his bottle down the embankment. It chimed and bounced against the earth, leaping in a graceful arc before landing in the mud. 'This is Newport Beach, boys. Cops can do anything they want. Don't forget that.'

15

Dennison and Dwight Innelman met them at the county impound yard. The yard was ten miles from the coast, and the late-morning haze had metastasized into a suffocating, corrosive smog. The four men stood looking at Ann's old Toyota as if a moment of silence was called for. Beside it stood Emmett Goins's Chevrolet.

Raymond gave Dennison an evidence bag with the tie tack in it, and told his chief the story. Brian held the bag up to the polluted light and jiggled it, then handed it over to the detective.

Innelman took off his aviator shades and studied the tack, probing at it through the plastic. 'How come he was so eager to give it to you, but not to me?'

'He doesn't like your attitude,' said Jim.

Smile lines formed at the corners of Innelman's mouth. 'Guess I'm losing my touch.'

'Plus, we plied him with truth serum.'

'Now I see.'

Dennison told his detective to take the diamond into evidence, get it to Robbins for blood and latents, then run a trace with the local jewelers. Innelman set the bag carefully in the briefcase that stood at his feet. Brian turned to Jim. 'Brief me on Blodgett and Kearns. You can talk in front of Dwight – he knows the . . . situation.'

Weir glanced at Innelman, who, still kneeling with his brief-case, regarded him deadpan from behind his sunglasses. For the first time since he'd taken on Dennison's task, Jim felt a tug of diminishment. The men were the men, and the blue was the blue, and quitting to do something else hadn't fully released him from that bond. But things were priorities now, and the first priority was Ann.

He told Dennison about Blodgett's fifty-minute 'coffee break' with the whole north-end patrol, the out-of-beat squad car that came off the bridge at midnight and headed south, the aborted fishing

136

expedition of the night before. Then Kearns's twenty minutes off-radio between 12:30 and 12:50 A.M.

Dennison shook his head slowly and muttered, 'Jesus.' His eyebrows furrowed and rose; then, an odd smile as he turned to Ray. 'You wouldn't spend an hour at the doughnut shop, would you?'

'The Whale, maybe.'

The chief chuckled. Weir realized how hard Dennison had to work to legitimize himself to his men: His rise from captain to interim chief to leading mayoral candidate had been too quick for anyone's comfort but his own. 'He's sure that unit coming off the bridge was one of ours?'

'No. He's not sure.'

Dennison stared off into the hovering smog. 'Too bad the chopper was down. Those guys see everything. Now, about Blodgett. He's some kind of fishing freak – spends every spare minute out in his boat. I wouldn't make too much of that. He might have been shaking down some new gear.'

'Was he on patrol?'

Dennison looked at Weir, then Ray. 'No. But I'm sure he's got a reason.'

Weir was surprised to see Dennison defending Blodgett, the only officer on his force actively working to defeat him in the election. Brian has a thin line to walk, he thought: Be thorough, be fair, but convincingly kick Becky's ass on June 5. Maybe the sheer publicity of Blodgett's dissension was what kept Dennison on the level – anything less than fair play on the chief's part would alienate his men, and make good fodder for the press. 'Blodgett wasn't out long enough to shake much down. Fog. Middle of the night, out on the same bay where we found Annie. Why?'

Dennison considered, his eyes again moving from Jim to Raymond. 'That's all, Weir.'

'That's enough, isn't it?'

'You don't understand me. You've done your part. It's over. You're done.'

Jim felt sucker-punched, a little rush of breath leaving his chest. 'Kearns and –'

'You're *done*, Weir. That's all, and that's it. You got enough for me to think about, so I'll think about it, right?'

'Kearns and Blodgett have a lot of answers to give,' said Jim. 'I can get those answers. Give me a few more days. I can –'

137

'You can't do a goddamn thing that Internal Affairs can't do better.' Dennison smiled at Jim with a wicked little nod that Weir supposed was to underscore the cunning of bringing in Internal Affairs. 'That's right. I'm taking this to them. It's in our lap now.'

Raymond stepped back and looked down, nudging at something with his shoe. He glanced up to Jim with a look that asked for caution.

Dennison clapped his hand over Jim's shoulder. 'Nice work, Jim. Look, we had a go at Goins's bedroom in Costa Mesa. There are some things you should see. Dwight?'

Innelman knelt again, pulled an envelope from his briefcase, and handed it to Raymond. Jim looked over his shoulder as Ray opened it and took out the photographs. The top two were of the peninsula ferry, the next of Poon's Locker – taken early morning, Jim could tell from the angle of shadow – then a picture of Ann's Kids taken after closing. The last shot was of the preschool during an outdoor break, the play area filled with toddlers on the move. Among them, bending over slightly to help a boy onto a rocking horse, her hair spilling down around her face, her smile calm and lovely, was Ann.

Jim felt a warm flush come to his face. He heard Raymond's breathing deepen and slow.

'It's a telephoto shot,' said Innelman. 'She doesn't know he's out there, is my guess. He sniped her. Robbins ran the originals and got what you'd expect – Goins's fingerprints on the edges. These are copies.'

'He shot from the water,' said Jim.

'Used the ferry,' said Ray.

'That's our guess, too,' said Innelman. 'Or he could have rented one of those little motor dinghys. Goins couldn't have much money unless he's been pulling some local jobs, so the ferry seems most likely.'

Raymond stared at the last picture. The silence widened. Ray looked first at Jim, then to Dennison and Dwight. 'Where the fuck is this guy? How hard can it be to –'

'We've got extra men on a door-to-door right now,' said Dennison. 'The newspapers will help. We'll get him, don't worry.'

'Who developed the originals?' Raymond's voice had taken on a calm that Weir could vividly recall – the adrenaline cool of pursuit.

138

'He did. He moved out the hardware when he left the Island Gardens.'

Weir asked about a hair sample to match the one found on Ann's blouse.

'No match. Robbins already tried. But that hair could have been a floater, we know that. It doesn't let Goins off the hook – not even a little.'

Innelman gently took the pictures back from Ray. 'I'm having Robbins run my hair, and Roger Deak's. We contaminate things sometimes, no matter how hard we try. You and Jim ought to give him a sample, too, just to save time. But the other physicals match up, Ray – blood type B positive, right-handed, same weight as the guy who left the prints at the crime scene, same size feet. We'll run genetics as soon as we have him. I talked to Mrs Connaught – the old woman that Kearns kicked up. I looked out her bedroom window. Where she saw the car was where someone would park to take the path down. She looked at a picture I shot of Goins's car – from above – and she says it looks the same. We took soils from some of Goins's shoes – Robbins says one pair has some salts and silicas that indicate a saltwater estuary. He was down there, we just haven't established *when*. We're building, we're getting closer.'

Dennison took Raymond's arm and moved off to Goins's car. They stood examining the primer patch on the driver's door, but Weir couldn't hear what they were saying.

Innelman checked his watch, looked over at his boss, then came closer to Jim. His voice was flat and quiet. 'You should know this. Blodgett got drunk at a party a few weeks back and said he'd seen someone dumping in the bay. He couldn't catch up, or lost them, something like that. I know Ann had been out with him on Toxic Waste. Blodgett's got a terrible temper. There were rumors he burned out a gill netter last year, just for the fun of it. At the party, he's drunk and he says if he catches the dumpers, he'll sink their boat with them in it. He hasn't done that, yet, so far as anybody knows. But maybe Ann saw something. Knew something. I don't know, but I'll tell you this, I've known Blodgett for eight years and I don't know him at all. Internal Affairs is a joke. Got me?'

'Got you. Why would a cop burn out a commercial fisherman?'

'Blodgett's a fascist sportsman. He and the tree huggers don't like the netters taking out so many fish, choking all those sea lions

139

in the mesh. He volunteered for the Toxic Waste job. Blodgett's got the same attitude about the water that all these so-called environmentalists have – he thinks it's his.' Innelman glanced over toward the chief. 'None of what I just told you is Dennison's favorite topic, because if he gets in Dale's face, it makes Brian look bad. Politics. Personally, I think Dale's a loose cannon.'

'Thanks, Dwight.'

'There are people who know more about all that than I do. Your mother, for instance, or Becky Flynn. Just so you know, we haven't kicked up Ann's journal yet. Love to get my hands on that thing.'

Innelman turned and headed for the Crime Lab. Dennison left Raymond with a handshake and came back over to Jim. 'Thanks, Jim. You helped me out – helped us all out.'

'Let me stay on Kearns and Blodgett for a few more days. No charge.'

'No way. It's in our court now. Trust me, I'll get the answers we all want.'

He walked off toward the helipad. A moment later, the NBPD chopper lifted into the air and angled west.

Sitting in the driver's seat of his sister's car, amidst the faintly lingering scent of her perfume, Jim was drawn into memories of Ann so specific and immediate, they frightened him. The all-night talks they'd had, when Ann dispensed her greater wisdom – greater by two entire years – regarding girls, guys, parents and how to get around them, school and how to keep it easy, church and how to get out of going. He could see a picture of her taken when she was a few days old, wrapped in a pink blanket with a bow taped to her bald head, and he could remember being astonished that his older sister could ever have been so young; he could see her in a pair of overalls sitting in her wagon, grinning with two front teeth bucked enough to open a beer bottle on; could see her waddling down to the water of the bay with a green plastic shovel in her hand; see her on that same beach a few years later, thin and dark and hard as a piece of wood – much the envy of Jim's younger friends; see her on roller skates, flying down the peninsula sidewalk with a book in front of her face; see her tearfully boarding the plane one summer, bound for France, to, as Poon had put it, 'get some Frog culture';

140

see her coming down the stairway in the big house in a blue dress for the junior prom – it was the first time that Jim realized she wasn't actually a girl any longer, or perhaps that he was no longer actually a boy – and Raymond there at the bottom glowing with unabashed pride at this, his undeserved princess; he could see her folding helplessly into Virginia's arms when they heard about Jake; could see the sudden fury in her that night she pushed Ray off the pier, then, in shock at her own act, jumped in after him; could see her later that same night wrapped in blankets in front of the fireplace in the big house, her hair slicked tight against her head and her eyes filled with a profound distance, as if she was still in France, and yes, there was something different about her when she came back, something experienced but unspoken; he could see her just a few nights ago standing at Virginia's table in her silly, frilly skirt, bringing her own special class and dignity to a job that required neither; see her . . . see her . . . see her . . . fragments from the parade still going on inside him, if nowhere else.

In Virginia, he thought.

In Ray.

In whoever last touched her, took her life and left his seed, arranged the roses for her final journey into the unredemptive waters of the Back Bay.

A shiver rocked through Jim's body, all the way to his feet. His eyes were filled with heartbeats. The sound of Raymond's voice penetrated the reverie.

'. . . I said, what the hell is this?'

'Huh?'

'You all right?'

'I'm all right.'

'You don't look all right.'

Weir took a moment to bring it all together and try to make sense of it: this car smudged with fingerprint dust and festooned with impound tags, this smell of perfume, this absent woman who was his sister, this blood of hers – and his – spilled so generously on a ground that neither deserved nor wanted. 'It comes out of nowhere,' he said.

Raymond was quiet for a moment.

'I hate it, Ray,' he said, staring through the windshield, through the poisoned atmosphere of inland Orange County. The air looked like smoke. The car parked across from them was a red Porsche with bullet holes in the windshield and headrest. 'I hate what he did to her.'

'I do, too, but there's no time to hate, Jim. We have to find him. And when we find him, we kill him – like I said.'

'You know, that's actually starting to make sense.'

'Of course it does. You're not a treasure hunter. You're not a brother. I'm not a cop, or a husband, or a law student. Look down on us like God does, and what you see is just two men who have to kill someone. Because he deserves it, and because he's asked us to. It's simple.'

Weir regarded Raymond's calm face. He could almost believe him. He had tried his best to keep away from this kind of thinking, tried to keep his head clear, tried to act in a way that would lead him to the truth about Ann. But the grief would hit him without warning and he would realize how present it was, how small was the distance at which he managed to keep it. And the grief was married to the anger.

Raymond looked down at his hands. 'I sat in my study the other night and looked at all those beautiful law books. I love the law. I love the way it defines and clarifies. I love the way it's always ready to be more defined, more clear, more fair. But I realized what a gap there was between that law and what happened. You see, those are just *ideas*. Ann was real. Our baby was real. When I looked at Ann lying on the ground down there, it changed everything I believed. The law, and what I've *stood for*! It's an illusion. These ideas – that we're a nation of laws, that God in heaven watches over us like he does the sparrows – they're illusions. The only things that aren't are flesh and blood, and what we can feel and touch and see. What I'm going to do is take vengeance. You can hold vengeance in your hand. It's real. They could strap me into the chamber for it, and I wouldn't blink. I promise you, Jim, I wouldn't blink, not once. And don't tell me what Ann would have wanted me to do, how Ann would have wanted me to carry on and forget someday. That's the biggest illusion of all.'

Weir leaned back and stared at the torn headliner above him. 'I know.'

'I know you do. So what we have to do, right this second, is figure out why I'm holding this thing in my hand. I don't want to be holding it, because it's telling me something I don't want to believe. Jim, what is this?'

142

Weir looked down. 'That, Raymond, is the control for an automatic garage-door opener.'

'That's right. And we don't have an automatic garage-door opener at home.'

Jim took the unit. It was a standard brown plastic box with a clip for the sun visor and the words DOOR GENIE on it.

Raymond was quiet for a long moment. In the periphery of his vision, Jim could see him looking through the window at Horton Goins's Chevrolet.

Jim turned the thing over in his hand. It seemed inordinately light. Strange, he thought, how something so insubstantial, so mass-produced and impersonal, can land on a man's life with such tonnage. There was no way he could explain its presence, other than as a posthumous confession that Ann had been going somewhere she didn't want Ray to know about, sliding right into a waiting garage, leaving her approved world behind, making the leap into the invisible, the illicit, the secret.

Raymond glanced at him now, an expression of denial so feeble, it turned to confirmation before he could look away again. 'I thought at first she was dressed up that night because she was coming to meet me at the station. She used to do that – come down and meet me when I got off. She'd put on a sexy dress and makeup, do her hair. You wouldn't believe what a sight she was, done up that way, waiting for me. One time, we did it right in the Toyota, alongside Coast Highway. One time, we got a motel room because we couldn't wait. Just like kids.'

'I don't think so.'

'I don't, either.'

'The roses, the clothes she was wearing, the street clothes that Ruff saw, the diamond tie tack, a garage-door opener that doesn't work at your house.'

Jim idly flipped open the battery compartment and found it empty.

Raymond gazed out the window again and Weir followed his line of vision out past Goins's car, through the chain link, over the Health Department building and into the unemphatic sunshine of a cool spring day. 'She had enough opportunity. She could have done it easy enough, with me gone all the time.'

Raymond said nothing for a long while. Weir understood that for Ray to confront Ann's loyalty was to shake one of the foundations

143

on which he had built his life. 'I don't think she'd play the field. I think if, uh, if Annie was really going to see someone, he'd have to . . . mean something to her.'

The last words were so faint, Weir could hardly hear them.

'Any ideas, Ray?'

Raymond drew a deep breath. Jim never heard it come back out. 'No.'

Weir thought of Kearns's description, the capacity to go through with things, Ann the Ulterior. He told Raymond what Kearns had said.

Raymond looked at him again, layers of betrayal visible in his face. 'If he thinks what Annie really wanted was to get her ashes hauled, I guess that's no surprise. That's about how deep Phil Kearns goes.'

'Did you see anything between him and Ann?'

Raymond shook his head.

'What about Dale Blodgett?'

'Come on.'

The fundamental question still hovered in the air, furtive, unanswered. 'Say Ann had a lover. Did he kill her?'

'No one who knew Ann could have killed her,' Raymond said quietly. 'That's my opinion.'

'The crime stats would say you're wrong.'

'The crime stats would say I did it.'

'Did you?' The question came out before Weir could stop it. It was the kind of question a cop would ask a cop. Ten years of law enforcement lead to habits.

Raymond answered without a beat. 'No.'

'Sorry.'

Raymond shook his head. 'Don't be.' He sighed heavily, slid the battery-compartment lid back onto the opener, put the opener in his pocket. 'I'll get this into evidence, where it belongs.'

They rifled through the glove compartment and under the floor mats, through the usual oddments that collect in a car. Impound tags indicated the goods looted by Innelman, then by Robbins's minions, for further study: two coffee mugs, an unlabeled audio tape, the lighter and ashtray, an envelope of 'snapshots, personal,' two hairs taken from the driver's side headrest, one from the passenger's side.

Raymond opened the door for air and breathed deeply. 'I spent

144

some time in the hospital, realizing some things. Ann and I were good together – we had our ups and downs – but overall we were good. She'd had a hard winter; she was locked up inside like she'd get when she'd think about not being able to have a child. I knew the pattern, so I didn't go home. I went down and parked by the Whale's Tale, then I drove to where they found her car. A couple of things hit me. One was, Annie was probably going to see a lover. So I started wondering what kind of man he would be. What I think is, he would be different from me, totally different. You have affairs because you feel neglected or bored, right? So you seek out someone . . . fresh. I'm just a cop. I act like a cop, I think like a cop, I make the money a cop makes. So let's say she's met a high roller at work. Maybe a guy with lots of money coming in – a privileged man, a mover. She sees him, they come together, it's good. One night after work, she changes into something real sexy. She's offering herself to him, her body for his pleasure. Say for a minute that he was the one who killed her. What's hard for me to imagine is the arrogance, the waste of it. What I see is a guy used to getting what he wants, used to that kind of destruction. A guy with a towering ego, who could actually think of Ann as property, a consumer good. Someone with power and bucks. Some guy who thinks he's above the law. She goes to see him, he takes her to the Back Bay, and he's so sure of himself, he leaves her car in his neighborhood. I sat in my car on the street there, where they found Ann's, and it's the high-rent district – money and power. I think she got mixed up with a man who thought he owned her.'

Weir listened. Raymond's profile made sense. Ann would choose the opposite of Raymond, someone to be the jewel of intrigue in her secret life. 'It would be in the journal. The journal would be at home.'

Raymond brought his hands to his face, pressing his fingers into his temples. 'Innelman and Deak turned our place inside out. I spent last night doing the same thing, then I went down to the preschool and did it again. She either hid it awfully good, or someone else has it. Maybe, she took it to him.'

'Along with a dozen purple roses.'

'Right.'

'Why?'

They got out and shut the doors. Raymond didn't answer until they were back in Jim's truck.

'I think,' said Raymond, 'she was telling him it was over. She was going to be a mother and her fling was done. Maybe she took him the diary because it was like letters to him, his story, something he could have to remember her by.'

Weir played it through. 'It would make more sense to just chuck it in the bay, get rid of it.'

Raymond shook his head. 'That's not her character. Annie kept things – friends, memories, pictures – you name it. Annie was a keeper. If she wrote a diary, she wouldn't just toss it in the water.'

'She wouldn't give it away, either.'

'She gave more than that away, my friend.' Raymond went quiet for a moment. Weir could hear the hiss of his breathing, slow and deliberate. 'How old is Horton Goins, twenty-four? Maybe that's all it was. A tumble with a good-looking kid who turns out to carry a knife.'

Weir said nothing. It didn't play. But on the other hand, that's exactly what Horton Goins had been to a girl named Lucy Galen in Hardin County, Ohio.

'Let's get the hell out of here,' said Raymond.

16

They started off for the coast, threading first through the barrio side streets of Santa Ana where the houses stood behind wrought-iron fencework to keep the thieves out – even the windows were latticed with metal that tried to look decorative but was, in fact, a barrier against the junkies, crackheads, gangbangers, drifters, home invaders, cutthroats, and occasional killers who wanted in. Then down Fourth Street, past the cafés and shoe and taco stands; past the record stores blasting mournful Mexican ballads; past the pawnshops and the beauty parlors; through the crosswalks filled with women in dresses, burdened by groceries, laboring flat-footed from the marketplaces toward home. Men moved even more slowly along the sidewalks, men with cowboy hats and heavy jackets and sun-darkened faces, men without work, without applicable skills or pressing destinations, with weary legs and exhausted backs and expressions – barely visible beneath their hat brims – of acceptance, resignation, and faith that the Virgin Mary or certain saints would eventually deliver them from this hostile land of dreams mañana, mañana, mañana.

Raymond watched them go by from behind his sunglasses. 'I wish they had more to do,' he said finally. 'They're wasting their lives.'

'They're trying,' said Jim.

'They don't understand the system. If they understood the system, they'd be running this place. All they are now is cheap labor. This whole county's nothing but a day-work center for them. It's pitiful.'

'Another ten years, things'll be different,' said Jim. 'Someone will get them together, and they'll find out what numbers mean.'

Raymond's relation to his own race always had baffled him. Sometimes Ray seemed proud of his blood, other times ashamed of his people. What struck Jim was Raymond's indecision, his unpredictable swings between sympathy and contempt. Raymond,

147

for instance, hadn't associated with the other Mexicans in school. He hung with the white kids, and took German. He had devoted himself to an Anglo – two years his senior – from an age so young that Weir couldn't specifically place it anymore. But Raymond, among his family, was different. Weir spent hours with Ray at the Eight Peso Cantina when they were boys, eye-high to the great bar that runs the length of the place, checking the floor for dropped change, running minor errands and accomplishing minor chores, always under the quietly watchful eyes of Raymond's father and mother, Nesto and Irena Cruz. And there, among parents and relatives, Raymond's Spanish rolled off his tongue with rapid grace, his face took on a fresh new physiology as his lips and cheeks formed the words, even his eyes seemed to glitter with a new energy when he was in the Eight Peso. Later, Weir had come to understand it as the face of belonging.

One incident stood out in Jim's memory. They were high school sophomores, standing together in the quad one afternoon before lunch. Ann was with them. A fight broke out between a big white kid named Lance and a little Mexican named Ernie. Later, Jim found out it was something about Lance's girl. Lance was a football player, a nice-looking boy with an athlete's body and a head of sun-bleached hair. Ernie was a dark, silent boy nobody seemed to know. A crowd closed in on them as Lance's fist slammed into Ernie's face, the sudden eruption of blood hushing the students, but drawing them closer, as if in witness of some holy act. Lance threw Ernie against the brick wall of the cafeteria and started punching again. Jim could hear the pop of knuckles on flesh. Ann begged Raymond to stop it. And Weir could still remember the look on Ray's face as he turned to him, a look of sadness so profound that he stood paralyzed, deaf to Ann's entreaties, hypnotized by the heavy precision of Lance's big arms as he slammed away at the Mexican. Without looking at either Jim or Ann, Raymond simply said, 'Watch.' And to Jim's astonishment, Ernie began to slip the punches and dodge the blows. His face was bleeding hard. Lance tired and slowed, hit the wall with a fist intended for Ernie's stomach, and suddenly, the Mexican was all over him. His hands were lighter and faster than the big boy's, and no single punch seemed to take more out of him than another, but they chopped away at Lance – straightening him, backing him up, moving him away from the wall and back into the open space, where for a moment he swayed, his head tossing side to side like a

148

treetop in some violent storm, before his knees buckled and he fell – one comely, well-developed muscle group at a time – flat on his face, moaning already and trying to cover himself with the fallen brown needles of the quad's centerpiece pine.

Raymond had looked at Jim once, sickness and fury in his eyes, and walked away. It was two weeks before he showed up at school again – flu, he said. Years later, Jim realized that what had made Raymond so sick wasn't a virus at all, but deep and gnawing anger: at Lance for his stupid white arrogance; at Ernie for the stitches it took to close his stubborn macho face; at himself, for not trying to stop it, for knowing that no one would really win, for letting down Ann, and, most of all, for his failure to take a side, commit himself in this momentary crucible of life to a position that he could defend with dignity and truly call his own.

'They deserve something better,' said Ray. 'But they have to earn it. Nothing comes free, nothing comes easy. You want your treasure, they want theirs.'

Jim guided the truck down Fourth, out of the barrio and into the white suburbs of Tustin, a city that, for years, had actually maintained a sign on this boulevard that read WELCOME TO TUSTIN – THE BEVERLY HILLS OF ORANGE COUNTY. Jim could remember thirty years ago, when there had been an odd bit of truth in this. There were big stately homes in the foothills, small ranchos tucked behind stands of eucalyptus and avocado overlooking mile upon mile of emerald green citrus groves. The smell of the orange blossoms – visceral, opiate – rose on invisible thermals. Main Street looked like a dictionary definition of itself – solid brick buildings housing the five-and-dime, the garage, the pharmacy, and an occasional Victorian manse converted to professional offices. But in the late sixties and early seventies, Tustin had sold out. Franchises now ruled every street corner – the Golden Arches, the Jack in the Box, the garishly unmistakable logos of oil conglomerates, grocery chains, convenience networks, and fast-food distributors – all bawling for consumer attention. It was astonishing to Weir, as he gazed out through the eye-watering smog, that in the city of Orange, just a few miles from here, a special plot of ground had been planted with orange trees so people in the future could see what they really looked like. They had literally paved over the trees and put up a tree museum. At some point, he thought, isn't enough enough? The Beverly Hills sign had been taken down years ago.

Then onto the freeway at a crawl, merging at ten miles an hour into a slow lane doing thirty, max, a restless river of cars stretching from as far as he could see in his rearview all the way out of sight ahead of him, where they vanished, brake lights flashing and exhaust systems belching, into the dominating pollutant haze in the west.

And yet, incredibly, thought Weir, the beat goes on. Jackhammers tore out old asphalt to widen the offramps and add freeway lanes; foundation crews and framing teams scurried to cover the last inches of unbuilt land; developers crammed thousands of identical units over hillsides and small valleys while city council and the Board of Supervisors approved it all from on high with furtive sweeps of the ballpoint. It seemed to Weir to be less the land of dreams than the land of disregard. It's all for sale under the spacious skies, he thought, every last amber wave of it, view lots with a peek of purple mountain majesties, God shed his grace on thee.

'This why you wanted to get out?' asked Ray.

'Yeah.'

'People have to lie somewhere.'

'I know that. I'm not so sure Virginia's right, the way she looks at things. But I'm still young enough to pack it in and light out for the territory. She's not.'

'Trouble is, there's no territory left.'

'I guess we just eddy back, or maybe north,' said Jim. Friends of his had joined the rush into the Pacific Northwest and were now busy trying to shut the gates behind them, much as Virginia was doing in Newport. But the question remained: When do you stay and fight, when do you get out and quit complaining? Jim could think things through only so far. Maybe it was as simple as just following one's heart.

But he was beginning to understand that Ann's death had nearly severed some cord in him, a cord that once had included Poon and Jake, that connected him in blood and spirit with this place. There was in Jim a sense of things unraveling. It was down to him and Virginia now. And Ray, and maybe Becky. It felt like the Alamo.

Forty minutes later, they rolled down the peninsula and into the neighborhood, into the heart of what would soon become the Balboa Redevelopment Project, if PacifiCo and the other builders had their

150

way at the polls, sank Virginia's beloved Proposition A, and staffed the mayor's office with friends like Brian Dennison, so eager to exercise the city's power of eminent domain. Weir looked out at the huddled duplexes and small bungalows, the unassuming 1940s-style cottages, the boulevard palms that had grown to majestic height through the decades.

It was the opposite of the suburbs here: no uniformity, no franchised street corners, no 'planning,' no slick production values at all, just the clean air that blew in off the Pacific, miles of thundering ocean butting up against the land, and the unrepentantly modest houses that had stood here for half a century.

Jim had seen, in the papers, concept sketches of the redevelopment. The 'theme' of the new Balboa was Early California, a faux mission look featuring red tile roofs, arching colonnades, and courtyards and fountains. The Eight Peso Cantina was a two-story restaurant called the Newport Sailing Club. Poon's Locker was part of a financial-services minimall. Ann's Kids was a sushi and burger emporium called Taka-Fornia. Virginia's house was a maritime museum, to feature 'elements of Newport's historic past.' Ann and Raymond's house was gone completely, airbrushed away to make room for a three-story parking structure that would be 'architecturally integrated into the Early California look.' The pier would be made over with a mock-adobe material that was waterproof and 'seismically forgiving,' and would feature a 'five-star' restaurant at the end.

Weir remembered now that Virginia and Becky and a handful of other citizens had been arrested near the entrance of PacifiCo Tower for protesting this plan and ignoring repeated warnings by security. They had termed the project 'Mission Impossible,' and gotten the local news stations out for the march and arrest. Cantrell had refused to file charges, and pointed out that they were less concerned with the opinions of the protestors than the safety of their employees, some of whom had been 'harassed' by the demonstrators.

Looking out at the old neighborhood, Jim could only conclude that it wasn't right to change what was working fine to begin with.

Working, he thought, except for the traffic, which had stopped dead on Balboa Boulevard.

Working, he thought, except for the flashing lights of cop cars gathered down the street.

151

Working, except for the helicopter hovering low over an old yellow motel called the El Mar.

Working, except for the black-clad Newport Beach Police SWAT team, bristling with armament, crawling all over the place like ants.

He could see Phil Kearns standing in the motel courtyard, talking to the SWAT captain.

'They found Goins,' said Raymond. 'I *knew* it.'

Weir pulled along a red curb and parked. Raymond was already out, running down the sidewalk.

17

Above the heads of the curious, Weir could see the roof of the El Mar Motel, the ancient fading sign that read VACANCIES, REFRIGERATION, the people hanging out of apartment windows nearby to enjoy an aerial view of the action. The police chopper hovered over the El Mar, tail circling slowly as if the nose were pinned to some invisible axis.

They ducked under a crime-scene tape already in place between the outer wall of the El Mar and a parking meter on the curb, and Weir's first thought was: They shot him. Raymond badged his way past the SWAT team, all attired in black, heavy with automatic weapons and side arms, in boots shiny enough to make a storm trooper blink. Unit 4 was open, a forest of bodies darkening the doorway. The door itself, torn from its hinges, leaned against the outside wall. Officers Hoch and Oswitz stood aside as Raymond went in, but stepped in front of Jim and started pushing him toward the street. Hoch's nightstick drove against his sternum and sent a bullet of pain into his chest. Weir knocked it away with a forearm just as Oswitz drew his baton – gripping it far down on the handle for a punishing swing – but Raymond suddenly reappeared, coming up on them from behind with a quick little push that left Hoch off-balance and Oswitz standing face-to-face with Raymond, who cursed him viciously and drew Jim past them.

He stepped into the tiny motel room. It smelled of a disinfectant supposed to suggest pine. There was little light, the one window being closed off with a thick plastic curtain that looked as if cut from a picnic tablecloth. There was a twin bed, made up, along one wall; a furnace in the corner by the door; a worn green carpet; a Naugahyde chair. The room was too small to hold much else.

The first thing on which Jim's eyes fastened was the city map pinned to the wall next to the bed. Dwight Innelman was photographing it. Jim didn't have to lean close to see the two routes marked out in black and red markers: from the El Mar to the Back Bay via the ferry in black, via the boulevard in red. A cool finger traced its way up his back.

'You guys get him, Dwight?'

Innelman turned from his tripod, then back to it. 'No. He wasn't here. Couldn't have gone very far on foot, could he?'

Roger Deak squeezed from the bathroom with a small, eroded bar of pink soap and a razor inside a plastic evidence bag. 'Prints on everything in here,' he said, with a nod to Jim. 'His darkroom.'

Weir leaned into the bathroom. Metal racks had been screwed into the wall above the toilet, on which stood three trays still shimmering with developing fluids. Plastic containers were grouped neatly beside the john. A small window inside the incredibly tiny shower stall had been covered over with tinfoil. A drying line was hung from the shower head to the wall, affixed to the highest tray rack. The plastic clothespins positioned along it were all red, all empty. Sitting on the sink were a pair of scissors, a red grease pencil, and a loupe. The room smelled like chemicals and mildew. Everything was covered with fingerprint dust.

Past the living room/bedroom was the kitchen, a small rectangular space with a two-chair dinette, a sink and counter, a miniature oven and two-burner stove. It was roped off and guarded by Tillis, the fat plainclothes who had vibed Weir at the station that morning. 'Chief,' he said, turning only slightly toward the kitchen, 'we got a pain-in-the-butt concerned citizen here. Bounce him?'

Jim stood back from the yellow tape that ran across the doorway, and looked into the room. He could smell the natural gas. Brian Dennison was squeezed into one corner, huddling with PR man Mike Paris. Brian had a hand on Paris's arm. Paris was nodding, looking up at Dennison with the beseeching face of a penitent, his shoulders slumped submissively and his head bobbing. Dennison finally looked toward Weir. His expression froze momentarily, then took on a dreamlike calm.

'Out,' he said.

Tillis clamped a hand on Jim's arm. Quickly, Hoch and Oswitz were on him again, sticks jostling into his rib cage and kidneys, fists grabbing his shirt and hair.

Raymond was there in a flash. 'What the —'

'Back off, Cruz!' Dennison yelled. 'Cruz, back the *fuck* off.'

Jim stumbled, raised his hands for balance, which gave Oswitz

154

an excuse to drive the short end of his stick into Jim's armpit, then press up and shove him into the wall. The three men closed him off suddenly, forming a tight little circle around him. A knee shot into his groin, but before Weir could even bend over, Tillis had straightened him, pulled him off the wall, guided him to the front door, and pushed him down the steps. At the bottom, Jim crashed into a hapless photographer, who went down under him in a clamor of cameras, lights, and power packs. Two SWAT cops dragged Weir to the yellow crime-scene tape and prodded him under with their boots. The photographer was allowed to retrieve a shattered flash unit before he was hustled into the crowd on the other side of the ribbon, into which he disappeared like a man pursued by lions.

Jim stood slowly, nauseous from the groining, walked with short measured steps through the parting crowd, and leaned against a parking meter on the sidewalk, breathing deeply. Raymond appeared in the doorway of unit 4. Jim looked at him and shook his head: Okay; go back in. Raymond snapped something at Hoch and Oswitz, who regarded him with attitudes of puzzled contrition. Laurel Kenney, the Channel 5 reporter who'd covered Virginia's arrest at PacifiCo, came toward him with her microphone extended and her minicam operator trailing along behind. Weir had met her at the jail on the day Virginia was released.

'Can you tell us what is happening in there, Mr Weir?'

'No.'

'Where is Horton Goins?'

'At large.'

'Are you active in the investigation into your sister's murder?'

'No.'

'Is it true that she was stalked by Horton Goins, the sex offender?'

'Ask the cops.'

Laurel stood for a moment, looking at him, her microphone at her side. She was a big pale woman with a head of long red hair and dazzling green eyes. She held up the mike to Jim, switched it off, then turned and waved away her cameraman. 'What in hell happened in there? Off the record?'

Weir looked at the curious faces around him, heard their prodding silence. 'I'm not sure what's going on, Laurel. That's all.'

He pushed his way through the crowd, walked south down the sidewalk, then at the first alleyway cut through toward the bay and came up on the El Mar from the back. He picked his way through the trash cans and litter, an old bicycle, a stack of cardboard boxes loaded with empty bottles, a lawn mower completely covered with black residue, a brittle tan Christmas tree still trailing bright stringers of tinfoil. He worked his way up to the small, windowed rear door of unit 4. Goins's escape hatch, he thought. Two high cement steps led up to the door, but standing in the alley, Weir was scarcely more than head-level with the window. He looked in through a long horizontal slot between the blinds. A refrigerator blocked half his view. It took his eyes a moment to adjust to the deep shades of the little room, but when they had, he could see the kitchen and the cops clearly, like players up on a stage viewed from the front row.

Phil Kearns, in a loose-fitting silk shirt and a pair of jeans, was briefing Tillis. Kearns had a retrospective, 'what a game it was' attitude, leading Weir to conclude that Kearns was the one who'd first stumbled on to the El Mar and Goins, thus, MVP. He looked at Paris with a self-satisfied nod. Two more plainclothes were going through a closet built into the wall that divided the two rooms. Weir recognized one of them from the Sheriff's – Mapson, who turned, looked at Dennison, shook his head, and mumbled something to his partner. They brought in the whole fucking department, thought Weir. Raymond, by himself, was staring at the knotty pine wall.

Ray turned to Innelman and indicated something in the wood.

Jim could see Raymond passing his fingers over the wall, then Dwight doing the same. He followed Ray's gaze down to the stained linoleum floor. Raymond stooped, collected something, and stood. For a brief moment, Raymond looked up and through the blinds, straight into Jim's eyes. Then he came across the room, blocking the tiny window with his body, and reached out his hand. Weir stepped back and rested against the wall. He saw the blinds shift open just a little, then Raymond's voice: *need a little goddamned light in here*. Looking from an angle between the widened slats now, he saw Raymond's hands open to the light that filtered through. He had collected thumbtacks from the floor. Jim considered. What had Goins hung on the walls? Whatever it was, he had taken it with him: It was more valuable than his developing chemicals, his map, or his razor. More pictures?

Raymond's hands retracted from view and Jim angled out of sight. He could barely see in, just enough to make out Dennison whispering some final command to Paris, who then turned and

156

shouldered his way past the uniforms, under the ribbon and out through the front room.

As Tillis went through Goins's closet, Jim could see the odd schizophrenia of Horton's wardrobe: impossibly bright Hawaiian shirts and pants; three pairs of tennis shoes – one red, two white; a couple of painter's-style caps in Day-Glo green. Then, pushed to one side as if unwanted but still somehow necessary, were two sport coats, two white dress shirts, a pair of dark dress pants and a pair of light ones, and a handful of neckties on a hanger. Tillis examined a pair of penny loafers, holding the bottoms up to the light. Jim could make out the shape of a skateboard that sat beside the shoes. Innelman bent down, flipped it over with a fingertip, and spun a wheel. *Didn't use this much*, Weir heard him say.

A kid from Ohio, he thought, comes to California and gives himself a make-over. Takes a new name. Gets a job, saves his money, tries to look like he's one of the natives. He gets a skateboard but doesn't have time to use it. He's too busy making plans, taking photographs, studying maps, moving closer and closer to a woman he's probably never even talked to. Of all the women in the country, he thought, why would a messed-up kid in a mental hospital pick Ann? Chance – the horrible randomness of chance? If someone else had been standing in the play yard of Ann's Kids the day he shot her picture, would he have become obsessed with that woman instead? Raymond stepped forward and fingered each necktie. Looking for the telltale hole of a tie tack, Weir ventured. Raymond shook his head helpfully. There was none. Horton Goins doesn't wear half-carat diamond tie tacks. Horton Goins wears Day-Glo painter's caps and red tennis shoes. Reconcile the two, he thought. Somewhere is an explanation.

Hey Paris, said Dennison. *What's the deal on the press, anyway? They're ready when you are.*

Dennison checked his watch, then stepped forward to confer with Innelman.

Tillis brought over a chair and stood on it for a look at the top shelf. He looked like a circus elephant on a stool. Innelman broke away from the chief with a shrug, and joined Deak in dusting the kitchen counter and the oven door. Raymond was standing with Kearns now. He cast a quick glance at Jim through the blinds.

Christ, thought Weir, if a Newport Beach cop killed Ann, what he has here is carte blanche to contaminate, conceal, tamper

157

with, remove, adjust, or plant any evidence he wants to. It was an incredibly sloppy job.

The idea hit him that the cops would be happy to have it this way, if one of their own had killed Ann. They'd be happy, too, to let Goins stay one step ahead of them for a week or so, to put him in the spotlight and keep him there. What if they were orchestrating this circus, letting Goins run off ahead like a mechanical rabbit? Maybe Kearns isn't after Goins at all, he thought. Maybe he's *running* him. Why was it Kearns, out of everyone in the department, out of every citizen on the peninsula, who caught up with Goins? For a moment, he wanted to burst in, beat the shit out of anyone who got in his way, grab each offending invader by the throat and drag him outside, leaving Innelman and Deak to do what only Innelman and Deak should have been doing in the first place. Stupid. There was nothing he could do about it now.

He watched as Dennison clapped his hand onto Kearns's back – a job well done – then onto Raymond's, too – we'll get this guy – like this was some cocktail party and he was three martinis strong. There was an ingratiating tilt to his head as he said something to Kearns. Then Paris the flack shouldered back into the kitchen and leaned close to Dennison. The chief's hand dropped from Raymond's back. *Carry on*, he said, and headed toward the front room door, buttoning his linen sport coat, running his fingers through his hair, straightening his back, a sense of mission now returned, now palpable in his stride.

When he was gone, Paris turned to Tillis, straightened his back, brushed a hand through his hair, and echoed *Carry on*, in a voice that approximated Dennison's. Weir noted that it wasn't very good. Muted chuckles came from behind the window glass, anyway. Raymond shot him another glance.

Parrot, he thought. Public Relations officer Mike Parrot. Another fucking clown with a badge and a gun.

From his elevation on the chair, Tillis's voice boomed clearly through the general hum of the kitchen. *Hey, hey, hey! Young Tillis delivers.*

Weir watched him step down, with a large manila envelope between one thumb and forefinger. He walked it gingerly to the kitchenette table, set it down, and worked open the flap with a pencil. Tillis shook out the contents – a stack of eight-by-ten glossies, black and white. Using the pencil eraser, he separated them, spreading them around the table.

Jim heard the silence that descended on the room. Three backs blocked his view – Innelman's, Ray's, and Roger Deak's. Past them, he could see only the surface of the cheap table, the stack of photographs, and the dick's pudgy hand still holding the pencil.

Man.

Fuckin' nutcase.

Look at this.

Weir could see that someone with a pair of tongs had lifted one of the pictures to the light. He couldn't make it out. Raymond's face, in profile now, looked conspicuously pale. Raymond accepted the tongs, held up the picture, made a show of not being able to see it well enough, then came toward the window. Bending down, his back to the room, he held the photograph to the weak inrush of light.

And there was Ann in all her beauty, captured unaware by Goins in a moment of her everyday life. She was coming out of her front door in the morning, one arm still trailing inside to turn the lock. She had a fresh expression on her face, the look of mild optimism with which some people anticipate their work. Raymond flipped it over. Written in grease pencil were the words *New Morning – February 25.*

Then he was looking at Raymond's back as Ray returned to the table and got another one of the pictures, which were now being circulated like snapshots of a wedding. Raymond made his rounds, careful to keep himself between the other cops and the window.

Ann swinging open the chain-link gate at the preschool while a gust of offshore breeze lifted her hair back from her face. *Work – February 25.*

Ann walking down the sidewalk along the bay with two large grocery bags clutched to her chest. *Groceries – March 2.*

Ann on the same sidewalk in her short work skirt, an old sweater, her purse slung over her shoulder; Ann amidst her children at the preschool – similar, thought Weir, to the shot that Innelman had found in Emmett's Costa Mesa apartment; Ann and Raymond, in uniform, chatting through the chain-link fence of the play yard; Ann and Ray and Phil Kearns – a night shot this time – walking arm in arm down Balboa Boulevard just past the theater; another

159

shot taken the same night of the three of them standing outside the entrance of the Studio Café.

The last three were the ones that hit Jim hardest, however. The first was a shot of the window of Ann's and Ray's apartment, taken at night, from an angle below the glass. Ann was staring out, with a vacant expression on her face. She wore dark lipstick, and a string of pearls around her neck. Her hair was up, and her shoulders were bare to where the dark material of her dress covered them, her dangling earrings throwing stars of light toward the camera. She looked, to Jim, lost. *Window Thoughts – March 14*.

In the next shot she had her back to Goins, stopped in an alley that Jim recognized as the one behind her apartment that led toward the boulevard. The alleyway glistened with puddles and the asphalt shone in the aftermath of a storm. The sides of the buildings were slick and reflective as mirrors. Goins had managed to get the moon in there, a forlorn sliver peering down from between two apartment structures. Ann was framed in the middle, not walking, legs together, up on her toes just a little, looking down, an umbrella visible in her left hand, apparently deciding how best to negotiate the puddles that looked from this angle to have penned her in. *Ann in Moonlight – February 25*.

In the last, only her legs and shoes were visible, where they were about to disappear behind the door of a limousine being held open by a stout man in a dark suit. His back was to the camera. No license plate was visible. *Joyride – March 21*.

'Woowee,' said fat Tillis. 'Goins is a definite fan of hers. Definite fuckin' whacko. But they let him out. Don't they always? What do they think, it's a way to keep us busy or something? Chief ought to see this shit. Hey Parrot, get the chief back in here!'

Led by Paris, Dennison came gliding in a moment later, his brow furrowed, a fresh sheen of sweat on his face. Backing away from the glass, Jim could hear him mumble something about three locals *and* three networks.

Paris brought him to the corner by the refrigerator for a confidential chat, right in front of Jim.

'The news crews can use one of those photos as an insert, sir.'

'What good would it do?'

'Up to you, sir, but it will set this story aside from all the other homicides they have. It's a nice piece of airtime and it's free. If Becky Flynn could get this kind of coverage, she'd climb to the top of PacifiCo Tower naked and set herself on fire. Which, come to think of it, is a scene I'd like to see. Take advantage, while you can.'

Dennison was silent for a moment. Weir could see the line of his linen jacket through the slats, the way the lapel folded back over his big chest. Paris's wrist turned over, exposing his watch.

'Better get on it, sir.'

Dennison's coat shifted back now and his hands slid into his pockets. Weir could see the worn patch on the elbow of the jacket.

— What about the feds?

— This would be an excellent time to mention them, if you can work it in.

— I still don't see why. It implies we're not doing a good job in our own backyard.

— Either we co-opt them and imply we invited them in, or Flynn uses them against us. Take your pick, sir.

— No.

— No what?

— Nobody needs to see these pictures. I run one and every shutter nut in the state's gonna see it and send us his candids of pretty blondes. No.

Paris was quiet for a moment.

— What about the handle?

— I'm working on that.

— I still think the Bayside Slasher is strong.

— He didn't slash her, he stabbed her.

— *Stabber's* not a good word — too focused, gory but not graphic in the right way. We need something with motion in it, something they can *see*.

Another pause. Weir could hear Paris sigh.

— Any word at all on Goins, Chief? If we could announce the arrest it would —

— You think if we'd caught him I'd be standing here talking about fuckin' *handles*?

A muted light came to the glass as Dennison moved away from the window. Paris's back then crushed up against the blinds. Weir heard Paris mumble, in a poor caricature of Dennison,' . . . talking about fuckin' handles?'

⋆   ⋆   ⋆

161

Weir, Raymond, and Phil Kearns leaned against the outside wall of the El Mar Motel – VACANCIES, REFRIGERATION – and watched Interim Chief Dennison give his interviews to the TV news. The crowd had pressed up close to the crime-scene ribbon and the SWAT team provided security, an idea that Jim overheard Paris suggest to Dennison when the news crews were setting up.

'How'd it go down?' asked Jim.

Kearns shrugged. 'I got lucky. Went to the realty people and the lady sent me here. I called Brian and he ordered me to hold off. That's how SWAT got into it and the whole circus started.'

Dennison sweated intensely in the tepid overcast sun. The minicams pressed in close, spotlights glaring, technicians linked umbilically to their machines, jostling for the best angles. Dennison was talking down Goins's prior offense – already treading lightly on his way to the courtroom – but he adamantly linked the MO to Ann: '. . . waitress here, waitress in Ohio . . . knew his victim . . . swampy area, in this case the Back Bay . . . apparently a photographer who had been "aware" of her for some time.'

Weir turned to Kearns, who was looking to Dennison with the expression of an on-deck hitter. 'What did his room look like when you got in?'

'Neat. The furnace was on. There were two pieces of white bread on the kitchen counter, like he was getting ready to put them in the oven.'

So, Weir thought, Goins was home all right, gathering up his things and heading for the back door while Dennison's production got going. Was that part of the plan? 'Any idea what spooked him?'

'I don't know. It could have been me. I waited across the street where I could see his front door. I thought I was cool, but if he was watching . . .'

Raymond shook his head.

'Dennison called SWAT, not me,' Kearns snapped.

'Dumb,' said Raymond.

'Fuckin' dumb is right,' said Kearns.

Dennison had launched into a law-and-order spiel, focusing on the peninsula here, where 'the overwhelming majority of crime in our city is committed.'

The implication, thought Weir, was that the whole place would be better off torn down and built again, but Dennison wasn't mercenary enough to mention the Balboa Redevelopment Project. Paris, his hands stuffed down into an overcoat, lurked behind Dennison like a bad conscience.

'What makes Newport Beach a great city is great people,' the interim chief was saying. 'And these people deserve protection from the less fortunate, like Horton Goins. This city can no longer afford to provide an environment that encourages violent crime. The citizens of this peninsula deserve more.'

As if the less fortunate were all committed sex offenders, thought Weir, as if you can redevelop someone like Horton Goins out of existence, as if a low-profit, low-tax-base neighborhood was the reason for it all.

'Chief Dennison, is Horton Goins now officially a suspect?'

'Horton Goins is a prime suspect.'

Paris leaned forward and whispered something in Dennison's ear. Dennison cupped his hand around the nearest mike, as if national security might be at stake.

The chief nodded and turned back to the cameras. 'In the search for the Bayside Slasher, Horton Goins is our *only* suspect.'

18

Joseph Goins rang the doorbell once, then took a step backward on the creaking, uneven porch. He turned to look again at the immense avocado tree that cast its shade around him, at the weed-choked walkway up which he had just come, at the looming shapes of hibiscus and citrus and bamboo that stood tall in the yard, their tops connecting skyward, hushing the lot in shade and sealing off the house from the street. He already liked it.

A shriek issued from behind the door. The hair on the backs of Goins's hands rose. Maybe it was more like a cackle, something containing a word.

'*Mmmyyaa?*'

What a grating tone, he thought. He rang the bell again, looking down at his box of cameras, photographs, clothes. The image came to him again of that man loitering across the street from the El Mar, the one with the tight jeans and the fancy billowy shirt. An idea had screamed up Goins's backbone when he looked out and saw him, and he had listened to it telling him to get out while he still could. Cop, it said. See the cop who's found you. It was part of the same idea that, the day before, had told him locate another room in case this happened. Thank God for the clarity, he thought, thank God for back doors.

'*Mmmyyaa?*'

'Mrs Fostes?'

'*Mmminute!*'

Joseph took the newspaper from his box. A nice touch, he thought, like in the movies. He folded it back to expose the right column. His hand was still shaking. And whose wouldn't? he wondered.

Carrying his box of things, he'd slipped out the back door and then walked down the bayfront to the video arcade, where he lost himself in the dark pinging metropolis of buzzers and bells and alarms. Everyone was looking at him. These California people *know* when you're not one of them, he'd thought.

Aching inside, his mind swirling with contradictory messages, his face on fire with the heat of discovery and flight, he had sat on the seawall for a few minutes and just given up, just waited for them to come get him and take him away. A SWAT detail had pounded past him with martial precision, heading for the El Mar. The helicopter had settled over the motel, its rotors beveling the silence with chop-chops that he could see inside his eyelids – harsh, red-black blades cutting down from a blue sky. Three uniformed cops had marched by him, too, quick with purpose. And there he had sat, sunglasses and a bright painter's cap on, his box of things beside him, wondering why they just didn't stop and cuff him. Then he'd kept to the side streets, hefted the box up onto his shoulder to block his face from view, and headed south down the peninsula toward the address.

The door swung open and a withered, robed, white-haired woman beheld him with the palest blue eyes that he had ever seen. Her shoulders were curved over on top, like a paper clip. Her face was sunken, but the skin looked soft. With one bony dark-spotted hand she clawed her robe up close to her neck.

She's lovely, thought Joseph Goins. He lifted the folded newspaper up to her, and watched with extreme care what she did now. 'Are you Mrs Fostes?'

'I am,' she said. Her eyes wandered, focusless, over the folded paper. Perfect. *Sighted older woman seeks companionship for room and board*, it said. To Joseph Goins, 'sighted' could only mean almost blind. He was right.

'I'm Joseph Gray. Is the room taken?' he asked, smiling.

Her blue eyes locked on his face for a moment, and he took off his sunglasses to return their assessing gaze. 'No. Come in.'

Even her speaking voice was a shriek, he noted, but it was a quieter one. He picked up his box and followed her bobbing down-white head into the house.

It was dark, warm, and filled with competing, unpleasant smells. A cat curled atop an end table, as if mounted to the lamp base. There was a slouching green sofa, an overstuffed chair in a floral pattern, a coffee table, and a television set, which was turned on. A dog the size and shape of a fluffy bedroom slipper zipped in tight angles around Joseph's feet as he followed Mrs Fostes toward the

165

furniture. She sat slowly in the middle of the couch and lifted a bony finger to indicate the chair.

'If I could find my glasses, I could see you better,' she said. 'I can hardly make out the TV from here. What's on?'

'A soap opera, I think.'

'Where could they have gone?' She dug into a shoe box that lay on the table before her, a box filled with dozens of prescription bottles. 'I don't need them for these,' she said, tapping the box. 'I can go by shape. But I can't see the tube. Do you see them anywhere?'

Joseph looked around the room, his gaze moving to the top of the TV set, where a pair of black-rimmed heavy glasses sat. 'No, Mrs Fostes. I don't.'

'I lost them for a month this winter,' she said. 'Didn't slow me down a bit.'

'What a lovely home,' said Joseph. The cat's tail dropped off the tabletop, swung, twitched.

'It'll do,' said Mrs Fostes. 'Are you a student?'

'I'll be going back full-time in the fall,' he said. 'UCI.' He knew all about the University of California, Irvine – the medical-research facilities, anyway.

'What's your major?'

'Computers.'

'That's the best field there is right now. My husband, John, he always said computers were the future. That was way back. He died in 'sixty-two.'

'I'm sorry.'

'So am I,' she sighed. 'Where are you from?'

'Irvine.' May as well stay consistent, he thought. 'My dad's a computer salesman. My mom's a homemaker.'

'Do you have a job?'

'I'm living off my savings right now. But I'll be seeking a position in computers in the near future.'

'You're certainly well spoken for a local boy. Your mouth isn't loose when you speak. Do you surf?'

'I skateboard some.' Joseph chuckled, remembering the few dizzying moments he'd spent on the eighty-dollar board he'd bought, moments of vertiginous peril, banana-peel quickness, absolute befuddlement. 'But I'm a good swimmer.' This much was true. He'd spent every available moment in the City Plunge, up until Lucy. Even through the long years of the state hospital, he had held an undiminished feeling of what it was like: the cool water parting before him, the way it would support you if you kept moving, the peacefulness of it.

She looked at him, a little off center with the soft blue gaze. 'In the ad, I said companionship. What I like most is someone to read me the paper every morning. Perhaps discuss the major stories for a few minutes. Then, someone to talk with after dinner. Only for half an hour or so. We'll make dinner together – the other meals we just fend for ourselves. I pay for groceries. You have to pay long-distance telephone, but that's about it. You empty the wastebaskets and take the trash out Thursdays. Sometimes I need help out of bed, but once I'm up and moving, I'm a hellcat. I prefer a young man or woman because I might need your strength occasionally, and, quite frankly – old people depress me. You're welcome to bring a friend over when you want.'

'You can't read the papers yourself?'

'No.'

'What about the pictures?'

'Only a blur – even with my glasses. *Damn*, where could they have run off to?'

Good, thought Joseph. His nervous system seemed to exhale. 'Don't you have other boarders?'

'Just Dolly, that's the cat, and Molly, that's the dog. There was a young girl living here until two weeks ago. She disappeared.'

'Disappeared?' asked Joseph. There was something about the way she said it.

'You know. Packed up and went.'

Joseph nodded. His fingertips were stinging now. As the days passed, they would crack and begin to bleed. They seemed just to come apart along the whorls, as if whatever holds skin together dried out. In the nine years he'd spent at the hospital, not a single doctor could explain this condition. It happened twice a year or so – no explanation. But Joseph had noted that it seemed to come either when things were going very well for him or very badly. It would become painful before long. 'I'll be more reliable than that, Mrs Fostes.'

'Would you like to see your room, Joseph?'

He stood, smiling. 'Sure.'

He followed her from the living room, lifting her glasses off the TV on his way by, and dropping them into his box.

*   *   *

167

The room was upstairs, at the end of a short dark hallway, last on the right. It was larger than both rooms of the El Mar Motel put together, with one window that looked over a sideyard crowded with trees and another that faced the street. The floor was hardwood that no longer shone. A cheapish fluffy blue rug lay in the center. There was a large desk along one wall, with two box-shaped items on it, each draped with a folded white sheet that was then taped snugly to the desktop.

How interesting, thought Joseph. He set his box on the floor, and asked what was under the sheets.

'A computer and a printer,' said Mrs Fostes. 'I bought them for my granddaughter, but she never used them. I have no idea how it all works.'

Joseph, who had never used a computer, nodded. 'They all operate on the same . . . principles.'

'Well, the principle I use is to keep the dust off it in case she ever decides she needs it. There's a bathroom across the hall.'

Mrs Fostes walked slowly to the window, felt for the curtains, then grasped them in both hands and threw them open. 'You could see the water when the trees weren't so high.'

'I like the trees,' he said.

In the pale stream of sunshine, Joseph studied Mrs Fostes's eyes, the way they absorbed the light like old glass but didn't send much back out. It must be sad to have your eyes quit working. Magdesh, at State, had taken out his own eyes with a pencil nub.

Suddenly, Joseph sensed a third presence in the room. He turned quickly. Standing in the doorway was a pretty young girl – she couldn't have been more than eighteen – with her arms crossed and her head at an inquisitive angle. She had on a pair of stone-washed jeans, high-tech athletic shoes, and a Fine Young Cannibals T-shirt. Her hair was honey-colored and fine, and she wore it straight, gazing past a shining wall of it now as if she was looking around a corner at him. 'The computer's mine.'

Mrs Fostes's head turned suddenly in the girl's direction. She had been trying to get a closet door open to show the new boy where his clothes could go. 'I thought you were out, dear.'

'I'm going out.'

'This is our new boarder.'

'I'm Joe,' he said.

'I'm outta here,' said the girl. She turned and vanished, then her diminishing footsteps sounded down the stairway.

'She's my granddaughter, not very manageable,' said Mrs Fostes.

'She lives here?'

Mrs Fostes nodded. 'She won't read me the paper, or cook with me, or take her meals with me. She's at an age. I understand . . . I was like that once. I'm surprised she was still home.' Mrs Fostes gathered her robe up close to her chin again, and started toward the door. 'She won't bother you, Mr Gray.'

Joseph knew some nicety was called for, but he couldn't imagine what.

'Come down now and we'll sign the agreement.'

Joseph heard the front door slam. 'What's her name?'

'Lucinda.'

Joseph's entire inner being felt as if it were about to wrench itself inside out, like a sock. *Lucy*. For a brief moment, everything in the room went bright, so bright that he could hardly keep his eyes open. He slipped his sunglasses back on. His legs felt thick and his heart was throbbing up in his temples. 'Well,' he said quietly. 'That's a nice name.'

'Don't worry, she's hardly ever here. Let's go down and sign the paper now. Then you can unpack and get to know your room. I like to eat at seven, so we can start the dinner at six.' Mrs Fostes hobbled to the door, steadying herself against the wall as she passed through. 'I sure wish I could find those glasses of mine.'

An hour later, Joseph was lying on the bed, his hands crossed behind his head, staring up at the ceiling. Would Lucinda recognize him from the TV, the papers? She didn't seem like a cognizant person, but who could know? Maybe the best thing was just to avoid her. His temples were still pounding, but not as hard now. The sun had gone past the window and a comforting shade had crept into the room.

The more Joseph tried to relax, the clearer became his memory of what had happened in the last few hours. They were on to him. They were close. They wouldn't give up. That first electric shock he'd felt as he watched the cop loitering across the boulevard repeated itself up his backbone now, a dizzying comet of energy that shot into his head, dashed against his skull, and showered sparks back down onto the tops of his eyes. His fingers were beginning to burn.

He climbed off the bed, took the leather-bound journal from the closet shelf, and sat down at the desk. He had to pull up the tape to move the computer away to make room. He peeked under the sheet: a tan plastic box with a Japanese company name on the front.

Joseph smoothed his hand over the soft leather of the journal, arranging it perfectly before him. He took a deep breath, turned to the postcard of Poon's Balboa, and opened. Seeing Ann's handwriting – her actual handwriting – was something that still loosed armies of emotion inside of him. He could hear her voice as he read.

MARCH 26

I sent my letter to Dave Smith at Cheverton Sewer & Septic, not exactly a romantic address, but romance was not what I was after – not yet. David's letters back to me were waiting in box 2212. My father was the one who gave me that box, not long before he died. He used it for the same kind of thing and told me to keep it secret. I'm always up for a secret – secrets are soul-builders – but I ended up telling my mother a year or so later. She wasn't surprised. Living with Poon for thirty years is enough to take the surprise out of anyone.

Our first letters – this was late January – were all about the big, general things – politics, religion, people. Funny how the better you know someone, the smaller the things you talk about get. I think that David was getting the same pleasure I was from writing: When you tell someone about what you really think, well, it can seem interesting in new ways. Why do we share things with strangers we never tell our closest friends and family?

At the end of his third letter, David asked if I would tell him about Paris. Now, David was one of the few people who knew I never went to France, and he knew basically what happened that summer when I was fifteen. But he asked the question so tentatively,

170

I realized how little he actually knew, how deeply he had buried it all.

So I told him about the conference between Mom and me and that lawyer – Nathanson – and how we made arrangements to give my baby away when she was born. Nathanson must have gotten some of his instructions from David's father, but Blake Cantrell never once came and talked to me. By the time all this happened, David was already shipped back to Montana by his family, to finish out the school year, then work around the ranch. I missed him terribly then, and I wish I'd had Dad's P.O. box then, because I knew he was writing me from Montana, but not one letter got past Mom. I wrote him every day, but found out later, of course, that he didn't get my letters, either. Of all the minor cruelties surrounding the time, that stealing of the letters always seemed the cruelest.

The agreement that Mom and I made with Nathanson was that the baby would be given up at birth to an unidentified couple that Nathanson had located in upstate New York. I was not told their name. I signed several documents, Mom signing each time first because I was a minor. The empty lines across from our names were for Blake Cantrell and David. I tried to sneak a look at who was getting my baby, but I couldn't see any names in the thick legal paragraphs. They all assured me it was for the best.

And as I wrote about these times to David – what, twenty-five years later? – it all came sweeping back to me, all the strangeness of that trip back to New York, the little house that was waiting for me on the lake, the nanny, Ruth, who turned out to be a fine lady and friend, the long summer months when I finally started to show, then got big, then the rainy morning in September when we left the lake and went to the hospital.

The delivery room was so bright and metallic; I remembered lying on my back and the terrible pain that came in waves. And the doctors and nurses behind their green masks, little eyes peering down on me, their voices steady and so matter-of-fact. Then the rising pitch in those voices when things started going wrong, the hemorrhage and the cesarean section, and finally, through the fog of anesthetics and the horrid sounds of instruments being applied to me, there, from between my upraised knees, this tiny bloody form that they pulled out, tangled and not moving and barely human it looked, and after all the kicking it had done inside me, so still and peaceful. And that one dream-like glimpse of Little Warm – I had taken to calling it Little Warm because that's how it felt inside sometimes – was the first and last I ever had. A few minutes later, they gave me something to put me out and when I woke up I was in a hospital bed, all cleaned up and changed into my favorite nightgown and Mom was standing there over me. The doctor came in a few minutes later and told me that Little Warm had been born 'still.' It took me a moment to understand what he meant, but then it sunk in.

I think I knew that there would be something wrong with her – I had a terrible virus during my second trimester and David had it, too. I wondered what the fever would do to Little Warm.

As I lay there and looked up at Mom, there seemed to be some great cool depth opening up inside me, and I fell into it, eagerly, like running into the ocean on a hot summer day. I cried so much. Mom said it would get better, that nature had done what it had to do, and Little Warm was in a better place than she could ever be in the real world.

For nine months, Dear One, David and I had had a daughter.

Joseph looked up from the journal and stared out his window, past the cypress trees to the pale eastern sky. He heard the door downstairs slam. This part of the story always made him the saddest and the most furious, the fact that the world can push around a soul so pure and young as Ann's, the fact that she was so alone then, so small against the system. He thought with disgust about David Cantrell, out on some ranch mending fence while Ann

172

went through the fires of childbirth, thousands of miles from home, surrounded only by those so ready to lie and cheat and use her for themselves.

How little she knew, he thought. He looked down at his fingertips, already starting to split along the whorl lines, not so much split as just open up. Next, he'd start hitting his fingers on things and the cracks would widen, bleed, widen more.

What a terrible thing it had all become.

MARCH 29

I had to wait three days to write again. My memories of Little Warm make me ache, as if it all had happened a year ago instead of a quarter century. And Raymond has been so moody these last few days — snapping at me about the house and my cooking, looking at me for long minutes with nothing to say.

David and I arranged to see each other again in late February, the twenty-fifth, I think. He sent a limousine that waited for me in the alley while I hobbled down in my heels, trying to get around the puddles.

When I climbed inside, there he was, offering me his hand. The coach smelled like leather and cologne; it was like stepping inside a man's body, it felt so . . . *inner*. I sunk into the seat as the car moved away from the curb.

He told me I looked nice, and I told him nothing special.

In truth, I was so nervous, I could hardly keep myself in one piece. This moment was all I'd been thinking about since the day we set it up — an entire week to feel, well, a lot of very different, very strong things.

First, I was scared. I was scared that Ray would find out. I'd made sure he wasn't working the peninsula shift; I'd made sure the limo wouldn't be on the boulevard, in case the neighbors, or Mom, or Phil Kearns, or someone else I knew just happened to come by. My sense of betrayal was deep, and I fought it by telling myself that I was simply meeting a very old

173

friend for a very innocent talk. Then why the new nylons? I wondered as I unrolled them up my legs. Why the hesitation about perfume – which one, which mood, how much – I wondered as I touched just a little behind each ear. Why these heels? Why did I stand in front of the mirror when I was finished, up on my tiptoes, turning a little to see if my butt was still high and firm and the silk dress was flattering? (It was.) I know why. It was because I was betraying Raymond's trust, a trust that he had offered to me for twenty years of marriage. Every commonsense, conventional voice inside me told me to call this off, honor my pact as Mrs Cruz, resist. But the other voices were there, too, assuring me that meeting an old friend – especially one with whom I had undergone so much – was an act not of betrayal but of affirmation. These voices told me my fear was not of Raymond but of myself, a fear that I could not be trusted, a fear of testing my commitment, a commitment that I could reconfirm *by going ahead with this*. Dear One, if only I can tell you someday to be careful of the things we tell ourselves, of the things we'll believe. The strange part is that in many ways, they're true.

Also, I was just excited as all get-out to be dressing up, meeting a nice guy I used to know well, getting out of that cold, miserable little apartment and, well, to be letting someone else do the driving. I felt like a young woman again, not some tired lady with two jobs, pushing forty and putting her husband through law school. I felt so light, so . . . *interesting*.

I'm glad you came, he said.

I asked him if he thought I'd chicken out. I told him I almost did, because it wasn't my habit to cruise around in limos while my husband was at work.

He said he didn't set this up to compare notes on how guilty we felt. He was hoping we could just keep it light, maybe do something silly.

Like what? I demanded.

Like this, he said.

He flipped open the cooler beside him and pulled out

174

two champagne glasses. Mine had a purple rose tied to the stem with a purple ribbon. David had sent me roses like that in high school – it was our flower. I laughed and so did he. He poured some bubbly and we toasted.

To years gone by, he said.

And years to come, I said, and we drank. For a minute, I looked through the dark windows at the rain coming down again, the slick blackness of Coast Highway, the wet faces of the buildings shining in sign light. I felt like every inch of road we covered was an inch I'd never cross again, that I was moving on into unmapped territory, unsettled frontier. For a moment, I let myself believe it was true. And in that moment, I let myself admit how deeply I was rutted in my life, how numbingly familiar things had become, how astonishingly easy it all was, and, of course, how hard I'd worked to make it that way! David was looking at me when I turned to him.

I do this a lot at night, he said. I like to sit back and watch things go by. If you don't think about anything while you see it, it seems new.

I said it must be nice to cruise Orange County, when you own half of it. A flicker of disappointment crossed his eyes.

Forget what I own for a while, he said. I'd like to. No one owns things, anyway – we're renters. We all just rent, until the landlord comes.

We went out the boulevard to Coast Highway, south past the restaurants, through Corona del Mar, down into Laguna. I opened the window to get some storm. The waves were big at Main Beach, I could see the white foaming walls towering into shore; I could feel the power surge through the air when they broke, a sound you get in your chest, not through your ears.

You're getting wet, he said.

I let the rain hit my face.

Same flake you were in high school, he said, and down went his window, too, and we sat there for the next five minutes riding through town while the wind charged in and the rain slanted through. He filled our glasses again and I could see the raindrops hitting the pool of champagne and bouncing off the rose. Neither of us said anything for a long time. It was just him and me and a couple of feet of leather between us, and a storm the shape of a window swirling into me.

I don't know why I'm doing this, I said. But that was only partly true. Parts of us remain unrevealed to ourselves, but we catch glimpses of these missing pieces sometimes if we are awake and looking for them. So I had a notion of why I was doing this. I was surprised by the smallness of it. I was doing this as a simple way of not caring for a few minutes, a way not to have an experience but to let the experience have me.

'I never thought that Little Warm would be the last chance I'd get to have a child,' I said suddenly, and the words shocked me as I heard them.

He was brooding and quiet a long while, then finally said that when he learned that Christy, his wife, couldn't have children, he wondered if it was some vengeful, poetic consequence of what had happened to me.

Then I caught myself saying things to him that I'd never said to anyone but myself, about the hugeness of what happened that fall in New York, and how long it took me to realize what my ruined womb would come to mean, how I'd look in the mirror or at one of the kids at school or see an expression in Ray's eyes and realize again that I'd never pass myself on in that way, never have the chance to offer my best to a little being who needs me, never give Ray that gift, never, well . . . *have one.*

David's window followed mine up. Getting pelted in the face by rain didn't seen much fun anymore.

'There was one thing I wanted to say tonight,' he said. 'It was the only thing I wanted to say. I'm sorry, Ann. I'm sorry for how it worked out.'

I shrugged. There have been times in my life when those words would have brought tears to my eyes and I'd have started blubbering, but after a while you just

176

accept what is and don't beat yourself up anymore about what isn't. I mean, how much can a girl take?

'Me, too,' I said. 'But it wasn't your fault and it wasn't mine, so what can you say?'

David was quiet for a long time. 'Just that if I had the chance to do it again, do it right, do it now – I would.'

I looked at him for a moment. Always beneath the rational good sense in David's eyes, I've seen the gambler that he is, the willingness to take a chance. He meant it.

'Well, that's a fat, bitter pill, at this point,' I said.

'Remember our plan to run away and have it? Think of how different things would have been if we'd have had the guts to carry it out.'

I told him I'd thought of that every day for twenty-five years. And suddenly, I was aware of myself, unexpectedly, acutely aware of myself: the makeup running from the rain, my hair all a mess, my dress soaked, my husband almost off shift, my almost-forty body trying its best to stay young, my barren womb waiting there like some cute little house that nobody's ever going to live in, and I thought, What in the fuck am I doing here?

'I turn into a pumpkin in about half an hour,' I said.

David tapped on the privacy glass and the driver headed for the left lane.

He said he wanted to ask me something.

Ask away, I said, though I knew what it would be.

Why did you marry Raymond so soon after . . . us? You were hardly out of high school.

Dear One, though I'll probably never give this book to you, I must say that there are certain decisions made in life that are best left unexamined once you make them. Some things we must have the luxury of taking for granted, because if we entertained doubts about them, we simply wouldn't be able to move ahead with life. I admit that I had asked that same question over the years, but never deeply, never with a passion to really

177

know. I've always let the answer sit just out of reach, an unexamined mystery that requires no attention.

So I told myself then what I'd always known: that Raymond Cruz has a heart the size of California, and I was content to be a villager in it. I came to know Raymond as a girl of fifteen, secretly attached to a college senior of twenty-one I simply fell for in one lightning instant at a party, and was later made pregnant by. I came to know Raymond as a girl who'd just been through a secret death about which she could speak to no one but her parents and this college senior now exiled to Stanford University. I know now that I easily became lost in Raymond Cruz's dimensions.

I told myself this, too, and I will tell you, Dear One, though I'll never have the nerve to give this book to you: Besides the breadth of Raymond's decency, I was seduced by his patient, tender, unwavering devotion to me. It would be a lie to deny that. I'm not sure when I first became aware of this devotion, but it was long before I turned into a woman, long before we went as a couple to our first dance, when he was sixteen. I think it started when we were children in the neighborhood. I came to bask in that devotion like someone in the sun. It surrounded me; it waited for me; it was a dependable constant in a world of motion. And it would be a lie, too, to deny that I reserved the right to ignore it; to control my intake, to simply free myself of it when I wanted to be in a world that lacked the burden of someone else. That was often, in those first years, reeling as I was from what had happened in New York.

So why, as we walked the bayfront that fine spring afternoon, my eighteenth, Raymond holding my hand and respecting my distance with the silence I desired, did I ask him to marry me? Why?

178

More than anything, as I ponder the question in
the silence of this house I now share with him, I
believe it was because I had seen the quickness
with which life can take things away: my brother
Jake just killed in Vietnam, David banished to the
north, Little Warm to some medical-waste-disposal
unit – I didn't know what they did with her and
I still don't. No one can tell me that a girl of
fifteen doesn't feel genuinely. I felt with a depth
of heartache that I still won't let myself remember
in any but my worst moments. And as I walked
along the bay that day, I was aware, Dear One,
excruciatingly aware that there was no God watching
each footstep, no parent or friend powerful enough
to guide my unsteady feet, no one devoted to
my protection. There was nothing but him, Ray,
walking beside me without words, holding my
hand with just the right amount of possessiveness
and tentativeness. He was my companion. He
was my friend. He was soon – that night, in fact
– my lover. Why did I marry him so soon after
David?

'Mainly,' I said to C. David Cantrell in his limousine
twenty years later, 'to have something that wouldn't
go away.'

'But did you love him?'

'More than anything in the world,' I said.

Joseph Goins looked up from the journal, his heart heavy and his
eyes misting over. Such a pure young thing, she was, he thought,
so innocent.

And a plan started forming in his mind. It was still unclear,
the actual details, but those would fall into place as they always
did.

What he began to see was a way to end all of this running, a way
to escape without having to leave, a way to make sure that people
got what they deserved. A little wobble of excitement crept across
his back as Joseph let the ideas come, let the plan take shape. He
fingered the sheet taped over the word processor that sat on the
table in front of him.

179

The late-afternoon sunlight warmed the avocado leaves outside his window, throwing a soft golden shade into the room. His fingertips burned with the terrible dryness that came when he began to feel this way. Joseph looked at the tree leaves outside, then pressed his fingers gently against the table. There was only so much of the world that he could take at a time, then he reached his fill and, like water brimming over the top of a cup, he simply had to go somewhere else.

Open your arms again, Sweet Ann, he thought. And let me in.

APRIL 2

What happened that night after our first ride in the limousine is important. I got home at quarter 'til one, half an hour before Ray did. I took off my wet clothes and put them on hangers far back in my closet; I washed and brushed my hair; I put on fresh makeup and lipstick. Then I got out some of our adult toys – we called them 'learning aids' back when we used to use them – a red lace teddy that snaps under the crotch, a garter belt and some fishnet stockings, a very slinky black silk robe, some ridiculously high heels. My skin felt so warm and sensitive as I put it all on, opened a bottle of wine and poured two glasses.

I felt like a prehistoric flower inside, one of those kind that can gobble up a man if he steps in.

When Ray came home, I took him in my arms and we kissed, but it was mechanical and disembodied, and I could feel that Raymond was somewhere else. So he moved down and tried to please me another way.

But that night, well, it wasn't going to happen.

So we ended up so strangely, with Raymond sitting on the bed where I had been, and me standing in front of him, quivering on those dumb high heels for balance. I poured another glass of wine, closed my eyes, drank the wine, said to myself, If you can't make him happy, at least let him make you happy.

And I'll admit now what I refused to admit then, what I drank the rest of the wine to deny – that I was

180

hungry not for Raymond that night but for David. Although I could certainly not have said that I loved Dave Cantrell then, what I craved that night was not to be pleasured but to be loved, not to be worshiped but simply to be needed, not to take satisfaction but to give it. Sometimes I think of life as an elegant party going on constantly inside our heads. Mine is a masquerade. It was David's role to wear the mask of love. Could I have known he would be so eager? I admit that from the first time I saw him again on *Lady of the Bay*, I believed he would be.

Ray had not played that part in a long time. Five months, two weeks, and eleven days, since the last time we made love, or held each other with true affection. I know because it was my birthday last year.

But the masquerade kept going on, despite my confusion. As the days went by, I was afraid, then elated. I was content, then desperately thirsty. Sometimes I even felt that I was being watched! I turned and saw no one; I scanned my mirror when I drove; I peeked from my windows when I was home alone. My conscience, Dear One, hounding me already. Once I thought I saw a young man — standing at a distance from the playground with a camera around his neck, staring directly at me. But when I looked again, he was gone. So, I thought, my conscience is a cute guy, dogging the heels of my betrayal, logging every step of my treachery. I was disgusted with myself. I was angry. My confusion was very real.

Joseph placed the Poon's Locker postcard on the open page, then shut the journal over it. Things were beginning to make sense now, like an image coming through fog, as if Ann's confusion were becoming his clarity.

It was too hard to get close to C. David Cantrell. Joseph was not allowed past the PacifiCo Tower security booth; he was hustled off the steps by security men three days running; he could neither walk nor drive past the guard house of Cantrell's private Newport Beach neighborhood. He hit upon a simple alternative.

Joseph had just turned to lie down on his bed again when someone knocked on his door.

It was loud, so loud it sent a riot of alarm into his ears, a terrible clanging noise. As it settled into a quieter roar, he turned, to see Lucinda, halfway into his room and halfway out, studying him with her dark brown eyes. She brushed away a long golden band of hair and offered a very small smile. 'What are you doing?' she asked.

'I –' Joseph's tongue wallowed against his dry mouth, trying to get positioned. The roar was better now, but he couldn't seem to get his thoughts down into his lips. His cracking fingertips felt as if they'd been held against dry ice. 'I . . . was reading.'

'What a drag.'

Joseph thought with new terror of the leather-bound journal sitting on the table in front of him. He gathered it up without looking at it and slid it into his box beside the desk.

'Aren't you gonna unpack?' she asked.

'Yes. In a while.'

'What were you reading?'

'Just a story.'

'Horror is my favorite,' she said. 'If I really have to read.'

Joseph nodded. The ringing in his head lowered in volume again.

'My grandmother will talk your ear off. That's why I'm gone a lot.'

'She seems like a nice old lady.'

'Old people are so, like serious. How old are you?'

'Twenty-four.'

'I'm eighteen. My name's not rilly outta here. It's Lucinda. Not Lucy. Lucinda.'

Joseph cleared his throat with some difficulty. 'I've always . . . liked that name.'

She continued to regard him from behind a corner of bright straight hair. 'So, can I come in, or what?'

'Sure,' he said calmly.

Lucinda slid in with an air of secrecy, and shut the door. She looked at him with a cumbersome, self-conscious expression – kind of a smile – then glanced around for somewhere to sit. She picked the bed. A deep updraft of warmth spread into his genitals.

'What beach do you go to?' she asked.

'Any beach.'

'I go to Fifteenth.' Lucinda apparently intended for this information to do something once it sunk in. 'Older guys,' she prompted. 'Even the cops there are cool. Cute, too.'

Joseph wasn't sure why it mattered what beach you went to. It was all the same beach really, street numbers or not. Did Lucy . . . *Lucinda* like cops? 'Cool,' he said.

'You're not very tan. Where are you from?'

'Irvine.'

'Inland. Bummer. What do you listen to, like, for music?'

'I don't listen to music.'

'That's fully unbelievable.'

'It's too . . . fast.'

'There's slow ones, too. Slow stuff is old people's music. I like it when in makes me all amped and crazy. You know, gets you through the day.' Lucinda sighed. She looked around, suddenly bored. Her eyes were quick, and they seemed to be looking for something specific. 'Do you have a car?'

She's looking for car keys, he thought, of course. He hesitated. 'Yes.'

'What kind?'

'Porsche.'

Lucinda came back to life. 'Get out of here!'

'But it's in the shop.'

'Yeah, right.'

'It's blue,' he said.

She looked at him, askance but hopeful. 'Maybe we can drive around in it when it's fixed.'

Joseph was suddenly clear of head now – no ringing, no interference. His plan was crystalizing. 'Sure. But there's some trouble with the mechanics. I've got to get my lawyer involved.'

'You got a lawyer?'

'On retainer.'

'The only retainer I had was when I was thirteen, but it hurt my gums.' She laughed at her own joke. Her smile was dazzling. 'So, you really got your own lawyer?'

Joseph, for the first time in his life, was discovering what it was to impress. It seemed to come to him like a revelation from heaven. He'd always gotten by before by being the boy, the wonder-struck youth, the innocent. How well that had worked in

183

Hardin County. *It's out by the swamp, Lucy. I swear. I couldn't believe it, either. . .*

He wondered whether this was his first taste of adulthood. 'And I need to write him a letter on good paper, with a good word processor. It's got to look important, because he is.'

'Well, like write it then, and we'll go for a ride. I got lots of friends you'd like.'

'My computer's in the shop also.'

Lucinda laughed, more of a snicker maybe. 'Everything you have is broke. I suppose your lawyer's in the hospital, too?'

'Can I use this one?' Joseph looked at the shrouded boxes on the desk before him.

'Fine with me,' she said. 'Grandma bought that for me for college. A little like, early. I'm not ready for college.'

'I'm not familiar with this model.'

'Even a nerd can run one. It's totally easy.'

'Will you show me how?'

'So you can write your lawyer about the Porsche?'

'Yes.'

She looked at him, torn between trust and her somewhat dim view of the stuff guys try to pull on you sometimes. Then she stood and offered him a coquettish smile, peeping out from behind that wall of hair again. 'First, Joe, you got to take the covers off.'

19

Just after midnight, Jim was poring over the department file on Phil Kearns when the phone rang.

'Jim Weir?'

'Yes.'

'This is NBPD Dispatch. Brian Dennison wants to see you immediately. He's at Three-forty Leeward. It is urgent.'

'I'm on my way.'

Jim pulled on his boots, grabbed a windbreaker to cut the night chill, and got down the stairs as quietly as he could.

He choked the old Ford and let her idle high for a minute. Leeward, he thought, the industrial zone of Newport, home of Cheverton Sewer & Septic. Goins? Why would Dennison call if they'd gotten Goins? Maybe Dale Blodgett and *Duty Free* were off on another mystery cruise.

The peninsula traffic was light at this hour. The houses squatted together closely in the fog and each streetlamp wore a damp halo. Up the boulevard, over the bridge, past the hospital, then across Superior and into the poorly lit blocks of body shops and boat yards. Leeward was one block south of Cheverton. Jim turned left, steered around a gaping pothole, and followed a chain-link fence topped with concertina wire to a gate held open by an old truck tire. The numbers 340 were painted in Day-Glo silver along the top curve of the rubber. He cranked the wheel and bounced in.

While dust settled down in the beam of his headlights, Jim considered the stucco building, one of dozens of 1950s houses now converted for commercial use. The porch light was on, aswirl with moths. The sign below it read DAVIS MARINE INDUSTRIES. The front room was dark, but a steady light issued from the back and the pale yellow of a window stood out on the south wall. A late-model Jaguar sat in front – Dennison's unreliable import, thought Weir – and beside it a white van.

He stepped out, pocketed the keys and crunched across the gravel, and went up a couple of steps and rang the buzzer by the front door.

A man's voice issued from inside. 'Weir?'

'Yeah.'

'Door's open. Come on back.'

The living room/lobby was cool and dark. Jim walked toward the hallway and the light. He could make out the shapes of an old table and some folding chairs, a sofa, a couple of file cabinets in one corner. At the end of the hallway, a door was cracked open and the light from within sprayed out calmly against the opposite wall.

Jim pushed through the door, stepped inside, and was just about to bring up his arms in defense when the baseball bat, swung by the figure on his right, slammed into his stomach and sent him down on one knee.

Shapes around him: ski masks, gloves, dark clothing. A surge of adrenaline brought him up and he caught the man with the bat square on the jaw with a hooking left. Movement to his right, squaring to meet the onrush, driving his right fist straight into a masked nose that cracked and flattened and sent the man down. It hit him sooner than he thought it would, a heavy blow to his lower ribs, a blow that sent the breath gasping out of him and a bright red luminescence burning in his eyes. Then another to his stomach, followed by a weighted shove – two men at least, he thought – from behind, hurling him forward in a tripping run that ended abruptly when he hit the wall. He spun away and caught a chin with his elbow, but the movement left him open and he saw it coming before he could do anything about it, the short side-chopping swing of the bat again as it *thwumped* into his stomach. He hit the floor hard, landing on his hands and knees. For an oddly peaceful moment, Weir believed that he could simply stay here like this – immovable, safe. The kick he knew was coming lifted one side of him up and crumpled an elbow. He rolled onto his back, looking up through his own hands held before his face.

Six, he thought, wanted to count, but couldn't concentrate. No words. No Dennison. No one built like Dennison. Heavy breathings, a sense of purpose. A burning down in the ribs, the rise of nausea, dizziness. Looking straight up now, he saw the hangman's noose fixed to a beam exposed by a hole in the ceiling.

'Having fun, Weir?'

He grunted as they descended on him and he tried to struggle up, but his legs were too slow to move him, and one well-placed foot on his chest pressed him back to the floor. Then the strangest sensation, of being swept up feetfirst, his head dangling and his legs above him. Grunting, a curse, then a sudden jolt and Weir was swaying back and forth, gently as a limb in a breeze. When he looked up he saw his boots, cinched into the noose. When he looked to his side, he saw a belt buckle, a stomach, a pair of gloved hands on hips, the walls rotating dizzyingly – not just left to right but up and down, too. When he strained his neck up, he could see the masks, which was to see nothing at all. A gag was jammed into his mouth. He felt the knot being tied behind his skull.

One of them nodded. Two others stepped forward and Jim saw the lopping shears; the ones with the long, long handles and the short curved blades that can take off a limb the size of a man's wrist without great effort.

In that moment, Jim Weir knew the greatest fear of his life. It settled over him like a box with thick walls, a cold, contained finality with which there was no argument, no negotiation.

Two more men moved in close, stripped off Weir's belt, and yanked his trousers up. He could see their elbows, their chests, their chins covered by the masks, their gloved fists that held his pants up by his ankles now while the lopping shears moved into his field of vision, opened and shut like the mandibles of a great ant, and moved between his legs.

Jim summoned everything he had. It was a blind surge, a screaming release of fear that brought his torso up level with the floor and guided his hands for the neck of the man with the cutters. But his body swung away with the lunge and his fingers missed the neck by inches, and his stomach, bruised and aching, surrendered. His head dropped back down and he tried again, but his strength only brought him up halfway, and for a moment he swung there, arms reaching out like some infant groping for its mother while he swayed in a lazy circle and the men around him laughed.

Laughed. It was a sound, Weir knew in an instant, that he would carry with him to his grave.

'Say goodbye to someone you love, Jim.'

He felt each of his arms taken and held fast. Looking up the length of his body, Jim could see his stomach, his groin, his thighs and knees, his trousers bunched and held tight around his boots, his boots locked in the noose. The curved blades settled in his pubic hair, cold and hard. Weir tried to jerk himself up, but his arms were pinned and it was utterly useless. A strange high-pitched buzzing then came into his head, almost electric. He watched the blades lift, open, and slide into his crotch. The buzzing in his ears was louder now – it sounded like a barbershop when he was six.

Then it happened. The cold blades touched him and a sharp pain shot into his groin. Weir screamed against the gag, and his back arched and he felt his eyes getting ready to leave their sockets. Red everywhere. If you can scream loud enough, it will go away. The buzzing so loud, so electric; the metallic shearing sound as the blades opened and closed. Something falling down now and hitting his face, something warm and light – *oh my dear sweet God, you let them do it.*

You let them do it.

Dear sweet God.

'Don't fuck with us. You know who we are.'

'Ever.'

'Anymore.'

'Got it?'

'Enjoy your new look, Weir.'

He could hear them leaving, but he couldn't open his eyes. And he couldn't, for the life of him, figure out why the pain was not excruciating – just a cool stinging patch that felt open and foreign. His head throbbed with each wild heartbeat.

Then he felt someone grab him by the shirt and lift him up, followed by a sawing sounding above. Suddenly, his feet broke free and he dropped to the floor in a backbreaking flop cushioned only by his hands.

He lay there on the cool linoleum for a long moment, listening to the footsteps departing, then the cars starting up outside, then only to the racing gallop of his heart against the floor.

Then he was strangely, insanely, profoundly happy. He could feel it there beneath him, and he knew they hadn't taken it. He rolled over and parted his trousers, hoisting himself up on one elbow. There it was, in all its terrified, recessed glory, lying on a plain of white flesh. He lay back, turned his head to the side, and saw the clump of hair a few feet away. The barbershop sound, he thought: electric clippers – the lopping shears were strictly for show. He managed to get his zipper up. Then he rolled over to the wall and scrunched himself up against it and peered out the window to the dark sky outside. His heart wouldn't stop racing. It sent the blood rushing into his face, into his ears and eyes, into his hands and fingers, into his legs and his feet, and he lay there a long while thanking God for the blood that still pumped inside him, every precious, eager, frantic drop.

The moon came into the window. When his heart finally began to slow, the pain came to take its place. It was mostly surface now: his back and stomach and ribs, but he knew it would sink down deeper over the hours, settling into the bone and tendons.

He stood slowly, bracing against the wall. By the time he got to the living room, he had found a tremulous balance that threatened to give out at any second. He fell once going down the steps, and once more standing beside his truck, trying to get a trembling hand into his pocket for the keys.

20

On the day of Ann's funeral, the ocean died. The first victims were the small fish that washed up before sunrise – anchovies, smelt, grunion, young bass. By nine, there were halibut, mullet, mackerel, bonita, stingrays, skates, mud sharks, sand sharks, blue sharks, and thresher, carried by the tide to shore, where, bloated, eyes protruding, bladders ejected from their mouths, they lay either dead or in final twitching demise. Half a dozen sea lions were beached, too, but still alive at first. They lolled in the shallows near Poon's Locker, entangling themselves in mooring lines and issuing their last agonized groans before turning belly-up and silent in the dismal, fog-clenched afternoon. Last to go were the seabirds – the ducks, the gulls and pelicans, a few heron deep in the Back Bay – which floated, limp-necked and feet folded, onto the beaches around noon. By 2:00 P.M., the smell was getting strong.

The old-timers of the peninsula mumbled about a red tide – a deadly buildup of plankton that robs the fish of oxygen – but none of them had ever seen a sea gull die of too much air. Besides, the water wasn't the telltale orange-brown of a plankton surge, but its usual gray and unassuming self. Charter trips were canceled and the harbor tours were postponed, but the Newport-to-Catalina ship weighed anchor at the usual 8 A.M., dividing with its prow the thousands of bobbing bodies that littered the bay. The ferryboat continued its runs, pushing through the carnage with the glum efficiency of a snow plow in winter. By noon, the EPA, the California Department of Fish and Game, the Coastal Commission, the Coast Guard, the County Sheriff's, the city Marine Department, the mayor, an aid to the governor, and the press had all arrived to evaluate the problem.

Jim saw it from the window of his old upstairs room in the big house. He had spent an aching night tossing on his bed, sweating, plagued by visions of lopping shears and, later in a state of light

190

sleep, again by the dream of someone holding a single purple rose up to Ann's trusting, lovely face. Before first light, he got up and read the files on Kearns and Blodgett, searching for something that had gotten through, something he hadn't seen, something he hadn't understood. The words danced on the paper in front of him, cloying and ineffable. When he finally looked up from the files, he saw the hundreds of pale, shining shapes lining the curve of shore to the south. In the first light of day, they looked like coins spilled from a treasure chest. To the north, he could see a crowd that had gathered on the sidewalk, just past Ann's Kids. Becky Flynn stood off to the side, talking on a portable telephone. Some of the people were still in their robes. Downstairs, the phone started ringing.

And through it all, the hunt for Horton Goins continued. When he went down to the Locker for coffee, Jim saw a team of uniforms working the motels around the El Mar. When he sat in the window of the café and drank it, Tillis and Oswitz walked by with copies of Goins's photograph in their hands. The morning paper said that south-county sporting-goods stores were reporting brisk gun sales; Goins's picture ran again; a front-page article recounted the death of a fifteen-year-old Newport boy who was shot by his own father while trying to sneak back into his house – through his sister's room – after a night away. Later when he drove Virginia and Raymond and Becky off the island toward the cemetery, they had to stop at the roadblock – with about a thousand other cars, it seemed – set up to find Goins. Officer Hoch, with a swollen purple nose and two black eyes, waved them through. Ray commented on it, but Weir said nothing. He was feeding his anger on silence. The Newport cops had taken him down a notch. So what? He'd quit their world and gotten a less-than-welcome back. The shoulder holster and Poon's old .45 felt strange against his ribs, troublesome allies.

The helicopter hovered noisily, in and out of sight through the windshield, always audible, always there. An OCTD bus groaned ahead of them and cut straight into the cortege, Dennison's face smiling back at them through clouds of black exhaust. Two young motor officers provided escort alongside his truck. They never once looked over.

From the chapel in the hills, Weir could see the city below them, the Pacific beyond that, a faint horizon dotted with sails. The aroma of flowers was so heavy that he had trouble drawing breath. Everything seemed to be happening slowly and every movement

191

brought him a rush of pain. The Cruz clan sat across from them, shapes in black, many already sobbing. Ernesto and Irena sat in the first pew on the left, motionless and reduced. Raymond remained erect in a black suit, his face locked safely around something terrible. When Irena turned to look at him, Jim was met by a sadness too complete to behold. He looked away, sat down beside Virginia, and took her big knotted hand in his.

The obituary was offered by the Rev. Matthew Martell, then eulogies by friends. Jim sat, sunk by the ballast of mourning, and considered the black-clad figure of Becky as she stood at the podium, looked out from behind a veil, and cleared her throat.

'One of the blessings of my life,' she said, 'was to know Ann Cruz.' A blessing she counted as a great one. Her voice to Jim sounded brittle as glass, ready to crack. But he knew she wouldn't: Becky was always toughest in a clinch. Behind the black netted veil, her eyes were a dark, wet brown, and her lips below were red as apples. To Jim's mind, assaulted by the cruelty of reminiscence, staggered by the heavy smell of the flowers, surrounded by the people with whom he had grown up in this crowded small-town neighborhood, she seemed to be talking only to him. He lost himself in her.

'We were girls, then women together. When I was confused, Ann was clear. When I had doubt, Ann had certainty. When I was undecided and afraid, Ann had judgement and courage. And when there was something I had to do, and right and wrong weren't clear, I could always ask myself what Ann would do, and know that that would be right. She loved me with generosity and good humor; she felt my sadness and shared my joy. There was something at the center of her that I came to realize was in her blood, the blood of Virginia and Poon, the blood that runs . . . that ran through all their children. If I had to say what it was, I'd say it was dignity, the refusal to be diminished by the things in life that try to diminish us all.' Becky looked out to the mourners, her eyes pausing on Jim. 'That, and a willingness to put herself on the line, to commit herself to what she believed and act accordingly. In the time I knew her, Ann was never cruel for the sake of cruelty. She never laughed at someone who didn't have what she had. She never assumed that she deserved what she had — there was no arrogance in her, no pride. The one person she could always laugh at was herself, and she did that often. You . . .' Becky wiped a tear away with a slender finger slid up under the veil. She took a deep breath. 'You all know what an

192

honor it was just to hear her laugh, to see the sparkle of her eyes and the sparkle of her soul coming through. I think that . . . I think that where Ann goes will be a better place for her presence, and that what she leaves us is a place much lessened by her loss. To say that there are no words for all of this would be a lie. There are words, too many of them, too many thousands of words used over and over to express what we feel. They are not designed to carry such weight. That burden is left to us. I will just say one more thing, that I hope God in heaven will treat her with the gentleness and respect that is due to Ann, that He didn't . . . offer her on this earth. That is my hope and my comfort. In honor of Ann, I will love and smile and laugh, and consider her, forever and in perpetuity, among us.'

Jim sat, asking himself the usual huge questions: Was there something he could have done or should have noticed; why was there such misery for the people whom God is supposed to care about as much as He does the birds of the air and the beasts of the field; is Ann really going to a better place or is that a fiction told by the living for themselves?

Irena and Nesto Cruz were sobbing openly as Becky stepped down. She fixed her eyes on Jim's, as if they were the sole known coordinates in a storm, following them to her seat.

Raymond's head was bowed; he was so still that he seemed to be a statue of himself. Weir felt the tremoring of grief inside, the tectonic shelves of one emotion shifting against another. Becky wrapped an arm through his. He put his head in his hands and his elbows on his knees and felt the tears welling into his eyes from a part of him that seemed filled with them.

Then everyone filed out and watched as Ann was put into the ground. The fresh dirt was covered by a black tarp. The grave was neat, precise, deep. Through the flowers and perfume and sweat, Jim could smell the city below, the smell of death and sea and muted sun.

Somehow he got them back to the big house for the gathering. Three different radio stations reported that toxic levels of the solvent, 1,1,1-trichloroethane had been found in Newport Harbor. Beaches were closed until further notice.

Weir, Virginia, and Ray greeted the mourners at the door. Jim clasped hands, returned embraces and kisses, mumbled his appreciation of whatever was said. Each condolence seemed to take something out of him, open up a new grief. The odd, slow motion of the funeral service was still upon him, as if the afternoon was taking its rhythm from a time signature he'd never heard. Everyone looked bigger when he met them at the door – the solemn faces, the moist eyes, the unsure chins. Raymond stood straight beside him, his voice calm but somehow disembodied. His smile was withered; his usual animation and quickness were gone. Of all the people in the room, thought Weir, Ray's the only one who hates this more than I do. When most of the people had arrived, he joined them, went to the bar, poured himself a double shot of scotch, downed it, and took a beer from the cooler.

As he looked around the room, the world seemed to divide into two camps – them and us. Us was himself, Virginia, Raymond and his family, Becky, Them was everybody else. There they were, standing in his home, Ann's home. There they were, drinking Virginia's booze, eating her food. There they were, dressed up, talking of who knew what, advancing their own private ambitions, seductions, concealments, and betrayals under the same roof that had protected the child Ann. There they were, all doing what Ann would never do again, all honoring her in death in a way that they would never honor her in life. You hypocrites, he thought, you latecomers, you fakes. You dispensable, minor, alien fucks. It was a sacrilege. He caught the eye of every cop he could and sent his clearest message: You changed the game last night; you will pay. He was not exactly sure how. He finished off the beer and poured another scotch. Mayhem was calling.

He watched Dale Blodgett come through the door, find the law-enforcement contingent in a far corner, then head in the other direction. Dennison's droop-eyed Judas, thought Jim, odd man out. Was he one of the six from last night? There was no certain way to tell. Clever to have brought along a Jaguar. He took another drink, watching Virginia trail across the room to meet Blodgett, where they hugged for a long, almost motionless moment. Blodgett's big, thick-featured body somehow complemented the wiry, windburned Virginia.

Becky took his arm. 'Watch the stuff,' she said, tapping his glass. 'You've got that expression – all wound up and nowhere to go. Hang on to it, though. You're going to need it.'

194

From across the room, Virginia gave him an odd look. He was about to head over when he realized it was for Becky, who excused herself and worked through the crowd toward her. Jim watched as Blodgett hugged her, his big hands open against the black back of her dress. Brian Dennison, Jim noted, was watching, too. Then Becky broke away and followed Virginia down the hallway and into Ann's old room, where they shut the door. Politicos, thought Weir: They never stop.

Phil Kearns and Crystal from Oklahoma edged over to Jim. Kearns looked like a model – hair gelled back, face tan, a black linen suit with black shirt buttoned to the top, no tie. Crystal was small, pretty, pink from her morning sun on Kearns's deck. She gave Jim a small, somehow inviting smile.

Kearns talked on about Ann, and Weir sensed a genuine sadness in him. But Kearns wouldn't use her name, as if he felt obliged to hold something he didn't want to touch. When Crystal went for drinks, Weir stepped in front of Kearns, sealing him off from the rest of the room.

'You didn't answer four calls from Dispatch that night, Phil. Between twelve-thirty and twelve-fifty. Explain.'

Kearns blushed, even though his eyes narrowed – A contradictory response, thought Weir.

'Not true. Dispatch calls my squad, I answer. If I was quiet for twenty minutes, that means she was quiet for twenty minutes. Jesus, Weir, this is a funeral.'

'The trouble is, I got a copy of the Dispatch tape. Carol tried to rouse you four times. What she got back from you was nothing. It's all right there, on record.' He was bluffing. 'I'll play if for you anytime you want to hear.'

'Chief might like to hear his Dispatch tape is floating around Newport,' he said. 'Unless he already knows.'

'Fuck the chief,' said Jim.

Kearns eyed him with a look of amusement.

'I want some answers, Kearns. If I don't get them from you, Dennison will. If he listens to the tape, he's going to haul your ass onto the carpet.'

Kearns's face lost its self-satisfied glow for a moment. Without it, he had a hollow, hard expression. The expression, thought Weir,

195

of someone capable of going through with things. 'I'll talk about that on two conditions. One, if you believe me, you won't go to Dennison with it. Two, if you believe me, you'll stay the hell out of my life.'

'Agreed.'

'You look like a guy who'd agree to just about anything to get what he wants.'

'That's what I am. Talk, Kearns.'

The expression of amusement on Phil Kearns's face turned to contempt. 'I gave a citizen a ride home.'

Weir imagined said citizen, said ride. Would it jibe with Blodgett's story of an out-of-beat squad car coming off the peninsula that night? 'Did you use the bridge at midnight, come onto the mainland?'

'No. It was eleven-thirty and I didn't stop off at the Back Bay. But don't believe me, Weir. You want to talk to my alibi, she'll tell you herself what happened. I'll pick you up outside the Whale's Tale tonight at ten. I want you to listen to her and listen good. Then I want you out of my face.'

'When did you make your play for Ann?'

A cool, predatory look came to Kearns's face. 'Never.'

Jim drank again, studying Kearns. 'Why not? I think if I were you, I might have. I think you liked her a lot. I think it drove you crazy that she looked like an animal in a cage – your words – and you could let her out so easily. 'Cause you know what you saw when you looked at her? You saw a woman you could stand five of *her* next to' – Jim nodded toward Crystal – 'and Ann would still add up to more. You saw a woman, not a girl. You saw someone in the same boat as yourself.'

The sergeant studied Jim's face, then looked away toward Crystal. 'You're right. That's what I saw. But I didn't act on it, not once, not consciously.'

'Why not?'

'Ray.'

Kearns locked eyes with Jim. In the calm strength of Kearns's expression, Weir believed he saw a man telling the truth.

'Tell me what you thought of her, Kearns. Just for me. I want to know what you thought of Ann.'

Kearns looked away. 'I thought Ann Cruz was the most desirable woman I'd ever met.'

'But you never told her that.'

'Never.'

'What about Ray?'

Kearns sighed quietly. 'No. God, Weir, what's it fucking matter?' He watched Crystal coming back toward them, this pale lovely girl from Oklahoma willing to make him happy, two glasses of champagne in her red-nailed hands. He stared at her, a long moment of assessment, then at Weir. 'I don't know about you, but I'm here to mourn your sister.'

Kearns took the glass from Crystal and aimed her toward the cop corner. Weir caught Dennison watching. Doesn't miss a trick, he thought.

He drank again, then worked his way over to Dale Blodgett, standing alone by the bar. Blodgett shook his hand and apologized for missing the service. His scarred, sun-lined face was all the more pronounced above the collar of his ill-fitting suit jacket. His heavy left eye bore into Weir. 'I was with the EPA and Fish and Game people, trying to figure out how five hundred gallons of TCE got into the bay.'

'How do they know it's five hundred gallons?'

'Just an early guess, from the damage. The ocean side isn't touched yet – just the harbor. They said five hundred gallons would do it. Strong stuff. They'll find out who dumped that shit. There's only a few companies licensed to use it around here.'

'What's it for?'

'Solvent. Breaks down just about anything. Grease, paint, rust.'

'Maybe it'll give Becky an edge in the election. Get some more people out for the Slow Growth thing.'

'We'll take it,' said Blodgett. He poured himself a vodka on the rocks, then lit a cigarette.

Jim heard the phone ring, then saw Virginia and Becky both moving down the hallway again.

Blodgett shook his head. 'Lots of covert ops for a funeral,' he said.

'That's Mom.'

'Fine woman. Tell me, Weir, how goes your investigation of the Newport cops?'

'It goes fine. You find out a lot of interesting things.'

'Like what?'

Jim didn't answer. He watched as Becky came back up the hallway, without Virginia.

Blodgett grinned. 'Tell me, Weir. Which one of us did it?'

Jim followed Blodgett's glance toward the cop corner. Half of the men over there were looking at him now – Innelman and Deak, Tillis and Bristol, a few patrolmen that Jim had never met. Dennison stood in the middle of them, his attention fixed on Jim.

'I'm not sure yet. But I'm curious about a couple of things.'

'I don't talk about those guys. I told you that in my driveway that night, and I'm telling you that now.' Jim noticed a couple more heads turning his way.

Weir saw how hard it was for Blodgett to be part of Dennison's force and still stay loyal to his own politics. This little show is at my expense, he thought, to prove to the men that Dale's really just one of them.

He spoke loud enough to reach the cop corner. 'The only cop I'm curious about anymore is you, Blodgett. You and your big ugly face and your fishing boat without any rods in it. You and your buddy from Cheverton Sewer.'

Blodgett's face went red; the heavy left eyelid faltered down a notch. He turned his back to the cop corner, screening them off. His crooked teeth revealed themselves. 'You followed me? I take offense at that. Definite goddamned offense.'

'Let's weep, fat man.'

Blodgett lit a cigarette, blew the smoke into Jim's face. 'I make an albacore run on my night off, and you follow me. I'm starting not to like you very much, Weir.'

'Funny albacore run, Blodgett. Can't catch much in forty minutes with no rods, no tackle, no bait. The pole racks on *Duty Free* were empty. You didn't catch any fish. You weren't even trying to. What was under the tarp? Official police secret?'

Blodgett smiled, a wholly vicious exercise. He clasped Jim's shoulder with a heavy, powerful hand.

'Step outside, Weir?'

'Love to. And take that thing off my shoulder.'

They stood on the sidewalk outside the big house, up next to the seawall, staring out at the dead fish bobbing on the shoreline. The bodies stretched up the bay as far as he could see. The smell had risen in pitch.

Blodgett drew on his cigarette. 'You ask too many questions that aren't your business. You insult me. But I'll tell you what we were doing, because you're Virginia's son, and because you're the kind of guy who needs things spelled out real clear. That's okay – your mother's the same way. Weir, trichloroethane isn't new here. The levels have been rising since last spring, when Fish and Game came out to test salinity and find out why the fish were croaking off. Not enough for anyone to notice – strictly trace. Virginia got the EPA on it, and they came back out every two weeks, figured the dumps were being made once a month or so. City council got the news in session; they budgeted Dennison an extra five hundred a month out of the general fund to have someone out there once in a while. That five hundred barely covers the gas for my boat, not to mention the wear and tear, or the head gasket I blew that night, or my precious goddamned time. I do it because it needs being done. I'm the entire goddamned Toxic Waste patrol, Weir – me and whoever I can get to lend a hand. We were on the bay, watching for whoever dumps that shit in my backyard. We missed them. One boat isn't enough. Dennison can't get any more money from the city, and he won't budget us for another boat because a few dead fish don't mean squat to him when he can get a new chopper or a few new uniforms on the street. That's one of the reasons Becky Flynn should be the mayor of this town. And that's the whole reason I took off fishing that night with no gear. My gear's at home. When I fish, I *fish*, man, I go for days – down to Mexico. I wouldn't eat anything out of the local ocean if you paid me, anyway. Nobody's going to for a long time, now.'

'What was under the tarps?'

'Oh, for chrissakes, Weir – my fighting chairs. What else do you find on the stern deck of a fishing boat?'

'Who's your buddy from Cheverton Sewer?'

Blodgett jammed his finger into Weir's chest. Jim leaned a little into it, gave no ground. 'None of your business. It varies, though. Some nights, my buddy is Virginia Weir.'

Jim said nothing. He's been expecting this. What he really wondered about was something else. 'And some nights, it was Ann.'

Blodgett showed his equine teeth again. 'Some nights, it was Ann and Virginia. Never Ann alone. Not once.'

'Was she with you when Virginia took the samples?'

'That's part of what we do, and we do it every week. Annie was there for that a couple of times.'

'So Annie knew there were trace levels, someone dumping – out in the open ocean probably?'

'Ann knew that.'

Weir tried to figure Ann's place in all of this. Had she found something more than what Blodgett and Virginia were looking for? 'What else did she know? Why hide the tubes in her refrigerator?'

'She hid the tubes because Virginia told her to. What else did she know? I've got no idea.'

'When was the last time Ann went out with you?'

'Month ago or so.'

'Was it the night you took the samples?'

Blodgett looked hard at Jim. A tight smile came and went. 'No. We got distracted. We saw the boat.'

'The dumpers?'

Blodgett nodded.

'What did it look like?'

'Not much in the fog. We couldn't catch it.'

'Where?'

'Two miles straight west of the harbor mouth.'

Jim watched a halibut, eyes paired by eons of evolution, flipping disconsolately on the sand. 'Did Ann see it, too?'

'We all did. Ann, Virginia, and me.'

It suddenly made sense, why Virginia hadn't been forthcoming with what she'd seen. 'You reported it all to Brian, but he wouldn't go public with it because it makes him look asleep on watch.'

Blodgett nodded and grunted. 'My watch, too, Weir.'

'He was hoping the problem would go away. Virginia was hoping it would get worse. Trace levels in the bay don't get headlines. This does.'

Blodgett pointed his cigarette out to the dying harbor. 'Now it's a matter of who plays it best. My money is on Becky.' Blodgett eyed him silently for a long moment. 'You've got an untrusting mind. I like that. But it's not focused. You should get clear on some things.'

200

'Like what?'

'Like who your friends are, for one.'

'That's supposed to make you a buddy of mine?'

'It's supposed to let you back off and get to the heart of the matter.'

'Which is what?'

'Your sister was cheating on Ray. That's where she was the night she got cooled. Find him, you find the perp. It doesn't have anything to do with this ocean here.'

'How do you know she was cheating?' Jim said it and listened for the how.

'How much evidence do you need? Dressed up like that, driving around late at night? Some guy with flowers and a diamond fucking tie tack? No struggle getting her down there. No struggle later. Come on, Ann didn't go down there with some freak like Horton Goins. She didn't go down there with some cop working with Raymond, I don't care what Mackie Ruff thinks he saw. Don't you know your sister any better than that? I barely knew her but I could tell she was decent enough. Ann had a foot in another world. That's the world that got her dead. It doesn't have a thing to do with that Goins kid. The DA's along for the ride with Dennison, for now, but things will look different after June fifth. Don't forget, Frank D'Alba's been district attorney here for eight years, and he's up for reelection, too. It's all just a fuckin' headline grab for him and Dennison. They're all after a piece of your sister.'

'What about the pictures Goins took? What about the girl in Ohio?'

Blodgett sighed and looked out across the dying bay. 'I'm just saying what I think is right. I don't think it was Goins.'

'I don't, either, but he was following her. That's more than just a coincidence.'

'Maybe you're not as dumb as I thought.'

Blodgett leaned forward on the seawall, still looking across to the mainland. 'What a fucking shame,' he said. Then he turned to Weir. 'Jim, if I catch you doggin' me, hanging around, I'll bust you up real good. I don't care whose kid you are. Nobody follows Dale Blodgett, nobody sneaks around, nobody calls what I do into question. I got a sense of right and wrong that does all that for you. Back off and stay off. Other than that, I'll help you with Ann, all I

201

can. She seemed like a real good woman. It's a goddamned shame – all of it. Everything.'

They looked for a moment out to the bay. Blodgett popped his cigarette into the water. For a moment, Weir was aware of the man studying him. Finally, Blodgett spoke. 'That boat I saw? The dumpers? I haven't told anyone this, because I figure I'm wrong. I want to be wrong. I figure it's a coincidence, you know – lots of boats in Newport Harbor.'

Jim waited.

'It was a thirty-foot Bayliner, set up just like that one.'

Weir followed the line of Blodgett's pointing finger, up the bayfront to Becky Flynn's dock. Her boat – once *our* boat, Weir thought – rocked against her lines.

'I don't understand anything anymore, Weir,' said Blodgett. 'I'm getting to the point where there's too many things I don't want to know.'

They headed back into the house.

Dennison broke away from Ernesto Cruz and came over to Jim. His suit was a dark blue chalkstripe, expensive, but cut too tight around his barrel chest. His eyebrows were furrowed, his face flushed. From captain to interim chief to mayor, all in one year, thought Jim. But Brian could pull it off. His confidence was astounding, contagious. And somehow – maybe it was his face, or his modest public demeanor, or maybe it was the perpetual air of the underdog that Dennison employed so disarmingly – you forgave him the sin of ambition. You wanted to root for him.

He rested a hand on Jim's shoulder. 'What a day. I'm awful sorry, Jim. It was a lovely service, for what it's worth.'

'What have you gotten from the tie tack?'

'Ann's blood, no prints. We're still working on a trace, but nothing yet.'

Weir was aware of the men looking over at him again, trying to appear as if they weren't.

'Kind of like yours, isn't it?'

'Yeah, yeah, yeah. I figured some genius would make that point. The difference is, mine wasn't found with Ann.'

Dennison reached down and fingered his tie tack. It was a dark blue stone set in gold.

'God knows where Ruff really found it,' said the chief. 'For right now, I'll believe him. He's a great witness, don't you think?'

Jim followed his hooking thumb to where Ruff was attempting to stuff a bottle of rum down his pants. He wouldn't put down his drink to do it, though: It sloshed in one hand as he aimed the bottle through his waistband with the other. He swayed like a man in a hurricane.

Weir caught the laughter from the cop corner as Dennison glanced with satisfaction toward his men.

Becky angled her way over to Jim and Dennison. Weir could feel the interim chief stiffen at her approach. Whatever she and Virginia had been hatching must have worked out, thought Jim; there's a glow on her. The warmth of the room had brought a fine glistening to her upper lip and cheeks, and her wavy brown hair had loosened in the humidity. She offered her hand to Dennison, who took it with a formal smile. 'Tough precinct for you,' she said.

'It sure is.'

'It's the heart of the city.'

'It's a big city, Ms Flynn.'

'Really it's just a small town, Chief. It needs to be treated that way, by people who care about it.'

'We'll see what the people think in June.'

Becky made a show of looking out over the crowd, settling on the cop corner. 'Which one of them did it?'

Dennison actually choked on something, washing it quickly down with a sip from his drink. *'What?'*

'Come on, Chief,' she said, turning an inquisitive smile on him. 'Everybody knows what Ruff saw. Everybody knows you put Jim here on the case – the department's case. Everybody knows your secretary copied the time cards and personnel files so Jim could take a look at your people. Like I said, this is a small town.'

Dennison's unsure eyes found Jim, and Becky heard the unspoken line.

'He didn't tell me a goddamned thing, Brian,' she said. 'He kept his end of the deal. So I'm asking you.'

'What do you want?' he asked.

'I want to know if you're going to continue investigating this case or not.'

203

'Of course we are.'

'After you get Goins?'

'It's up to the DA after that. If he indicts, our work is done. You can't prosecute two people if only one of them is guilty.'

'Exactly,' said Becky.

'We've already got a solid case against him, and we haven't even talked to him yet,' said Dennison. 'D'Alba's given the green light to George Percy. Percy's satisfied they can indict on what we've got now.'

Weir remembered George Percy, an Orange County assistant district attorney, from his days with Sheriff's. He was a lithe, good-humored man with thick black hair that cascaded down onto his brow like a cheap hairpiece, which it wasn't. In court, he was courteous, disingenuous, and cunning when he needed to be. There was something about him of the front porch, the family picnic, the station wagon. Juries liked him because he reminded them that the state was made up of people just like them: a little bewildered, a little overworked, and, of course, outraged at what had happened.

Becky laughed, curling her mouth up in a mocking smile. It was the look that, when turned on Jim, had always brought his blood to a boil. The sheer depth of its disdain made the ground shift under you. 'Saying he can indict doesn't mean he can, and pulling it off still leaves him with a long, hot jury trial to handle.'

'What's this,' asked Dennison, 'you think Goins is innocent?'

Becky shrugged. 'Let's include that on our debate topics.'

Dennison colored. 'I'm looking into that.'

'Got to get Paris's expert opinion on whether you should talk in public? You're going to have to start guiding your own ship, Chief. Your hesitation on the issues is starting to show.'

No wonder he doesn't want to argue with her in public, thought Jim; she'd cannibalize him.

'Don't confuse hesitation with prudence and good judgment,' said Dennison.

'I don't know how you got them into the same sentence, Chief.'

'There's a lot you don't know.'

'Come on . . . let's debate. Let's fire up this election.'

'Politics isn't a spectator sport for me, Ms Flynn – it's serious business.'

Becky nodded, a little condescendingly, Weir thought. 'I should think that bringing a case against Horton Goins would be pretty frivolous business,' she said. 'No physical evidence putting him at the scene; an eyewitness – undependable as he may be – who saw a cop. No motive except his own illness, which you can't use because Goins already did his time and took his cure. We get a change of venue out of Orange County, half your steam goes out.'

Weir suddenly realized what Becky was saying. He felt himself blink. Becky Flynn had never, not once in her life, lost her ability to astonish him.

It took Dennison another moment to get it. 'You're going to *defend* him?'

'I intend to. If you catch him before you kill him, that is. I've already talked to his parents.'

What does she know, thought Weir. It's an incredible risk, unless she knows something that we don't.

Dennison's battered expression indicated the scope of his discomfort. He looked toward his men again, a reflexive search for Paris, Weir decided. 'Then I guess we don't have a lot to talk about,' he said.

'I'll get it through discovery anyway,' she said.

Dennison nodded, then bowed slightly, a gesture intended to be courtly but that came off instead as backwoods and clunky. 'Good luck with the election, Ms Flynn,' he said. 'And the trial.' Weir could see the fury building in Dennison's eyes.

'Give the people of this town a debate,' she said. 'It's the least you can do with Cantrell's bankroll behind you.'

'My financing is no secret,' he said. 'Everything's above the board.'

'Except who that diamond tie tack belongs to.' Becky fingered the sapphire stone that held Dennison's tie to his shirt. 'Could be anyone.'

Dennison's mouth parted for a beat, before he turned and walked away. Becky looked at Jim impishly, the same expression Ann used to get when as kids they'd put masking tape on the kittens' feet. She took a sip of her drink, then a longer one, then finished it right down to the ice. She leaned up close to Jim. The musky smell of perfume and sweat enclosed him. 'Virginia and I found out who ordered the roses for Ann,' she whispered. The end of her tongue, cooled by ice, slid very lightly along the outline of his ear.

205

Jim pulled back and waited, looking into the deep brown of Becky's eyes. It crossed his mind that Counselor Flynn was a little drunk.

'And?'

'Talk to me, Weir. Please come talk to me.'

He offered his arm, which Becky took, and they headed for the back door.

21

They looped through the alley for a block, then came out on the sidewalk, past the reporters who were still hanging around outside the big house. Laurel Kenney stood on the seawall, looking down at the dead and dying fish that continued to float toward the shore. For once, thought Weir, she looked questionless.

Becky aimed Jim onto the dock just short of her house, let him climb aboard her boat while she took off her heels, then steadied herself on his arm as he eased her aboard the *Sea Urchin*. It was a thirty-foot Bayliner that Weir had always loved – fast, eager, joyful in motion. They had bought it together when Becky got her PD job and Weir made detective, then she had bought him out before he quit the Sheriff's and started outfitting *Lady Luck*, two years later. He noted with pleasure how well Becky had kept her up.

He climbed back out and untied the lines while Becky stripped the canvas cover and turned over the engine. A moment later, they were motoring into the bay, heading south toward the harbor mouth. Becky had put on an old pea coat to cut the breeze. Standing barefoot at the helm with her hair curling back and the black silk of her mourning dress protruding from beneath the tattered coat, she looked, to Jim, wonderful. He stood beside her and felt the reassuring vibration of the motor coming up into his feet.

'Who bought the roses?'

Becky spoke without turning her eyes from the yacht-littered bay in front of her. 'They were bought by phone, on a company credit card on Saturday, the day before Mother's Day. The florist was the Petal Pusher, way up in LA – that's why it took so long to trace. The company was Cheverton Sewer and Septic of Newport Beach. The man who called it in was Dave Smith.'

'Do you know him?'

'No.'

'Talked to him yet?'

'No way. We've got some groundwork to lay.'

'Tell me about that.'

'Wait until we're outside. I want to get past all this.'

A small sand shark floated by upside down, its pale belly glistening. Along the shore, the body count had grown; the smell on the water was stronger than on land, borne by onshore breeze. Sunlight struggled through a thick spring cloud cover, mixed with pollutants, cast a brownish pall over the city. Jim watched in rapt disbelief as a sea gull labored exhaustedly across this dire sky, then suddenly folded up as if shot and plummeted down into the water. A moment later, *Sea Urchin* slid by it – nothing but a lifeless mass of feathers with a wing protruding at an unlikely angle.

Becky turned to Weir, her face a mask of anger. 'If we can't turn this to our advantage, we're the stupidest people I know,' she said. She sighed deeply. 'It breaks my heart.'

'How'd you know I was looking at the cops?'

'Just put the pieces together. Ruff's statement, your early-morning visits from Dennison, all the personnel stuff you had up in your room.'

Virginia had provided the intelligence, thought Jim. Should he have assumed she'd spy on him? 'How come you didn't tip the papers?'

Becky glanced at Jim, the tiredness showing in her face. 'Because you'd have been on the hot seat, Jim. I'm not without loyalty.'

She'd have put me on the hot seat in a second, thought Jim, if she thought I'd have sat still for it. Weir thought back to his days in the miserable Zihuatanejo jail, the long stinking hours he spent, marinating in the juices of his own regret over Becky. The feeling of being trapped in an eight-by-eight-foot cell while Becky lingered in freedom, unattached, lovely and perhaps even lonely, nearly drove him crazy. He imagined every pivot point he could as he lay there and watched the roaches trace frantic patterns on the walls, relived every moment when they had drifted further, entrenched deeper in opposing positions, or simply – as they had so often toward the end – hurt each other so as not to be hurt first. At each of these events, Weir had paused to imagine what he could have done better, but the sheer volume of those missed opportunities quickly overwhelmed and sunk him further into depression, fear, and hopelessness. In the end, sickness just burned it out of him. He lay trembling cold as the fever finally broke, realizing that he and Becky hadn't made it because they were simply unable to make it – they were ill-suited, mismatched, star-crossed – whatever you want to call it. It seemed to Jim, in postfever clarity, that somewhere along the line, the trust had disappeared. Toward the end, it was an ugly little war. But the fever hadn't burned out his desire; it simply had reduced it to elemental constituents. When he had come out of jail, rode the bus north, and finally stood on the ferry and watched the lights of the old neighborhood easing toward him, it was, with regard to Becky, a journey of strange new hope, of wild, impossible expectation. Neither he nor the fever had been able to change the fact that, in the center of his heart, he loved her and he always had.

Sea Urchin motored between the long rock jetties that frame the harbor entrance. The swell and chop met her as she crossed the visible border between bay and open sea, lifting her slightly, welcoming her into the maw of the Pacific.

Becky sat behind the wheel and Jim rested against the shining gunwale. She shook her hair against the wind and gave him a pressed, limited smile. 'Cheverton Sewer is owned by Cantrell Development Group, which is a wholly owned subsidiary of PacifiCo. That's what all the hugger-mugger was at the gathering. We had a couple of paralegals making the connections.'

Weir understood Becky's smile now: She was trying to conceal her joy. If she linked David Cantrell's company to Ann's killer, he could suffer mightily. Becky Flynn and Slow Growth – both heavily opposed by Cantrell – could sail to victory, and Dennison would go down with the losers.

'Before you say anything, Jim, I want you to know we're going to move very carefully on this. We'll employ the press when we need them and not until. The way Virginia and I call it – it's all or nothing.'

'Meaning?'

'We find out who killed Ann, then we use it to our best advantage. We don't try to capitalize yet. If this Dave Smith killed her, we need him in the bag first.'

'So you offer to defend Goins now.'

'I need it. First, it will give the media something new to cover me on. The *Times* poll yesterday had me down thirty-nine percent to Dennison's forty-three. I could use a nudge, two weeks before election. Second, if Goins needs a defense lawyer, he may as well get a good one. Third, if I'm Goins's counsel, I can hire my investigator to gather evidence that will prove his innocence, and that's exactly what I intend to do. It's the only logical way to get to Dave Smith and PacifiCo while I'm a candidate.'

Weir saw it coming.

'Interested?'

'I'm interested in Dave Smith.'

'But not in helping my campaign?'

'As long as they're one and the same.'

She cast him a long look, some slight amusement lingering beneath its surface. 'I just told you they are.'

'Anybody with the number and a verified employee name could have used that card. It could have been stolen, lost, borrowed.'

'Those are all possibilities you'd be looking at. I'm not stupid, or did you forget?'

Weir looked off toward the horizon, one panel of gray set atop another. 'You know about Blodgett's special beat, patrolling the bay for dumpers?'

'Of course I do. Virginia goes out with him sometimes.'

'So did Ann.'

'Funny the things you learn when you stick around home.'

Weir ignored the sucker punch. To Becky, nothing was a sucker punch. He told her about his tail of Blodgett, the forty minutes on the water, the blown head gasket, and the buddy from Cheverton Sewer & Septic.

'*You sure?*' she asked.

'No, I dreamed it.'

Becky considered. 'Dale Blodgett, Cheverton Sewer and Cantrell Development,' she said. 'Interesting, isn't it?'

'It raises the question of Blodgett and Dennison.'

Becky glanced at Weir and nodded. 'Some of the stuff he's pulled . . . hard to imagine him playing both sides.'

'Dennison could sit still for a lot, with an ear inside Virginia and you.'

Becky shook the hair from her face. 'You've got that right.'

'How tight are you with him?'

'I've always kept my distance. Something about him. Virginia likes him a lot, though.'

'Not like her to read someone wrong.'

'No one's perfect, Jim.'

210

'Mom and Ann were with him the night he saw the dumpers. Blodgett told me the boat looked just like this one.'

Becky studied him, open-faced. 'And?'

Jim studied her closely. Becky betrayed no emotion he could recognize.

Then she throttled *Sea Urchin* all the way back and cranked the wheel to starboard. The engine whined, the bow rose, and the little boat threw up a rooster tail of spray that arced and flattened in the wind. She hit the swells hard, riding high and fast. Becky's expression was one of controlled fury.

She had to scream over the engine and the thumping of *Sea Urchin* on the water, and the blasting rush of wind. '*Do you believe that story? Do you trust Blodgett?*'

Weir had to think about it while the spray swirled against his face and the boat charged west. '*I'm afraid to!*'

'*That's right — you're goddamned afraid! That's why you need to get to Dave Smith at Cheverton!*'

'*I'm not even licensed as a PI!*'

'*You don't need no stinking license! I never thought I'd have to plead with you to find who killed —*'

'*Shut up, Becky! Just shut up for once in your goddamned life!*'

Becky cranked the boat hard to port, cutting a wide angle south, then cinched her into a tighter and tighter pattern, a dizzying concentric rush until *Sea Urchin* came to rest in a roiling sea of white water and exhaust.

Weir's ribs ached from the force. When he looked over at Becky, he saw the tears running across the sides of her temples. She cut the engine and buried her face in her hands. 'I hate it, Jim,' she said. 'I hate what happened and I hate the way I feel and I hate it you don't trust me and I'm just so goddamned afraid.'

He hesitated a moment, running his hand over her head. 'Trade seats,' he said. 'I'll steer.'

They swapped places and Jim took the wheel. Becky huddled inside the worn coat, turning up the collar. Her feet, covered only in nylons, were pushed together for warmth, toes curling against the cool, clean bridge.

'I thought five drinks would keep me warm,' she said.

'Here.' He put an arm around her and brought her close. She nudged up next to him, kind of hunkering into the curve of his ribs, the old position. They used to tease each other about how

211

well they fit. Her hair blew against his cheek. 'You're as bad as I am, holding it all inside.'

'I almost *was* a Weir, once.'

Jim was still amazed at Becky's ability to frame him as the perpetrator of their demise, when it suited her. Certainly they had argued about it enough. But the whole topic, to Jim, had been rounded smooth by too much talk, like a stone by water. Yet at the center of it, there was still something jagged and inaccessible. Jim could never figure whether identifying this final truth was really what they needed, or if it was just another mystery best left unsolved. He had long suspected that in certain matters, the truth was overrated. Some things were more important. If he had carried away one bit of treasure from the whole dismal escapade in the Mexican jail, it was that, in order to go on, he had to forgive.

'I know we've talked it to death,' he said, 'but I forgive you, Becky.' He realized it sounded a little ecclesiastical.

'Well, if it's any consolation, while you were rotting in jail, I was rotting in freedom. I missed you.'

Jim felt tidal stirrings inside: anger on the ebb, love on the flood. 'Maybe we could just forget it all and start again. Fresh.'

She pressed in closer to him but said nothing. Becky the lawyer, he thought, was an unlikely party to such a glib treaty. There was always the fine print. 'You should have written to me.'

'I was trying to get over you.'

'And you're telling me it didn't work?'

'It was a miserable failure.'

She rested her feet on the deck now, toes still curled under in the nervous way that Becky had. Jim looked at them, fixed on the idea that they were probably the only feet in the world besides his own he could identify without the rest of the body attached. Did this count for something? The boat was clunking in the swells, adrift and at rest.

'I thought about leaving when you did,' she said. 'For a while, it seemed you were right just to get out and find something more. I'd always been happy to be in Newport. But with you gone, I looked around and thought, Well, it's a nice little town, but so what?'

'Don't tell the voters that.'

'No. After a month or so, it passed. I mean, if you stay involved, it answers a lot of questions for you. Now I'm thirty-seven, I've realized that you can't do everything. For every thing you decide to do, there's something else you decide to leave undone.'

'Amen to that.'

'I'm changing inside, Jim. I'm getting to want a family. I want to settle in, raise 'em up, all that stuff I didn't want before.'

'I hope you do all that. The world could use some little versions of you.'

She paused then. 'You interested in that kind of thing?'

'Yes, I am.'

'All of you or part of you, Jim? The usual ambivalent mix?'

'Part, I guess, to tell the truth.'

'Which part?'

'The part that's here right now.'

'But not the one that likes being away, that wants to be diving for somebody's gold?'

Jim thought it through. 'It's not being away, though I like that. It's not the diving, really, even though I love it. It's not even someone else's gold, although the idea of a few hundred grand in the bank sits rather well with me. It's dumber than all that. Simpler. It's . . . owning my time.'

'Oh, Christ, not that again. We're all just borrowing, anyway.'

'The illusion of owning my time, then.'

'But couldn't you have the illusion anywhere? In a nice town with a good girl, maybe a little boy to teach about diving and boats? Trade *that* for an *illusion*? You're a romantic and that's good. But the real romance is taking a stand, kicking ass to make it work. You gotta admit one thing, Weir – I was never in your face for long. You had a pretty long leash, about as long as one can reasonably get.'

'The length of the *leash* you offered isn't exactly a selling point, Becky.'

She groaned, the wind yanking the sound toward shore. 'I know. God. A fucking leash.'

For a second, she looked confused. It was an expression he hardly could remember seeing on her. But in that moment, Jim saw for the first time – truly saw and understood – that Becky wasn't young anymore, that she was no longer the girl he had known, the teenager he had lusted after, the young woman he had come to love and almost married. It seemed a wholly intimate finding. She looked like what she was now: a thirty-seven-year-old woman with no husband and no family and the dictates of biology pulsing away

213

inside, a woman whose primary fear in life is that she is smack-dab in the middle of missing it all.

He told her she was beautiful.

Becky studied him, then squinted out to sea. 'I know I could have just stuck by you a little more. But Jim, you're so . . . so touchy. You never tell me what you want or what you're feeling. You're worse than a Sicilian when it comes to holding a grudge.'

'Guilty, with an explanation.'

'Proceed.'

'Unavoidable genetic defects. Plus, I loved you.'

She smiled, settled closer against his side, and sighed. Jim wasn't sure whether it was exasperation or something akin to contentment. There was always in Becky an elusive center; she was a moving target. She had turned her face into him and he could feel the softness of her cheek in the crook of his neck. The top of Becky's head always had been one of his favorite smells. Jim partook.

He leaned his head against hers, closed his eyes for a moment, then gazed through windblown strands of her hair to the horizon. The swells rolled under them, not actually water, but the invisible energy that moves the water.

'Why don't you find us a reef, Weir?'

He hesitated, weighing the consequences. 'I think I will.'

The cabin was musty and cool. Becky opened the curtains over the portholes and locked the door behind them. She looked at Jim with solemn brown eyes and sat on the edge of the narrow berth, hands folded in her lap like a schoolgirl's. The coat was still pulled up close around her neck, and her hair was a windblown nest.

'You okay?' she asked. 'You're moving funny and you're carrying.'

'I ran into some irate police last night,' he said. He told her the story.

She listened intently, as Becky was good at doing. Weir almost could see the legal pad in her mind. She deduced that 'Dispatch' was someone's girlfriend, now guilty of impersonating a police officer. She counseled him to bring suit and, in the near future, cover his ass.

'Can we drop it?' he said. 'I don't want to think about that right now.'

214

She patted the mattress beside her and Jim sat down. He had scarcely settled when her mouth found his and her hand moved up between his thighs. In this, as in all things, he thought, Becky was a fast starter. Through the layers of coat and silk, hose and underwear, Jim prospected, finally stiffening two homesick fingers onto which Becky slid with expressed ease. *'Ooohhh Weir, you're wicked.'* Then he found himself disengaged, guided gently onto his back, looking up at her as she got rid of his pants, unfastened a few key buttons and straps, wriggled away her underwear and climbed on.

'Oh, God, what they did to you.'

'I asked you to drop it.'

'Dropped. Dropped forever.'

In the chilly cabin, with the sea air damp around them, their connection formed a warm center, a literal home fire burning. She rested her hands on his stomach and settled. His back was killing him.

For Weir, it was like being shot from a cannon into yesterday. He could anticipate every movement and every pleasure that branched up through him. He was as dead center as a man can get. To Jim, this act suggested a closure around what had happened since they had fallen out, seemed to set aside those years of numb detente as a containable unit, a stage that they had to go through, something to be endured and learned from, as if being apart had been a simple component of coming back together. Beyond all that was the touch of Becky's fingers on his scrotum, this upward, milking motion of hers. He looked up and saw her in profile, eyes closed, mouth open, her hair sagging in the heavy salt air, still wrapped in the old coat with the dress unbuttoned to reveal beneath the dark layer of silk her pale, smooth body, exposed like a new pearl, working upon him, breasts heavy and round, sweat glistening low on her neck where an artery throbbed fast with blood beneath the shining skin. When Becky came, she balled her free hand into a fist and clenched it beside her straining face like a singer hitting a high note. Jim joined her, a rigid, quaking arc that left nothing of them touching the mattress but the back of Weir's head, his outstretched palms, the bottoms of his feet, and Becky's trembling knees.

A few minutes later, Jim was looking at Becky beside him, bathed in the minor sunlight that came through the porthole and landed upon her face. He had forgotten how intimate, how secret, a boat

215

can be. She spoke without opening her eyes, from what he had thought was a deep and satisfied sleep.

'Are you going to find Dave Smith at Cheverton Sewer and Septic, or am I going to have to get someone else?'

'You know the answer to that.'

A small smile crossed her lips. 'Two hundred a day is what I told Emmett and Edith.'

Jim considered. 'That'll break them. I'll take expenses for a week and see what I come up with. And I'll tell you right now, I haven't forgotten Horton's pictures of Ann, or the fact that his physicals match up, or what he did back in Ohio. I call my own shots.'

'No leashes ever again, Weir.'

'Then do me a favor, keep me out of the headlines you'll be getting.'

She squeezed his hand. 'I'm going to hog those. Starting with a press conference tomorrow morning at ten.'

'That sounds like you.'

'Please be there.'

'Okay.'

'I still love you, Jim. I loved you even when I didn't. I've got an idea where we're going, and I know where I'd like to end up. My heart's coming back alive, Jim. I want you to stay with me. Stay here in Newport, with me.'

Jim, in the afterglow of love, imagined himself a knight errant, questing for the grail – in this case a man named Dave Smith. He told himself as *Sea Urchin* rocked under him that he would pursue the matter with all his might, that somehow, solving the larger problem of Ann would set this and all things right.

Voices outside jolted him out of his reverie, off the berth and to the porthole. Becky sidled up against the hull, bringing her dress to her breast.

Through the glass, Jim could see the sportfisher, forty feet of glistening white with a swordfish plank, a cabin with blacked-out windows, and the name *Enforcer II* written in blue script beneath the bow. There were three men on the deck, one on the plank, another two sitting casually in fighting chairs. He recognized Tillis, Hoch, and Oswitz; the others he knew by face but not by name. Six again, he thought, my lucky number.

'Who are they, Jim?'

'Newport cops.'

'Shit.'

Weir climbed into his pants, pulled on his shirt, pulled Poon's .45 from its holster. He slapped out the clip, checked the six shells waiting like missiles in their silos, then shoved it back and slipped the gun into the front waistband of his pants.

By the time he got abovedecks, *Enforcer II* had nosed closer. The man on the swordfish plank popped a cigarette into the water, then drew deeply on a bottle. The three men on the deck were all leaning against the gunwale and looking down at him like tourists spotting a whale. They all had drinks in foam cups. The boat's exhaust puffed white from the stern, billowing against the water. She was thirty feet close before anyone said anything.

'Everything okay down there?' asked Hoch.

'Looks fine to me,' said Weir.

'Thought you might be in distress.'

'I just told you I'm not.'

'Got some company belowdecks? Female variety, perhaps?'

'None that I'm aware of.'

'That's funny – smells kind of fishy out here.'

Chuckles came from the boat, carried away quickly by the breeze. She had drifted closer now – twenty feet off Weir's bow, idling slowly. The man on the plank stood, tossed his bottle overboard, and picked up a rope. It astonished him, very briefly, that these guys would think about boarding. Weir saw clearly that things could get ugly fast.

'Don't think about coming aboard,' he said.

'Maybe you need our help,' said Tillis. 'Engine trouble?'

Becky chose this moment to come on deck, repackaged in her funeral black and pea coat. She waved to the men on *Enforcer II*. 'Hi, guys.'

All six broke into yips and yipes, the idiotic screams that men must learn from Hollywood Indians in Western movies. Weir, in a flash, foresaw the fall of his nation. *Enforcer II* was close enough now for him to see the CF sticker, the custom rub rail, the pinstriping down the hull. He felt *Sea Urchin's* engine rumble behind him, then stall out. Fuckin' great, he thought. The yips got mightier and the man on the swordfish plank dropped his rope onto the back of *Sea Urchin*.

'Tie us up,' he called.

'Not a chance,' said Weir. He threw the coil of rope into the water and cast a quick glance back at Becky. She was working the ignition with an insouciant look on her face, the kind of look that can advance from boredom to panic in a heartbeat. But Becky wouldn't rattle: She caught him with her brown, unperturbed eyes and tried again to turn over the engine.

'Hey,' she called over the laboring starter. 'You guys are Newport pigs, aren't you?'

Oswitz yelled back. 'Just plain old guys trying to help a vessel in distress. We're looking for a way to be useful, *mayor*.'

'Then pool your IQ's and get out. You touch this boat of mine and I'll sue your ass straight into the twelve-mile bank. Trust me.'

'We trust you, mayor. Got any tits under that coat?'

More yipes and yips. Weir cast a shut-up look back to Becky, but she was visibly riled: a shade redder in the face and this icy glint of murder in her eyes. Becky's nature was to fuel the fire. 'Sure. You've never seen one?'

The *Sea Urchin*'s engine finally caught.

Hoch asked whether someone could come aboard and have a look at them.

Becky said sure, then, to Jim's absolute disbelief, nosed the boat closer to *Enforcer*. The man on the swordfish plank dropped onto the deck of *Sea Urchin* and caught the rethrown rope. Weir was on him in an instant, grabbing a fistful of hair with one hand, jamming the .45 into the man's ear with the other. He pivoted his prisoner to face *Enforcer* and called out. 'Any excuse'll do to blow his brains out. One more of you shitcakes boarding this boat comes to mind as a handy example.'

Becky had already put *Sea Urchin* into reverse and motored back. *Enforcer* slid momentarily to a thirty-foot distance. There was a look of befuddlement on the faces of the three men on deck. Oswitz actually looked to Hoch, as if for direction.

Jim forced his man's head down to the deck and put a knee to his neck, jamming the gun in harder. The kid seemed about twenty-five, and scared. Weir's whole body hurt. 'What's your name?'

He shook his head, then when Jim lowered his weight onto his knee, changed his mind and nodded a frantic yes.

'Name, bubba. Cough it up.'

'No.'

'Don't know your name?' Jim really bore down now, jamming his knee into the crook of neck. There was an outside chance it might give.

'Needham. It was their idea, I just went along to —'

'Um-hmm, yes, I see, Needham.'

Weir hauled his man up, stood him upright and rabbit-punched him. It was a perfect blow that left Needham shuddering for a helpless moment, during which Weir pushed him overboard. It felt great, as if the report of Weir's fist on hostile flesh was a form of cutting through the crap and lies, bringing him one step closer to the truth about Ann. Jim watched as he gasped and thrashed in the cold ocean, a wholly rejuvenated young buck.

He turned to Becky. His stomach was nothing but pain. *'Step on it, Errol.'*

22

The office manager of Cheverton Sewer & Septic was a dour, fat-nosed woman whose desk plaque read MARGE BUZZARD. Her hair was brown-gray, straight and thick, and lay upon the shoulders of a white blouse whose high, frilly neck suggested Victorian primness. Her eyebrows were thick, threatening to connect. She looked to Weir like Charlie Watts in drag on the old Stones album. To her left was an ancient punch clock in olive drab, with a slotted stand beside it for time cards. To her right was a dirty window that looked out to the oil-treated dirt that served as the Cheverton equipment yard. Next to that was a framed photo portrait of a middle-aged man. It appeared to be the only clean thing in the office.

Jim introduced himself as a researcher for attorney B. Flynn of Newport Beach. He told her whom he was looking for.

'I've been here ten years, and we never had a Dave Smith,' she said conclusively. 'We had a Don Smith, back in 'eighty-five, one of the pump crew. He only lasted a month.'

'You've got quite a memory, Ms . . . is it Buzzard, like the bird?'

'It's Miss Buzzard, Mr Weir, like bazaar with a d.'

Weir invented a tale involving Counsel Flynn settling out of court for a client in Laguna Beach. A Mr Dave Smith of Cheverton Sewer & Septic now had a substantial sum in court escrow. 'Something on the order of seven hundred thousand dollars,' he said.

'That's something on the order of impossible, like I already told you. We don't have any Dave Smith. Never have.'

'I'd like to see the operations manager.'

'That's impossible, too. He's out in the yard, and to get there you either have to go over the fence or past me. You are not coming past me to bother him about an employee we do not have. Those are the rules.'

'Rules just got changed,' he said, lifting the wooden partition in the counter and going through.

Marge Buzzard, nearly as tall as Weir, was on him in a second. She scolded up close like a schoolteacher, then blocked his way to the back door. Jim poked his index finger under her larynx, lifted up just enough, and guided her out of his way. He slammed the door behind him, latched it, and, finding the necessary item available, padlocked her in. He pocketed the key. He could hear her fists hitting the wood as he walked across the yard toward the manager's trailer. The new red Corvette he'd seen the night with Blodgett was parked outside it in the shade.

Beyond the pump trucks and portable generators, Jim could see *Duty Free* sitting on her trailer, engine compartment open, and two men on deck steadying winch cables that disappeared into the opening. One was flannel shirt and baseball cap – Blodgett's companion on the Back Bay – the other was a youngish blond with big muscles and long hair.

Jim walked over. 'Operations manager in?'

'That's me,' said Baseball Cap. He peered at Jim from the shade of his bill, then turned back to his task. 'No work, if that's what you want.'

'I'm trying to give some money away, is what I'm doing.'

Baseball Cap glanced down again. The big kid looked at Weir and shook his head. 'Just bring it right over,' said Baseball Cap. 'Dump it anywhere.'

'Are you Dave Smith?'

Both men leaned down into the guts of *Duty Free* now. All Jim could see were their rumps, legs, and elbows. When they stood back and signaled, the winch revved and the cables tightened. Jim looked to the winch operator, sitting quietly behind the glass of his cockpit, a cigarette dangling from his lips.

He heard a door slam from the main office, and looked back to see Miss Buzzard clomping toward him across the yard. Her arms swung purposefully at her sides, and her eyes were fastened on Weir. She stopped three feet away from him, breathing heavily, the wind hissing past her teeth. 'Remove yourself from this property *immediately*,' she said.

'Sorry, Miss Buzzard, but I'm in now.'

She pointed toward the chain-link exit gate. 'You will leave this `instant`.'

221

Jim saw that the two men on *Duty Free* had risen from the engine compartment and now stood watching from the deck. The blond was smiling. Baseball Cap wasn't.

He climbed down from the boat and came toward Weir, wiping his hands on his pants. He introduced himself as Lou Braga and offered his hand. Braga was younger than Jim had thought, about his own age, with plenty of dark hair curling out from under his cap. His face was all sharp angles, nothing round except the big Roman nose. His eyes were almost black, and his handshake was strong. 'He's okay, Marge.'

'He is trespassing, I remind you.'

'I'll talk to him.'

'I'd rather you did not,' she said. Jim noted the fury with which she glared at Braga.

'But I'm the ops manager around here, so I'll manage this operation. Thank you, Marge. It's all right.'

She looked at Weir with unalloyed hatred, then back to Braga. 'This didn't happen when Dick was alive.'

'I miss him, too, Marge. Go inside – it's okay.'

Weir tossed her the key. She regarded him with a final disdainful look, then turned and marched back the way she had come.

'After all that, I hope you're not selling somethin'. I'll be on her shit list for months now.'

Weir explained his mission – the settlement and Dave Smith's seven hundred grand. Braga listened closely, nodding. 'Trouble is, there's no Dave Smith here.'

'Know where he is?'

'That's what I mean, we never had a guy named that.'

Jim wondered whether this was the party line here at Cheverton Sewer, or if Becky and Virginia had simply gotten it messed up. 'He used a Cheverton credit card a few weeks ago, minor purchase. He's got an authorized name.'

'Gotta be some mistake. You know, we're owned by about ten other companies. He must have been with one of them.'

'He said Cheverton, gave the card number and expiration date.'

'You TRW or something?'

'I'm on the level. Never thought I'd have so much trouble giving away seven hundred grand.'

Braga nodded, studying Weir's face. Then he turned and watched the motor of *Duty Free* rising like some steel Lazarus from the

222

engine compartment. The big blond steadied the cable, jumped off the boat, and helped guide the block onto a waiting tarp. 'Looks like they're doing fine without me. Come in, maybe we could straighten this out.'

The inside of the manager's trailer was neat and minimal: a master calendar on Braga's desk, an old coffee can full of pens and pencils, an upturned car piston full of cigarette butts, a smudged telephone, the usual girlie calendars on the walls, and a photo of Braga and his family hanging over the air conditioner. There were a couple of faded pictures from fishing trips, too. In one of them, Dale Blodgett stood beside Braga, holding a heavy yellowtail toward the camera so it would look bigger.

They sat on either side of the battered gunmetal gray desk. 'What's the deal with Marge?' Jim asked.

Braga laughed, both rows of even white teeth showing. 'She's been here too long to get rid of. Everybody's scared of her but me. She's not so bad, but this is her whole world, so she guards it like a Doberman.'

'Mr Cheverton passed away recently?'

'Five years ago. He was doing a cesspool when one of the pump trucks jumped into gear, and he was standing in front of it. Knocked him out and pitched him in. It was bad.'

'That his picture in her office?'

'You don't miss much, Weir. You a PI?'

'No. Just doing basic research work for attorneys now.'

'Used to be a PI?'

'Sheriff's Department for a while.'

Braga nodded, studying Jim with his black unhurried eyes. 'Marge loved him to death. She was bad before. After Dick died, she's been pretty much out there. Keeps that picture of him wiped and polished like it's the Virgin Mary or something.'

Weir accepted a cigarette from Braga, who lit his own, waved the match out, and tossed the book toward him. Braga placed the piston in the middle of the desk. 'Now about this Dave Smith, there's gotta be some mistake. Like I said, our corporate credit cards are issued from headquarters, so who knows who actually called it in. What'd he buy?'

Jim hesitated. 'Minor purchase. Hardware, I think.'

'If you're not TRW, how do you know who charges things on a Cheverton card?'

223

'I'm a legal researcher. That stuff isn't too tough to find out.'

Braga shrugged. 'Guess not. Thanks for the tip, though. If someone here is charging personal things to a company card, I want to know. What's the number?'

'I'd think so.' Jim copied it from the slip Becky had written out for him.

Braga glanced at it. 'What about this settlement?'

Weir remained vague: class-action suit, settled out of court; couldn't reach him at home for over a week; Smith said his current employment was here.

Lou Braga listened without interrupting, then shook his head slowly. 'Just a mistake, I guess. Maybe he was just using us to look legit or something. I don't know. But he isn't here, that's a fact.' Braga waited then, as if expecting something from Jim, an air of suppressed curiosity surrounding him. He sat up a little straighter, drawing on the cigarette. 'You're Ann Cruz's brother, aren't you?'

Jim nodded.

'I'm real sorry about what happened.'

'We buried her today.'

'I guess they've got it narrowed down to that nut from Ohio.'

'There's not much evidence, to tell you the truth.'

Jim could see from Braga's eyes that he was rising to the bait, but he wouldn't take it. Braga said nothing.

'So,' Jim said, 'the family is doing a little investigation of its own. Trying to keep everything covered.'

'Sure. I would, too. This whole business about Dave Smith wouldn't be about Ann, would it?'

'Not unless you know something I don't.'

Braga smiled uncomfortably, both rows of teeth again. He raised his open hands. 'Hey, hey, I was just thinking out loud.'

Jim waited.

'No, not at all. It's just this story about a settlement seems so goddamned weird. Like a sting the cops would pull, or something.'

'How many people are verified to use the Cheverton company card?'

'Three of us here – Marge, me, and the field supervisor, Manny Rueda. But like I said, that card is issued from corporate, so they might keep some other names on it. For verification, I mean.'

'Who is corporate?'

'Cantrell Development owns us. PacifiCo owns them. They call the shots.'

'They have a Dave Smith?'

'I sure wouldn't know. Look, I'll make a call and find out, if that'd help.'

'I'd appreciate it. So would Smith, if he's got seven hundred grand coming his way. Know of anyone around here who might take the number from your statements, figure out a verified name, use that card for himself?'

Braga considered. 'We've got a couple dozen on crews. Some are good men, been with us a while. Some are kind of edgy. You take what you can get at that level. We had a break-in a couple of months back. Some junkie could have lifted the number, if he was smart enough.'

'Would you mind passing along a name, if someone comes to mind?'

'Sure. Sure will.'

'I'd like a list of your employees, too.'

Braga shook his head. 'I won't do that. I don't give that kind of thing away. Court order comes along, I'll be happy to. You gotta understand, Weir, I hired most of these guys. They're my men.'

The more Jim talked to Lou Braga, the more he liked him. And the more he believed that Braga was caught between a rock and a hard place. The hard place was Dave Smith. It was time to turn things up a notch. 'You know my mother?'

'I've heard of her.'

'You have a friend in common – Dale Blodgett.'

Braga just nodded.

'When you can't make the patrol runs with Dale at night – like the night you blew *Duty Free*'s gasket – she goes with him instead. A few times, Ann went with him, too.'

Braga looked at Jim with a mystified expression. 'Every time you ask me about something, you end up knowing more about it than I do. In fact, we've been talking here for twenty minutes and I don't think I've told you one thing you didn't already know. I got work to do, so if you're just fucking with me, I think I'll get back to it.'

Jim rose and followed Braga back into the oil-covered lot.

'I need Dave Smith,' said Weir. 'Bad.'

'I can't help you,' said Braga.

225

Jim gave him Becky's card, with his number written across the back. 'Just in case.'

Braga nodded, then joined the big blond at the engine. Weir stood and watched a moment as both men ignored him. A few feet away from him were the life preservers, toolboxes, tarps, engine cover, and bait tank from *Duty Free*, all cleaned and ready to go back aboard, all arranged neatly on a new canvas tarp. The fighting chairs, removed from the deck, leaned against an old truck parked in the shade. The vigilante patrol boat, he thought. The fishing boat that catches no fish, carries a bait tank that holds no bait. Why bother putting it aboard unless they're fishing? Jim wondered. Why bother with the fighting chairs?

'Hey Weir! Beat it now. I said I'd do what I can for you.'

Jim waved at Lou Braga, and started off toward the gate. He was sure of two things as he climbed into his truck: that Marge was watching him from the side window of her office, and, more importantly, that Lou Braga would be talking to Dave Smith as soon as Weir got his truck out of eyeshot.

Halfway down the peninsula, two Newport Beach units pulled him over. Weir sat tight. Two officers came to his truck. One loitered behind it as the other came to Jim's window. Weir read his nameplate – Lansing – Blodgett's buddy, drinking coffee during the hour in question. He asked for Weir's license, clipped it to his citation board, and went back to the car for the check. It took twenty minutes. When it was done, Lansing wrote him up for a broken taillight.

'Have a nice day,' he said with a smile, flicking the defendant's copy of the ticket into the cab of the truck. 'Been feelin' scratchy down there, treasure boy?'

23

Raymond hustled up the sidewalk from his house, still dressed in his funeral suit. He was carrying a paper shopping bag. He had it pinched between his thumb and first finger, holding it slightly out to his side, as if it contained something foul or dangerous. Whatever it was, Jim could see that it was light: A gust of breeze swayed the bag out toward the odorous water and Raymond's arm extended, giving it play.

Ray's face looked exhausted, but his eyes were sharp and clear. 'He wrote me. At first, I thought it was a joke. It's not.'

Jim could see the agitation on Raymond's face, the need for movement, release. Raymond smiled and shook the bag as if it was a reward long overdue. 'It came with the afternoon mail.'

Becky stepped forward and held out her hands to receive the bag, but Raymond shook his head and didn't offer it. 'No,' he said. 'I don't want it contaminated any more than it already is. Robbins is waiting for it.'

Becky asked what it said.

But Ray was too energized to answer directly. His eyes betrayed an almost-religious excitement, and the sack shook in his hand as if there was something live inside it. 'It's the real thing. I could feel it as soon as I read the first words. He's close. I can smell him, man, smell his fuckin' breath.'

Becky caught Ray by the arms and kissed him. 'Good luck, boys. I don't think my presence would be appreciated in Ken Robbins's kingdom. Call me, please.'

Brian Dennison and Mike Paris were already with Robbins in his office, locked in a murmuring discussion that ended quickly when they walked in.

'Beautiful work,' said Paris.

'Getting your mail out isn't too tough,' said Ray.

The Crime Lab was empty this late in the evening. The hallways echoed with their footsteps and the overhead lights seemed hungry for bodies to shine on. Robbins took them into Hair and Fiber Analysis, put on a pair of latex gloves, and turned on the light of his examination table. The surface was glass, with a clean sheet of butcher paper taped over it. The fluorescent tubes threw a bright clean light up around the corners of the paper. Using a pair of kitchen tongs, Robbins lifted the envelope up and held it steady against an overhead wire. He clipped it on with a red plastic clothes-pin – the same kind of clip, Jim noted, that Horton Goins used in his makeshift darkroom. Weir looked at Dennison and Raymond, but neither seemed to catch it. Dumb coincidence, he thought; put it out of your mind. Then Robbins clipped up the letter, one page at a time, three sheets.

He spoke from behind his magnifier, his breath making little condensation clouds on the bottom of the lens. 'Printer paper, eight and a half by eleven, continuous feed, blank letter edge. Common as dirt. Twenty-four pin dot matrix printer, ten-point Courier font, set to low speed for high resolution. Not fancy stuff, just the basics. Now.'

He pulled a standard stainless-steel table knife with a nonserrated edge from an alcohol jar like Weir's doctor used for thermometers, wiping it on a cotton cloth. Robbins's forehead glistened with sweat. 'Don't get your hopes up – paper doesn't hold much. Tell me again where you touched it and when.'

Working from the top down, he tapped the knife against the envelope. Weir stared at the crisp fluorescent light for falling debris, but saw nothing. Robbins's lined tan face stayed eye level with the pages, following the descending pattern of the knife. He finished the last page, then started in again, this time working the backs. 'Squat,' he said. 'Inside the envelope might be bonus time – things collect.'

Using the tongs again, Robbins reversed the envelope and clipped it upside down. With the gloved tip of his index finger, he lifted out the flap, then slid the knife blade inside and held the pouch apart. He tapped the outside with his finger, across the bottom, the middle, the top. 'Zip,' he said. 'Don't worry. There's the adhesive to check, and under the stamp.'

Next, Robbins photographed the pages, swinging the big camera into place like a dentist positioning the X-ray machine. He took a second set of photos with magnification, shooting each page four times. When he was finished, he went back over each sheet with his glass. "'A heavy heart",' he mumbled. "'My own shock and fear of self . . . I am a brave man . . . helpless against me . . .'" Robbins looked at each of them in turn. 'These guys are always so florid.'

'Is it genuine?' asked Dennison.

'It's a genuine letter from a genuine nut,' said Robbins. 'The rest is up to you.'

In the Fingerprint Lab, Robbins aimed the others to some stools beneath the counter. A window overlooked the parking lot. Weir sat down next to a cabinet filled with vials of chemicals, fingerprint powders, and sprays. A helium-cadmium laser setup dominated one corner, bedded for the night beneath a blue plastic cover. In a far corner stood the light oven for boosting chemicals.

Robbins threw off the laser cover and turned on the machine. 'We hardly ever get friction-ridge impressions from paper,' he said. 'Unless they use a messy ink pen, or have something pretty obvious on their hands – blood, food – I got one from engine lube once. We'll use the laser, try to fluoresce the sodium and potassium chloride – body oil.'

He worked the envelope first, adjusting the eyepiece to read the scan. 'Smudges, boys. The kind your mailman would leave. No . . . nothing clear at all.'

Three sheets of paper later, nothing gave. 'He was careful, used a tissue or something to keep his fingers off the paper. Careful son of a bitch, but not as careful as I am. We'll atomize with ninhydrinacetone, which will bring up things pretty fast on this paper. Heat boost'll help.'

He mixed the solution fresh, drew it into the atomizer, then hung the sheets again and misted both sides. 'Kalb, who usually does latents, soaks her things. Too much spray and you drown the ridges. The oils manifest as purple and pink after the heat boost.' The sheets went into the oven one at a time, then the envelope. *'Bloom, my little violets, bloom in the spring.'*

Weir could see the purple smudges developing, like Polaroid film, in the upper-right corner of the first page and the top-left of the last, backside.

Robbins pointed and looked at Ray. 'Yours?'

'I'd guess so.'

Robbins picked up the phone, ordered from Index a full set of prints for Raymond Cruz and Horton Goins. 'ASAP'll do it,' he said, 'I need them five minutes ago.'

He worked the camera into place and shot the developing blossoms. 'Now, if you don't mind, I'd like to read this thing before the Index people get here.'

Robbins read out loud and slowly, grunting at certain lines every few seconds, wiping the sheen of sweat off his brow with a paper towel.

Dear Lt Cruz:

It is with a heavy heart that I write to you in this time of our great, shared grief. My genuine sympathy is with you, because I know now what it is like to lose someone you love very dearly. And I know that for you, as an officer of the law, this death of your beloved must lie like a tumor in your very soul, because of the fury you feel with the loss, and the impossibility of finding, or even naming me.

This letter is an apology to you, but it is more than that. It is my explanation. Over this last week, as I have recovered from my own shock and fear of self, I have thought about surrendering to you many times. But I couldn't do it. I am a brave man, yes. But I couldn't bring myself to you because I will not hurt those around me. I am greatly loved, surrounded by those who appreciate my talents and energy. I have them to consider, not only myself.

But to you, Lt Cruz, I must confess, and do what little I can to put your soul at ease. I know you are tormented by guilt and shame. Did you know that we – Ann and I – drove past two patrol cars that night? I'm sure that in retracing Ann's steps you have guessed that might have happened. I tell you this not to further your anguish and helplessness – and you are truly helpless against me – but to establish my empathy for you. If I were you, what a hell my life would be.

First, so you are sure that I'm not offering a false

230

confession for unstable reasons, let me tell you some
of what I did that night. I made love to your wife,
Ann Cruz, in a lovely room overlooking the sea. It
was satisfying to me, in almost every way. Because it
was not satisfying in all the ways I require, I struck
her twenty-seven times with a Kentucky Homestead
kitchen knife (freshly sharpened six-inch blade). She
suffered very little because I am strong. I placed one
long-stemmed purple rose into her sexual opening as
a gesture of affection, and ten others I put into the
waistband of her skirt, which was red and short (she
had worn it to please me). The other, I now possess.
I moved her into the Back Bay approximately two
hundred yards north of Galaxy Park, then I walked
back to my car and drove away. Now you know that
what I tell you is true.

I knew Ann very well – far better than she knew me,
and far better than you knew her yourself. Don't be
surprised. Ann was not an easy person to get to know.
She had a large secret area inside her, which was not
available to most people – even you. But I recognized
that place in her because I have one of my own, and
our two great privacies were drawn to each other. She
revealed all to me, in the end. She opened herself in
every way. I was her mentor, her confessor. She was my
angel, and finally, my anguish.

Why did I do it? Two reasons. The first is that I had
to protect her from you. You were her falsehood, the
one that had brought Ann to the brink of madness.
I knew that she was in your influence, and that she
needed me to guard her from you. She begged me to
protect her from you. You tried to own her, but you
could not.

Have you ever known complete possession of a
woman? For many years of my life, I did not. There
was always that distance in them, always that place I
couldn't go to. You can imagine the anguish it caused
me to see Ann's private world – what a temptation
it was, what a challenge! Always between man and
woman there is the distance, the difference, the

apartness. The woman is, to us, Raymond, the eternal
other. And how can true passion adjust to that? What
I require is simple devotion, submission, and complete
surrender. For years I wondered how that could be
accomplished. It cannot be done with money. It cannot
be done with love or affection – women make careers
of exploiting those very weaknesses in us. It can't
be done with sex, however vigorous, because for the
woman there is her pleasure, her self, her other. Do
you understand my need? Do you know what it is?
I think you can, if you forget what you have been
taught by a cowardly society and remember only what
you are.

Robbins looked up from the letter to Raymond, who sat staring
without apparent focus through the window at the receding evening.
He looked, to Weir, so alone and so exposed. Robbins turned back to
the document.

Yes, I made love to her that night, in a comfortable
place beside the sea. I made total love to her. I begged
with my body for her complete surrender. I pleaded
with my entire being for her devotion. I aspired to
possession.
And yet, she resisted.
Can you begin to imagine the crush of this?
You can't, because you could never fathom the
depth of Ann, you never knew through all those
years what great treasures in her went undetected.
And in my darkest hour I had a vision of Ann as my
own, as a complete possession. If my own love and
seed could not convince her, then I saw my only
alternative.
You understand, Raymond Cruz, that Ann was with
child. My child. She convinced you that it was yours,
but I know the truth, and so did Ann. And I will admit
that the very heart of my anger and frustration was
this lie that she offered to you, rather than offer that
great gift of life – my gift to her! – back to me. When
she told me that night that she was going to bear my
child as if it were yours, and retreat from me forever in

232

order to establish her cheap charade, well . . . I saw no choice but to become her God.

So I loved her purely. We drove in my car, past police and your pitiful ideas of enforcing the law, to a place where we had been before. And after embracing her, I plunged the knife deep into her heart. I felt the flutter of outraged muscle through the blade and in my fingers, heard the sound of sharpened metal parting her. Then I saw it on her face, finally, the surrender, the helplessness, the absolute dependence on me she never had before. If only for a moment! It was the moment I had prepared a lifetime for. It validated everything I had done. It released her forever from your banal torment, Raymond. There was such love in her eyes, such relief, such . . . splendor!

Robbins's voice had lowered. Weir's heart had grown heavier with every line, heavy with the knowledge of Ann's terror. Raymond sat with his head in his hands. Paris gazed down at the floor. Dennison appeared to be praying. Robbins sighed quietly, and continued.

And still my heart aches for her, Lt Cruz, for her touch, her laugh, her flesh and spirit. I know that yours does, too, because while you loved her in a small way and loved her imperfectly, to have partaken in Ann was to have touched the heart of all women. I know you loved her. She loved you, too, in her confusion and weakness. She died as she had lived: content in me. In a very real way, I provided for Ann what she had always wanted.

I don't expect you to comprehend this brief explanation. You are, after all, a simple police officer. Words are such feeble tools for the task of explaining love. It is my sincere desire for you to know that Ann did not die in vain, but that her heart was full for me. Ann was finally complete.

I wrestle with the heaviness of my own heart, with the need to tell the world what I have done. Perhaps it is as humble a thing as guilt, or as simple a thing as pride. And if that day comes, Lt Cruz, I will deliver myself to you and only you. Because truly, for

233

Ann, there was only us. Truly, everything we did, we did for Ann. We are connected through her, though our battle for her body and soul was conducted with cunning and fury.

With My Understanding and Sympathy,
Mr Night

A kind of roaring silence filled the room, a silence too crowded with emotion to admit anything as insignificant as sound.

Weir felt as if he'd been sucked down into some funnel cloud of insanity, left spinning with it, unable to find balance or escape.

'Brian,' said Robbins. 'This sound like Horton Goins to you?'

'I can almost hear his voice,' said Dennison. 'It's perfectly him.'

Robbins turned to Raymond. 'Ray?'

'It isn't him. He's too young. Mr Night knew Ann and she knew him. It isn't Goins.'

'Jim? Your vote?'

'I'm with Raymond. Goins couldn't have written it.'

'Mike?'

'Brian's right — it is Goins, right down to the schizophrenic delusions of grandeur. It's all in his hospital records.'

Robbins sat back, crossed his arms, and looked down again at the letter.

Weir asked him what he thought.

'I'll keep my opinions to myself for right now,' he said. 'We'd do best to focus on the text itself. Let's take it through, okay? First, rage and sorrow. He's got a lot on his mind.'

Ray nodded. 'He wants to talk about it.'

'Not very much, he doesn't,' said Dennison. 'He wants to obscure.'

'I think Raymond is right,' said Robbins. 'It's half his reason for writing — a need to confess. And the other half?'

'His confidence needs bolstering,' said Weir. 'He's waving the trophy, bragging.'

'That's my take, too,' said Robbins. 'And speaking of trophies, I'll bet he's kept something else of hers from that night, besides the flower. He thinks he loved her. According to his definition, maybe he did.'

'Her purse,' said Raymond. 'All the personal things — the smells.'

'Her shoe,' said Jim.

234

Robbins nodded. 'Both good bets. Okay, this is what I hear. Educated, middle or upper class. Probably has some kind of job – that stuff about being talented might even be true. Obviously, he's got access to a word processor and printer, and he knows how to use them. He isn't delusional, seeing visions, hearing voices. Raymond, I just have to ask you this straight out – what about this affair? Did Ann have a lover?'

'I never suspected,' Ray said quietly. 'Until I saw the pictures. Of Ann in the limousine. She was completely discreet about it – if it's true.'

If it's true, thought Jim. Raymond buried his faithful wife today, and he'll keep her faithful to the bitter end.

'*If* he was really seeing her,' said Dennison. '*If* his love affair was anything more than sniping her with a camera, following her around the neighborhood. Maybe his trophy was a photograph of what happened.'

Robbins shook his head in disagreement. 'That would certainly make our jobs easier. But what good does it do to lie about an affair he never had?'

'Building up his confidence again,' said Dennison.

'Throwing us off the track,' said Paris. 'He's built up this whole romance in his mind. There wasn't any romance. He followed her; he raped her and killed her. He wants to believe in an affair – that's why he wrote it down.'

'Maybe,' said Robbins. 'He's got a big ego to keep feeding. The whole letter about a woman he allegedly loved and allegedly killed? It's about *his* feelings, *his* needs, *his* confusion. He's arrogant. When they write, there's always an element of taunting, too. He's challenging us, rubbing our noses in it. Especially when the man he writes to is a cop.'

The heavy silence hovered in the room, disturbed by nothing but the whirring of the air conditioner.

Raymond spoke next. 'Goins wouldn't be so linear.'

'I wonder,' said Robbins. 'I read his file yesterday for the third time this week. The boy – man, I guess – is ineffable. He's committed for rape and attempted murder at the age of fifteen, and two years later at the state hospital he's already teaching photography to the chronics. He's taking correspondence classes in everything from astronomy to genealogy, for chrissakes. His favorite subjects are the nuns that come through; he takes their portraits and gives them

235

away. Probably the only women he saw. Maybe that's where he gets his religious bent – himself as God, Ann as an angel. At the time they committed him, he'd had a Stanford-Binet intelligence test in school and tested out at eighty-six. They gave him another one in the hospital four years later and he scored one thirty-nine. Goins is formless. I think he could have written this, but it's nothing more than a guess at this point.'

Dennison cast a quick, satisfied looked to Weir and Raymond. 'I mean, if he was her lover, why rape her anyway? He was . . . you know . . . getting it for free.'

'He didn't,' Weir answered. Certain particulars of Ann's beating had been bothering him for days. In this new context, something that he had dismissed as improbable suddenly made twisted, brutal sense. 'He didn't. We assumed it was a rape, but it was consensual. Yee found bruising on the mons, but he said it was done close to the time of death, could even have been postmortem. He beat her *after* they had intercourse, to throw us off, to create a dimension that wasn't there. He as much as told us that.'

'Dumb,' said Dennison.

'I reached the same conclusion Jim did,' Robbins snapped. 'By the third paragraph. Call it what you want, Brian. I don't think she was raped.'

Dennison stood, head at an incredulous angle. 'But why does lover boy kill her in the first place?'

Raymond spoke next, his voice trailing off to a whisper. 'I think Annie got herself into something she couldn't get out of. Maybe she tried to, and that's what set him off. That's all he talks about – how he can't ever . . . *own* her.'

'The roses,' said Weir. 'He sent her the roses because he sensed the end with her. He dressed up, wore a suit, a slick diamond tie tack. Ann did the same. She made love to him one last time, asked *him* down to the bay for a moonlight walk. She was going to lay it on the line. The footprints showed no hurry, no struggle. They walked with their arms around each other, Ann thinking about what she was going to say, how she was going to break it off, not wanting to hurt him or light his fuse. Maybe they'd already talked about it, worked out the basics, and this whole night was supposed to be just a long goodbye. Either way, he knew. He already knew what was coming. He was ready.'

236

'But how come she was going to dump him?' asked Dennison. '*Assuming* this was a real affair?'

'Simple,' said Weir. 'She found out she was pregnant. The child wasn't his.'

The unasked question filled the room. No one seemed willing to give it breath. After another roaring silence, Raymond did it himself. 'The child was ours. I know that. We had names, the announcement party, everything. . . .'

'How would Ann know?' asked Robbins. 'For sure?'

Raymond considered. 'Maybe they used birth control. I know we didn't. Maybe she didn't have intercourse with him until April. It was April twenty-seventh when she saw the doctor. That puts her conception back to late March.'

'It could fit,' said Robbins, but Weir detected something disingenuous in his voice. It was not like Robbins to feign. 'It could also fit that she hadn't been intimate with him for long. He was still in the heat of passion for her. No sooner had he consummated than she tried to cut him off. Less than a month. He thought he loved her; she was using him for a fling. That's a perfect trigger for someone as unstable as this guy is.'

Dennison began pacing the room, shaking his head. 'Bunch of fuckin' baloney. You guys are suckers if you believe much of anything in that letter. The guy's a *nut*. That have any bearing here?'

'Quite a bit, I'd think,' said Paris.

'I realize it's contradicting your assumptions,' said Robbins. He turned to Ray. 'For the sake of argument, say the child was his. What would she do, if she knew?'

Raymond stood and looked out the window a long while. The evening had fallen. Headlights crept past on the boulevard below. Ray's voice was so quiet, it hardly rose above the hum of the air conditioner. 'Ann wanted a child badly. If she had gotten pregnant by someone other than me, I think . . . I think she might have kept it, and told me it was mine. That's speculation, though. Maybe that's just a way to convince myself that she loved me more than she really did.' He turned from the window and sat back down, crossing his legs and looking at Robbins.

'And what would she tell *him?*'

'She sure as hell wouldn't discuss it with me,' said Ray. 'But why speculate? We can't test the . . . Ann's fetus now.'

Weir looked at Robbins, whose face was visibly paler. The medical

237

examiner crossed his arms and shook his head slowly. 'We already did. We used the blood they took at the hospital when you were in, ran all the chemical panels. The genetic typing confirmed it this morning. Ray, the child wasn't yours.'

Jim watched Raymond look out the window again, his eyes as black as the night outside the glass. He seemed to have shrunk inside the funeral suit, which hung loosely on him, pant cuffs sloping down to the floor. He turned and looked at Weir, then at the others in turn. His face had deepened in color. 'Well,' he said quietly. 'That's nice to know. It might have shaded my decision when we were picking out names.'

He moved toward his chair, snapped a kick, and sent it toppling and skidding quick along the floor before it slammed into the far wall. Jim watched the eyepiece of the laser scope wiggling with the impact.

'You should have just fucking said so up front.'

'We're not sure what it means, so far as the case goes,' said Robbins. 'There wasn't any gentle way to tell you. I wish I didn't have to.'

Raymond stood over his fallen chair now, then reached down and picked it up. He slumped into it, arms crossed, eyes lost to some distance near or far, Weir couldn't tell, and it didn't seem to matter. Raymond then straightened himself, composing his face by sheer force of will. 'The fact,' he said quietly, 'the fact that he mentioned the child means she told him she was pregnant. Ann . . . she couldn't have known who the father was, not for sure. She must have just assumed, *prayed* it was mine. Maybe I'm flattering myself. Maybe she didn't care enough, even for that. Maybe she was going to make me the father, when really I wasn't. But it would explain why she was breaking off with him – her in a family . . . way.'

'I would have to agree,' Robbins said quietly.

Dennison seemed ready to speak but said nothing.

The silence that fell again was merciless and impenetrable. Weir watched the headlights below, studied the dark shapes of the county buildings through the window. Then the door flew open and a courier from Index came in with the print cards.

Robbins took the slides to the laser scope and set Raymond's prints against the ones taken from Mr Night's letter. The latents, as Weir knew they would, belonged to Raymond.

'We've got two last shots,' said Robbins. 'The possibility that our man used his own saliva to seal the envelope or the stamp, and the off chance that we get something from *under* the stamp. The serology will take a day or two to work up. We can do the stamp now, with permission from Mr Eliot. Say your prayers.'

Weir watched as Robbins used an autoclave to steam it off. It curled up on the edges, a folding poet, loosening by degrees. The idea struck Jim that the key to this case was never going to be found under a goddamned postage stamp.

Raymond continued to stare out the window. Jim walked over and stared with him. It was an ugly city on an ugly night.

He was aware of Robbins removing the envelope with his tongs and placing it back on the light table. Dennison leaned over, his hands crossed behind his back.

Then, a sudden motionlessness came over them. Dennison still stood, his hands still folded behind his back. Robbins had straightened, his head bent down toward the light table. He turned to Weir and Ray.

'He left a hair under the stamp,' he said. 'A beautiful half inch of dark brown hair.'

Ten minutes later, Robbins had run it against a sample taken by the Newport cops from a brush in Goins's old bathroom at the Island Gardens, and another taken from a T-shirt hanging in the closet of the El Mar Motel.

No match.

Then Robbins compared it to the hair taken off the blouse that Ann was wearing that night on the Back Bay. 'Same guy,' he said finally. 'I can put him with Ann; I can put him with the letter. Killer at large. Killer unknown. I need a warm body, gentlemen.'

Dennison considered. He looked at Paris, who seemed to take it as a signal for something.

Paris's voice dropped in pitch, took on a weight that suggested certainty. 'Goins has an IQ of one thirty-nine. He's bright enough to slip someone else's hair under that stamp. It's too convenient. It's too pat. I'll go far enough out on a limb to suggest it's a frame.'

'Parrot,' said Jim. 'You can do a good imitation of Brian here. You can do a good imitation of a man who knows what he's talking about. But deep down, you're dumb as a stump and you ought to be chained to your desk writing press releases.'

*   *   *

239

It was almost eight o'clock by the time they left the crime lab. On the damp steps of the building, Dennison stopped and took Jim's arm, aiming him away from Raymond and the suddenly subdued Mike Paris.

'I've got a proposition for you, Jim. I want to put you where you belong, back on this case. You can come on as sergeant of detectives – that'll be a level-five pay grade. Violent Crimes will be your section, and you can focus on Ann. Interested?'

'No.'

'Care to explain why?'

'I quit that life five years ago,' said Weir. 'Because chasing after people to put them in jail just doesn't do it for me. And you know something else, Brian? Some of your men are real assholes.'

Dennison regarded him with suspicion as Jim told him about his shearing at Davis Marine Industries the night before, and his encounter at sea with some of Dennison's finest. As Jim looked at him, he saw that the chief had lost weight the last few days, that his coat seemed large and his pants were slipping down. The outdoor floodlight threw a waxy shine onto Brian's face.

Dennison listened carefully, then, to Jim's surprise, actually apologized. He pulled a roll of antacid tablets from his pocket, chewed down a small handful. 'Jim, Jesus . . . I'm going to kick some ass tomorrow. I swear to God.'

'You might mention to them that at this rate, someone's going to get killed.'

It was clear to Jim that Brian Dennison finally believed that he was in over his head. His campaign was plodding, his suspect was still at large, and he couldn't keep track of his own men. Something between worry and panic showed in his eyes.

'That's why I need you,' said Dennison. 'You quit the Sheriff's on your way up. You were good. I've checked around – everybody thought you were good. I'm giving you a chance to do what you're best at.'

'I've got a new trade and I'm going to ply it.'

'Hunting treasure?' Dennison asked. There was a whisper of near-woe in his voice. 'Or working for Becky Flynn?'

'She asked me to do some work.'

'And you took it?'

'She's moving in some interesting directions.'

'Care to share these with the police?'

240

'Not right now. She's got a press conference tomorrow. The papers should be full of it.'

The few cars in the lot were misted with condensation, windshields opaque as dirty mirrors in the lamplight. Weir could smell the moisture rising from the asphalt.

'I could really use you, Jim.'

Weir looked again into Dennison's uneasy eyes. 'What you want is me off the case, Brian. You see it one way and I see it another. If I go to work for you, I'm paid to see it your way. No. But thanks.'

'I hope you changing sides won't loosen your tongue about the arrangement we had.'

'It won't. But you saw that Becky knows, same as your men and half the people at city hall. If the papers finally start to make noises about Ruff and a cop car, don't come to me.'

'No.'

'You're too eager for Goins – even you know that. Maybe your Internal Affairs people have kicked up something that doesn't smell right. Something about Kearns's twenty minutes away from his car that night.'

Dennison paused. 'Internal Affairs is moving carefully, as they should. But I'm not sold on Goins. There are some things that don't fit.'

'I noticed.'

'I took a beating in there just now.'

'Don't tell George Percy that.'

'Robbins will. Just don't forget, Weir, that two hairs in this universe don't make Horton Goins an innocent man. That guy's a dangerous son of a bitch and you know it. You can check my file for the pictures of what he did in Ohio, if you ever need to put Horton Goins in a clear perspective. He left one of her tits hanging by a piece of skin. He raped her the nice old-fashioned way, then he tried to do it again with his fist. Made the same kind of bruises we found on Ann, incidentally. Nice kid. Reliable. Innocent. A heartwarming individual.'

'We'll see, Brian. My guess is a lot of things might look different to you, after June fifth.'

Dennison's eyebrows fluttered above his flat gray eyes. 'You shouldn't make too much of that. Yeah, I'm using this case for the publicity. And Becky's found a way to do the same. She and your mother will be all over this chemical spill in the bay, like if

241

you don't vote for the Flynn, Slow Growth ticket, you may as well have dumped that stuff yourself. It's just the politics of politics, Jim. A year from now, we'll all be doing whatever we're doing and no one will even remember.'

'I don't care about the politics,' said Jim.

'Maybe you should.'

Weir stopped, took Dennison by the arm, and turned him. 'You know what I think? I think politics is just a circus full of assholes – everyone for himself. I think whatever happens to Newport is whatever Newport deserves. You and your developer friends can have it, if that's how the people vote. Dice up every last inch and sell it off. Mom and Becky can preserve the whole thing in formaldehyde, legislate flattops and bouffants if that's how it comes out. But Ann wasn't politics, unless you've learned something I haven't. Someone killed her and all you people do is try to fit it into your programs. I'm sick of the bullshit, Brian – the way you've used Goins to look good, the way you're playing up half the evidence and playing down the other half, the way you and Becky snarl at each other like a couple of dogs over a stinking bone. Anybody care about the fucking *truth* here? What I care about is getting that guy, sticking his ass where the sun don't shine.'

'So join up with me. Ann would be yours.'

'She already is mine.'

Dennison stopped at his car, put his hands in his pockets, and looked at Weir. He shivered once, bunching up his shoulders against the chill. 'Virginia and Becky are going to point some fingers on this spill, aren't they?'

'Christ, Brian – that's what I mean.'

'Do me a favor, will you?'

'No. No Brian, I won't do you a favor. I'm out of fuckin' favors for you and everybody else.'

'If Virginia knows who did the dumping, will you tell me? Just tell me if she knows. She's got some ideas, doesn't she? They're going to make an announcement, right? All I'm asking you to do is share some information.'

Jim was silent for a moment. There was just no way to get through, he thought, no way to get a train like Brian Dennison or Virginia Weir to stop and change direction. Maybe that was the way of the world.

'You know what your trouble is, Weir? You're afraid to put

yourself on the line, to take a side. Stand in the middle of the road, Jim, you get run over by traffic on both sides.'

'I'm off the road, Brian. It's your road. It's Mom's.'

Then Dennison offered a haggard smile. 'The only people who stay free are children and drunks. Life's a shitty thing sometimes.'

Dennison climbed into his car and rolled down a dew-dripping window. He turned over the key but the starter just kept coughing and the engine wouldn't catch. 'Becky can use you just like I can, Jim.'

'I know that. And I also know you've got to get Ray back on the job. He's got no business with Annie's case right now. It's hurting him. Get him out there on the streets where he belongs.'

Dennison's car finally started. 'One step ahead of you, Jim. Ray's on the day shift starting tomorrow.'

He pulled the Jaguar up to Jim, gunning the engine. 'I'll share everything I've got on Ann with you, if you'll share some of Virginia's and Becky's intelligence with me. It could work out in the best interests of us both.'

Weir shook his head. 'You know what *your* trouble is, Brian? You're an amateur.'

Dennison smiled, a little sickly. 'We'll see.'

When Jim got into the truck, Raymond was already there, his gaze flattened against the misty windshield. 'It's okay. Maybe it's better if I don't believe anymore that I put an angel in the ground today. Maybe it's better if she didn't have my child, that she was a fuckup sometimes like everybody else.'

Weir was quiet for a moment. 'This may not hold much water, but that last night I saw her at the Whale, her eyes lit up when she talked about you. She wanted to call you right then, let you know I was back. You were the first thing she thought about. I think she died loving you Ray, no matter what was going on at the end.'

Raymond nodded. 'Yeah. Sure. Thanks.'

Going over the bay bridge, Jim looked out to the fog-muted lights of the restaurants, the hushed spring calm of preseason Newport. The air was rank as they dropped onto the peninsula. A Newport Beach cop unit pulled in behind them and trailed along.

Raymond sat up straight, looked over at Jim, then out the window. He started drumming his fingers on the armrest, looked over at Weir again.

'What?' Jim asked.

'I want to go in the water, deep. I want to do it now.'

'Can't see much at night, Ray.'

'I don't want to see. I want to not see.'

Jim drove on for a while. 'Okay.'

They got one of Virginia's rental boats from Poon's Locker and took her down to Laguna. It was a nice little Whaler with a 35hp Yamaha on it. Weir could barely see the houselights in the fog. They anchored off of Moss Point and geared up. Jim found some glow sticks in his dive bag, and hooked one to Ray's vest and one to his own. He checked the light batteries and water seal: okay. Night dives were always a little strange, and Raymond wasn't used to them.

'Follow me down,' said Jim.

'How deep is it here?'

'Sixty. There's the eighty-foot wall about fifty yards out, but we're not going down it. Stay above sixty.'

They put on their masks, traded thumbs-ups, and spilled over.

The cold water filled Jim's wet suit as soon was he was under. It was a chilling, sobering cold, one that erases clutter from the mind. He knew what Ray was after. His regulator drew easily and he dropped to ten feet, looking upward through his bubbles to watch Ray descending, his glow stick burning bright green against the darkness.

Weir found the anchor line, turned on his light, and motioned Raymond down. The visibility at forty feet was almost nil: There was only the beam of light on the pale rope of the anchor line, the luminescent rise of bubbles, and Raymond's glow stick ten feet above him. The pressure mounted and Jim cleared his ears.

As he slowly descended, Jim felt the strange ebb of reality that always hit him when he was under, that replacement of the old order with a new one. Down here was the alternate world, governed by alternate law and principle. Down here, you were smaller, disenfranchised, considerably lower on the food chain.

Raymond joined him at the anchor. Jim's depth gauge said seventy

244

feet. He knew where the wall was, but Raymond was in no condition for the wall; not tonight – maybe not ever.

They traded okays again. Through the glass of Raymond's mask, Jim could see his eyes – wide and a little frightened. Raymond was working hard to stay down. Like a lot of people, he left too much air in his vest, as if that little extra would give them a head start on their way through seventy feet of water. Jim reached out and hit the deflate button on Ray's compensator. Raymond settled comfortably down beside him. Jim pointed to the rocks and Ray nodded.

Night is day for most creatures of the sea, Weir thought. They feed, travel, mate by night; the corals bloom and the anemones open; a rock outcropping that looks abandoned by day will brighten and bloom and teem with life in the darkness. Jim floated over the rocks, watching his flashlight beam. A garibaldi, bright as an orange, perused him from beside a round tan stone. A halibut wavered along the sand, its two eyes shifting alertly in Weir's light. Jim could see the antennae of a lobster in the deep crack between two rocks. The sea grass wavered in the current, blown left then right by a breeze of water. Two silver mackerel streaked by. Jim looked behind him. Ray had fallen back twenty feet. Okay, he thought, Ray is going to be okay. The suctioned tentacle of a big octopus swirled behind a rock. Jim swam over and picked up the creature in his light. The sand was settling where the octopus had squeezed under the rock, but he couldn't get all the way in. Three tentacles still wavered, rippling outward like whips cracked in slow motion. Jim pulled him out, felt the surprising strength of it, let go, and watched as it convulsed, hovered, then shot away from him toward the larger rocks. What an unlikely grace, he thought.

He felt the current pushing him to and fro, like the sea grass. He'd found that if you let go and let it take you, it was easy and natural, as if the currents around you and the currents inside you were the same. When you fought it was when you got into trouble, when you'd understand its ceaseless, unresistible power. That was what Raymond had to do with the current, he thought, with the current and everything else in his life. Go with it some. Don't fight every inch of the way. It was going to take time.

He checked his air and depth and watch. Just ten minutes down. He felt good.

When he turned to see how Ray was doing, Ray was gone.

He stopped, running his light beam through the congested deep.

245

He backtracked, swinging the light in front of him. The beam looked like a white rope for a few feet, then it frayed and dulled into darkness. He found the anchor line, but no Ray. On the surface, he trod water until he found the Whaler, which had swung north and west with the swell. The lantern glowed from the aft bench of the boat, but Ray wasn't on it. Jim understood in a flash that Raymond had gone to the wall.

He headed back down, along the rope, then swam west toward the open sea. The wall – more of a trench – was an almost vertical drop of eighty feet that formed a valley before rising almost as sharply on the far side. When he got to the drop, Jim floated out over it. In good water, you always got a little jolt of vertigo when you did this, the sudden fear that you were about to fall straight down for eighty feet. But you didn't. You hovered there, pinned to the sea, viewing the bottom below. It was like flying.

He could see Raymond's glow stick descending. His depth gauge said seventy-five feet. His tank had seventy psi of air. Ray would be using his air faster, breathing hard. Jim felt the anger gnawing at him: Divers didn't just leave each other and head out on their own – not at night. There were reasons, and the reasons had to do with yourself: What if your regulator clogged, your mask shield popped out, your tank strap got caught on a rock, your legs cramped? What if you just got lost?

Jim closed the distance, kicking steadily and strongly. The pressure squeezed in on his aching ribs. At one hundred feet, Ray was still ten yards ahead. Jim felt the first subversive lightness of the nitrogen buildup in his blood, brought on by pressure. Some people called it rapture of the deep. It made you loosen up, forget, take chances, get playful – all the wrong attitudes at depth. It was a hazard, and a good diver never forgot how dangerous it could be.

He caught Raymond at 150 feet, took his swim fin and pulled him back. Ray swung around lazily, smiled, offered the okay sign. Jim shook his head, thinking it isn't okay at 150 feet, you fool – it's too deep, too cold, too dark, and too far from the boat. Now we'll have to decompress on the way up – five intervals, three minutes each, starting at one hundred feet. That was fifteen extra minutes of cold, wasted energy, air. Jim hooked his thumb toward the surface, twice. Ray nodded, started up, then dolphin-dove and reversed direction, heading down again. Weir caught him by his ankle. Then he took Raymond's vest in his right hand and shook him. Ray was smiling again, drunk on the nitrogen and wanting to get drunker. Jim took Ray's chin in his hand, straightened it, and forced Ray to look at him. He wasn't smiling now, but he looked at Jim with a woozy expression containing something that sent a genuine shiver of fear up Weir's back. It was a look of defeat. Ray was moving toward the ultimate surrender.

Jim guided him up to one hundred feet, then stopped and timed the decompression rest. Ray floated there, staring down the wall as if he had left something precious behind.

At seventy feet, they used the anchor line to steady themselves. By the time Jim threw his mask and fins into the Whaler and climbed over the starboard stern, he was chilled and shaking.

He took Ray's equipment and helped him up the ladder. He already had the engine running and was cranking up the anchor by the time Ray got his weight belt off.

Ray set down the belt, lost his balance in the swell, and plopped down onto the bench. 'You pissed?'

'That was stupid. You're supposed to be there for me.' He drew up the anchor and settled it into the box behind the breast hook. 'You want to fuck with somebody's life, fuck with your own.'

Jim regretted his words as soon as he heard them. That's what you get for diving with an amateur. What he hadn't understood was how desperate Raymond was, how his despair was pushing him toward closure, toward anything that would end it. Now Jim was angry at himself for not knowing. Had Raymond let him down, or the other way around?

'I didn't mean that,' he said.

'You're right.'

'You scared me, goddamn it.'

'I scared myself. The deeper I got, the better idea it seemed just to keep going. For a while, nothing hurt and everything was okay. It was like washing it all away.'

Jim pushed the throttle forward and headed north for Newport. The Whaler bounced hard against the chop and the shoreline lights inched past them. He shivered, wrapped his jacket tight.

'But I realized something,' said Raymond. 'I realized where Ann

247

would keep the journal. It hit me at a hundred and twenty feet –
clear as a vision.'

Jim looked at him and waited.

'Stop at the *Sweetheart Deal* on the way in. That's where
we'll find it. That's where we'll find out who was . . . who her
lover was.'

24

Jim could see the outline of *Sweetheart Deal* fifty yards ahead of them. She slouched at her mooring, the mast angled skyward in an empty crucifix, the gull nest atop it an unmanned crown of thorns. Easy to see why the cops had overlooked it, Weir thought: All it looked good for was a fire hazard and a wildlife refuge. Raymond has got this wrong. Balboa Island lay at the far shore, then the mainland and Coast Highway; beyond them, the mirrored glass of the PacifiCo Tower presided from a near-distant hill, dotted like an *i* by the moon.

Raymond sat in front of him in the dinghy, his face pale against the night. He had not spoken the whole trip back; now he let it all out in a rush of words that seemed almost beyond his control. 'I waited for it,' he said. 'I knew it was coming, as soon as we found that garage-door opener. I think I knew, down somewhere, that I wasn't enough for her. Sometimes, it struck me as okay – it seemed like she was . . . underappreciated. I forgave her, in advance. Annie would surprise me when I came home from work. One night not long ago, she wasn't there to greet me as usual. I went into the bedroom and she was spread out on the bed, nothing on but a flimsy robe that was open most of the way, and a garter belt thing, and a lacy top. She was made up heavy, red lipstick, and her hair was pulled back the way I like it. There was a bottle of white wine on the nightstand, mostly gone, and she was holding a glass, resting it between her legs. Her fingernails were red, like her lips. She didn't say anything at all – she just pulled me down. Those were the times I wanted her the most and it wouldn't happen. I wanted her because she wanted me, but there was a short in the wiring somewhere and the whole thing got turned into fear. Mr Night is someone who doesn't have that problem.

'That night, I got to thinking about myself. Annie finished the bottle, got sick, passed out. I saw myself from the outside for a

249

while, and what I saw was a good guy. A good cop. A man who married his high school sweetheart and tried hard to make a good life for her. A man learning the law. A guy who didn't drink much or smoke. And you know what I wondered? I wondered if I might be better off – if we both might – if I wasn't such a goddamned Boy Scout.'

Jim pulled on the oars, said nothing.

'You know something, Jim? I've had this feeling ever since I saw Annie down at the Back Bay, that when I kill the guy who did it, I'll be . . . complete. That I'll be worthy of her. That all the times I couldn't do what she wanted won't matter anymore. That when I kill him, I'll kill that thing inside me that failed. That somehow, she ended up that way so I could become the man I always thought she wanted. Dumb, huh?'

'Yeah.'

'I want to tell you something else,' said Raymond. 'As soon as I read that letter about Annie and him, there was a voice inside my head. The voice says that Annie got what she deserved. I hate myself for thinking that, but it just happens on its own.'

'Some things aren't worth thinking,' said Jim. 'I'm not sure how you tune them out.'

Raymond's face was beveled in moonlight and darkness. 'Are you with me on this? If you're not, it would help me to know.'

Weir wondered whether Francisco Cruz had asked the same of his men, the men who had finally abandoned him to the bullets of Joaquin La Perla. For awhile, at least, the answer must have been yes. 'I'm with you, Ray.'

'Because you want to kill him?'

'Because I don't want him to kill you.'

'When we get way out on the edge, I hope you keep your footing.'

'I do, too, Ray.'

He eased up to *Sweetheart Deal* and tossed the line. Raymond climbed out, the Whaler shifting with the loss of weight, the beam of his flashlight crossing the rust stains on the hull. Jim took the lantern and followed him, feeling himself drawn into Raymond's net of logic regarding this ship: Ann protesting her sale after Poon's death, Ann cleaning her up once a year to beat the city dereliction notices, Ann clinging to this rotting vestige as if it was a direct link to Poon himself. In a sense, he realized, it was. He could see Ann in his mind's eye, reaching from the dinghy to steady herself against *Sweetheart Deal*, fingers touching the rough deck, knowing that the sea in which the old boat rocked was the same Pacific that had accepted Poon's scattered ashes, perhaps seeing herself as an agent afloat upon this great separating river, as a connection between Poon's underworld and the world of which she was still a citizen. Touch the ocean, touch the ship, touch the Father, a finger from above meets the finger from below, each outstretched and yearning. Ann, Daddy's girl. Ann, like Poon, the unfettered, the ulterior, the unloyal.

Jim realized as he climbed aboard that he hadn't been on *Sweetheart Deal* since his father died, a decade ago. The deck was pliant under his feet. She smelled of mildew and the acid of bird waste that had piled up behind the mast, blown in flight just slightly astern by the prevailing onshore breezes. Raymond's light led them through a squeaking door on which hung a lock too rusted to fasten anymore, and into the cabin. Jim, still shivering, lit the lantern. As the mantles glowed and the light gathered, he saw nothing that he was expecting.

The floor, repaneled in teakwood, was clean and shining. The walls were freshly painted a gleaming white, and there were bright flowered curtains over the portholes. The table was lowered from its stowed position, and covered with a simple white and pink checkered cloth. A single director's chair was pushed up neatly under it. The air smelled faintly of flowers from the multitude of sachets that hung, sat, dangled, rested in every possible nook or cranny. A bud vase stood in the middle, complete with a purple rose. Jim touched it with a fingertip: silk. Beside it were two candles in short glass sticks, each half-burned. The berth was made up carefully, with a spread that picked up the background blue of the curtains, a couple of fluffy pillows, and a knitted afghan folded on the foot. A half dozen stuffed animals were tucked up against the pillows: floppy-eared dogs, a rabbit, a koala, a big Mickey Mouse.

'I thought . . .' said Raymond. 'I thought she just threw this stuff away. It was . . . years ago.'

'I remember that dog from when she was a girl.'

'Didn't she used to have curtains like these in her room?'

'Yes. Mom made that afghan.'

'The pillows look familiar, too.'

'They're thirty years old, Ray.'

'Jesus. I can't believe this.'

Weir couldn't, either. It was like stepping into Ann's girlhood room, right down to the horse miniatures that now stood upon the Formica pasture of the galley counter. He looked at Raymond, whose mouth actually hung open, a slow waltz of astonishment circling in his eyes. The lantern hissed, glowed brighter. But the more Jim looked, the more he saw that this was not just a girl's cabin at all, but a woman's. Behind the model horses sat a row of books: the Hardy and Eliot that Ann always had loved, May's *The Courage to Create*, three volumes of Neruda, two of Marianne Moore, Márquez's big novels, Fitzgerald, Toni Morrison, Joan Didion, Anne Tyler, and Elizabeth George. Holding up the books at each end were two bottles of wine, all four of them expensive cabernets. Two wineglasses stood to the left of the books, a bottle opener beside them. Next to that was a pack of cigarettes, with two extending from the open hole as if in casual invitation. Atop the pack rested a lighter in a simple silver case, around which was wrapped a roll of U.S. postage stamps. Leaning against the galley wall was one large bar of Belgian chocolate, unopened.

Jim's vision moved again to the fold-out table. At the far end, away from the chair, was a tumbler – one of Poon's old scotch glasses, he knew – filled with pens and pencils.

He looked at Raymond, who looked back. 'Where she wrote,' he said. 'The journal can't be far.'

But the leather-bound book was nowhere obvious. They searched the drawers and shallow cupboards, the stowage space beneath the berth and benches, the tiny shelf in the water closet, the railed compartments behind the countertop. It was not under a pillow or stuffed animal, not tucked into the space behind the fold-out table, not beneath the round pillow that Ann had set on the seat of the director's chair.

'Outside,' said Jim.

'She wouldn't leave it outside,' said Raymond.

'Well, Ray, it's not here. I'm checking outside.'

In the lantern light, Jim unlatched the two stowage holds. Raymond's flashlight beam sprayed across the life jackets and faded orange preservers, the buoys and nylon lines, the ancient green wool blankets, flares, spear guns, fishing tackle, Poon's old lever-action .22. They unfolded the blankets, pulled out the preservers and life buoys, then put them back.

'Engine compartment,' said Weir.

'It's going to be a mess,' said Raymond.

And that it was, an oil-caked Hades of grime and rust, what was left of a once-proud diesel that seemed to have somehow shrunk with time to little more than a blackened mechanical artifact.

Jim was lifting the lantern up for a better look when he saw the corner of plastic sticking up from under the plug wires. When he pulled, it slipped down and almost away – a surprising weight and mass. Carefully, he worked it out. The plastic was cut from drop cloth, with the four corners joined at the top by twine. Inside it was a brown grocery bag, folded over. It weighed at least a pound.

'We just passed Go,' said Weir.

'Take it inside.'

Jim set the package on Ann's table, carefully unknotting the twine and pulling out the paper bag. This he sat upright and unfolded, holding open the top with both hands. Raymond shone in his flashlight. Weir could see at a glance that there was no leather-bound journal. What there were was a small bundle of letters held together with more twine, and a stack of old school notebooks with covers of various colors. He took the letters out, untied the twine, and spread the envelopes over the tablecloth.

He picked up the top one, addressed in type to Ann Cruz at a post office box in Balboa, no return. Jim recognized the PO box number, one of Poon's old 'secrets' that somehow everyone in the family knew, one that Jim had long assumed was buried with his father ten years ago. The letter was postmarked on May 15 of this year, the day before Ann died.

> My Dearest Ann,
> Your decision leaves me broken and scattered, but
> I stand with you in this as I will in all things. I will
> wait for you on any distant shore. Go to your husband
> if you want; maybe that is best. Please, dear one, no
> mention of *Duty Free*, ever, to anyone?
> With Love and Affection,
> Mr Night

For the next hour, while Dwight Innelman and Roger Deak collected specimens and dusted for fingerprints, Jim and Raymond read through the letters to Ann, holding them to the lamplight in rubber-gloved hands, looking for the sentence, the phrase, the

253

word that might identify Mr Night. But it was almost as if they had been written with this in mind – they were general, obscure, shadowy.

In the end, to Weir, only three things were clear: that Mr Night loved Ann in a passionate, reckless way; that she was carrying his child, that he had known her, and she him, for at least a quarter of a century; that she was planning to end the affair.

He met Raymond's stare from across the table, a look so fraught with shame and helplessness that Jim wanted to turn away. But Raymond did first. He gazed down at the letter in his hand with the spent expression of a man whose entire flotilla of belief has just been blown to sea by a storm of cruel, undeniable fact. The comfort of denial was finally gone.

Dwight Innelman stood over the table with one of the wineglasses from the counter. 'The whole place is crawling with prints,' he said. 'Check this.'

Jim studied the white dust, saw the perfect thumbprint halfway down, the two lovely fingertips opposite.

Raymond looked up at him. 'What did she know about *Duty Free* that Mr Night was afraid of?'

'She saw the dumpers. Blodgett said they weren't close enough to make them, but maybe he was wrong. Maybe Ann saw more than he did. Maybe she recognized the boat.' Again Weir thought of Blodgett's implication, that Becky was doing the dumping, or at least someone using her boat was. No, he thought. Take a stand.

Raymond considered. 'Dave Smith?'

'Or call him Mr Night.'

Jim stood.

'Where now?'

'Phil Kearns,' he said, 'has an alibi for us to meet.'

Half an hour later, showered and changed, they sat in Jim's truck outside the Whale's Tale, watching as Sgt Kearns pulled away from the curb in a new Miata convertible.

Kearns had said it wasn't far. Jim followed him back out to the boulevard, then left. Fog was settling in again; the traffic was light. A fat moon hung like a spider in a web of clouds. Two miles down the peninsula, Kearns pulled into a driveway all but hidden by towering avocado and dense orange trees. Jim looped around and parked along the curb. Kearns nodded at Weir as he shut his car door and disappeared into the foliage around the old house. He was wearing a pastel linen suit, loafers, and no socks.

'He's got to quit watching so much TV,' said Raymond. 'And his alibi's going to be a chick.'

'He's got enough of them.'

Ray shook his head, tapped his fingers on the outside of the door.

Weir looked out. He could see a lit fraction of upstairs window through the trees, the silhouette of someone standing there. Kearns? The girl? How much had he rehearsed her? It shouldn't be hard to tell.

A moment later, Kearns came from the house, winding his way through the front-yard jungle. In front of him was a girl with bright blond hair. As they headed for the truck, Weir pushed his briefcase under the seat and Ray got out to let them in.

She climbed up and sat down beside him in a halo of perfume. Kearns squeezed in next to her, then Ray. She had on a pair of complex athletic shoes, thick socks pulled up over faded jeans, a T-shirt, and a denim jacket. Her hair was pulled up over her head, held in place at the roots by a rubber band, the rest of it falling down willy-nilly. She had a high forehead, a round little nose, pouting pink lips. Her eyes were large and filled with the confidence that comes from unwavering male attention and the notion, as yet unchallenged, that a girl can get by with a bod and a smile. She looked thoughtproof, about sixteen.

'I'm Lucinda Fostes.'

'Jim Weir.'

'Cool.'

Jim pulled out and headed back down the boulevard.

'Jim's got a few questions for you about last Monday night,' said Kearns. 'Answer him honestly. You don't have to hide anything, or protect me in any way. Got it?'

'Yeah,' said Lucinda. She was chewing gum. 'Go ahead.'

'Tell me what you were doing at midnight.'

She popped the gum, leaning forward to look out the window and point. 'My friend Kimber lives there. She's rich.'

'Sunday night, Lucinda,' prompted Kearns.

'Why don't you just tell him?'

'He wants to hear it from you. Go.'

'Okay, all right.' She sat back, crossed her hands over her knees, and shrugged histrionically. 'First I went down to Fry's – that's the market – and got a guy to buy me a six-pack. Then I went down to Thirteenth to drink it. I was kinda like pissed off at my ex-boyfriend, Sean, so I drank four of them and went to his house up on Twentieth. He wasn't home, his dad said. So I drank the other two rilly fast and went over to Charlie's Chili for a burger.'

'This is before midnight?' asked Jim.

'This is like, quarter 'til eleven. So after I ate, I stood around Rumple's for a while and listened to the band. I used to get in, but they carded me last month and I'm fully eighty-sixed now. So I just started walking, heading up Newport Boulevard.'

'Off the peninsula?'

'I don't know. I can't keep the peninsula and the mainland and like, all the islands, straight. I walked up the road, you know, toward like Costa Mesa. I was coming down off that swirly bridge when Phil pulled up in his cop car to talk.'

'How long have you known Phil?'

'Oh . . .' She chewed, gum snapping. 'A few months. He's my bud.'

'Then what?'

'He told me I should get home because it was almost eleven-thirty, and I told him I was hyper. So he said get in and he'd drive me around a minute, then take me home. So I did.'

Lucinda turned to watch Fifteenth Street go by. Weir noted Fry's Market on the corner, wherein she had scored her beer. He glanced over to Ray at the far end of the seat.

'That's where we like to hang in summer,' she said. 'Cool guys, hard bodies galore. Over there's where Lauren lives. She used to be Sean's girlfriend.'

'Where did you drive?'

'Well, over the bridge, then down Coast Highway to Balboa Island. We went across on the ferry and Phil dropped me off at home. It was one-fifteen when I got in. I remember because my grandma said something about it the next day. I'm supposed to be in like one at the latest.'

Raymond's voice had an edge. 'An hour and forty-five minutes to go from the bridge to the ferry to the peninsula? That should take half an hour. You barely made the last ferry run.'

Lucinda popped her gum and looked first at Kearns, then over to

256

Ray, then left to Jim. Weir watched the spray of her ponytail bobbing with the bump of the truck. She said something to Kearns that Jim couldn't make out. What Kearns said back was, 'Go ahead.'

'Well,' she said. 'We like walked.'

'Like walked.'

'Yeah. And talked. *He* talked. That took maybe an hour. Phil's always telling me to get my shit together and make something of myself. He's always telling me not just to give it away to anybody. By that, he means my body. He's always telling me if I get good grades and a couple years at a JC, I might get a clerk's job at the station. It starts at nine hundred sixty a month, so it's good pay.'

The hour in question, thought Weir. Kearns is clean if Lucinda is on the level. The idea hit him that she wasn't complicated enough to lie for anybody but herself.

She leaned toward Kearns, whispered something, then turned to Jim again. 'I might as well tell you I tried to get him to like do me right there in the car, but he wouldn't. Plus, I'm eighteen, so I can do what I want.'

'Guess so,' said Jim.

'Anything else?' she asked.

'No.' Weir looked past Lucinda's ponytail to Kearns, who was leaning back, eyeing him with a certain grimness. Kearns's eyes trailed down to her, then back to Weir, a regretting expression: Look what I passed up.

Jim suddenly U-turned on Coast Highway and headed back toward Balboa.

'Cool,' said Lucinda.

'Sure there's nothing else you want from her?' said Kearns. 'Ask away, Weir. It's now or you're out of my face for good. That was the deal. I'll have to tell Internal Affairs the same goddamned thing, if that makes you feel any better.'

'That's enough.'

Jim headed back down the boulevard in silence, while Lucinda pointed out highlights to him and Ray. Kearns had apparently had this tour before. It seemed as if she knew everybody on the peninsula: Colin lives here, Ryan here, Kate and Max right there. A thought struck him. 'You get around, don't you, Lucinda?'

'Well, I've been living here for a year, and visiting every summer from Michigan for like, ten.'

'See a lot of faces.'

'As much as anybody else, I guess.'

He slid his briefcase from under the seat – nudging her legs, at which she giggled – laid it across her lap, and flipped open the two latches. Copies of Goins's photograph lay on top, Dennison's enlargements for the door-to-door.

He turned on the interior light, shut the lid, and set the photo on top of it.

'How about this one?'

'Joseph?'

Weir felt a dose of adrenaline kick in. Raymond's clear, fierce eyes held his glance for a beat. He backed off the gas and held the truck in the middle of the lane as he turned to look at Lucinda Fostes. Kearns already had placed an assuring hand on her knee.

'Yeah, Joseph,' said Weir. 'Where can we find him?'

Lucinda held up the copy, gum popping as she studied it. 'Who's the lady?'

'His mother. Do you know where he is?'

She sighed, put the picture on the briefcase lid, and looked at Jim. A kind of snotty vacancy crossed her face, then dissolved. 'His name is Joseph Gray and he has a blue Porsche that's in the shop. He's Gramma's new boarder. He moved in yesterday.'

Weir floored it. From the corner of his eye, he could see Phil Kearns reaching under his coat to snap off the safety strap on his holster. He pulled up to a liquor store and slammed on the brakes. Ray was out before the truck stopped, throwing someone off a pay phone to call in backup. Thirty seconds later, he was back in and Jim's truck was screeching away from the curb in a cloud of tire smoke.

'Whoa,' said Lucinda.

'Was that his light I saw upstairs?' asked Weir.

'I guess so,' she said apprehensively.

'How many rooms upstairs?'

'Mine, and his, and the bathroom.'

'His is on the right, facing the street?'

'*Yeah*. Are you guys after Joe now, or what?'

'When we get to the house, you stay here,' said Weir. 'Don't move from this truck, not one inch. Do you understand me?'

'Yeah, but like, whoa . . . this truck's *fast*. What did he do? What did Joseph *do*?'

'Shut up,' said Kearns. 'I'll take the back door, Jim. You two head up front. Is there another way out, Lucinda?'

'No. You guys are like all over it.'

'Who's home besides your grandmother?'

'Nobody I know of,' she said, bracing herself on the dash as Weir ran the red light at Dillman's.

'Does he have a gun?' asked Kearns.

'I don't know.'

'No car?' asked Weir.

'It's in the shop.'

'What are you going to do when I stop this truck, Lucinda?'

'*Stay in it*. Gawd . . . wait 'til my friends hear about this!'

'Got a piece, Ray?'

'Ankle biter. Let's go.'

Jim slowed down before the house, turned into the driveway, cut the lights and engine, and pocketed the keys. He looked once at the girl.

'I'm staying,' she said. 'Don't worry.'

On the porch, they waited ten seconds for Kearns to find the back way in. Then Ray tried the door, found it open, and stepped inside. Looking down the entryway to the living room, Jim could see a white-haired old woman sitting up asleep on the couch. The stairs were to his right. He heard Kearns in the kitchen, saw his shadow on the floor. Two at a time, he took the stairs, wood creaking under the runner, one hand on the railing and the other holding his father's old .45. Ray was two steps behind. Jim stopped on the landing. Lucinda's room, away from the street, was dark. Down the hall and across from it was Goins's, the door shut and a faint light coming from beneath it. Jim lined himself up opposite the door, flicked off the safety, reached to the knob, and turned. Half an inch was all it rotated before stopping against the lock.

Weir stepped back and lowered his shoulder for the charge, but Raymond flew past him and slammed into the door.

With a shriek of breaking wood, it flew open, shot all the way back, and slammed against the wall with a thud. Jim, in a crouch, swung the gun, far left to right, his eyes drinking in the room as fast as he could make them. Ray moved left. Jim spun right, backed into a corner and scanned again over the automatic's sight. The curtains of the open window swayed inward. He swung, held. The curtains swayed back. Weir dove to the floor, landing hard on his belly, the gun pointing under the bed. He rolled up, ran out of the room, down the hallway to the empty bathroom, then into

259

Lucinda's perfume-heavy lair, a place of rock-star posters, stuffed animals, clothes thrown everywhere.

Raymond was already there, slipping his gun into its ankle holster.

Back in Goins's room, Jim really looked at everything for the first time: the computer on the desk, the cardboard box beside the bed, the pair of old-fashioned ladies' eyeglasses sitting on the pillow with a piece of paper under them. The paper said, 'I found your glasses, Mrs Fostes. Love, Joseph.' Standing at the window, Jim guessed the distance to the thick branch of the avocado tree. Six feet max, he thought, easy enough.

Kearns blew in, a storm of pastel linens with a shiny 9mm auto.

'He cleared,' said Jim.

'I'll call Watch. Window?'

'That's my guess.'

'*Shit.*'

'He can't get far. Hurry up, Phil.'

Weir waited in Horton Goins's room while Kearns went into Lucinda's and made the call. He slipped the gun into his holster and knelt down beside the box next to the bed. Shirts, shorts, two cameras, a sheet of proofs, a razor and shaving cream, a hairbrush, toothbrush, and two pairs of white and black checkered tennis shoes.

A sudden shadow in the doorway sent a fresh surge of alarm up his back. Mrs Fostes, squinting terribly, steadied her rocking head of white hair at Jim. 'Who *are* you?'

'Police, Mrs Fostes – kind of. I'm sorry.'

She stepped in slowly, Kearns standing now in the hall with a 'Let's go' expression on his face. Raymond slipped behind Mrs Fostes – taking advantage of her considerable blind spot – and started down the stairs.

'Where's my granddaughter?'

'She's okay. She'll be right up.'

'Is Joseph here?'

'He left. I don't think he's coming back.'

Mrs Fostes's tired old eyes did their best to behold Weir.

Jim fetched the glasses from the pillow and slipped them on her. They settled perfectly into the dark indentations on either side of her nose. Mrs Fostes's eyes burned into Jim's.

260

'Where did you find these?'

'Joseph did,' said Weir. 'If you see him again, call the Newport Beach Police immediately.' He could hear Kearns's footsteps pounding down the stairs, and Lucinda's voice in the entryway.

'Why should I call you?'

'He's a murder suspect, Mrs Fostes.'

'Oh my.' She looked around the room once, as if her new eye-sight were a gift from God. 'There was something strange about him. But he was decent enough to return my glasses, wasn't he?'

25

Knees pumping, the thin tire vibrating on the road just below him, the curved handlebars of the borrowed ten-speed tight in his clenched bleeding hands, Joseph slid through the fog and blurring lights of Bayside Drive, drawn by a growing, beckoning purpose.

The urgent breathing around him – did it belong to him, or was it the scoffing recognition of every light that bore into his eyes, every car that swept by so close that he could feel its accusing breath on his arm, every set of eyes behind the darkened windows calling down to the hunters of the world, *the killer you seek is southbound on Bayside – surround him, capture him, shoot him down in the dust of his own madness?*

Joseph thanked God for the city map he'd studied so long and hard as he charted Ann's movements all those lonely, thrilling weeks. Darkness here, a narrow winding road, banks of ivy green-black in the night, the comfort of fog and close houses all the way into Corona del Mar, all the way to The Meeting.

His legs were burning and his lungs seemed too small, but Joseph did his best to find a rhythm to sustain him. The biking helmet fit perfectly. His hands upon the bars were sticky with blood; the splitting flesh sent blades of pain up into his wrists and forearms. *Up, down, in out, keep to the side, forget your hands, I was a fool to think I could live in the same house as a girl who thinks cops are cute.*

He could feel the pack balanced on his back, the weight of Ann inside it, beside his best 35 mm, ten rolls of film, a few portraits stuck inside a *National Geographic*, a clean pair of socks and two T-shirts, two ripe avocados from the tree he had used to escape. The black road charged under him, split by the trembling narrow tire. He pushed up on the handle-bars, raised his aching head, then settled back into the rhythm.

At Marguerite, he waited for the WALK sign while his chest pumped and his legs jittered with the effort of standing. When he stepped off the curb, his knees buckled, spilling him into the cross-walk, the bike toppling on top of him. Music blasted from a café on the corner. Two young men helped him up, looked at him strangely, and told him to take it easy. A black Porsche screamed off Coast Highway and flew past, its blond driver screaming with the radio, her hair trailing back like a white-hot flame. So many lights, he thought. So much noise. The helmet helps hide me. Cross the street, Joseph – you are not a child – put one foot in front of the other . . .

Across finally, climbing carefully onto the curb, he leaned forward into the long, gentle uphill road that would lead him to Ann, to The Meeting. Ann would be there, but would he show? Did the letter get through, did it convince him? He put the thought from his mind. He was too tired to believe that anything more could go wrong. He checked his watch: early.

Joseph stood at the foot of Ann's grave, just a rectangle of earth still darker than the ground around it. Why was there no headstone? He listened for her, and in his mind he talked to her, trying to offer comforts that, even though he meant them from his heart, still sounded inadequate and thin. It was hard to believe that only a few feet of earth now separated them, after he had worked so hard, come so far, come so close. It was good to feel this close. It was like a small drop of contentment added to an ocean of confusion, and a small drop was better than none at all.

He climbed back up the walkway to the big marble mausoleum, sat down, and rested his back against the cold wall. He turned and looked around the corner at the path down which he would come, if he came, a few minutes from now, according to the letter. His chest ached; his hands were swollen and filled with pain. The bicycle rested in the grass beside him, one wheel turning slowly in the cool May breeze, the helmet resting on the spokes of the other.

He closed his eyes and listened to the chatter of the dead. There is still time to leave all this, he thought. Enough money for a bus to somewhere. Emmett and Edith might help him flee – or would they? No. This is the path I've chosen.

As his heart began to still, Joseph pried into his pack and took out the tattered *National Geographic* of January 1987. It opened automatically to his picture. There he was – his brain, rather –

263

displayed in the eerie neon colors of positron emission tomography. He looked down at the picture again for . . . what, he wondered, the millionth time in his life? His mind, as displayed, was a swirl of yellows and green, with the offending thalamus burning red-hot against a background of white. That is it, he thought, the source of schizophrenia, the key to me. He read the cutline again, although he had long since memorized it.

> Peephole on mental illness (above) is offered by this positron emission tomography (PET) brain image of a violent schizophrenic. An overactive thalamus (red – right of center) is compensated by a correspondingly active frontal lobe in healthy people. This young man's frontal lobe, as graphed by the PET scan, shows what scientists are finding with increasing frequency in the mentally ill – suppressed activity. The lobe (top – dark blue) shows little metabolic life. Scientists are now wrestling with the question of whether the suppressed frontal brain and overactive thalamus are genetically developed. Early findings of Dr Winston Field at University of California, Irvine (top right), suggest that schizophrenia may have viral causes that can be traced back as far as the second trimester of fetal development. Two percent of Americans suffer from schizophrenia.

Joseph looked at the picture for a long time, focusing on his agitated thalamus, trying to imagine in his real brain a calming, a deceleration of all that . . . *speed*. That is what it felt like in there: something going faster than it should, slipping and burning while one part careened out of control, like a tire flung from a race car as the rest of it choked in the smoke caused by the fire.

This is the reason, he thought. This is the reason I am what I am. I am not cruel. I am not hateful. I simply am wired wrong. I am defective in production.

He folded the magazine shut and slid it back into his pack. He felt better. But even with this picture of his trouble, Joseph could never find absolute rest. There was always a part of him that was afraid of the other part. What scared him most wasn't the strange faraway feeling that sometimes gripped him and seemed literally to pull him a few steps back from reality. He, with the help of the Navane and later the Clozaril, could control that slide away from the actual. What scared him was that at some point he became unaware of himself, and could not for the life of him explain where he was, what he was doing, or how he might have gotten there. One of the first times it had happened was with Lucy Galen in Hardin County. He could remember the story he had told her about the swamp – the money he'd found in the suitcase. He could remember her driving them out there, and he could remember the odd fact of having taken along a knife. But after that, there was no clarity, no remembrance, no hint. He recalled nothing of their walk to the swamp, nothing of ever pulling the knife, certainly nothing of stabbing her repeatedly as Lucy had testified that he had. Nothing of rape, no . . . nothing of ever having touched Lucy Galen.

Nothing of having ever touched Ann Cruz.

No, he thought, *I did not do that. I did not do that. I did not . . .*

Joseph looked out over the graveyard toward the fog-hidden Pacific. He spun the tire on the ten-speed, checked his watch: one minute to go. He lay his hands palms up on his lap and felt the burning pain.

Joseph stared at Ann's grave. How stupid, he thought. How stupid and young and wrong I was – none of it, none of it, none of it should ever have happened. It had all begun to change just two years after Lucy, in the Lima State Hospital, with Dr Nancy Hayes. Slowly, she had unraveled him, then put him back together. Slowly, the pieces began to fit. Slowly, he reconstituted himself, one sharp, angular, painful shard at a time, until the vessel was complete again, or at least as finished as it was ever going to be. It was Dr Hayes who had taken him to Dr Field, who had seen his problem for the first time, and given him, finally, the right drugs. Strange to think back now, thought Joseph, and understand that it all begins with knowing who you are. You know nothing in life – even with a color picture of your own brain – until you know who you are, and where you came from. Everything that is good follows from that.

Joseph heard the engine growing louder as a car wound up the cemetery road, came into the parking lot, circled around to the chapel. It was a muscular, throaty engine that shut down without a ping or a rattle. A door opened and shut. There were no footsteps for a moment, then the dry tap of shoes on concrete.

He has come, thought Joseph.

He leaned back against the cold marble of the crypt, drew up his knees, and held them close. The footsteps crunched down the gravel walkway behind him, each one louder, each one more filled with the specific sound of parting rocks. The smallest breeze issued past Joseph as the man moved past him, toward Ann. From the back, he looked tall, wide-shouldered but slender. He wore an overcoat. Both hands were lost in the side-pockets – would he bring a gun? Him. The man continued on to Ann's grave, stopping where Joseph had stopped, at the foot, looking down now, hands still deep in the pockets of his overcoat. He stood there a long while, looked once to his left, once to his right, once behind him up the path that he had taken.

Joseph's heart slammed into his chest. He could feel it knocking against the dried-sweat crispness of his shirt. He stood. 'I'm here,' he said.

The man's head turned, then his body pivoted toward Joseph. Joseph sensed threat, but he moved onto the path anyway. One step at a time, he drew nearer: twenty feet, then ten, enough, close enough to see the breeze lifting the man's dark brown hair, close enough to see the lined shadows around his mouth. A thousand voices inside Joseph were screaming a thousand different things. Beneath the roar, he heard himself speak.

'I'm Joseph Goins.'

'Hello, Joseph.'

'All of the things I said in my letter were true. The papers I copied from the lawyers are genuine. They never knew I was there.'

'I want to believe you. Come closer.'

His voice sounded so honest. Joseph moved into the dull moonlight. He watched the man's eyes prying into him. It was one of the hardest looks he had ever felt. It was more penetrating than any doctor's, but more curious and forgiving than any cop's. 'I'm not sure what I want,' said Joseph.

'I think I understand what you want. Some of what you want.'

'I didn't kill Ann. I would never kill Ann.'

The man said nothing. Could he blame him?

'I followed her for nine weeks, and took pictures of her. I wasn't sure . . . what to do. I saw her, up close, only once.'

The man looked down at the grave for a long moment. 'I might understand what you felt.'

'I'm afraid. The police are everywhere. Did you bring them with you?'

The man shook his head. 'No. There are things about you, Joseph, I don't want the police to know.'

'And things about Ann.'

'Yes. Things about Ann.'

'Do you want me to go away?'

The man hesitated. 'I wish you hadn't come. But now, you're here.'

'Do you wish I hadn't come enough to kill me?'

A long silence. 'No. Of course not.'

The breeze blew against Joseph's face, swaying the eucalyptus beyond the graves. The man's hard look came back: It seemed to dismantle him. 'I don't know what to say now.'

'Do you have a place that's safe?'

'No.'

'I can give you one, if you want it.'

Joseph's heart jumped. It was beyond the very wildest hope he ever had allowed himself to have. Was it a lie? 'I need a place.'

'Will you be quiet, until we figure out what to do?'

'I'll be silent.'

'You can come closer.'

'I'm afraid of your hands.'

The man pulled them slowly from his pockets, then let them fall to his sides. His face was handsome, lined, sad. It reminded him of his own. He offered his hand. It was strong and moist and confident. 'Did you see me that night?'

'Yes, sir. I saw a lot that night.'

'You must be afraid.'

'I don't believe I killed her. I wouldn't do that.'

'No. We should go, Joseph,' he said.

'Let me get my things.'

As Joseph gathered up his pack from beside the bicycle, he looked down the pathway to see Mr Cantrell standing at the grave of Ann – his mother – head bowed in silence.

In a way that he could not comprehend, Joseph Goins had more peace in this instant than in all of the twenty-four anguished, bewildering years that had led him here.

267

26

Thought: the first temptation. Small thoughts at
first, always pleasant, always manageable. But betrayal
and love both happen by degrees. They're like two
snakes, patiently swallowing the mouse of marriage
from different ends. To be honest – honest to myself
– I have to say that I think about David incessantly.
Mostly, I wonder about who he really is, how he's
managed to affect me so strongly after not seeing him
for twenty-five years. I want to expose the change in
him, see for myself exactly what his success and power
had cost him. I want to know what he was hiding.
Aren't we all hiding something? Sometimes, though,
all I can think about is *what if*. What if we'd run away
like we said we would, what if we'd had that girl and
she'd been born alive, what if we'd married each other
like we promised we would when we were young,
dumb, gloriously in-love kids? I want to see him. Not
to be close, really, but just to see. Who is this man?
Who am I, to be drawn to him, still, again?

Over the past three weeks, I've seen him seven
times, always at night after work. Twice, he's come in
for a late dinner, where, of course, we are polite and
formal. We write every day, almost. He signs his letters
Mr Night because we joked about not existing in
daylight. The first three times I saw him, we took the
limo, but I made a crack about preferring something
on a more human scale. So there I am, walking
through the alley at 11:30 on a cold, windy night, and
there's no limo in sight. There's just a busted-up old

Volkswagen bug, and David's at the wheel, all wrapped up in a thick coat. No Egyptian cotton and Italian linen, just a pair of jeans and a faded rugby shirt and the jacket. But the windows of the bug are darkened so no one can see in. Pure David. We roared down Balboa to PCH, then headed south into the Back Bay. He had a bottle of brandy wrapped in a brown bag, which we passed back and forth. Cut the chill, and went straight to my head. We drove through a chain-link gate and into a dock that said PRIVATE.

I gave the bottle to him and he took a swig. The sight of C. David Cantrell drinking brandy from a paper bag was something just too wonderful for words.

So we walked the Back Bay with the wind to our backs and the brandy going back and forth between us. When we were way out in the middle of nowhere, he turned to me, offered his arm, and I took it. Ann, he said, I can't get you out of my mind. I saw you on the *Lady of the Bay* and something jumped up inside me I didn't know was there. I get up in the morning, and there you are. I go through my day, and every second I'm not completely focused on something, there you are again. I go to sleep, my head a few inches from Christy's — and all I'm thinking about is you. I'm afraid she can hear it, sometimes.

You might be surprised, I said.

He looked at me sharply and we walked farther. The moon was low over the hills, a perfect half, like it was cut with a knife and the other part had fallen out of the sky.

Can I ask you something? he said.

He brooded for a minute. What is there about a brooding man? Please ask me something, I said.

What . . . what are you *doing* here?

I was surprised at how little I wanted to be asked that question. I'd managed to avoid it. Not so much to avoid it, but to glide over it, consider it a mystery unfolding, a flower not to be picked. But the moment he asked, I knew the answer. I asked him if he remembered the Seabreeze.

269

He looked at me, his face a pale oval in the darkness.
I knew he remembered it, *our* place, just a dumpy
motel down the peninsula – no view, no pool, no
TV. That was where he took me when I was fifteen
and he was twenty-one and still in college, our little
love nest, our world of damp sheets and sweat and
smells. It sounds now like nothing more than an
almost-grown man taking advantage of a girl, and
maybe in a court of law you could prove that's what
it was. But that wasn't it at all. It was the place and
time I first felt love for a man, and it was a love so
pure and uncomplicated, I never forgot it. One night
we had spent hours in each other's arms – like the
other nights there – and we just knew it was time.
I wasn't terrified – I was famished. I wasn't after
pleasure – I was after completion. I told him I was
ready for him, and he unfolded my arms from around
him and my legs from over his, and he touched me
from top to bottom with his warm, patient hands, and
a hundred years later he kissed me and I guided that
hard, wet knot into myself and I felt totally, absolutely
invaded, punctured, possessed. I could feel myself
hurtling through dark space. I could feel Ann the girl
falling away from me. And it wasn't an anguished fall,
but a contented one, and in her place I felt for the
first time Ann the woman stepping forth into being.
I felt trembling, given, and, strangely, empowered. It
didn't hurt as much as I thought it might. What I
remember most about that night is lying there with
him afterward, my head against his chest while he
stroked my back, feeling, *knowing*, that I now occupied
the world as a woman, that my world was small and
simple and bursting with love, and that this world
would never be so secure again, never be so complete,
never be so welcoming. These were moments to
be honored. Nine months later, lying knees-wide in
that hospital in upstate New York, came the coda I
somehow knew would end this lovely little beach-town
symphony. Life and love, truth and consequence,
birth and death, all neatly arranged in a bacteriostatic

room of gleaming metal and hovering, masked forms
– the employees of fate itself. And not once, not even
when the pain finally took me out – or was it the
drugs – would I have done it any differently, as if that
mattered at all.

'I wondered if I could feel again what I felt then,'
I said. 'I know that there aren't many things in the
world that could sound more ridiculous. I guess I've
gotten dumber in the last twenty-five years.'

'No,' he said quietly. 'No.'

And what of Raymond, my husband of two decades,
my companion, my brother, my man? Dear Raymond,
if you ever were to read this, your heart might break,
but if I could explain it right, you would see that what
I did was never meant to be at your expense. Is this
my grandest lie of all? Maybe. I will admit this: My
love for Raymond was never like my love for David.
To me, Raymond was a refuge from the loss of Little
Warm and David, a way to put aside what I'd felt at
the Seabreeze. David was a world; Raymond was a
living room. But I needed that room so badly. And
if I never felt for him what I knew I was capable of
feeling, that never once meant I could not treat him
with respect and kindness, help build him as a man,
be proud of him, focus my torn, divided affections
on him. It does not mean I ever once wavered in my
duty to him as a woman and a friend. It does not
mean that I ever stroked his dark hair with anything
but tenderness, that I ever diminished him in order
to control him. I invested in Raymond all the faith
I had to give, the ultimate faith, maybe. I believed
he would love me forever, even when the days came
and he would want a child that I could not give him.
And there was one other difference, too, between the
two men, a difference that became more and more
important to me as the years went by. David may have
called up something I couldn't find again, but Raymond
needed me. I may have craved being in the orbit of
something larger than myself, but I was honored that
Raymond would let me be that for him. No two people

271

can love each other equally. I loved Raymond less than
he loved me, but never – at least never until now –
did I exploit that. Years ago, Raymond's look began
to harden and his movements took on the first jittery
attitudes of anger. His distance grew wider and deeper
and his silences seemed to stretch for week upon
week. The basic struggle of life finally began to dull
him and transform me – in his heart – from someone
he wanted to please into someone whom pleasing was
an exhausting, impossible obligation. But never, *never*
did I ask him to love me more, or better, or again, or
even at all. Not once did I make a demand or utter
a disappointment. Half a year ago, when he stopped
making love to me, stopped touching me at all, in
fact, I let him without complaint move into whatever
thing was calling him. It seemed the very least a barren
woman could do for the man she'd married, fully
aware of her limited future. But right now, incredible
as it seems, I can truly say that the more I think about
David – and what happened that night – the more I
believe that my marriage is not in question. I believe
that my marriage is strong enough to take this. If
there is a wrong calculation here, there will be much
suffering ahead, for all of us.

So we drove to the Seabreeze. I registered. Same
room, same smell off the ocean, same traffic spinning
by just a few feet away, same damp mildewed air and
wrapped water glasses and little bars of pink soap. It
was all the same, only smaller. When we took each
other in our arms, it felt like we were coming together
from a thousand miles apart. I was absolutely terrified.
The room was spinning and I was spinning with it,
around David the fixed center. I almost laughed at how
preposterous this was, but he kissed me. Then, slowly,
his familiarities began to come back: the stiff muscles
in his neck, how long his lashes were when he closed
his eyes, the patient hunger, the comforting smell of
his breath through the brandy – the same after twenty-
five years! So I didn't feel like laughing anymore and I
just fell into the spin and let him take me to the bed.

272

Did I get it back, that feeling I'd had all those years ago?

Partly. What I felt when we were done this time was not that my whole life lay in front of me, but how profoundly it all had changed. I did feel again that lostness inside this man, the irresistible pull of him. But as I lay there beside him and looked out to the cold, clear night, I knew that what was ahead for us was not a love that promised togetherness and marriage and a family, but a love that promised heart-break, confusion, and treachery. And yet, for a few moments, I was someone different; I was not Ann Cruz of the two jobs and the distant husband and the dumb routines of the same neighborhood I'd lived in for all my life. I was Ann Weir, a woman desiring and to be desired.

And let me say this to you, Dear One – even though you'll never read this – I knew when we finished that night – the blessed night of March 23 – that you were inside me, beginning to grow. No scientist on earth can tell me that a woman can't *know*.

I knew. It was like stepping into a dream you've always had. I lay back in that little motel bed and closed my eyes and said a prayer of thanks for *you*. And I asked God to show me what to do, this unvirgin Mary with child whose husband hadn't touched her in so many months.

Joseph Goins marked his place in the journal and went to the big sliding glass door. Through the vertical blinds, he could see below him the soft illuminated blue of the lap pool, the palms and bird of paradise lit from beneath, the grounds receding into darkness and fog. The ocean surged and crashed somewhere far below.

It had been the most remarkable ride of Joseph's life – not the ride itself but what was going through his mind as it happened. Down the hills from the cemetery, sitting beside *Mr Cantrell*. Down Coast Highway, off on some side streets, through a gate that parted with a remote control, up a long pine-lined driveway, and into the wood and glass compound built around a huge central fountain. Mr Cantrell had said it was a house he maintained but

273

rarely used. He said that for now, it was his. A man named Dale would be there, too, to get Joseph anything he needed. Dale was large and pale-eyed, with sandy hair and a battered face. Long before he noticed the subtle rise of a gun in the small of Dale's back, Joseph recognized him as a man capable of extremes. It had to do with the arrogant way he moved his body through space, the unwitting craving of resistance. He was a man who had prepared himself to be deployed. But there was a certain truth in Dale's handshake, even though Joseph's fingers were split and burning. Dale said that he'd be around until morning. Mr Cantrell told him he'd be around as long as he told him to be.

David Cantrell had hugged him once rather formally, then turned and marched across the pavers, past the fountain, and back into his car. Dale showed Joseph to his room, then disappeared.

Joseph, dislocated as a Mandingo slave newly arrived at a Key West dock, had sat stunned in the fancy rattan chair in his new 'home.' Ideas streaked and fell across his mind like shooting stars. His heart raced, then slowed, then pounded, then seemed to stop altogether. He needed focus. He needed a purpose. He needed his mother.

He looked out the window now, feeling again the rush of confusion, the pull of too many possibilities. Dale lumbered lightly across the pool area below. What a weird guy, thought Joseph. He went back to the bed and picked up the journal again.

APRIL 6

I can't stop. I don't want to. On the nights I can't
see him, it feels like my body just might drive over
there on its own and wait. I can't go when Raymond is
working the peninsula beat – that would be an insane
risk. When I don't go to David, I take one of Mom's
dinghys out to *Sweetheart Deal* and write in this
book. We meet in his beach house down the peninsula
now – safer than the Seabreeze and a lot nicer, too.
Sometimes we go aboard his yacht, *Lady of the Bay*.
It was *his* boat we met on again, and I didn't realize
it for weeks! I get there at eleven, after work, use the
garage-door opener he gave me to slide in unseen, then
shower upstairs in the big bedroom, put on some fresh

clothes – or not – and wait. Sometimes, if I'm late, I'll change at work in the downstairs rest room and hope nobody sees me between the door and my car. I can see the ocean from the bed, twinkling across the sand. He always comes at eleven-thirty. Then we have until twelve-thirty, when I have to shower again, then dress myself on trembling knees, and go home. One hour. I live for it, and I feel, all this time, your presence inside me, Dear One, so patient and so warm. You, my miracle of all miracles, my secret life!

To my shock, Raymond has begun to seem happier these days than at any time in the last year. There is a minor intimacy in his looks, a gentle, growing lightness when we talk. I see him watching me sometimes when he thinks I'm not noticing. Little bits of that old adoration seem to be coming back to him. It is wonderful to see. And it is so necessary, so absolutely important, to what I want to accomplish.

Dear One, though you will never read this, I must tell you that I know what I will do, already. There was never any doubt about it. In the strangest of ways, *you* have given me everything that I had ever wanted in my life, and in the strangest of ways, *you* have given the same thing to Raymond.

APRIL 10

I believe I am being watched. I will also be the first to admit I am afraid, vastly afraid of being discovered, but still, when I discount my fear and look at the facts, I have to believe that I am being watched.

First was that time back in February, at work. I was lacing Tyler's shoestring and I felt eyes on me. When I looked up, there was this kid up the sidewalk, standing still while a gaggle of tourists parted and passed by him, looking straight at me and Tyler. He turned, joined the crowd, and disappeared. I say a kid: He looked about twenty maybe, an average beach kid.

Then a couple of days later, I got the feeling again. When I looked around, I didn't see anyone, until I

275

noticed one of those little dinghys they rent at the
Pavilion, and there was a man sitting in it right
offshore, with a camera held up to his face, aimed
at me. A big yacht slid by between us, and when I
looked again, the dinghy had taken off. The first thing
I thought was Raymond. He hired a man to shoot me
and expose my unfaithfulness. But why shoot me with
the kids? Then I wondered if it was David. No. Why
would he want me photographed?

I asked Ray about it, and he said I was probably just
making it up. But, he said, the best way to expose
a tail was to double back a lot, and keep an eye out
for who was still behind you. So I tried that a bunch
– walking to work on the nights I wasn't going to
David's, going back and forth to the preschool, strolling
down the bayfront on my Sunday afternoons off. It
never worked. Like I said to Ray, it wasn't that I was
being followed, I was being *watched*.

He said it was the mark of a guilty conscience.

We were up early, Ray getting ready to head up to
school for a contracts examination, I bound for the
preschool.

But I don't *have* a guilty conscience, I said. You can
imagine, Dear One, how guilty it truly was.

Maybe you just think you don't, he said with
a smile.

Well then tell me, what is it I feel so guilty about?

God, I wonder if my color showed. I have to hand it
to myself, I'm a pretty good liar. So was Poon.

I don't know, he said. You'd have to tell me.

He was looking at me with calm interest.

I nodded, glanced at the newspaper spread out on the
table before us, and thought before I spoke. 'The only
thing I feel guilty about is not being able to have your
children.'

'Then you'd have felt followed – watched – for
fifteen years. Have you?'

No, I told him. Just a couple of weeks.

Ray was quiet for a while, looking down at the paper.

I could arrange surveillance, he said.

276

I told him not to. God, imagine that.

I'm serious, he said.

For a moment, he looked like a boy, *acting* serious.
There is something so decent, so genuine about
Raymond. That something, if I had to name it, is
generosity. Even if he thinks I'm making something
up, he's generous enough to suspend his disbelief
and put himself in my shoes. Jim – your Uncle Jim –
always said Raymond was a good cop because he could
anticipate. I think he's a good cop because he can put
himself in the bad guy's shoes. Sometimes I think that
it has broken my heart to betray him. But it hasn't,
because my betrayal has yielded you, Dear One, the
great gift to us.

A long pause, Raymond looking at me. I can tell
you, as a thirty-nine-year-old woman who isn't totally
dumb, that Raymond Cruz has the most penetrating
eyes on earth. They cut in without hurting you, they're
so sharp. I have always found it astonishing how hard
Raymond tried to turn them off, how often he just
blinks and turns away while his eyes are cutting in,
ready to snip off the truth like a cluster of grapes from
the vine. Sometimes I think it's because he's afraid
of what he'll find. Sometimes I think he's just being
polite. I'm sure he doesn't offer his suspects such
courtesy.

But that morning, he didn't turn them off me.

Is there something going on, Ann? he asked.

Like what, baby? I don't understand what you're
asking.

His eyes kept coming in – exploring, finding?

'I'm asking *you*, Ann.'

'Well . . . no. I feel good. Everything except that
feeling of being watched.'

He waited. Raymond can wait for hours.

But I can escalate.

Maybe you're right, I said. I'm still willing to talk
about adoption.

He looked back to his newspaper, sipped his coffee,
shook his head. No.

277

I have held out for adoption for years. Sometimes I could almost feel that bawling little bundle in my arms. But deep down inside, whenever I imagined that bundle and knew that it was neither mine nor his, all the joy drained out of the scene and I felt only falsehood in it. Even though I'd offered this option to Raymond as unflinchingly as I could, there was never the conviction behind it I would have wanted. Certainly, that Ray would have wanted.

But beyond that, there was the other reason we never adopted, the bigger reason. Hope. We were still both under forty. We were still healthy, even though my uterus was destroyed – damaged, I know now – by infection after Little Warm. Raymond thought the scar and the damage was from an acute appendectomy I had had in France. France is where Poon and Virginia told everyone I was going, as an exchange student. I told Raymond about the operation before we got engaged, when he was sixteen and I was eighteen, and there was never any question from him. When the gynecologists later pronounced me unable to conceive or carry a child, I pretended to be as shocked and disappointed as he was. In so many ways, ways that I'll never be able to express to Raymond, I truly was. But still, there is that grand, eternal, lifesaving illusion called hope, and Raymond would never let it go. Maybe it was the saints he prayed to, maybe it was his faith in the Virgin Mother, maybe it was the only log floating in the stormy sea around him that he could grasp. Since we first 'discovered' I couldn't bear children, Raymond never once has capitulated. He never once admitted defeat. He used to read to me all the biblical tales of women who were barren, rewarded by God with sons and daughters. He used to pray with me for long hours, begging for a child. Only in the last two years have I thought that Ray really began to doubt, when he enrolled suddenly in law school, when his embraces started to vanish and his words to dry up and his interest in me as a woman seemed finally buried by the thousand burdens that plague this decent, trusting man. And I? Who was I to blame him? I wish I could tell you this, Dear One, that until you came along I had begun to lose hope, too. Hope. Perhaps we will name you that, if you're a girl.

We can keep on trying, I said.

I'd like to, he said, his ears flushing red. He swigged down his coffee, stood, and leaned over and pecked my cheek.

I'm late, baby. Have a great day.

You, too, I said. I'm okay, baby. Don't worry. This thing about being watched, just my dumb imagination.

'I love you,' he said.

'I love you, too,' I said, like I always did. There was more truth in it than I knew, Dear One.

APRIL 15

I am three weeks pregnant, as confirmed by the drugstore test. Of course, I already know that!

I stopped by St Mary's Church and went in, and knelt down before the pew and prayed. But I prayed with one hand in my lap and the other upon my womb, feeling for you, Dear One, feeling for you. And I prayed for Raymond to make love to me, *soon*.

APRIL 17

David sat on the bed as I told him. At first, he disbelieved, then, slowly, it all sank in. I told him I had decided to have you, Dear One, for Raymond, as Raymond's. I told him that for a while – a long while, probably – he and I should not see each other. It was simply too dangerous, and too difficult for me. He listened to me, then he came over and put his arms around me and let me cry on his shoulder. I still can't tell you whether they were tears of sadness or tears of joy – maybe both. Then he pulled away and looked at me and said that he would help me in any way he could. Love me, I said. Let me count you as a friend.

I do, he said. You can.

He went to the window and stood with his back to

me, looking out to the sea as if it were a future that he hadn't planned, developed, built, created for himself. A future imposed on him, instead of his imposed on everyone else. Truly, it was. He looked so helpless.

I assured him that your future, Dear One, was in my hands, and mine alone. That you and I had a family to start, that we would orbit away from him to form a little galaxy of our own, that we were really a family of four and that I would be tied to him by love and by you, Dear One, until the day I died. And as I looked at him, I could see the trenches of disappointment in his face, the etchings of defeat.

I understand men. I understand that greatness is a louder call than decency, that ambition is a stronger desire than love. I understand that to be a great shortstop you must love a white leather-covered ball of twine more than anything in life. That to be a great general you must love the risk of war more than peace. And that to be a land developer you must love buildings and land and money more than you could ever love a near middle-aged waitress you knocked up in high school and knocked up again twenty-five years later in a motel that smelled like mildew.

So I understand what he said next, but I will never forget how small it made him seem, how small and shrunken it showed him to be.

'You won't ever talk about the *Duty Free*, will you?'

The *Duty Free*. She was a cute little Chris-Craft that belonged to Dale, a Newport cop. Mom rode along with him on the Toxic Waste patrol, to find out who was dumping in the harbor. I went along, too, twice with Mom. One time, we saw the dumpers' boat, but I could hardly see it at all in the fog. Only Dale really saw it, or *said* he did. Another time, I tried to go out, because I was home alone on a night I couldn't see David and I was out of my mind with nerves. So I went to where they kept *Duty Free*, where Mom and I had gone to meet these men – Cheverton Sewer & Septic – and I watched Dale and Louis Braga fill the bait tank with canisters of something from Blake-Hollis

Chemical, and load on a bunch of fifty-five gallon
drums, too. Their jaws dropped as I walked up and
asked them if I could go along. But I played dumb.
I acted like I hadn't seen them fill the tank or load
the drums on board and cover them with a tarp. And
when they told me it wasn't a good night for me to go,
I humbly accepted and apologized and gladly left. Of
course, I knew who owned Blake-Hollis. So one night
later, being more frivolous than anything, I told David
I knew his secret: I knew the Toxic Waste patrol was
dumping more into the ocean than they ever prevented,
and if he had a heart as big as I thought he did, he'd
stop it. Since *he* owns Blake-Hollis, that is.

You would not believe, Dear One, the look on your
father's face when I said that.

He was furious. I thought I knew by then when he
was innocent and when he only wished he was. He
asked me for everything I knew about *Duty Free*, over
and over again. What I'd seen and who had been there.
He even wrote something down. While he paced the
room, he gave me the most hateful glances.

Then later, so very casually, he asked me if I'd
said anything to Mom about loading the stuff onto
Duty Free.

I told him no. And I wouldn't. I don't mix politics
and love, Dear One, and I hope you never do. As far
as I was concerned, David could just as easily get his
henchmen to dump somewhere else. I told him I was
doing him a favor, because deep inside, I knew that
Mom or someone like her would catch him sooner
or later.

He said again he knew nothing about any dumping
by one of his companies, and that he would look
into it.

I doubted then that he was telling me the truth,
but never since that day have I had a solid reason to
doubt him. David is too thorough to have something
so obvious land in the lap of someone so disinterested
as me. It wasn't like there were fish dying everywhere,
or birds dropping from the sky. The drums might have

281

been full of water for all I really knew. Plus, with all
the money he gives away to charity and hospitals and
the college – millions every year, I've read – I figured
maybe he really *didn't* know what Dale was doing
with the Blake-Hollis Chemical waste.

But I was surprised to have hit such a sore spot. I
decided to leave it alone. I was not put on earth to
rectify David Cantrell's soul, I thought. There are more
capable agencies around – in heaven and on earth – to
deal with that.

But there it came again, on the day I told him about
You, that fantastic fear he had of what I had seen. Dear
One, I was shamed for us both.

'David,' I said quietly. 'Your secret will die with me.'

APRIL 18

Raymond found me in the bathroom this morning,
sitting on the toilet seat, crying. His eyes looked down
on me, those cutting dark blades, and I almost told him
everything. Almost. But I diverted him again. I played
into the one thing I can always get his attention with –
and told him I was crushed for the millionth time that
I couldn't have his child.

Then it happened, what I had been craving for so
long, what I needed to accomplish my plan. He reached
down, pulled me up from the toilet, and kissed the
tears off my miserable, slobbering face. He led me into
our cold little bedroom and put me under the covers
and climbed in naked beside me and covered with his
tender mouth every inch of my body and made love
to me. And when I looked up at him, Raymond – my
husband, my brother, my man – he was crying, too,
big tears spilling down onto my face, and I drank them
into me along with everything else he had.

And when it was over, he said to me Ann, can we
start again? Can we please start it all over and love
each other like we used to? It's been so long and I
want you so much and there's nothing in the world I
love like you.

It is amazing how clear the answers can be, once the questions are put. From the very beginning of this whole thing, in my mind at least, there was never any doubt about what I wanted from Raymond, where I hoped that we would someday arrive.

'Please,' I told him. 'Please let's do that.'

I have never in my life uttered a sentence that I meant more, or that seemed more filled with the glorious scent of hope.

I will wait two weeks before I do another pregnancy test. We will run it together, so my surprise will be his surprise. We will have a party to announce the unannounceable!

Joseph marked his place and slid the journal under the bed. Outside, the night was at its tightest, the deep weave of darkness and silence at 3:00 A.M.

It's amazing, he thought, that Ann didn't see what was going to happen. Even I can tell, just from reading it.

27

By the false light of dawn, Jim pulled his truck into Virginia's garage and wearily climbed out. He had dropped Ray off at the station and Kearns at Lucinda's. His body was aching; his thoughts were racing to no particular destination. They had spent four hours cruising the peninsula, the island, the mainland, hoping for a sight of Horton Goins, but the man had disappeared like smoke.

Jim let himself in through the front door and immediately sensed the emptiness of the big house. Mom will be at the Locker, he thought, getting ready for the breakfast crowd.

But the sign on the window of Poon's Locker read CLOSED FOR THE DAY. Weir noted his mother's hurried handwriting, looked through the smoked glass to the lifeless interior – chairs still up on the tables, salt and pepper shakers on a tray for refilling, the grill cleaned and waiting.

Back in the house, he found her note to him on the kitchen table: 'Be back in a day or so. Patriots purloined this tape from the developers and I want you to view it and watch carefully. See if you can find why they decided to reshoot. Love, Mom.'

It was a standard videocassette. The label on top said 'GROW, DON'T SLOW! spot for June 1–5.' Jim groaned, took it into the living room, slipped it into the machine, and hit Play.

C. David Cantrell – slender, groomed, wearing a white shirt, a striped tie, and an open cardigan sweater – stood atop an overpass on the San Diego Freeway. Behind him, a river of cars was stopped in both directions for as far as the eye could see. Cantrell, arms crossed in friendly adamance, said that this was the daily scene in coastal Orange County now, thanks to unexpected growth, a booming economy, a lifestyle coveted by the nation. Taxes paid for this highway, he said, and all the new people will be paying millions more for the privilege of living here. The road – like so many others – was earmarked for improvement. Which would happen on schedule, *if* Prop A wasn't passed. Proposition A, he said, would do more to aggravate the traffic mess in Orange County than all the development put together: No new building meant no new business, no new taxes, no solutions to this kind of mess. Suddenly, the picture was changed to the same overpass at a different time of day – 6:00 A.M. – Weir guessed. Traffic was light, moving along behind Cantrell. He uncrossed his arms and put his hands on the railing, then leaned forward. Don't be suckered, he said, vote no on Prop A. *Grow, don't slow*. Leave Orange County's problems to the experts, not the elite, not the bureaucracy that got us into all this. Cantrell smiled as the cars whisked by behind him. A voice-over said this ad was paid for by the Citizens for Sensible Traffic Solutions. The picture went to snow and static.

Weir sighed, wondering when his mother would quit trying to convert him. She seemed too eager for life to conform to her dire predictions. Where was she now, out on the bay again, taking samples?

. . . view it and watch carefully.

He rewound it and played it again. So what? Big lies for gullible people. It was a story as old as the country itself: the land of dreams sold to too many dreamers. Maybe the committee was going to retape it because Cantrell's hair was messed by the breeze.

Jim was sitting on the seawall with a cup of coffee in his lap when a Newport Beach cop car pulled into the alley behind him and stopped.

Raymond, uniformed and fresh for the day shift, stepped out and nodded to him. He slipped his stick into his belt and walked over to the wall.

'Any Goins?' Jim asked.

'We're on the train stations and airport. OCTD has got the photos and a description. A lady down by Lucinda's said her son's bike was stolen off the porch sometime last night. My guess is that Goins used it.'

Raymond sat down next to Jim and slipped on his shades. 'Look at all those animals. It's a shame.'

Weir watched as a cormorant sloshed to shore, its dead webbed feet folded shut like little umbrellas. 'How's it feel to be back on the job?'

285

Raymond didn't answer for a while. His radio squawked and he turned the volume up for a moment to listen, then back down. 'It feels okay.'

'But?'

Raymond shrugged. 'How about taking a little drive with one of Newport's finest?'

Jim drained off his coffee and tossed the cup in a trash bin. 'Just like the old days, Ray.'

'Well, we keep saying that, but it sure doesn't seem true.'

They cruised down Balboa toward the Wedge, past the commercial district and then into the neighborhoods of the rich. Raymond was silent, locked behind his shades in that calm but alert way that he'd always had. For a moment, Weir was back ten years to his days on the Sheriff's with Ray; they were both still shy of thirty, both still filled with eagerness and the belief that the only direction their lives could go was up. Youth, thought Weir, what a blessed thing.

Raymond glanced over at him. 'Like I said, the idea was to get back on patrol and maybe just get too busy to think about things.'

'That doesn't really sound like you, Ray.'

'Yeah, well lift up the ticket log there on the seat and take the bottom stack of papers out.'

Weir picked up Raymond's log and slid out what was under it. The pile came apart in his hand like a new deck of cards: Horton Goins's photographs of Ann. So, he thought, Raymond has spent his first two hours of patrol working on the murder. Was there ever any doubt that he would?

'I don't blame you,' said Weir.

'Wouldn't do you any good to, Jim. Check the top picture – tell me what it implies.'

Weir slipped it out: Ann climbing into the backseat of the limousine on that cold March night. 'What was this one called?'

'Joyride – March 21.'

Weir stared down at it. 'She's real pleased to be seeing this guy. Look at her dress, the shine on her shoes.'

'What about him?'

'He's got money for a car and a driver.'

'How do you know it's his driver, not a limo service?'

'By the way he's looking away. He's letting his boss know how confidential this all is.'

Raymond nodded. 'That's what I figured when I first saw it.

Innelman ran an ownership listing for every home within three hundred feet of Annie's Toyota. I picked it up first thing this morning. It's under the pictures. Check the second page, halfway down, and see if you can put the name together with Cheverton Sewer and Septic.'

Weir found the listing and turned to the second page. C. David Cantrell's name was in the middle.

'He owns Cheverton Sewer and Septic.'

'Exactly. And a guy that Cheverton's people say doesn't work there is the one who sent the roses and wrote to Ann. Mr Night – Dave Smith. You do the arithmetic.'

'Dave Cantrell.'

Raymond's expression was a little pale, and a great deal agitated. 'Two days ago, Innelman got the credit card receipts for Ann's last night at the Whale's Tale. I found them in a pile of field reports about a foot high. Cantrell ate there, alone. Paid thirty-six bucks for dinner and left fourteen for Ann. I didn't think anything of it, until I saw the listing. Now I can't get all this out of my head.'

Jim let the possibilities sink in. No matter how he turned them, they wouldn't fit. 'Cantrell stands for everything Annie was against. I don't think so.'

Ray nodded, then cleared his throat. 'Jim – let's be honest about something here, okay? Ann was a great woman, she was bright and beautiful and good, but she was sick to death of our life together, sick of me, sick of that cold little house, sick of it all. I think we can assume that much. Say you were her, what would *you* want? What would your antidote be to all that?'

'Something different. Someone completely different.'

'Mine, too.'

Jim sat back as Raymond answered Dispatch – disturbing the peace complaint up on Fifty-sixth Street. Lt Cruz told her to let Unit 5 take the call.

'Too bad that garage-door opener is in evidence,' said Jim. 'We could run a little experiment.'

Raymond looked at him, grinned, opened the glove compartment, and took out the controller and two new AA batteries. 'Checked it back out an hour ago. It's mine until noon.'

* * *

They cruised back down to Cantrell's beachfront address. From a distance, Weir could see that it was a large but standard 1950s job – stucco, clean angles, a flat roof. It was painted white. Raymond was heading up the alley toward the garage door when he cursed and slowed. 'Down in front, partner,' he said. '*All* the way down in front.'

Weir slipped off the seat and into the foot space, hunkering with his head against the shotgun clipped to the dash. 'Company?'

'Umm-hmm. Cantrell's got security all over the place. I see one in the alley by the house, and another on the street. I'll bet there's someone out front, too, keeping an eye on the door.'

'Patrol cars?'

'No way. Dark sedans with cool dudes sitting in them. They look like FBI. I think I'll just run a little test, then keep on going.'

Jim watched as Raymond lifted the controller, pushed the button, then pushed it twice again.

'Up, stop, and down,' said Ray. 'It works. It's his.'

Weir felt the patrol unit start to move again. 'Why'd he leave it in her car?'

'He forgot. Like he forgot and left a hair under the stamp, like he forgot to get that car the hell out of his neighborhood. If he'd just stabbed her twenty-seven times – God only knows what was going through his mind.'

'I think our next stop should be the PacifiCo Security yard, down by the airport.'

'You haven't lost your chops, Jim. I was thinking the same thing. Maybe you should have taken up Brian on that job offer.'

Weir felt the car engine working beneath his knees, felt Raymond accelerate out of the alley and head for the boulevard. When Ray completed the turn, he pulled himself back up.

Raymond looked at him from behind his shades. 'Most innocent citizens I know have their houses patrolled by private security goons.'

'Everyone I know,' said Weir.

Raymond told Dispatch where they were headed, then guided the car back up Balboa Boulevard.

Ten minutes later, they sat outside the chain-link fence that surrounded the PacifiCo Security yard near the airport. In the middle of the yard stood a newish building with a wooden sign that read PACIFICO SECURITY SERVICES. Surrounding the building were a handful of jeeps, two dark Buick sedans, and a dozen or so patrol cars with PacifiCo emblems on the front doors.

'Mackie Ruff's cop car,' said Ray.

'I'd say so.'

Weir felt his scalp tighten. The circle is drawing itself now, he thought: purple roses to Dave Smith, Dave Smith to Cheverton, Cheverton to Cantrell Development, Cantrell Development to PacifiCo, PacifiCo to Cantrell himself. Annie, what have you done? Where do Marge Buzzard, Dale Blodgett, and Louis Braga fit in?

'Play it,' said Ray.

'They had a thing. She met him after work to tell him she was pregnant and it was over between them. Remember the letter? About how talented and important Mr Night is? It fits, Ray. Maybe they'd walked the Back Bay before. He took her down there for one last night, positive he could keep her close. He'd sent flowers – Mother's Day. It was his way of saying that pregnant or not, he wanted her. Then it was just like in the letter – he wanted to own her, but Ann wasn't for sale. He went over the top.'

Raymond was nodding slowly. 'Ann's car was jimmied open, right? Her purse is still missing, right? She left it in *his* car. When he got back home, he had to get her car out of the garage. But Ann had locked it. So he broke in and used her keys to move it a few blocks away.'

Jim felt another little dose of adrenaline move through him. 'No. She couldn't get into the garage because the opener batteries were gone. He took them. Ann parked a block and a half away because that was as close as she could get. That's what he wanted – Ann not able to use the garage that night. He jimmied the door to make it look like a stranger took her. But he forgot to ditch the opener.'

Raymond's face was pale and sweaty.

Neither spoke for a long while.

'Well,' Raymond said quietly. 'There you have it. C. David Cantrell. He's handsome, isn't he? Rich. A rich, handsome, powerful man who took my wife and used her like a toy. God, wait until Dennison hears this. He's going to hate the good news.'

'Dennison won't do anything but get in our way right now. What we've got is all circumstance, Ray. We need to put Cantrell at the crime scene. We need to connect him to the Back Bay that night, with Annie. Sit tight. Don't spill anything to Brian yet. We need more.'

289

'We need to cancel him.' Raymond guided the car down Mac-Arthur toward Coast Highway. He looked out to the PacifiCo Towers looming in the west.

'Ray, let's take this one step at a time. We don't know anything yet. We're not sure. When we are – then we'll move.'

Raymond wiped the sweat off his face. His skin hadn't lost its pallor. 'I'm going to take him.'

'That's what Francisco thought a hundred years ago, but he didn't do it right. Patience, Ray. We'll get him.'

'Francisco didn't have something that I do. A friend like you.'

The 10:00 A.M. sun leaked meekly through the morning haze, warming the bayfront sand in front of Becky's house, where a volunteer crew of cleanup workers wearing FLYNN FOR MAYOR T-shirts had been employed by the candidate to coincide with the arrival of reporters at her press conference.

Jim stood with his back to the hedge of oleander that protected Becky's front yard from the usually tourist-laden sidewalk. The thought crossed his mind that he had hunkered against this same hedge years ago to ID one of Becky's lovers. He watched the cleanup crew dumping dead fish into burlap bags. The press conference was already in progress behind him, questions and answers at rapid-fire.

– Why did you take on the Goins case?

– It isn't a case yet. I'm trying to keep a miscarriage of justice from happening. Horton Goins is innocent and I can prove it if I have to.

– Who killed Ann Cruz?

– That's for the police to determine. My job is to protect the rights of a twenty-four-year-old man who's being hunted down for something he didn't do.

– What about what he did in Ohio?

– What he did in Ohio was nine years ago.

– The police have photographs of Ann, taken by Goins.

– Taking candid photos of various subjects has long been the photographer's stock-in-trade. Goins has been an enthused amateur photographer for five years. We'll show those pictures for what they are: pictures of a pretty girl taken by an admiring young man. The police also found pictures of boats, local landmarks, kids, sea gulls, houses, tourists, dogs, sunsets, and waves. I haven't read a single word about those in the papers you publish, or seen a mention of it on the shows you produce.

— Miss Flynn, this move to represent a defendant —

— A *suspect*.

— before he's even arrested or charged, is going to be construed by some people as a publicity move to promote your campaign.

— That's exactly what it is. Part of my promise as a candidate for mayor of this city is to see that the innocent are protected, the guilty punished, and Horton Goins isn't tried for a crime he didn't commit.

— Why attach yourself to such an unpopular issue?

— If it's so unpopular, why are all you here?

— Do you have inside information on the murder — being linked to the victim yourself?

— Yes. And I wasn't *linked* to her. She was the best friend I had in the world.

— What is this information, generally speaking?

— I won't speak generally.

— Anyone can make promises, Miss Flynn.

— That's why I'd rather speak specifically, Marcia. We have evidence showing that Ann Cruz was being harassed by an employee of Cheverton Sewer of Newport Beach.

— What evidence?

— I won't say until we have the man identified by name. That will be shortly — within the next forty-eight hours.

Good Christ, thought Weir. Shut up, Becky. You're only driving him underground. The idea came to Jim that Becky would pillory Cantrell whether they had enough to question him or not.

— Harassed in what way?

— He followed her, wrote her suggestive letters, sent her certain gifts, possibly confronted her bodily.

— Killed her?

— That's for Assistant District Attorney George Percy and Brian Dennison to discover.

— You don't agree with the way the chief of Newport Beach Police has handled this?

— I don't agree with the way he handles anything. Look out at that bay. Thousands of dead fish, hundreds of dead birds, water so poisonous that the sharks can't even swim in it. Brian Dennison has

291

a Toxic Waste squad of *one* officer, who works part-time only, who is paid almost nothing for his efforts, who has to furnish his own boat. The boat blew a gasket, then a rod, on a toxic-spill patrol a few nights ago. The bill is going to run about twelve hundred dollars, and not a penny of that is coming from Chief Dennison's department or the city of Newport. I'm making arrangements to pay it myself. At the same time, Brian Dennison has requested funds for ten new patrol units, eight more officers, a new computer network for the station, and more sky time for that five-hundred-dollar-an-hour helicopter he likes so much. He's got six point five million dollars in lawsuits pending against his department for brutality charges, a great many of which were brought by people who live in this neighborhood, grew up on this peninsula, and contribute regularly to the health, welfare, and character of this city. I believe that Brian Dennison can run his department any way he wants, but I do not believe for a moment that he should apply his dubious talents to guiding this city. Here, I'd like to show you something. This is Art. He's a little western gull who ate enough trichloroethane to make him good and sick; maybe he'll even die.

Jim peeked backward through the hedge and saw Becky coddling a sea gull. She stroked the bird's body, then held his blinking, astonished face up to the cameras. Becky's shamelessness had never lost its ability to surprise him, even though she'd learned most of it from Virginia. Maybe that's why men marry their mothers, Jim thought.

– My volunteers picked him up yesterday, huddled against the seawall right out front. This is what I'm talking about when I say we've got to manage the growth in this county, and start to take care of what we've got left. We all know that we didn't inherit this place from our parents; we're borrowing it from our children. Until Art can swim in Newport Harbor and eat his fish without getting sick or dead, I think we have work to do. Brian Dennison's campaign is bought and paid for by C. David Cantrell and the other big developers, people who believe that the first responsibility of this land of ours is to bring them huge profits. Developer Kathryn Thompson recently threw up a new mass-produced housing tract, named it the Laguna Audubon after courts decided she could appropriate that naturalist's name for her own marketing concerns. She used Laguna Beach's name, too – her Laguna Audubon isn't even in Laguna. Ms Thompson named the streets in her development after birds. And, of course, Ms Thompson assigned a 'theme bird' to each phase. Wipe out the birds, name housing after them. That, in my mind, is the kind of arrogance that typifies the development cartel.

– Why don't you debate with Dennison?

– Ask *him*. He's the one who refuses. Thank you, that's all. I'm going to get out the eyedropper and give Art here a bite to eat. I'll keep you all informed on these issues.

Weir listened to the communal grumble as Becky's front door slammed shut. He started for the gate, feeling an inclination to strangle her. A handful of print reporters hustled down the sidewalk for the nearest telephones. A couple of television crews shot Becky's cleanup crew loading up dead animals on the bayfront, cutting in front of each other for the best angles.

'Comment for Channel Five, Mr Weir?'

It was Laurel Kenney, looking lovely in her usual pinched way. She leaned her microphone toward Jim's face. The minicam operator behind her aimed his lens at Weir like some giant mechanical eye.

'None at all.'

'Is Becky Flynn making a campaign issue of the death of your sister?'

'Say what you think.'

'I asked what you think, Mr Weir.'

'I don't think there's anything I can say right now that wouldn't be construed the wrong way. No comment.'

'Are you and Becky Flynn still personally involved?'

Three or four bodies moved around Weir; notebooks flipped back open; cameras clicked and strobes flashed; another minicam pressed in, red light blipping. Laurel positioned the microphone closer to Jim's mouth. 'Are you and Becky Flynn still romantically linked, Mr Weir?'

'Oh hell, Laurel, who could possibly care?'

'Do you think Chief Dennison's investigation has been fair and impartial?'

'Sorry, I'm not going to answer –'

Suddenly, Weir was aware of a figure cutting between him and the media people. It was a broad, tallish shape, with a white blouse buttoned to the neck and an improbable ruffle at the throat. The thick gray-brown hair was up this time in a bun of severest attitude. Marge Buzzard shoved away Laurel Kenney with a large knotted hand, then turned her fury upon the minicam operators, pursuing first one, then another until they had backed off to her liking. They kept shooting. She marched back on thick heels, and brought the full focus of her intensity upon Jim.

'*Come with me,*' she ordered. 'You will tell no more lies about Cheverton Sewer and Septic.'

'God, you look good this morning,' said Weir, taking her by a trembling arm. 'Right this way.'

Wielding her like a weapon, Jim guided Marge past the clicking shutters and whirring video cameras, up the sidewalk past Raymond's place, past Ann's Kids, around the corner of Poon's Locker, and finally through the back door and into the coolness of the supply room.

Marge Buzzard wheeled and measured Weir with enraged eyes. 'You have no idea what you're doing,' she said.

'I was standing by the oleander.'

'Then that smart tart of a girlfriend you have – she doesn't know what she's doing.' Marge poked a stiff finger at Jim's face.

He caught it in his hand, squeezed, and guided her backward into the empty café. 'Don't you poke me again, Marge. You want to do business, you learn some manners. Now sit down on your butt, shut up, and get yourself together. I'll get some coffee.' He let go of her finger and took a chair from one of the tables.

He watched her as the coffee brewed. She sat primly, back straight and off the chair, head erect, one hand in her lap and the other dabbing her eyes with a lacy white handkerchief. Weir concluded that Marge Buzzard was – as Poon was fond of saying – crazy as a shithouse rat. He liked her. He set the cup of hot coffee down in front of her, along with a creamer and sugar.

'I suspect you've got something to tell me,' he said. 'I'm all ears.'

Marge's eyes bore into Jim's with a suspicion he could only characterize as boundless. She made Virginia look trusting. At the same time, she started sniffling again, a helpless, tiny sound like a five-year-old might make, accompanied by a dignified quivering of the chin. 'I've had enough of you people,' she said finally.

'What people, Marge?'

'Disrespectful people – hustlers, gossips, liars, cheats, ingrates
... just ... just people in general.'

'You lost me. Start from the beginning.'

Marge clamped her purse into her lap. 'Cheverton Sewer and
Septic was founded in 1959 by Richard Cheverton. We called him
Dickie. I was his first and only secretary. His wife ... well, that's
another matter. He was the finest man I ever knew, and our business
was honest. *Honest*, Mr Weir, do you hear me?'

'I do,' he answered, noting her ringless left hand.

'In 1986, when our company was bought up by Cantrell Development as part of PacifiCo, we had annual revenues of five point
eight million dollars against expenditures of two point six million.
Our after-tax profit was two point one million. It was a happy little
company of fifty-six employees.'

Marge dabbed her eyes again. Jim was beginning to see what
it was about the bottom line of a sewer company that meant so
much to Marge. 'After 1986, we maintained a profitable status
for another two years, but we were finally folded into Cantrell
Development's contracting division and all we were was a part of
PacifiCo's development wing. Our profitability suddenly became
...' She sniffed again, then straightened her back and looked at
Jim. 'Nonpriority.'

'I'm sorry.'

'Don't be supercilious with me. You think it sounds stupid, but
to me, Cheverton Sewer and Septic was a way of life.'

Weir was silent.

'They gutted us. They folded our septic and cesspool operations,
so our name wasn't even correct. All we were used for was sewer
construction on PacifiCo's new tracts. Even at that, PacifiCo
sub-contracted out sewer installation if other bids came in lower
than ours. The division we were part of made huge profits, and
ours got upstreamed as part of them. But we weren't allowed to
do outside work, so if no new houses were going up, we stood
still. I continued to keep a set of books as if we were a viable
company, and I can tell you we would have continued to grow
at an annualized rate of six percent if we'd been allowed to. Of
course, those books didn't mean anything.'

'No.'

'No.' Marge wadded the handkerchief into her big hand. 'As soon as PacifiCo bought us up, Louis Braga – the corporate flunky they sent – started getting all this attention from corporate. Dickie, who was retained as manager, didn't understand it, and when he questioned it, there were no answers forthcoming.'

'Attention?'

'Mr Braga received sealed pouches from PacifiCo headquarters, up on the hill in Newport. Louis Braga got calls from them. Louis Braga got a corporate credit card under the Cheverton Sewer and Septic name – even though we were really just part of PacifiCo. Well, Mr Weir, once a month when I organized the payables and billables, I'd go through our expenditures with a fine-tooth comb. Every other month, there'd be a nine-thousand-dollar cash withdrawal on our card, made by Dave Smith of Cheverton. Braga told me to pay it and account for it as a consulting fee. I demanded to know where nine thousand dollars of Dickie's – Mr Cheverton's – money was going, *with a man who didn't work for us.* Corporate called me up to Newport and told me not to 'modify' the way they were doing the books – Mr Braga knew the new system, if I had any more questions. The next week, I got a raise. But I know for a fact they'd have fired me if it wasn't for Mr Cheverton. He defended me to them.'

'So Braga and Smith could use the card. Who at PacifiCo had access to the Cheverton number?'

'I have no idea. We've never been a part of PacifiCo, as far as I'm concerned. It's what accounting calls an O and I card. That stands for Open and Incidental. Everything else is O accounts for Office charges or M for miscellany, or T for Travel expenses, like that. They're all credit accounts with suppliers. But PacifiCo can call nine thousand dollars every other month on a credit card incidental because their sales ran over six hundred million last year.'

Jim waited while Marge unraveled a corner of her balled handkerchief and dabbed an eye. It was time to go fishing. 'Did Mr Smith ever get mail at Cheverton?'

'Yes. It was occasional and often marked 'Personal and Confidential.' I never opened an envelope addressed to Mr Smith. I was under orders from PacifiCo not to. I gave it directly to Mr Braga.'

Letters from Ann, he thought, to Cantrell. 'There really never was a Dave Smith?'

Marge's expression suddenly looked more hurt than hurtful. 'I *told* you that when you first came out.'

'But you've been covering for him for five years.'

She nodded, a new storm of tears gathering in her eyes. 'When Mr Cheverton died in late 'eighty-six, I vowed to continue with the company, to do what I could to restore it to its former integrity. But it's not the same. It's shameful. The only thing the same is the picture of him I've got on my office wall. That's why I won't stand still for Dave Smith casting a shadow on the ghost of Mr Cheverton. Mr Cheverton *hated* what was happening to what was once his company, and I simply will not let his memory be further trampled. Not by you, not by that strumpet for mayor, not by the papers.'

'Are the nine-thousand-dollar cash withdrawals still coming through?'

She nodded. 'Every other month.'

'Who takes the cash?'

'Louis Braga, I assume.' Marge straightened her back and fixed her formidable eyes on Jim. 'I have no idea where it goes after *he* touches it.'

Jim waited as Marge took a deep breath. She composed herself behind wet, steel-hard eyes and stared down at the Formica tabletop in front of her.

'None at all, Marge?' he asked quietly. 'You of all people have no idea where the money goes?'

A flash of beseechment crossed her face, then vanished. 'No, really.'

'Ah.'

She glanced up at Jim, then away.

'But you've seen something that doesn't fit, haven't you? You're not stupid, Marge. You've hung around a little after hours, maybe? Checked the books real close to see if there's a legitimate reason for it? Spun by late at night, or maybe on the weekends to see what's happening? Maybe? For Mr Cheverton? Am I right?'

She cleared her throat and nodded. 'I intend to defend Mr Cheverton, not to cast suspicion.'

'Wake up, Marge – Mr Cheverton is being used.'

'Yes,' she said quietly. 'Yes, I do know that.' She blinked wetly, and wiped her eye again. 'It's just so difficult to know when to fight and when to retreat. All we really have to go on is our own convictions, sooner or later.'

'That's true,' said Weir. He leaned back in the chair. Give her room, he thought. He sipped his coffee and waited.

Marge Buzzard glanced quickly at him, then down into her coffee cup. Her perfume smelled of lilac. 'I've been thinking of retiring,' she said finally. 'It's not the same. Nothing is the same.'

'It's a terrible thing, to lose someone you love.'

Something indignant flashed in her eyes. 'He was the finest man I ever knew. Honest, caring. He . . . deserved more than he got from life, I believe. Yes, I loved him. But I was never improprietous. He was a married man, and I a . . . single woman. I honor the marriage contract, Mr Weir, whether it's mine or someone else's. If I had one, I mean.'

'Not everyone is so noble.'

'I'm a big ugly woman, Mr Weir, but I do have my strengths. Loyalty, conviction, a certain amount of bravery when it's called for.'

'I admired the way you tried to throw me off the property,' he said.

She looked at him in assessment. 'And here I come with the same things I was trying so hard to keep you from finding out.'

'Why?'

'I knew who you were from the papers when you came to us looking for Smith,' she said. 'I heard about Becky Flynn's press conference and I thought she might try to exploit us. But I'm deeply affected by what happened to your sister, and though I'm sure there's no connection between the larceny at Cheverton Sewer and Ann, still – your sister's death helped me see the importance of . . .'

Jim waited, but she didn't finish the sentence.

Marge's fingers wrapped around her coffee cup. She didn't look at Jim when she spoke. 'Louis Braga gave money to a policeman named Blodgett, on at least two occasions. I heard Mr Braga putting the cash into a shopping bag once while I was waiting for him in his trailer, and I saw him give Blodgett the bag that evening when I was working late. I can't say that all the payments have gone to him, but two did. I suspect the others have, as well.'

'Why does Blodgett get nine grand of PacifiCo's money?'

'*Cheverton's money!*'

'Cheverton's, I mean.'

298

Marge studied Jim intently for a moment, her eyes narrowed, her big nose pink from crying. 'I have my suspicions.' She brought her bag up from her lap and zipped it open. Out came a small jar. 'The bait tank of *Duty Free* was filled with this material last week. There were six large canisters, too. They always take out the boat after a truck from Blake-Hollis Chemical comes. I know because Louis Braga never reports to work the following day until evening, and the boat is not there. I believe that this . . . substance is delivered by the Blake-Hollis Chemical truck. When *Duty Free* comes back the next day on the trailer, the tank is always empty and the canisters are, too.'

'Is Blake-Hollis Chemical part of PacifiCo?'

'A subsidiary.'

She offered the jar, but Jim shook his head and refused to touch it. He asked her instead to open the lid.

The fumes were sharp and alien. The fluid looked like water. Solvent, he thought. 'It's probably 1,1,1-trichloroethane,' he said. 'That's how it got into the bay.'

'That's what I believe. I'll leave it to you to find out and proceed as you see fit. I *am not willing* to tell the police what I know. Not the Newport Beach Police. Not with a man like Dale Blodgett in charge of toxic waste.'

'How about a federal grand jury?'

'The grander the better, Mr Weir.'

'Miss Buzzard, you can't leave that with me. Take it and hide it somewhere safe, but don't let anyone else handle it. If you want to prove that this was dumped into the bay, you're going to have to account for the sample. I can't touch it now. Do you understand?'

She nodded.

'I'm going to ask you a question now that I want you to think about for a minute. The answer is extremely important.'

She snuffed, stiffened her back.

'Did you ever see my sister, Ann, at Cheverton, going out or getting ready to go out on *Duty Free*? She was blond, tall, pretty – I'm sure you saw her pictures. She may or may not have been with an older woman. Please think.'

Marge blinked and focused her fierce, wet eyes on Weir.

'No. Never.'

'Think again.'

299

'Never. I don't forget things. But I do remember this. One day about a month ago, Blodgett had come to see Louis. It was the same evening I saw Louis give him the pouch of money, the day after they'd had the boat out. They were in Louis's office, talking and laughing. I was watering those miserable geraniums outside his trailer, the ones that he will never stoop to water himself. The following is a rough translation of what I overheard. Louis said, "That was a close call last night." Blodgett said, "She had no idea." Louis said, "She walked right past the truck when she came in." Blodgett said, "There's a dozen trucks in this yard. Don't sweat it. If it was her mom, then we might have to worry. Virginia's the one to watch."'

'Virginia?'

'Yes. "Virginia's the one to watch." I'm positive. Who is she?'

Weir's vision had blurred for just a moment, then focused with remarkable clarity. 'Virginia is my mother. Ann's mother. They'd gone out with Blodgett and Braga on the Toxic Waste patrol. Apparently, Ann tried to go out once alone with them, on a night they were dumping.'

'Oh, my. And now she's dead.'

Weir stood up. 'Don't do anything for now. As far you know, everything is fine. Wait until I call you. Do Braga or Blodgett have any idea you know this?'

'I've been the model of circumspection for thirty years at Cheverton.'

'You've done a good thing, Marge.'

Marge stood, arranged the frilly collar high on her neck, and patted down her skirt. 'I feel like Judas must have felt,' she said.

'Judas betrayed Christ,' said Weir. 'You've just busted a couple of profiteers who might be killers, too.'

'I think I will take a few days off and complete my letter of resignation.'

'Don't do that yet. Be quiet. Act like everything is normal.'

'Normal? Really. We're going to be flooded with questions because of what that awful Flynn lady has said. We have something in common, Mr Weir – we both work for manipulators.'

The statement struck Jim with a certain force. 'Stand your ground, Marge.'

'I've never had any trouble doing that. It just always seems to have been the wrong ground. My letter of resignation is half-written. I shall finish it and mail it.'

'No. If you upset them now, it could be a disaster for you. I'm serious, Marge. They're serious.'

'It includes a one month's notice,' she said. 'I wouldn't leave Mr Cheverton with anything less than that courtesy.'

'Wait a month to send it. Will you do that?'

She sighed. 'I've stuck it out long enough with Cheverton. Another month won't hurt.'

'It might save your life.'

Weir was holding open the heavy back door for Marge when Becky came in. The two women stopped and stared at each other for a moment. Weir could hear Marge Buzzard's breath catch as she raised a hand to the collar of her blouse.

'You are simply egregious,' she said.

'You can call me Becky, Ms. . . .'

'Buzz*ard* with a *d*, like bazaar.'

Becky offered her hand, with a worried glance to Jim.

Marge let out a wavering breath, and walked past Becky into the dull spring morning.

Becky's face was dappled with sweat and her hair was sticking to her forehead. 'Did you watch it?'

'You're way ahead of things.'

'Not the press conference, the tape Virginia left.'

'I watched it.'

She looked at him for a moment, then sighed and wiped her hand across her brow. 'You didn't see it, though. Things are now in motion, Jim. You've got to see things for what they are.'

'I'll say they're in motion. You all but fingered Cantrell out there. We can't link him with the roses yet – not for sure. We can say he had an affair with Ann, but we can't prove it yet. We've got nothing to put him down at the Back Bay. Nothing. You're going to blow this if you don't slow down. You're going to drive him away.'

A cunning smile came to Becky's face. 'Come with me, Jim. You have to learn to *see*.'

Back in the big house, Becky pushed the tape into the VCR and stood back. Weir sat down at Virginia's desk and tried to avoid Becky's impatient glances. He read his mother's note again: . . . *view it and watch carefully.*

301

As Cantrell's image and homilies went past him, Jim searched the pictures for whatever it was he had missed. The first half of the spot was innocuous enough. Then the background switched to the blissful flow of maximum-speed traffic and Cantrell leaned forward onto the railing for his heart-to-heart plea. His sweater shifted with the move, his tie swung forward, then stopped. The camera moved in on his face.

Something tugged at Weir's brain. What was it?

He stopped the tape, rewound it briefly, then let it play again. Cantrell leaned forward, his sweater shifted, the tie moved and stopped, caught by the tie tack. *The tie tack.* There was a tiny reflective flash amid the stripes, two-thirds of the way down. The camera came in to his face; the little gleam dropped away offscreen. Jim rewound again and stopped the frame just as Cantrell's necktie caught on the tack chain. The focus wasn't great. But the shape was right; the size was right.

Jim could feel his skin tighten, his heart speeding up. 'We've got him. He was there.'

'We're miles from getting him, but he *was* there.'

'How did Virginia know about the tack?'

Becky shrugged. 'Ways.'

Jim was about to call Robbins when the phone rang.

'Jim Weir?'

'That's right.'

'My name is David Cantrell.'

Jim said nothing. Cantrell waited a moment. 'I think we have some things to talk about.'

'I think you're right,' said Jim.

'Can you be outside the Balboa theater in half an hour?'

'I'll be there. Hope you don't get stuck in traffic.'

Weir hung up.

Becky studied him closely, her dark brown eyes shifting across his face. 'Was it him?'

'It was him.'

The smile came to Becky's face, that cunning little grin that always put him on edge. She took a deep breath and exhaled slowly. Then she came to the table and knelt down beside him. 'From now on, everything has to be done right. You've got to go through Dennison to get to Robbins, and Brian won't help. What he will do is everything he can to cover Cantrell's ass. We need

302

the DA, and I can get to the DA. We're going to nail him, Jim. We're going to hang that guy.'

Weir sat back and stared for a moment up at the ceiling. Hang him? Ray is going to kill him.

'How long until you meet Cantrell?' Becky asked.

'Half an hour.'

28

The silver limousine appeared in the fog as if born from it. Weir stood under the theater marquee, back from the gathering mist that hung along the edge, then rolled off in droplets and darkened the sidewalk below.

A tall, crew-cut man in a gray suit stepped from the car, nodded to Jim, offered a tight smile, then reached into his coat and brought out a metal detector, which he ran over Weir's body – front, then back.

'Smooth operation,' said Weir.

'Sorry for the inconvenience, sir.'

'No piece.' The detector chattered unemphatically.

'We're more concerned with a wire, sir.'

'No wire, either.'

The man's eyes went past him, toward the driver, confirming harmlessness. He slid the scanner back into his jacket and opened the door for Jim. 'Thank you, sir.'

Weir climbed in and sat. Cantrell reclined in the far corner, the gentle beam of an overhead reading lamp trained on a folded copy of *The New York Times* that lay across his knee. The coach smelled of leather and cologne and executive decision. He offered Jim a manicured hand. 'Dave Cantrell,' he said. His voice was formal and smooth.

'Jim Weir.'

'I'm glad you agreed to come. I'm sure you're a busy man.'

'Business is a little slow these days, matter of fact.'

'I understand. You've had a lot on your mind with everything.'

'I imagine you have, too.'

Cantrell studied him, a wrinkle of surprise crossing his face. 'Well, yes I have. Jim, I want you to know how sorry I am about what happened to your sister. She was one of my favorite people at the Whale's Tale – she could brighten up a whole

304

night. I'm ... genuinely, deeply affected by her death – that way.'

Looking into Cantrell's face, Weir found a perfect correlative to the man's words: He actually looked crushed. Astonishing, thought Weir. The proposition hit him right then, that Cantrell was crazy enough to write Mr Night's letter to Raymond, and mean every word of it. 'I'm touched by your depth of feeling, Dave.'

Cantrell nodded and stared at Jim. He was medium height and build, dressed in a navy suit, a pale pink shirt, and a necktie with a bold abstract print. He wore tassled loafers and socks that matched the shirt. His face was tanned, and the smile lines at the corner of his mouth were there even when he wasn't smiling. Cantrell's hair was dark brown, wavy, combed back from a high forehead. His eyes were blue, the eyelids just a shade heavy on the outer edges, giving his face an air of understanding and wry humor. His hands were strong and heavily veined; the wedding band thin and simple. He looked like a man used to making decisions that didn't please everyone, then living with them. The beam from the overhead lamp formed a pale circle on his folded newspaper. To Weir, Cantrell looked just as he did on TV.

The car eased onto Balboa Boulevard, the privacy partition already up.

'I'm sorry about the shakedown,' said Cantrell. 'I want to keep things as informal as possible right now.'

'Bodyguards lend a friendly air.'

'So do tape recorders.' He leaned back and regarded Weir openly. 'Your relationship to Becky Flynn, and, of course, Virginia, aren't lost on me. I'm a cautious man, and I apologize if it comes off as suspicion.'

The limo made a U-turn past the ferry landing, then headed east up the boulevard. Weir sat back, committed to the idea of playing this one close to his chest, for right now. Let Cantrell put up his ante – whatever it is – then raise the hell out of him. If all Cantrell wanted was an early look at Jim's cards, the best idea might be to give him a peek at his best. While that was going on, there were two things he needed. The first should be easy; the second might not.

'I try to stay clear of the politics,' said Weir. 'It's not my game.'

'It's certainly Becky Flynn's. I watched a closed-circuit broadcast of her little press conference this morning. The media should love it. She's gunning for me through Cheverton and whatever she's dug up on those people. Would you say that's an accurate assessment?'

'I'd have to say so.'

'I thought you would, since you're doing her legwork.'

'She's got a client to defend and I'm working for her. Her case for Horton Goins took her to Cheverton, among other places.'

'What did you find?'

'Pretty much what she said to the press.'

'There's more than that or she wouldn't have been so bold.'

Weir shrugged. 'We'll see.'

'I'm sure we will, knowing Becky. And I wish her all the luck in the world defending Horton Goins, because I believe he is only partly guilty.'

Weir said nothing.

'The Newport Beach Police and the district attorney have damaging evidence against him. Brian Dennison and George Percy are competent men.'

Jim studied Cantrell again. The party line, he thought. No surprise.

Cantrell sat back. The reading lamp still shone down on him, its beam brushing his shoulder, then passing on to illuminate the circle of newspaper. A hair lay caught on top of his coat shoulder, wavering slightly in the draft from the air conditioner.

'However, I believe that Goins was merely used to commit the act. He was employed on behalf of certain people who are opposed to my political views – paid handsomely, I would hope. Now, the flowers found on Ann were allegedly ordered by someone at a company I own. They were bought over the phone, on a company credit card, so it could have been anyone with access to the card number. At PacifiCo, that makes about eight authorized people; at Cheverton, two more. Unauthorized possibilities? About twenty-five hundred. The card could also have been used by anyone outside the company who knew the number, or got lucky making a number up. It certainly could have been used by the same people who employed Mr Horton Goins. But who is the card holder? Cheverton. And who owns Cheverton? I do. Are you with me, Mr Weir?'

'So far.'

'Second, a tie tack was stolen from my beach house last month, along with some other things. It turned up at the murder scene, in

306

the hands of Mackie Ruff. A Detective Innelman traced it to the jewelry store where my wife bought it.'

'It also turned up on your video blurb against Prop A.'

'I know that. It was planted at the crime scene by Goins, as ordered. I'm positive of it.'

'How can you be positive?'

'Because, Jim,' said Cantrell, leaning forward, 'I wasn't there. I didn't kill her. I didn't know her. She waited on me at the Whale – occasionally – and we got along just fine. The sum total of my relationship with your sister was professional. She was a lovely, bright young lady and I liked her very much. I never physically touched her. I never made a pass at her, or her at me. And I'm not going to sit still while someone tries to set me up. Are you listening?'

'Very closely. Go on.'

'It's not lost on me – or you and Becky – that Ann's car was found a block or so from my beach house, or that I ate at her station the night she died. The police know it. Did you?'

'Yes. And nobody's accused you of murdering Ann. You're the first to do that.'

'Mr Weir, be as honest with me as I am with you. I'm not a stupid man. Becky is getting ready to make that claim; it's the trump card in her election run – and she's using you to gather evidence.'

'Becky's framing you?'

Cantrell said nothing for a long moment. 'Mr Weir, I'm a lot less eager to accuse my accusers than they are to frame me. If I knew who was behind this, I would go straight to Brian Dennison and George Percy. For now, I would have to consider Becky Flynn a prime candidate. Her offer to defend Goins might not be purely for the publicity. Have you thought of that? At some point, she not only could be defending Goins but defending herself, or people sympathetic with her views. Of course, she'd be immensely better off if Goins was simply found dead, wouldn't she?'

Weir silently acknowledged the monstrous logic. 'You'll never convince me that Becky had her best friend murdered. I've know her for more than thirty years. She's known Ann for thirty-plus years.'

'And I'd known her as a waitress for a few months. Where is *my* motive?'

Jim smiled slightly. 'Maybe your conscience is a little over-worked. There isn't enough to charge you.'

Cantrell shook his head at Jim, the lines of his face deepening. A plain and simple anger flickered in his eyes. 'Becky doesn't need me *charged*. She knows, as a lawyer, that she doesn't have a case. She just needs me slandered before June fifth, dragged in for questioning, linked to Ann in any way possible. God, Weir, open your eyes. You're being used, and so am I. One more point here, since you brought it up – you don't know the first thing about my conscience.'

Jim considered the unabated anger in Cantrell's eyes. 'You're probably right about that.' He took one of the fresh copies of Horton Goins's photo from his jacket pocket and handed it to Cantrell.

Cantrell took it, placing a glorious thumb directly onto the bottom-right corner of the print surface. 'Horton Goins,' he said.

'Have you seen him?'

Cantrell was incredulous. 'What? I've seen this picture in every newspaper in the county for a week, and you ask me if I've seen him? All of a sudden, under your intense cross-examination, I realize I've seen this guy?'

'All that must mean no.'

Cantrell handed back the photo, shaking his head. 'Idiots,' he said, mostly to himself.

Jim looked at the picture again, then slipped it back into his pocket. Fingerprints, he thought; one down. 'Sorry, never hurts to double-check.'

Cantrell stared out the window for a while, seemingly oblivious to Weir.

'I guess you'll be happy to see Horton Goins arrested,' said Weir. 'He can finger his bosses if George Percy puts enough pressure on him – I mean, if he's got any bosses. All in all, I'll bet you'd like to see nothing happen until after June fifth.'

Cantrell nodded. 'Dennison is using Goins to look good, and so is Becky. It's fair. What I'm saying is, the more Becky comes rapping on my door with "evidence" that I was involved with Ann, the more I'm sure that someone is creating a case against me. I'm asking you to consider the possibility.'

Cantrell studied him from the padded recess of the corner. The reading lamp was still trained on his paper. The hair stuck to his shoulder still wavered in and out of the beam. 'Weir, some things are more important than who wins this election. A woman's life has been lost. At least one innocent man – I –

308

am being implicated. Forget the election. You don't think Goins did it. Fine. If Goins didn't do it, he'll walk. But you and Becky should either get off my case or get into it far enough to find the truth.'

'What is the truth?'

'I didn't know her. I didn't kill her. The end.'

'Where were you the night she died?'

'At the beach house, reviewing a TV spot.'

'Alone?'

'Alone until almost midnight. Then home. I was with my wife from twelve o'clock on, but I'll be extremely unhappy if she has to make a statement to that effect. In fact, if it comes to that, there are a few things I want you to know. Mr Weir, you're entitled to your own uneducated, undocumented opinions. But if anything about my "relationship" with Ann gets to the press, or to my wife, I will take that as a personal attack. I will call on every resource I have, every bit of influence I've earned, every favor owed me, and employ every power of my organization to crush you, Becky, and your mother. Completely and without restraint. One fault of mine, Mr Weir, is that I relish destroying my enemies, almost as much as I enjoy rewarding my friends. First off, my attorneys have drafted a defamation of character and slander suit that will take your last dime just to defend – whether I win it or not. And I will. We'll be asking one hundred million dollars for personal and punitive damages – more than that if Prop A passes on the heels of a scandal. Named are Becky Flynn, Jim Weir, and Virginia Weir as chair of the Proposition A election committee. If the proposition fails, I'll see to it that Dennison exercises the city's right to eminent domain in your neighborhood, and that Virginia's home, Becky's home, Poon's Locker, Ann's Kids, and Raymond's house are the first to be leveled. I can do these things, Weir, and I will. Maybe you forgot, but I own that land – you just *lease* it from me. I met with you here of my own free will, to clear up some very unfortunate suspicions. I guessed that you are a reasonable man, and I see no reason to change that supposition. I'm asking you to show me enough respect to examine any suspicions before you make me crush you. You might think this is an economical way to steal an election that will affect the way I make my living. But I'll tell you – it will cost you, your mother, and Becky Flynn everything but your lives. Everything. I hope I'm communicating to you how serious this is.'

Cantrell knocked his knuckles on the partition and the driver moved into the left lane for a U-turn.

Jim watched Coast Highway revolve around the windows, saw the yacht basin to his left as they headed toward the peninsula bridge. 'Nice town, isn't it?'

Cantrell's face hardened again: A vein that Jim hadn't noticed before manifested itself above the pink shirt collar. 'Let me guess what you're thinking now,' said Cantrell. 'You are sitting here in this pretentious limousine, realizing what a pig I am. How my vision for this county is an abomination. You see me and people like me, and the Irvine Company, and William Lyon and Kathryn Thompson as just pumping dollars out of the ground, cramming more and more paying customers into smaller and smaller places, ruining what was once a lovely, simple place. Close?'

'I see that, sure. Who couldn't?'

'Consider this: I've built over eighty thousand homes in this county over the last twenty years of my life. People live in them, make love in them, and raise families in them. My homes keep people warm in the winter and cool in the summer; they don't leak, they don't crumble, and they don't fall down. Every year, they're worth more to the people who own them. I employ over twenty-five hundred people, from professional architects down to the night custodians. I pay close to sixty-five million dollars a year in various taxes, support artistic and charitable groups with another eight million, offer a scholarship fund every year for about a million more, and I offered to build a homeless shelter anywhere in the county, but the homeowners won't let me *because they don't want it in their neighborhoods*. Neighborhoods that I built for them in the first place. This is what you call rape? I'm not a gangster. All I'm trying to do is build houses, for chrissakes.'

Jim watched Cantrell settle back into his leather seat. 'There's a point when enough is enough,' said Jim. 'There's a point when you're selling an illusion and nothing more. I don't think a man like you knows where the point is.'

'Becky does? Virginia does?'

'I think so. They just live here, like they always have. This land

310

isn't a business proposition to them. You people aren't artists. You're merchants.'

'High sentiments from a man who scrounges for gold that other men have died for.'

'I'll die for it, too, if I stay in the game long enough. I've assumed that risk. Are you willing to die for the Balboa Redevelopment Project? Or when the pickings get slim, will you just pack it in and go somewhere else?'

Cantrell leaned forward and looked out the window. 'Look at the peninsula, Weir. Look at that grotesque Fun Zone. Look at the bars, the beat-up old houses, the traffic piled up, and the air full of poison. What's wrong with giving people a better place to live and work?'

'You're *selling* it to them, Cantrell. Besides, people don't want your gifts – they want you to leave them alone. And don't try to tell me – like you're trying to tell the voters – that all your new buildings and neighborhoods and shopping centers and roads are going to make the traffic better around here, are going to make the air cleaner.'

Jim was quiet for a long moment. The old neighborhood slid past the smoked glass of the limo. 'Too bad you didn't know Ann better,' he said. 'She was a lovely person. She was smart and happy most of the time, and she worked hard. She didn't complain. She enjoyed things. You'd have liked her.'

Weir studied the changes in Cantrell's face. What he saw was confusion.

'I *did* like her.'

'Did you know she was pregnant when she died?'

The shock that registered on Cantrell's face look practiced. 'No. Did she have kids?'

'You know she didn't have kids.'

Cantrell said nothing.

'Ann grew up here. Right here. She was a child of this place. Every time I look around me, I see something Ann did, something Ann would have liked to see.'

Cantrell looked at Weir without speaking. Jim watched the hair on his suit wavering in the draft. He pointed. 'Like right there, for instance. That little house coming up with the fence around it? That's where Annie had her first baby-sitting job.'

Cantrell studied the house more thoroughly than Jim had expected, then turned back to him. 'Nice place to grow up.'

311

'Then, there at the corner is where she wiped out on skates and got five stitches in her chin.'

Cantrell looked again, with apparent interest. Jim saw a distance in his eyes, a detachment.

'Over there was where her best friend lived, Becky Flynn.'

Cantrell was nodding now, still staring off at some indeterminate point. When he finally spoke again, it was in a dry, flat voice. 'The thing I liked best about Ann was her sense of humor. She'd say things that would sound cruel coming from anyone else. She'd say things like that about herself. She could cheer me up, just waiting on my table.'

'Right there,' said Jim, 'is where we got our first dog.'

When Cantrell turned to look, Jim leaned slightly toward him, pointing to the exact house. He gently swept his other hand through the beam of the reading light, just above Cantrell's shoulder, then closed his fist and brought it to rest beside him. He smiled when Cantrell asked him what the dog's name was.

'Cassius,' he said. 'A chocolate Lab.'

'Cassius,' said Cantrell. 'Did he change his name to Muhammad Ali?'

'Always just Cassius to us. Ann picked it from Shakespeare. She liked to read. She liked to write.'

'Ah, yes.' Cantrell looked at Jim, an assayer's stare. 'I'm sorry about Ann, Jim. Please believe that. I didn't mean to land on you so hard. All this talk of elections and campaigns and slander doesn't really relate to Ann, the flesh and blood woman. Just don't let them yank your chain. You seem like a good enough man to me. And I wasn't involved with your sister.'

'You liked her, though.'

'I told you that. She was . . .' Cantrell's voice cracked, trailing off into a sigh. He stared out the window the rest of the way down the peninsula.

When they reached the theater, the car pulled over. The man with the crew cut flicked a cigarette into the street, then stepped from under the marquee to open the door.

'Let me know if I can help,' said Cantrell, offering his hand. 'You can find me at the beach house for the next few nights. I'm sure Becky Flynn has the address and phone number.'

Jim, still palming the hair in his right fist, looked at Cantrell's offered hand.

312

'Mr Weir, you should know that I am capable of making things happen very quickly.'

Weir climbed out and let the man shut the door. Crossing Balboa Boulevard, he almost could hear the hair in his fist bellowing out for Ken Robbins's Crime Lab, screaming that it would match the hair on the letter from Mr Night.

29

The first thing Weir saw as he opened the door to Ken Robbins's office was the gray, sweating, unhappy face of Brian Dennison. The chief's eyebrows went up in tired astonishment when he saw Jim, and he stopped talking, mid-sentence. Robbins, behind his desk, with his hands crossed over his stomach, looked exhausted. Raymond, yanked from duty and still in uniform, wore the expression of a beaten dog.

'Have a seat, Jim,' Robbins finally said. 'We were just talking about . . . well . . . Brian, maybe you should put your cards on the table.'

Weir sat. Dennison scooted back to face him better. Raymond sent a stubborn look his way.

Dennison poked a thick finger into Weir's chest. 'I think Becky Flynn is manufacturing a smear against Dave Cantrell. That press conference of hers was a self-serving circle jerk. She's making all sorts of wild suggestions to fuck over the antiproposition people.'

'She's doing a pretty good job on you, too,' said Weir.

'Well, she's sure not doing it alone,' said Dennison.

'I'm working for her, like I told you.'

'Who tipped you to the *Sweetheart Deal?*'

'I did,' said Raymond. 'It was my idea. We were looking for Ann's journal, and it was the one place we hadn't checked.'

Dennison didn't miss a beat. 'And all these letters from Mr Night were just sitting there waiting for you?'

Jim wasn't sure where Dennison was going, but he now understood that the same printer had been used on the letter that was sent to Raymond. 'They were stuffed down inside the engine compartment, wrapped in plastic.'

'Becky didn't suggest you look there, did she?'

'No.' Weir looked again at Robbins, who was following the

314

dialogue without expression. 'Becky never said a word about *Sweet-heart Deal*.'

Dennison shook his head in disgust. 'You know, Innelman traced the roses to Cheverton long before you did. Cantrell launched an internal investigation that afternoon.'

'What did he come up with?'

Dennison waved through Jim like a salesman overcoming objections. '*Twenty-five hundred* employees come and go out of the PacifiCo Tower every day. Any one of them could have gotten that number, and you know it. When Cantrell finds out who, Becky Flynn's going to take a bath. Tell me this, Jim – whose idea was it to call the goddamned Petal Pusher in LA? Becky Flynn think of that, too?'

'I think it was Mom who called.'

'That's a distinction without a difference.' Dennison sat back, shook his head, then leaned his face into Jim's. 'Now Becky wants to defend Horton Goins . . . for *free*. Isn't that just fucking sweet?'

'Goins doesn't have any money.'

Dennison exhaled through his nose, a short, bullish snort. His eyes were hard and eager. 'Generous,' he said. 'I got some little white printouts with lots of numbers on them from Pac Bell, Weir. Becky's first call to the Goinses came on May twenty-first, the day before she announced she was taking on the . . . *case*. That was placed from Becky's home, not her office. And they got calls from *your number* on May twentieth, twenty-first, and twenty-third. Explain.'

Weir hadn't called the Goinses. It could only have been Virginia. 'I can't.'

'Explain this, Weir – your mother was sitting in the Goinses' goddamned living room when Innelman went over with the tie tack. Want to tell me why you and Becky and Virginia are all of a sudden so cozy with the prime suspect in your sister's murder?'

Weir tried to track the logic, but it wouldn't come. Becky's calls were understandable; Virginia's weren't. 'I don't know.'

'I don't either, and Poon's Locker has been closed all day. Where is Virginia?'

'No idea.'

Dennison stared at Jim but said nothing for a long moment. 'We've seen the video. Cantrell reported that tack stolen a month ago, with a bunch of other things out of his beach house. I've got

315

forms downtown to prove it. He's on the level, Weir. He's being set up – and you're being used to do it.'

Jim nodded along, took the Baggie from his shirt pocket and set it on Ken Robbins's desk. 'If it matches the stamp, I've got our killer.'

Dennison swiped it up, squinted at the hair inside, then tossed it back to Jim. 'You're not going to use a county facility or county employees for this campaign of yours. You have absolutely no authority here, nothing you have could ever be admissible, and I flatly repudiate any connection you might have had to the Newport Beach PD. If there was any chain of custody to begin with, you fucked it up by getting involved. I offered you a job, Weir, a way to do all this by the book, and you told me to stuff it. Jim – lay off, get out, and, for chrissakes, save your own ass. It's over.'

The chief looked at Robbins, who shrugged.

'He's right, Jim,' he said. 'I can't help you anymore.'

Weir set the bag on Robbins's desk again, along with the glossy of Horton Goins. Robbins slowly shook his head.

Dennison slammed his fist down as a fresh gust of anger blew into his face. 'And I know about the goddamned garage-door opener you guys checked out of evidence this morning. Now the chain of custody runs through the victim's *husband*. I'll file an obstruction charge for that, if I have to.'

Raymond looked steadfastly at the floor. Robbins sighed.

But Dennison wasn't done. 'Again, where's your mother?'

'I don't know.'

'I'd find out, if I were you.'

The only way through Dennison, Weir saw, was around him. Percy might listen. If not Percy, then his boss, D'Alba. If not the DA himself, then federal prosecutors. They'd be more than happy to talk to Marge Buzzard, who could lead them to 'Smith,' Blodgett, Cantrell, Ann, Mr Night. No threats now, he thought. No tipping of the hand. He was alone here and he knew it. Raymond sat, neutralized between his suspicion and his career.

The phone rang. Robbins passed it to Dennison, who listened for a moment without speaking.

When he did talk, his voice was tight, low-pitched. Then a fresh rush of blood brought color to his gray face. *'Where? You're positive? Don't touch anything. I'll be there in twenty minutes. Get Innelman and make sure Paris knows.'*

316

He gave the phone back to Robbins and stood. A taut smile crossed his face, aimed first at Raymond, then at Weir. 'Okay, Weir – you want to know everything? You want to solve this case on your own? Get your ass up and follow me if you think you can handle the truth.'

Empire Plating was a smog-choked fifteen-minute drive from the county buildings back to east Newport. Jim pulled up behind Dennison to a big building in the industrial zone, just half a mile from Cheverton Sewer & Septic. Ray brought up the rear.

They followed Dennison through the front door, down a hallway, and into the shop. It was a massive high bay, with huge blowers that sent a breeze across the expanse, and hanging fluorescent tubes that did little to dispel the dismal industrial gloom of the interior. The dip pits ringed the perimeter – silver, chrome, brass – each a roiling storm of steam, vapors, and molten liquid metal. The heat was profound. The workers had been herded along one wall. Weir could see them loitering, drinking coffee, and smoking, eyeing them as they headed for a far corner. He couldn't keep his thoughts away from Virginia.

Three Newport PD uniforms, arms crossed and strangely reverent, stood back from a dip pit that Weir could see was boiling furiously with what looked like silver. Mike Paris stood apart, gazing in. A few feet away lay a body covered by a yellow plastic tarp.

Paris said something into Dennison's ear, then nodded briefly to Raymond and Jim, then to the long steel workbench beside the dipping pit. 'Must have been in here since morning. No one needed this silver until noon, but when they uncovered the pool, they saw it. Foreman told me it's twelve hundred degrees, so . . . well, you'll see. Note's on the bench over there, under the shoe.'

Dennison motioned toward the body, and the sergeant nodded at his officers. They pulled back the tarp and stood aside, each looking up and away in a different direction.

Weir had never guessed that something so inhuman could be so definitely human. The silver had stripped the fat and most of the flesh away, leaving in their place an oozing patina of bright metal. The eyes were pools of solid silver. The face was a bright, shrunken mask that followed more closely the contours of a skull than a face: no mouth or ears or nose, just the two high rises of cheekbones, a jut

317

of chin, the prominence of what was once brow and forehead. The body was little more than a twisted relic of silver-black in the shape of a man. Only his athletic shoes had survived the furious metal – they were plated smoothly in shining silver, like something to be worn on a moon walk.

He caught his breath and followed Dennison to the workbench. The note was held down by a red espadrille, which Weir recognized immediately as Ann's. The note was handwritten, and easy to read over Dennison's shoulder:

> To Whom It May Concern,
>   I am sorry for Lucy Galen. I am sorry for Ann Cruz. I could not help myself, so I think it is better I go away. Mother and father, I hope you understand. You can have my pictures.
> Joseph Goins

Dennison regarded Raymond, then Jim. He put his hands on his hips and shook his head. 'I'm sorry, Ray. I'm goddamned sorry about everything. Take the day. Go home. Get drunk or something.'

But Raymond had already turned away and was heading out of the high bay. Jim caught up with him out in the parking lot by Raymond's old station wagon. His chin was trembling and droplets of sweat covered his forehead. 'Too goddamned convenient,' he said. 'For Dennison, Cantrell, everybody but Horton Goins. Christ, did you see . . .'

Jim felt the outrage building up inside himself, a sharp, specific anger. Cool down, he thought; you must have a clear head for what is to come. 'We've got options, Ray. We've got evidence against Cantrell, and a DA who isn't stupid. We're not out of this yet – not by a long shot.'

'The case is closed.'

'Theirs is. Ours isn't.'

Raymond wiped his brow with his palm, took a deep breath, and sighed heavily. 'Let it be Goins. That's okay. It can be Goins.'

Weir grabbed Raymond by his shoulders, shook him hard, and pushed him back against the car. 'It wasn't Goins and you know it. We need a way into Cantrell's beach house. We need a scene out front, so I can get into the garage. Now listen. Get into your car, go down to the PCH bridge, and pick up Mackie. Meet me on the boulevard, a block north of Cantrell's house in one hour.'

318

'What about you?'

'I've got a stop to make in Costa Mesa.'

'Hi, Mr Weird,' said Edith Goins. She tenderly dabbed an eye with a wadded tissue.

'Hello, Edith. May I come in?'

She left the door open and Jim stepped in. Emmett was sitting in his usual place in his usual black robe, hosted by the shadows. There was a box of Kleenex on his lap.

Jim sat down on the couch and listened to Edith sniffle. 'I'm sorry for you,' he said. 'You two have been through . . . an awful lot.'

Jim's sympathy brought a fresh rush of tears from Edith. 'I feel like we failed. Like we raised a man who killed two girls, then himself. I can't . . . can't explain how disappointed I am. I thought he was going to be all right. Mr Weird – I'm so sorry for what Horton did to your sister.'

'He didn't kill her, Edith.'

For the next five minutes, Jim used all his powers of persuasion to convince the Goinses that their son had been falsely accused. Slowly, Edith's tears subsided and she leaned forward to receive every word he spoke. She was nodding in agreement as Jim described the political struggle in Newport, Cantrell and Ann, Horton's as-yet inexplicable haunting of his sister.

'Well, I might believe all that,' said Edith, 'as a balm to my grieving soul – but what can we do about it now? We know better than to tangle with those big boys out here.'

'First, you can tell me what Mom wanted from you, the last time she came out here.'

'Don't you talk to your own ma?' asked Edith.

'She wasn't too willing to talk about the visit. She knew I'd be seeing you – helping with Horton's defense – so maybe she just figured –'

'Thanks, by the way, for not charging us no money. We're just about broke. That nine hundred a month for Clozaril about breaks us. Ain't been here long enough for Medi-Cal.'

'You're welcome. Now, why was she here?'

Edith lit a long brown cigarette, inhaled mightily, blew out the smoke. 'She was mostly curious about Horton. Who he was with before us.'

'And?'

'All's we ever knew was Horton was on a farm up to Dayton area, and his mom didn't want him no more. Horton wouldn't have anything to do with the pigs, or something like that. His dad was paralyzed, in a wheelchair, they said, and Horton was too much for them. They had four other adoptions, if I remember right. The mom had "inappropriate behavior" with Horton, whatever that was. I told your mom all this.'

Weir tried to imagine what Virginia was after. 'What else did you talk about?'

Edith wiped her eyes again. There was a wonderful feminity to it.

'Lucy,' she said.

'Lucy in Hardin County?'

'That's right. Lucy Galen, that Horton attacked in the swamp.'

'What did you tell her?'

Just that, and the fact that Lucy was in the Manor View sanitarium last we knew. That was eight years back, though.'

Emmet moved in the shadows. 'You know something? I don't think Horton kilt your sister.'

'How come, Em?'

'He was too happy. He loved it here in California. He didn't have any of the anger he did when he was little. It was the drugs, maybe, but those are good drugs they gave him. I mean, the police is usually right about this kind of thing, but I don't believe Horton did it. I just don't.'

Jim waited a moment. 'Mom's been gone a day now. She didn't tell me where she was going. Did she give any hint to you where –'

'Not to me, she didn't,' said Edith. 'Your mom don't say much; she just asks questions and listens hard. She doesn't exactly converse in the normal sense. She wanted some old pictures of Horton, so we gave her a batch. She said she'd return them.'

Weir couldn't track Virginia with his logic, and his imagination wasn't up to it, either. The more he turned it over, the less good it seemed to do.

He sat with Edith and Emmett a few more minutes, checked his watch, then offered his condolences again and left.

* * *

320

He stopped at a pay phone on Harbor, called Peninsula Travel, and asked for Trish. Trish had sent the Weir family on vacations for as long as Jim could remember. At the funeral gathering, she had worn a hat with black silk flowers sewed to the crown, one of which had fallen off in the punch bowl.

Trish confirmed that Virginia had flown from LAX to Dayton, Ohio, last night at 9:00 P.M. Stopover in Chicago, one-way, no return flight booked.

'I was hoping she had a man to see,' said Trish. 'She told me this trip was a secret.'

'It's safe with me,' said Weir. 'Thanks.'

He hung up, fished out the right change, called PacifiCo Towers, and asked for C. David Cantrell. Three different secretaries moved his call along. A few seconds passed, then Cantrell was on the line.

'This is Jim Weir.'

'Yes.'

'Nice work on Goins. His parents are sitting in a rotten little apartment in Costa Mesa, wondering what they did wrong. I know you did it.'

Cantrell was silent for a moment, then he hung up.

Thirty minutes later, Weir was sitting in the back of Raymond's patrol car, one block away from Cantrell's beach house. Mackie Ruff was up front with Raymond, his profile visible to Weir through the mesh partition. Mackie repeated his instructions back to Ray for the third time: Come down the sidewalk, go right to the front door of Cantrell's house, knock, and if I don't get an answer, start pounding on the thing. When the security goons come running, make a scene. Any kind of scene, just make one for about a minute. Then walk away. At exactly five-eighteen, come back and do it all again. 'How's that?' he asked.

'Perfect,' said Ray. 'Go.'

'I get to keep this fancy synchro watch?'

'You'll get more than the watch, Mackie. *Go.*'

When Mackie had taken a shot of courage from a vodka bottle in his oversized coat and gotten aimed in the proper direction down the sidewalk, Weir joined Raymond in the front of the car. The garage-door opener was in his hand. Across his lap lay a briefcase containing the basics: Becky's video recorder, a flashlight, wire

321

cutters, latex gloves, a slim-jim, and a copy of the day's newspaper. Raymond drove slowly down the alley. Weir slipped down again into the foot space. He felt the car roll to a stop and watched Raymond shift it into park.

'I can see both security cars, Jim. Both the goons are eyeing me. I'm going to stay here for a minute, write up a report. When I see them move, I'll tell you.'

'I'm ready.'

'I'll be behind the garage at five-eighteen. Until then, all I can do is cruise, so you're on your own. If I see security decide to go inside for a look around, I'll honk twice and meet you here.'

The engine idled. Raymond scribbled something in his Citation Book, looking up every few seconds.

'Contact,' he said. 'One goon out, heading for the front. Goon two is on the radio. Like clockwork, Jim — there he goes. Hold on now . . .'

Weir took hold of the briefcase handle and tried to get his legs up under him as best he could.

'*Go*,' said Raymond, and Weir went.

Ten feet from the garage door, he hit the control button and the door started up. How long to take out the alarm, he thought, a minute, thirty seconds? Briefcase in hand, heart in his throat, he walked calmly into the open garage and hit the Close button on the overhead switch. When the door was down, he went to work with the slim-jim. The lock was an ancient single-slide that wiggled open in less than twenty seconds. Inside, Jim found the security system and cut the wires. A silent job, he thought, probably plugged straight into PacifiCo security *and* the Newport cops. His breath was coming short and fast; he could feel a wash of sweat working down his back. He put on the latex gloves and stepped back out to the garage.

Standard in all respects, he thought: no windows, a big old tool-box sitting along the plasterboard wall, garden implements hanging from hooks, a workbench with power tools neatly boxed at the far end, a stain of oil on the concrete floor, a lawn mower and gas can in one corner, two bicycles propped against the house, one trash can beside them. Calm. Calm. Calm. He pulled off the lid and looked inside – some empty deli containers, a few soft-drink cans, and, nicely, an empty bottle of Cristal champagne. He swung the camera into place, set the *Times* against the door, and took an establishing shot. At the end of it, he lowered the camera over the top of the trash can and got the champagne. *How I'd love to print that bottle,* he thought. He checked his watch: 4:20. Fifty-eight minutes to exit time.

He shot the kitchen and found nothing. There was no carving block on the counter, and no carving knives in the drawers. *Cleared out? How did he trim the barbecue steaks, slice the bread?*

He skipped the big living room downstairs and climbed slowly to the second floor. He could hear Mackie Ruff on the porch, arguing in his shrill voice that C. David Cantrell owes something to the homeless. The security men were trying to talk him down, but Mackie was turning up the juice.

He made the landing and checked the first two rooms off the hall: neat, unused, unpromising. The third was the master suite, consisting of a large bedroom that opened onto an enclosed deck outfitted as an office. There was room on the desk for a word processor, but Cantrell didn't have one. *Why not?* Jim stood for a moment in the middle of the room, listening to the ocean rumble to shore outside. *I made love to your wife, Ann Cruz, in a lovely room overlooking the sea.* The bed was to his right. He studied the fluffy comforter, the pillows, the polished mahogany four-poster. *Because it was not satisfying in all the ways I require, I struck her twenty-seven times with a Kentucky Homestead kitchen knife (freshly sharpened six-inch blade).* The pillowcases were light blue with little sailboats on them. For a moment, he understood why Raymond wanted to kill this man. *I understand, Raymond. I understand. But that's not the way it's going to go down.* He checked the drawers of both nightstands. The usual. He stood up and shot the room and the newspaper. It was 4:30.

Jim moved across the carpet to the office. He sat down in the wooden chair, which rolled with difficulty on the thick Berber. *Idea.* To the right of the desk, he found what he was looking for: four indentations still clearly left in the weave of the carpet, indentations left by wide rollers bearing weight. *A computer stand?* He shot the carpet, aware that the marks probably wouldn't show up on the tape.

He set the camera on the floor, then opened the top drawer of the desk. *Neat.* Cantrell was orderly, even in his home office: boxed paper clips, a roll of stamps – T. S. Eliot – pencils and an electric sharpener, a small cardboard box containing keys of various purpose, all with labels attached by safety pin – 'front door spare,' 'Mercedes trunk,' 'Christy's footlocker,' 'garage door,' 'gate padlock.' A Smith .357 K-frame wrapped in an oiled cloth sat behind a box of shells. Jim opened the box: six shells missing from their holes. He could see the lead tips inside the cylinders of the revolver. Hoisting up the camera, he filmed the drawer, closed it, and moved to the next.

He remembered Robbins's words: *and speaking of trophies, I'll bet he's kept something of hers from that night, besides the flowers. He thinks he loved her. According to his definition, maybe he did.* Something besides Ann's red shoe, he thought. Something else. Something more. Something personal.

But the desk offered him nothing. Neither did the closets, the dresser drawers, the guest rooms, the living room, the kitchen, or the garage. He sat for a moment at the dining room table, looking in the fading light at the china cabinet to his left, then the sofa, the curtained window that opened out to a small patio. *She was my angel, and finally, my anguish.* It was 4:50.

Jim tried to concentrate. The refrigerator hummed in the kitchen. A skylight above him admitted the kind of light that illuminates dreams. What does a man do, he wondered, who claims he is being framed?

He searches for the planted evidence.

When he's 'found' it?

He destroys it.

No. He hides it. He can't destroy it because it frames the framer – so he believes. He keeps it for that alleged purpose, for the day he will prove his innocence.

But I know there's another reason you keep it, David, you keep it because there is no frame, other than the one you hung on a kid named Horton Goins. You keep it because you want to be close to her. So much that you'd risk having her things. Something you can smell, touch, behold. Somewhere safe, but easy to get to.

He combed through the kitchen drawers and cupboards, took out the pots and pans and put them back, checked the cabinet above the refrigerator, behind the cereal, took out the boxes of extra wine-glasses, dug his way down into the appliance cupboard around the blender, popcorn maker, espresso machine, juicer. He looked in the freezer, the vegetable bin, under the sink, inside the trash compactor and dishwasher, put his gloved hand into the garbage disposal, stood on a chair and looked inside the light fixture.

Then into the living room, the same frantic attention to detail, sweat dripping down into his eyes: inside the big Chinese vase in one corner, under the sofa cushions, beneath the sphagnum moss in the fern pot, everywhere he could think to look, everywhere he could see, every angle that would accommodate an arm, a hand, a line of sight.

He climbed the stairs again two at a time, checking his watch: 5:00.

It was more of an attack than a search: both dressers, the desk again, the bathroom, the enclosed patio, the closets – up on the top shelves through the boxes and folded sweaters; down on the bottom through the shoes – under the bed and under the pillows, his eyes burning, his shirt clinging with sweat, his hands scalding inside the latex gloves. And everything, to the best of his ability, back the way he had found it.

He stood in the middle of the room, breathing hard, looking again at the bed where Ann had spent her stolen hours, where she had unwittingly conspired to bring her life to its sudden brutal end.

Where?

Here, but not here, he thought. On the property, but not on *his* property. He checked his watch again: 5:10. A car pulled up in the alley and Jim peeped from behind the blind. Looking down, he could see the light bar, the PacifiCo emblem on the driver's side door, the shotgun upright against the dash. It stopped. Weir could see the guard gazing casually toward the garage, then lift his face for a look at the second story. Tough old face, he thought: retired cop. Jim watched as the guard got out, shut the door, and walked toward the house.

Idea: Cantrell uses. He used Ann. He used Goins. Always someone else. Who else would he use? Someone close. His wife.

Christy.

Christy's footlocker.

It was 5:14.

He moved across the room, away from the window, and found the key in the desk drawer. Outside, the security car still idled. Jim went to the window and looked out again. The guard was back in his car. On the radio? Hard to tell. Writing down something? Lighting a smoke?

Weir ran downstairs, through the kitchen and into the garage. He could hear the engine of the security car just twenty feet away, the

325

proficient idle and the hiss of the air conditioner. Raymond would cruise by in another two minutes.

Christy's big trunk sat on the floor beside a heavy steel tool chest. The lock was rusty and the key went in with a rasp that continued through Jim's fingers and up his arms. Scrapbooks, stuffed animals, dried flowers, and photo albums were all arranged neatly in the top tray. Jim pried through them, then lifted out the section and set it on the floor beside him. He heard the car door open again, then saw the dark shoe soles of the guard as he walked the length of the garage door. Weir wiped his face against the shoulder of his shirt, and started emptying the chest. The shoes moved back the other direction, stopped, then came again.

Did he call in?

The goons are back in place by now. They won't make contact with this guy. Where's Ray?

Be cool. It's here. It's here. You will find it. . . .

A bright orange ember hit the asphalt just beyond the door. Jim watched the shoe snuff it, then disappear. The car door opened and shut. He heard another car approach, surely Raymond's. Voices outside now: the old man and Raymond in a 'them and us' chitchat. Get rid of the old bastard – but not for another minute or two.

He didn't find it until the trunk was completely empty. It was the last thing there, in the last place he looked – as all things are – sitting in the far bottom corner, under fifty pounds of a woman's memorabilia. He lifted it, retrieved the wallet, and flipped past the credit cards to the driver's license – the unflattering DMV mug that made her look like someone being booked on a felony rap. Ann's purse. Ann's wallet. Ann's picture. It was a dressy little thing, made out of white satin, with a gold chain. The satin was splattered with blood; the chain was clogged with it. It looked like it had just been born. The twelfth rose was worked through one of the links of the chain.

He filmed it atop the newspaper, date visible, the rubber eyepiece slick against his eye. When he had put it back into the trunk, he loaded in the rest of the things, then set the latch in place and locked it shut.

He sat back against the wall and listened to the idling of the security car. His body ached anew and he closed his eyes for a moment and saw himself hanging from the ceiling of the deserted building, looking up at his boots inside the hangman's

326

noose. His ears were ringing and he could smell his own sour breath.

Then one of the cars outside clunked into gear and Jim heard the tires moving on the asphalt. Raymond said goodbye, have a nice evening. A shadow crossed the space beneath the door, then was gone.

He ran back into the house, up the stairs, and returned the key to Christy's footlocker to its place in Cantrell's desk. It was 5:20.

For a moment, he stood in the living room, trying to imagine anything he'd left undone, anything he'd left out of place.

Mackie Ruff's voice shot through the door, 'The homeless shall not be denied!' The goons were talking back.

In the entryway, he spliced the alarm wires back together and shoved them back inside the plastic housing. 'You can tell that God loves the poor because he made so many of us!'

Jim locked the door behind him, pressed the garage-door opener, and moved across the alley in the gathering evening, toward Raymond's waiting car. He tossed the briefcase through the open front window, then dodged off into the alley. Raymond nodded and gave him the thumbs-up.

A few minutes later, Weir was standing on the boulevard, deep in the lengthening shadow of a wisteria hedge. His knees were shaking. The patrol car came toward him slowly and stopped. Jim climbed in beside Raymond and turned back to look at Ruff.

Mackie's red face was beaming, his eyes large with excitement. 'Great way to make a living,' he said. 'You guys need a few good men?'

30

Becky swung into the big house, clomped across the hardwood floors in her heels, and set her briefcase down on the couch. 'I'm meeting George Percy in one hour. What did you get?'

Weir, sitting in Virginia's chair, told her.

'*Fantastic*. Then where's the tape?'

'There.' He nodded at the coffee table.

'What's wrong with you, Weir? I know that look.'

In the lifetime that he had known Becky Flynn, Jim had felt many things for her. There was the draw of childhood friendship, the adolescent awakening to her mysterious otherness, the young adult love and the wild happiness it can bring, and finally the bitter disillusion of watching what he had long assumed was destiny coming apart in his helpless hands.

As Weir had thought back on his life with Becky – sitting alone in the big house, waiting for her to arrive – he knew that what they had failed to create between them for all those years was trust: absolute, unquestioning trust. Somehow it had gone undeveloped, and its absence had gone unacknowledged, in the same way that a three-legged dog hobbles about oblivious to what is missing. In the end, the lack of trust had loomed large, helped to send caving down around them whatever goodwill, friendship, and love might have managed to thrive without it. They had both exploited the lack in order to create power, at different times and in different ways.

Becky stood across from him. 'Spill it, Jim.'

'You've been ahead of this game from the start, Becky. You've been talking with Edith and Emmett – Mom has, too. You were the ones who traced the roses. You were the one who thought Ann was seeing someone. You were the one who made the jump from a Dave Smith who doesn't exist, to a Dave Cantrell, who does. You were the one who hired me to defend Horton, but all I've found is evidence that fingers Cantrell. You used Horton Goins like you used that sea gull — to illustrate a point. You were the one who knew I'd find something in Cantrell's house. I want to believe you've gone on brains and luck. Have you?'

Becky remained standing. She was wearing a navy blue suit and a plain white blouse that clung to her body snugly. He smelled a wash of fresh perfume. For a moment she seemed frozen, then she sat slowly across from him. 'Well, it sounds to me like you've been talking to Brian Dennison.'

'That doesn't answer the question.'

'The answer is yes. I've gone on brains and luck. But I do know I've . . . been exploitive of some situations. I knew Horton Goins was innocent, and I used him.'

'How did you know?'

'Does it matter to you?'

'Quite a goddamned lot, Becky.'

Becky fastened her dark brown eyes on Weir, then looked down. She sat back and stared up at the ceiling. 'Ann told me back in March that she was seeing Cantrell.'

'And you've used me to get to him?'

'Is *use* the right word, Jim? For getting the man who killed your sister? I sure couldn't go to Brian Dennison. I wouldn't go to George Percy until we had the goods. Now we've got the goods, and Cantrell has staged a suicide and confession that will probably keep him untouchable.'

'You could have come clean with me.'

'And you could have become a conspirator, if I was wrong. I left you free, Jim. I let you find out things in a . . . realistic manner.'

'A realistic manner. Things you knew all along.'

'Not all of them. Annie had told me under an oath of death — half-joking, I mean — about Cantrell. I was horrified, although I'll admit the man has his . . . attractions. She saw him briefly, while she was in high school. I understood. She said it was like being fifteen again. Annie was a lovely, good, strong woman, Jim. She was bored, fed up with Raymond, and wanted a fling. That didn't take her down a notch in my book — it never will. I opened the door to Cantrell, Jim, but you ran through it.'

'And you guessed he killed her?'

She nodded.

'And you guessed he'd have something in his home — Annie's purse, for instance?'

Becky nodded again, then looked down. 'I was right.'

'What about the tie tack?'

She offered a puzzled expression and said nothing.

'Cantrell's place was broken into in April – the tack was taken, along with some other things.'

'No. I know what you're thinking. No. Never.'

The dim light fell on Becky's face in a way that showed the years, revealed the simple consequences of age. Jim saw what he knew to be only natural: that she was drier, heavier, less adept at dodging the ceaseless punches that life throws. For a moment, she looked almost wasted. But through it all, at its very center, Jim saw again what he had been seeing in Becky for three decades: that the central theme of her character was to accomplish, to challenge, to conquer. Becky was a warrior.

'Where's Mom?'

'I . . . she told me she was going to Ohio. But that was all, Jim. It's got something to do with Goins, but I can't tell you what.'

'And the roses?'

Becky shook her head and looked away from him. 'He ordered them, not me. Please, Jim.'

There was a long moment of silence. The bridge of a massive power yacht came into view through the picture window, slid inaudibly down the bay, heading for the harbor mouth. In the distance, the brilliant reflective glass of PacifiCo Tower dominated the mainland hills.

Jim regarded Becky in the half-light of the living room. 'And *Sweetheart Deal?* Did you put that idea in Raymond's ear?'

'No. Ray thought of that. I had no idea Cantrell had written her.'

'What about Blodgett seeing *Sea Urchin* that night? The idea crossed my mind that you and Mom are profiting nicely from the spill.'

A cold, simple anger settled upon Becky's features. 'I'll forget you said that. Never say it again.'

Becky stood, brushed something invisible from her midriff. She collected the tape and briefcase, and stood before Jim again. 'That's almost the whole truth. I'll tell you the rest now, just to have it out in the open. Since we've been apart, I know you've had a few women, but I've never asked. I imagine you had one or two down in Mexico. You've never asked about my men, and I've appreciated

330

that. Well, I had a man. His name is George Percy and I cooled him the day after you walked into my house again, because I knew right then I was going to get you back. Anyhow, George isn't going to be all that receptive to what we've got on Cantrell. If I was as smart and lucky as I'd like everyone to think, I'd have stuck it out with him another week or two.'

She leaned down, rested a hand on Jim's thigh, and kissed him lightly on the lips. 'On the other hand – who knows what a guy'll do to get a girl back. Wish me luck.'

'Good luck, Becky.'

'Trust me, Jim. Trust me all the way this time. I need that from you now.'

He said he would, but even as he spoke, Jim was unsure that he meant it. It struck him then that the real deficit of trust, all along, had likely come from his own traitor's heart. Faith is easier to come by than belief.

'I will.' I must.

'Stick this out with me, Jim. I need a man who's going to be there, all the way. Let it be you.'

Jim looked at her but said nothing.

'Meet me at the Wrecking Ball,' she said.

31

The Wrecking Ball was in full swing when Jim walked into the Eight Peso Cantina at ten o'clock. The windows had been boarded up, and bogus condemnation notices were stapled to the wood. A crane stood in the alley beside the cantina, its boom extended over the roof, a huge gold foil dollar sign dangling where the ball should be.

The Newport police chopper hovered above for a long while, low and noisy, its searchlight trained on the entering guests.

Inside, a mock interior lay in ruins around the room: splintered wood, pieces of concrete with rusted rebar protruding at angles, sawhorses with blinking orange lights, piles of rubble cordoned off with bright red pylons in the hope of keeping people from tripping on them. The skylight had been removed, and a jagged border of papier-mâché glued around the perimeter of the opening, through which the cool May breeze swirled.

Weir stepped in and nodded to Dale Blodgett, who stood with the air of a bouncer just inside the door. He was dressed in a tuxedo. 'Thought you might not make it,' said Blodgett. His big face labored toward a smile.

'Trying to do my part,' said Weir. 'Mom back yet?'

'Back from where?' Blodgett's smile went down an octave.

'Doesn't matter. Did you get *Duty Free* back together again?'

Blodgett sipped from a martini glass with a toothpick and two olives in it. 'She's ready. We might make a shakedown run tomorrow night. Interested?'

'I'll think about it. Will that be one of the nights you and Lou Braga fill the bait tank?'

Blodgett blushed, finished off his drink in one gulp. 'You lost me, Weir. Hey, have a drink, loosen up. Maybe even try to enjoy yourself.'

Jim stepped past him to hug Ray's parents, the host and hostess,

Ernesto and Irena Cruz. Irena had on an elaborate fuchsia dress, with a matching silk scarf around her neck. Ernesto wore a tuxedo so old, the elbows shone. Weir wondered whether his own tux looked that old, too. What can you do? The thought crossed his mind that Ernesto probably had been married in it. They pointed him to a far corner, where he could make out the back of Raymond, who seemed to be pressing a diminutive woman into a corner filled with rubble. The rubble was marked by a sawhorse with a pulsing light. The woman sat in a wheelchair, her face and the chromed chassis of her chair throbbing intermittently orange.

Between Jim and the corner were a couple of hundred people, dressed in varying degrees of finery. Half of them were the neighborhood folks, the faces he'd grown up with, the faces that had loomed sympathetically before him at the funerals of Poon, Jake, and Ann. The rest were the Prop A partisans from around the county – the disgruntled adversaries of development.

Raymond, looking slender and composed in a white dinner jacket and bow tie, found Jim in the crush and handed him a glass of champagne. 'Any word?'

'None yet.'

Raymond looked at Jim without expression, then nodded very slightly. 'If anyone can convince Percy, it's Becky.'

'It's not in the bag, Ray. I'm worried.'

'What can a prosecutor say to a tape of Ann's purse?'

'He can say it was made during the commission of a burglary. No judge in the world is going to order a search warrant. The rest depends on how much energy the prosecutor's got – and where his boss comes down.'

Raymond cast Jim a wary glance. 'Cantrell's supported D'Alba for two elections.'

'My thoughts exactly.'

'Doesn't seem like there's a man in this county who can afford to have Dave Cantrell take a fall.'

'That's what Becky's up against right now.'

'I need another drink.'

Ray broke away for the bar and Jim watched him drain one glass of champagne, then another. Dressed as he was, alone at the bar, staring back at Jim from over his raised glass, Raymond looked small, stranded, lost.

The band reassembled onstage and launched into a Zydeco tune.

The kid playing accordion looked about twelve. The stage backdrop behind them was a painted pile of rubble with graveyard crosses placed atop each big rock, bearing the name of a neighborhood business or family home that would be ground up in the redevelopment deal. A banner across the top declared PACIFICO PRESENTS . . .

In the corner closest to the street, a booth was set up, where a dapper old gentleman sold chances for the prize, a Japanese subcompact. Weir wondered who had donated the car, until he got close enough to read the sign: CHEVERTON SEWER & SEPTIC. Tickets were a hundred bucks apiece, and business looked good.

Becky walked in an hour later. She had changed to a backless black velvet dress and gloves that came up past her elbows, and her hair was pulled back on one side with a big rhinestone comb. Her lipstick was dark red and her eyes were made up into twin brown mysteries that seemed to draw Weir straight into her. Jim wondered whether she'd changed before seeing George Percy or after, then decided he would never ask. 'God, you look good,' he said instead.

'It's all for you, Mr Weir. Come outside. Let's talk.'

They stood on the sidewalk, facing the bay. 'George is taking it to D'Alba right now. He's not going to make a move either way without his boss — way too hot to handle alone. My guts tell me he's with us.'

'And D'Alba's with Cantrell.'

Becky nodded and turned to Jim. She put a hand on each of his arms and drew him forward gently. Her eyes picked up the glow from the streetlamps, illuminating some new pain inside. She lay her head on his shoulder for a long while and held him in her strong brown arms.

'Dance with me,' she said.

He led her to the crowded wooden floor, guiding her across it into a kind of modified swing step that, like so many things from days gone by, came back to them as sure as instinct. Jim felt elevated. Becky's skin looked rich against the black fabric, and when he raised her hands for a spin, he caught the damp smell coming from her, saw the shine of sweat beneath her arms. Coming out of the turn, he pulled her closer.

While the room whirled around them, Jim began to feel for the first time in years the pieces of his life starting to settle into place. He could almost see them: surface meeting surface, side fitting side, corners snugging into larger corners to form a complete, harmonious whole. He entertained briefly a thought that had come to him dozens of times since returning home – a snippet of future possibility too precious and delicious to contemplate in any depth. A son. A daughter. The Weirs. My family. Even the loss of Ann had the feeling, as he pressed Becky's supple warmth against him, of something that would eventually fit, bringing with it not her absence but the years she had been alive, the hours they had shared, the moments that, as moments do, continue on inside the living.

'I didn't know what I was missing,' he said.

'I had an idea.'

'Can a mayor fit a love life into her busy schedule?'

'I'll adjourn for you anytime.'

'Maybe you should adjourn over to Ray. He looks kind of lost at that bar by himself.'

Becky looked at the clock, then over to Nesto Cruz behind the bar. He shook his head. No call from Percy yet.

Jim found a booth and drank more champagne. As the alcohol did its work, he sighed deeper down into his seat and looked out through the mocked-up crossbars on a condemned window. The night was damp, bringing halos to the streetlamps and dew to the glass that faced the bay. He could see yacht masts tilting slowly, and the ghost-pale forms of hulls steady on the water. Beyond the invisible horizon of the island, the PacifiCo Tower stood illuminated against a starless sky. Tower of Babel, thought Weir, tower of lies, tower of pillage, tower of death. And I'm going to bring it down, one mirrored window at a time, straight down into the dead sea of this little city. He smiled, sipped, looked to the dance floor.

Ray and Becky danced with the ease of old friendship. Raymond kept his hips in a respectful rhythm that he never showed with Ann; with Ann it was always deeper and more fraught with sex and abandon and promise. There was a stiffness to him now, Jim saw, a sense of going through motions. When Ray made a turn, his black eyes locked for a moment with Jim's, and in that instant Weir was reminded again that whatever the final tally would be, Raymond's loss was the deepest and least fathomable, that Raymond's memory would be forever tainted by the bitter scent of Ann's betrayal. Raymond looked away.

And when he did, another truth stood revealed to Jim: that from this point on, Raymond and he would begin to drift apart. Even now he could feel in himself the autonomic recoil when he stood close to Raymond, feel the self-protective urge to go away. It was the weight of Ann, he knew, of the tragedy that had bruised them all; it was something akin to returning, as he once did, to the hospital where Poon had breathed his rattling last, where a frantic voice had told him to get the hell away from there as fast as he could. But that was only part of it. In the future, Raymond would find another woman, and when that happened, Raymond would have to seal off some of this, if there was to be any chance at all of a happiness and a life. Jim saw that he would become to Raymond what Raymond already was becoming to him: a living reminder of pain, an agent of sadness, a fellow traveler on a road once shared but no longer passable.

Jim wondered, How do I keep that from happening?

Becky dragged Raymond off the floor and to the bar. Nesto handed her the phone. Jim watched her nod, freeze, nod again, then give it back to Nesto. She brought Raymond to the table.

'D'Alba's considering. George said to give them another hour. I can't stand this. Anybody got a cigarette? Look – it's speech time. This lady's great.'

Weir bummed a smoke and lit it for Becky. They sat back in the booth and watched two young men push the old woman in the wheelchair toward the stage. They forgot to lock the chair wheels and nearly lost her over the edge once they had gotten her up. She rolled to the microphone under her own power. The twelve-year-old accordion player lowered the mike for her, cinched it tight, bowed. There was a smattering of applause, which seemed to wither in the voracious stare of this woman, who sat glaring into the crowd. Her downy white hair, backlit by the stage lights, stood out around her head like a halo. She held her hands in her lap, wrapped around a tumbler of scotch delivered by Irena. It got so quiet that Jim could hear the ice clinking in her glass.

'Thank you so much for inviting me here tonight,' she said. 'I've come to the age where my humble meanderings are praised in public and giggled at in private, but I accept the mantle with whatever grace I can muster. My name is Doris Tharp.'

Weir was surprised at the resonance of her voice, a genderless

336

tenor that seemed launched from a hollow of smoothly polished teak. She sipped from her scotch.

'You deserve better,' she said. 'You deserve a Homer to chronicle these days, a seer, a sibyl. But this is not an age of prophets. It is an age of spokesmen . . . spokes*persons*. Even our sex awaits the leveling boot heel of conformity – but, I digress. At ninety-one, one's entire life becomes a digression. My grandfather fought at Shiloh in the Civil War; my father came west in a covered wagon. One of my grandsons flew last week from New York to Paris in three hours on a Concorde; another died two years ago from a virus that didn't even exist when John Tharp took up arms against the Union.

'I'd like to let you in on a little secret – there is no such thing as history. History is the name given to events in order to mark them for our forgetfulness. Nothing is really past us, in the same way that nothing is really with us – it all changes between blinks of the eye, no two moments the same. Those ignorant of history are not doomed to repeat it – that would be a staggering achievement. They are simply doomed to ignorance of everything else.

'But you asked me to talk about Proposition A, didn't you?'

Doris lifted her scotch glass and sipped. Her eyes – ice blue in the lights – peered into the crowd. Jim had the feeling they were seeing every detail of each face, every thought behind the face. It was quiet enough to hear the bay water lapping against the sand outside.

'We are a nation spoiled by excess, bored with the spoils, fattened on the boredom. We are a people not of ideas but of notions. We are a people hypnotized by the notion that we know what is good for the world, when in fact we don't know what is good for ourselves. The average American family watches television for seven hours a day. Television executives defend the slop they serve us as "what the people want." The Medellin Cartel sells us "what the people want." The President tells us, on television, that we must stop the invasion of drugs because that is "what the people want." Let me tell you something: People want everything. We are accumulators, hoarders, gluttons, and misers. We Californians produce more trash per person than any other state in the nation, than any other civilization in the history of the planet. But we want more. We want things that don't even exist yet; yes, we want those, too.'

Doris Tharp sipped her drink again, eyes fixed on the audience.

337

'Why? Because it was here. A bounty inconceivable – an ocean teeming with fish, endless valleys of fertile soil, month upon month of growing season, rivers overflowing with gold. We devoured it at first just to live; now we live just to devour it. And what have we offered in return but one great wrapper licked clean and tossed back – a dead ocean, dead air, and hundreds of thousands *more* people rushing in to lick the wrapper.

'You people out there, you who want to stop the building and preserve what is left, if that is all your imagination can muster, then go forward with my blessing. But don't forget your obligation to add something good to what is left. Don't forget the backs that labored to bring you here; don't forget that the roofs over your heads were put there by men you trained to do this, men you honored and courted and hired to protect you from the March wind and the August sun. Don't forget that *we* are the builders, *we* are the spoilers, *we* are the insatiable guests living off the host of great generosity.

'Narcissus drowned in the pool of his self-admiration, and I fear that we may do that, too. We are not morally superior here; we are not the great friends of Earth – look at us, we sit here for the benefit of ourselves tonight, and nothing more – we are only the few who have found enough. It is our duty to share, not to hoard; to offer, not to abscond. Why? Because we have been blessed far more than we have blessed; we have been protected far more than we have protected; and we are all in need not of being saved but of being decent. Thank you.'

There was a hovering, tentative moment of silence before the applause started – scattered at first, then fuller, then rising in pitch and volume until the walls seemed to participate. Becky stood, then everyone else did. Jim watched as the two young men lifted Doris Tharp down from the stage. She handed one of them her glass, then wheeled herself through the parting crowd and out the door.

Nesto was waving frantically from behind the bar. Becky shot up, powered her way through the crowd, took the phone again. For a long while, she didn't move. Weir's legs felt numb. Then she placed the receiver back on its cradle, said something to Nesto, and came back to the booth.

She stood there looking down on Jim and Raymond, wiped a tear from her eye, and shook her head. 'No. They'd reconsider what's in evidence already, if we can come up with a new way to look at it. Otherwise, no. One of you get up and dance with me, please.'

For the next hour, Jim and Raymond hurled and were hurled by Becky around the dance floor. The crowd thinned and the floor opened up, so that the last half hour it was theirs alone, Becky dominating it and them in a frightening choreography of rage that left her comb gone, her hair in a sweat-drenched mess, her makeup running freely, and her body glistening.

When the band announced the last song, she took Jim and Raymond each by an arm and steered them toward the door. 'Take me home,' she said. 'We have work to do.'

The police chopper made another pass above, razed them with its beam, then banked away with a battle groan and was gone.

They sat in Becky's living room in the dead quiet of early morning, poring over the crime-scene reports, the interviews, the lab conclusions, the coroner's findings, the Ruff statements, the recent press clippings on Cantrell and the GROW, DON'T SLOW! organization, the PacifiCo annual report that Becky had obtained from a 'friend' inside the company, the corporate profiles on PacifiCo and its holdings that her paralegal helpers had unearthed in their assault on Cheverton Sewer & Septic, even a copy of the Redevelopment Project for the peninsula – complete with artists' conceptions of the new and improved neighborhood.

Two o'clock became three o'clock. The documents that Jim was reading began to merge in his mind into an unfocused enigma that offered up the same refrains: Ann the Deceased, Ann the Victim, Ann the Supine.

At four, Becky drank off another cup of coffee and went into the kitchen to make more.

Raymond looked up at Weir through his attorney's spectacles and set the crime-scene report on the fireplace hearth. 'Jim?'

'I'm listening.'

'Let's kill him tonight.'

Weir considered Raymond's deadpan expression. 'I'd like to.'

'I'm serious. Use the opener, get him out of bed, take him out on one of Virginia's skiffs, waste him and dump him out deep, tied to some dumbbells. I've got them at home.'

Jim could see behind Ray's inscrutable mask a willingness that, for a moment, unsettled him. Justice of the Plains, he thought: Raymond and Francisco, chasing their stolen and beloved dreams across the rough terrains of fate, knights-errant, hell-bent on their way to the bullet marked for them. Would that bloody ending suit Raymond better than a lifetime of drinking, one bitter cup each day, the poison of knowing a truth that the system – the system he had served long and without complaint – would never allow him to prove? Maybe.

But for Jim, there was the breathing body of one Raymond Cruz: friend, brother, partner in tragedy. Life needs the living. 'No. I'm not going to the chamber for Cantrell. I'm not about to let you, either. He isn't worth it.'

'Ann was.'

'Nothing you can do will bring her back, Ray. Nothing. Ever. Least of all, that.'

The strangest of smiles crept into Raymond's face, a smile of such soaring disregard that Weir's scalp crawled.

'Just thinking out loud, Jim.'

'You let me know if you have any more thoughts along that line.'

The smile changed to something more grounded. 'I will.'

Becky came back with more coffee, slumped down into her sofa, and picked up the annual report for PacifiCo. 'Drink more coffee,' she said. 'It's in here. Something is in here. Robbins already has something that points to Cantrell – we just haven't found it yet. Look. Look until you go fucking blind, then look some more.'

At five o'clock, Weir placed his head back on the couch and watched the patterns in the stucco ceiling form shapes that looked like things he could identify. He and Jake and Ann had often lain on Jake's bed and done the same thing: there's the Indian chief, the state of Florida, the flat bicycle tire. Ann had spotted the pregnant lady first.

'Move around a minute,' said Becky. 'It'll wake you up some.'

'Think I will.'

He walked through the house, each room furnished with memories, both good and bad, of a lifetime spent on the perimeters of love for a woman. Time is running out for us, he thought. Time is running out for us to make legitimate what we've enjoyed so casually, so conditionally, on the sly. He wondered whether he and Becky had taken on, in the eyes of others, an aspect of the ridiculous. There was something comic in the hedging of life's big bets.

On Becky's nightstand was a vase with a dozen purple roses in it.

He sat on the bed and beheld these lovely flowers, so tainted now for him. He closed his eyes for a moment and saw again the image from the dreams he had had so often this last week – of someone's hand holding a purple rose up to the smiling, anticipatory face of Ann.

Against all the higher consciousness he could muster, Weir counted them.

Twelve.

Of course.

He sighed, closed his eyes again, and again saw the hand holding a purple rose up to Ann. At first, the rose was in focus and Ann was a blurred face in the background, then the rose lost specificity and Ann's face became clear.

Weir's head wobbled and he snapped himself up straight.

His eyes were so heavy. Just a moment to rest.

Of course, no rest. The hand holds the rose. A man's hand. The petals are purple and full. Ann's face becomes the place between her legs. The hand drips blood. This is unholy.

Weir stood to walk back into the living room. And when he looked again at the roses in Becky's vase, he understood in an instant what he had only been seeing all along.

He stopped. The understanding was still there. He ran through it once, then again, then again. He reached out and took a flower from the vase. His hand was trembling as he gripped it up on the bulb, just under the petals, the thick green underleaves snug against his fingers and thumb.

He was still holding the flower when he walked back to the living room and drew the worried stares of Becky and Ray.

'You look like you've seen a ghost,' she said.

'Give me the phone and Ken Robbins's home number. I've got it. I know what he has that we haven't seen yet.'

He dialed and got Mrs Robbins. She told him dreamily that Ken was still not sleeping well, had already left for the office. It was 5:30. Weir apologized, called the Crime Lab, and got Robbins on the second ring.

'Ken, this is Jim Weir. Get the rose from the evidence freezer. The rose he put in Ann.'

'Why?'

'We've got him. We had it all along, and didn't know it. Please, Ken, get the rose.'

Robbins was quiet for a moment. 'You're out, Jim. Dennison

made it clear. I can't be running evidence for you anymore. My hands are tied and you know it.'

'Listen, Ken. This isn't new. It's something you've got already, brought in by the Newport cops. The chain of custody is tight, it's admissible, solid, and sitting in your freezer twenty yards away. It isn't mine. I'm asking you to take another look. I'm begging you, Ken. Get the rose and put it on your light table. Get a good overhead on it and a pair of clean tweezers.'

Another pause. 'Wait.'

Becky sat still on the hearth. Raymond was at the front window, looking out toward the hedge of oleander.

Two minutes later, Robbins was back. 'Okay. It's on the table, I've got a light on it, and a pair of tweezers in my hand. Now what in hell am I going to do with this withered-up thing that I haven't done already?'

'We overlooked something because it wasn't visible. The green underleaves, right below the petals – what do they look like?'

'Nothing on this thing is green – it's plain goddamned simple brown.'

'The brown husks then – can you see them?'

'They're buried under the petals, Weir.'

Weir fingered the rose in his hand. Was it his hand in the dream? 'Are they folded down against the stem?'

'Yeah, Jim. In the same goddamned way they were when it came in here.'

'But they weren't that way when the flower went in. The force folded them back, closed them tight against the stem. Lift the petals and turn up the husks with your tweezers – all the way up to where they meet the bulb. Tell me what you see.'

Robbins set down the phone. Weir could hear him snapping on a pair of latex gloves, then the metallic shuffle of instruments in a drawer.

Jim felt his pulse beating through his ear and into the receiver. Becky hadn't moved. Raymond was facing him now, the beginnings of a smile on his face. A minute went by.

Robbins picked up the phone again and cleared his throat. 'Weir? It's beautiful. A partial thumb and probably a forefinger, drawn in blood, sealed by the underleaf when it went in. The seawater pickled the plant and sealed in the print. I can't . . . I can't actually believe this. You want a job?'

342

'I want you to run it against Cantrell's set.'

'He's never been printed.'

'That picture of Goins I left with you . . . with the hair in the Baggie? Cantrell's thumb is on the right side, halfway down. It ought to be clear as day. You still have the picture, don't you?'

'Dennison insisted I throw it away. I . . . well, kind of didn't quite throw it away. Give me fifteen minutes.'

'I'm at Becky's house.'

He left the number and hung up.

Becky looked at him with an air of perplexity that in thirty years Jim had seen probably twice. Becky always had chosen games she could stay ahead of.

Raymond smiled wholly, walked across the room to Jim, and hugged him. It was the longest, strongest embrace from Ray that he could remember. Still, he thought, something seems to have gone out of him.

Jim watched as Raymond looked out the window for a moment, then walked over and sat on the couch.

'Maybe we should have a drink,' said Becky.

'Maybe we should wait until Robbins calls,' said Weir.

Raymond shot a glance at Becky, then stood and walked toward the door. 'I need a minute alone.'

Jim caught the oddness in Raymond's expression. 'Don't mess this up, Ray. We're too close. We've worked too hard.'

Raymond smiled weakly. 'I want to say a prayer of thanks under the stars. That's all.'

'Stay with us, Ray,' said Becky. 'Please?'

Raymond looked at each of them in turn, his face coloring and a visible anger rising in his eyes. 'Don't worry, kids. I'm not going to do *anything* to mess this up. I promise. I'm going to sit on the seawall, watch the sun rise on the day we take down the man who killed my wife. You couldn't *pay* me to mess that up. You don't believe me, that's your problem. Keep an eye out if you want.'

Fifteen minutes went by. Weir paced the living room, looking out the window every few minutes at Raymond, who, still in his tux coat, sat on the seawall beside a lamppost, facing the bay and PacifiCo Tower. What terrible visions were his? Jim wondered. The darkness had begun to dissolve with the first hint of dawn.

Five minutes later, Robbins called back. His voice was subdued and he spoke very slowly. Weir remembered that this was Ken's

343

way of stretching out the pleasure, of letting the satisfaction of a job well done percolate down from the head into every inch of a waiting, exhausted body. Robbins lived his job. 'It's a lock,' he said. 'A perfect match.'

'What now?' Jim asked, the first waves of relief starting to wash over him.

'I'm not sure, Weir. I ran them twice against the photo, but it didn't match. So I ran them twice through the computer index, then did a visual myself. The prints belong to Raymond Cruz.'

Weir hung up and looked again out the window to Raymond. Raymond waiting for the truth, he thought. Raymond, who knew.

Jim closed his eyes for a moment on the world he had known, trying to say goodbye to it. Then he opened them to a world he could imagine but still could not believe.

'What's wrong?'

He walked past Becky, down the walkway of her yard and through the creaking gate. Raymond's tuxedo jacket was spread convincingly across two pieces of driftwood that were propped and balanced against the lamppost.

Raymond himself was gone.

32

Becky sped through the alley, out to the boulevard, then down the peninsula toward Cantrell's beach house. The sky was changing black to indigo, with an orange tint to the east, and Jim Weir was a man unraveling. He stared out the windshield at the old neighborhood. Nothing looked the same. He was aware of moving south-bound on the boulevard in Becky's car, hunting something he did not want to find. The feeling was of being borne to sea by an undertow, away from what he knew, from what he had relied upon and held to be true. He could almost see these things, diminishing on a retreating shore.

'What if they're not there?' she asked.

'Cantrell told me he'd be there. Raymond's going to try for him. I know him enough to know that.'

'God, Jim. There's got to be something wrong. Ray couldn't have done it. Something is wrong.'

Raymond's station wagon was parked behind Cantrell's beach house. The windshield was clear where the wipers had gone; the rest of the glass was heavy with dew. The house was dark except for soft lamplight in the master suite upstairs. One window panel of the side door was broken out and the door stood ajar.

'He's inside, and the alarm is banging away at PacifiCo Security,' said Jim. 'Stay here.'

'Don't be an ass, Jim. Call the police – this is what they get paid for. You don't know anything for sure. And if he killed Ann, what's to keep him from killing you?'

He brought the .45 from his holster, aware for a moment of its terrible heft.

'And what in hell am I supposed to do?' she asked.

'Stay here.'

'You're a fool.'

He let himself in, gave his eyes a moment to adjust then moved quietly through the living room to the stairway. The house was silent. He took the stairs slowly, calling for Raymond in a calm voice. His pulse throbbed in his ears with a bright, metallic clang. The bed was unmade, the bath was empty, and the air around him had the feeling of air that wasn't going to answer back.

'Ray?'

Jim slid out the desk drawer: Cantrell's revolver was still in place and the ammunition box was unmoved. Raymond surprised him, he thought, dragged him out of bed.

Jim looked out the open front window to the beach below. Nobody there but one surf fisherman and his dog.

From the back window, Jim could see the bayfront homes, the masts of the yachts at anchor, and between the homes a stretch of beach. A cloud of white exhaust rolled from the stern of C. David Cantrell's *Lady of the Bay*, the biggest vessel Weir could see. She eased away from the dock with a high-horsepower grumble that rattled the windowpane in front of Jim's face.

He flew down the stairs, out the door, and back into Becky's car. '*Sea Urchin*,' he said. 'As fast as you can go.'

'Raymond's taking the boat, isn't he?'

'It's already out of dock. Flog it, Beck.'

Three PacifiCo security cars quietly rolled up just as Becky turned for the boulevard.

Five minutes later, they were speeding down the center of the bay, Weir on the bridge, guiding the little craft around the yachts and buoys and moorings, throwing up a rooster trail of water as he carved into a stretch of open harbor and shoved the throttle all the way forward. He could see the settling wake of *Lady of the Bay* ahead of them, disappearing into the glassy calm of the early-morning harbor. Becky stood beside him, still in her back velvet dress, hugging herself against the chill. Jim yelled over the roar of the engine. 'Go get the anchor line clear and cut it off at the cleat – there's a knife in the tool chest!'

Becky vanished into the cabin, then reappeared on the fore deck. 'How are you going to get aboard?'

'Get the anchor line clear!'

'It's clear!'

'Cut it off!'

'It's off, goddamn it!'

Jim could see the stern of Cantrell's yacht now, squarely between the jetties forming the harbor mouth. The big boat was picking up speed as she approached the open sea. Outside the jetties, the ocean rocked deeply with the swell and its color deepened to near black and spray blew off the whitecaps, to dart windward in the breeze. Weir heard the engines of *Lady of the Bay* groan louder and lower, saw the settling of her stern as the prop blades dug in.

'Becky! Get back up here!'

She nearly tipped over in the chopping motion of the little boat as she reached his hand and rode his yank all the way back to the bridge. He already was yelling out the only directions he could think of to make this thing work. 'Cut close, stay with her, then fall back. Don't press it – the swell is wicked.'

He jumped to the deck and crouched for balance against the fore hull, took the anchor in his right hand and payed out line with his left. Ahead, he could see *Lady of the Bay* hit the full chop of the sea, plowing through with a majestic nonchalance, losing not a bit of speed at all. Becky swung the *Sea Urchin* wide to port, aiming her with the swell, and with a surge of velocity bore down on a collision course for the yacht. The engine screamed when they hit the open-water swell; the bow left the water and the stern popped out and the prop cut nothing but air. They landed with a bone-crushing jolt that nearly sent Weir overboard. When he glanced up at Becky, she was hunkered down like a racer, hair streaking, a wholly fearless being. She brought *Sea Urchin* astern, then cut the throttle to nothing. The little boat pitched in the swell. She rose, swaying precariously as her momentum died and the wake of the yacht swept her up again. It was like being pushed skyward by some huge hand. Weir felt his knees bunch and tighten. At the apex of this rise, he threw the anchor aboard *Lady of the Bay*, yanked down to set the flukes, then, feeling *Sea Urchin* beginning her deep drop and praying the anchor had bitten into something solid, he jumped into the sky and started scrambling up the rope. It was like holding the tail of a sea monster. He felt the rock and surge of the ship above him, felt the wracking tug as she lifted over the swell and almost pulled his arms out at the shoulders. He banged hard against the stern, sucking in the billowing clouds of exhaust. Fist over fist he climbed, his body reeling, his boots sliding on the wet hull. Then he was high enough to see the polished teak gunwales.

347

He whapped hard against the stern again, rolling with the yaw, but finally got his hands around the railing. He waited for a nudge from the ocean, and just as the yacht pitched down into a trough, Weir pulled up and rode the momentum up over the gunwale and onto the gleaming deck of *Lady of the Bay*.

He hit hard, rolled, righted himself, and stood. Ray was waiting for him, ten feet away. The bore of his .357 looked big enough to crawl into. There was a spray of blood on his white tuxedo shirt.

Ray lowered the gun. 'God, it's good to see you,' he said. He looked past Jim toward *Sea Urchin*, waved to Becky, and gave her a thumbs-up. Jim turned, to see Becky falling back, rocking deeply in the swell. She looked up at them from the bridge.

Raymond slipped the gun into his waistband and regarded Jim with clear dark eyes. 'Don't worry – the prints on the rose weren't mine. That's what Robbins tried to tell you, isn't it?'

'That's what he said.'

Raymond sighed and shook his head. His shoulders slumped as he looked past Jim again, toward the shore. 'I never thought Robbins would throw in with them. I wonder how they got to him. I thought he was tougher than that.'

'Throw in with whom?'

'Dennison. Cantrell. Paris. They've been manipulating all this from the start. Or haven't you figured that out yet?'

Jim felt as if he'd jumped off a diving board, only to hang midair: Hope wouldn't let him fall; dread wouldn't let him rise. 'Your prints, Ray. Your prints – nobody else's.'

Raymond came across the deck to him, took both of Jim's arms in his hands, and shook him urgently. 'Be careful, Jim. You've got to understand, that's exactly what they want you to believe.'

The gun in Raymond's waistband was exposed, just a foot from Jim's unresisting hands.

'Go ahead and take that piece if you want it,' Raymond said. 'But *think*, Jim. Think first. Look what a perfect setup they've got now. Cantrell killed Annie, Dennison covered it up, they got their prime suspect to confess – then they offed him. It's perfect, except for two things – you and me. They knew no matter how tight a case they made against Goins, we'd never go for it. You told Brian as much, back in Robbins's office. So what do they do? They try to pit us, like fighting dogs. Go ahead, pull that gun out of your jacket and waste me. Or here, use mine. That's exactly what they want.'

Jim couldn't speak. The rushing sound in his ears suddenly quieted. In the silence that followed, he felt a deep, spacious calm settling over him. Everything was becoming clear.

'Don't believe me, Jim – I might not if I were you. Come ask Cantrell. Get it straight from the source.'

Ray turned and climbed the ladder up to the bridge.

Inside the cabin, Jim took it all in: the carpeted floor, the richly paneled walls, the instruments recessed in wood, the captain's and navigator's chairs, the compass showing a southerly course, the wheel self-correcting on autopilot, and C. David Cantrell sprawled against the fore wall still in his bathrobe, a widening patch of red on his right shoulder. His eyes locked on Jim's, wild and clear as a wounded animal's. His jaw was clenched in a silent grimace.

Raymond walked over and prodded him with his toe. 'Tell Jim what you told me five minutes ago, Davey. Don't leave out the part about the fingerprints and the rose.'

Cantrell's eyes darted from Jim to Raymond, then back to Jim again. 'I never . . . I never hurt her. Never.'

Raymond, hands on his hips, looked down at Cantrell. 'Never hurt her? Twenty-seven times with your kitchen knife didn't *hurt* her? Oh, *man*.'

Ray stepped away and turned, and before Jim could read the movement, Ray pulled out his revolver and blew away the top of Cantrell's good shoulder. A slab of muscle and flesh slapped against the bulkhead. Cantrell shrieked, dug his feet into the carpet, and pushed, as if trying to press himself into the crack between floor and wall.

Raymond watched him, then turned to Jim. 'He's playing to the new audience. Still thinks he can set one friend against another. Arrogance. Pure arrogance.'

Ray looked again at Cantrell, who raised a hand for protection and whispered, 'No.' Raymond blasted a hole through the beseeching palm. For an instant, Jim could see one of Cantrell's terrified eyes through the gaping wound.

'You ought to get in on this,' said Ray. 'He'll fold up and die soon. Come on – get some of that revenge we've been waiting for.'

'I'm ready,' said Jim.

'I'd think so.'

Jim, with surprising clarity of eye and heart, pulled the gun from his shoulder holster, stepped forward, gripped the handle tight, and

349

swung it in a quick, vicious arc straight into the side of Raymond Cruz's head. In the paralyzing moment that followed, Jim kicked away Ray's gun, then slammed him against the bulkhead once, twice, three times before pinning him against the wall. He jammed the .45 into Ray's neck. 'It's over, friend. You killed her and framed Cantrell. They were your prints, Ray – nobody else's.'

Raymond's head lolled and his eyes wouldn't focus. Weir slammed a left hook into his ribs, dragged him back up, and pinned him to the bulkhead. 'Robbins wouldn't lie if you paid him ten million dollars – you know it and I know it. Cantrell won't even lie to save his own life, and he knows it's the only chance he's got.'

Jim could see Raymond's focus blurring again. A terrible energy spread through him. He slammed Ray up against the bulkhead again, and drove the gun up under his jaw. 'Look at me, Ray. *Look at me!* Every time I played that scene in my mind – Annie down at the Back Bay – I knew there was something missing. Now I know what it was. She didn't fight, did she? You know why? Because it was you who took her down there. You were the one who walked her along that path. Annie could believe a lot of things, but the one thing she couldn't believe was that you'd hurt her. She'd have fought a kid like Goins, with that baby inside her. She'd have taken a piece of Cantrell with her. But she wouldn't fight you. You were the only one she could trust that much.'

Raymond's gaze swam toward focus now. 'I'd never betray that trust. No.'

Weir jammed Raymond hard against the wall again. 'You did more than betray it. You employed it. *You* took the batteries out of the controller so she couldn't use his garage that night. You changed into street clothes right in your car, met her with the flowers you knew Cantrell had sent her. You were wearing a pair of Cantrell's shoes. You'd already filled out your logs – making sure the times would cover midnight to one. So you begged her to get in the car – 'Just for a minute, Ann, I have to talk to you.' And she *trusted* you enough to get in.'

'No.'

'Yes. But she'd just been caught in someone else's bed, hadn't she? So she was scared. Too scared to realize you were giving Dispatch bogus fixes. Between the peninsula and the Back Bay, you had her trust back again. You had her right next to you on the path. No struggle at all. You had your arm around her.

350

What did you tell her, Ray? How'd you make everything seem okay?'

Raymond tried to break away, but Weir's grip was strong and the gun barrel was too hard against his jaw.

'*How?*'

'No.'

'*How!*'

Raymond's knee shot up toward Weir's groin, but Jim caught it on his own and threw a punch into Ray's sternum. He slumped and Weir let him go. Ray settled on his hands and knees and looked up at Weir with a ferocity that Jim had never seen in him. He didn't even look like himself. 'I just told her I'd known about Cantrell all along. And that I . . . forgave her. She was always a sucker for that word.'

The last leaf of doubt broke away and blew from Jim's mind, leaving nothing but a naked black branch. He felt like his heart was impaled on it. 'Aw, shit, Ray. Oh God. No. *No.*'

Raymond looked toward his gun. Jim kicked it to a corner. A hopeless low groan came from Cantrell's throat. Jim moved to the instrument panel, killed the autopilot, and pulled the throttle back to idle. Raymond slumped back against the wall and watched him the whole while, his face white and his mouth clenched. His eyes moved from Jim to the window to the floor as if looking for somewhere to hide.

'How long did you know about them, Ray?'

'I knew everything about her. She was my goddamned wife. For better or for worse – all that crap.'

'You broke into Cantrell's house twice – once to take the tie tack and a pair of his shoes, and write the letter to yourself on his equipment. Once later, to plant Ann's things.'

Raymond looked to Cantrell, then back to Jim. 'Three times, really. The first time, I just wanted to see the bed she'd been in.'

It took Weir a long while to ask his next question. In the quiet, all he could hear was Cantrell's shallow breathing, and the slosh of water on the big yacht's hull. 'You practiced, didn't you? You *practiced* using a knife with your right hand.'

Raymond looked away. 'That's right. I practiced a lot. There was a heavy bag in my garage. I took it to the dump when it got too many holes.'

Jim followed Raymond's stare out the window to the somber

spring clouds. 'She believed in you, Ray. And you fucking snuffed her out like a dog. I'd blow your sorry brains out if it would do any good.'

Raymond looked at him with a vacant expression. 'Go ahead. I'm ready.'

But Weir couldn't do it; he couldn't even come close. This was too vast a thing to end now. There was so much of it he couldn't understand. 'Why, Ray? It was Annie. *Why?*'

'I explained it all in that letter to myself. I wrote it to ID Cantrell's printer, but I also wrote to try to . . . clarify.'

The twisted sentiments of Mr Night came back to Jim, this time in Raymond's voice. *Then I saw it on her face, finally, the surrender, the helplessness, and absolute dependence on me she never had before. If only for a moment!*

'Surrender? Dependence? What shit is that? She was your woman. You had a life.'

An expression of genuine bewilderment came to Raymond's face. 'It's like something laid an egg in my head, and it grew, Jim. I wanted to tell you so bad. I wanted you to take me out, once and for all. I wanted to keep on going when we were underwater – just never come back. You knew I wanted to end it, but you didn't know why.'

Raymond turned Cantrell's chin with a finger. 'Still ticking, isn't he?'

'Take off your shirt and plug him up.'

'Let him die.'

'Do it, Ray.'

Raymond worked off his bloody shirt, tore off some pieces, and jammed them into Cantrell's wounds. Cantrell bellowed, arched, then fainted.

'This guy ruined my life,' said Ray. 'Now I'm trying to save his. I knew from the beginning about them. Ann's looks. Later, the clothes coming back from the cleaners that she hadn't worn for me. The little come-ons when she tried to make me look like the father I knew I wasn't. That stupid little boat and journal of hers. I tapped my own phone to get their pattern down, then took off the bug and chucked it in the bay the day I killed her. I kept wondering if a dead fish would wash up with it wrapped around its head.' Raymond looked straight at Jim for a second, then away. 'Ann always thought just because she hid things from herself that

352

she hid them from me, too. For all her cheating and sneaking, she really wasn't careful. That first night – it was March twenty-third – I could smell him on her when I got home. She'd showered but it didn't matter. I could always tell because she'd be showered and still have that smell. The baby was the last straw, Jim. It wasn't mine – it was his. You know how bad that made me feel?'

'Made *you* feel?'

Ray beheld him for a long moment. There was a dullness coming into his eyes now, as if clarity and purpose were draining out as fast as Cantrell's blood. 'Yes. Me. I just couldn't believe she'd do that to me.'

'So you killed her. God Ray – it was *Ann!*'

Raymond shook his head slowly. He looked out the window, then toward Jim, but Weir could see that his gaze traveled far past himself, all the way to some destination that Jim could neither identify nor imagine.

'There are certain things a man can't put up with in this life,' Ray said. 'You can't borrow his wife, use her, then hand her back with your kid inside. I tried to take it, but I couldn't. The more it ate at me, the more I needed to see some justice done. You won't understand this, but to me, Ann was proof that I was good. When I had her, I believed that. She was my badge, my . . . validation. When she betrayed me, I fell apart.'

Jim could hardly keep a rein on his charging thoughts. 'You were always good enough, Ray. You were the only one who didn't think so.'

'I don't know. It's something you either have inside or you don't.'

'I stood up for you when you married my only sister. I stuck up for you anytime you needed it. You never had to prove anything to me. You're right – I don't understand.'

Raymond looked again at Cantrell, then he worked himself up to his hands and knees. He stood slowly, eyes fastened on Jim. 'You don't understand because you've never let yourself go. You always wash around in the middle. Ask Becky. We've had enough talks about the way you drift. You're a good, strong, decent guy – but you're afraid to go all the way. I was never like that. One thing you can say about me, Jim, is I've always been willing to go all the way. Want to hear something strange? When I found out she was carrying this asshole's child, was going to try to fool me, I felt like

353

everything I'd believed in was a lie. I sat there with her journal in my hands, crying like a baby. And God, I was furious. I didn't believe in Ann anymore; I didn't believe in the God I'd been praying to for thirty years. I didn't believe in me or my job, or the law, or anything at all. I realized I was still living my life according to all the things that had failed me. I felt like a fool. Then, after I killed her, they all came rushing back. That's why I stabbed her so many times – I could feel the old beliefs coming back. So I just flailed away, trying to make them disappear again. But it didn't do any good. After she was dead, everything was back in place. Just like before. I missed her and I hated myself. I believed in God again and knew he was going to waste me. It took killing Ann to get my faith back – not that I really care about my soul anymore. I came *that* close to telling you, Jim, that night we went down the wall. I'm sorry. But I'm not sentimental enough to think I can change anything by saying so. I'm prepared to carry this through. I always have been.'

Ray looked down at Cantrell once again. 'Pull that trigger if you want, but I'm going out on deck so I can breathe.'

He walked past Jim and out to the bridge deck. Jim followed him three steps back, the gun still in his hand. They were five or six miles offshore, ten miles south of Newport, Jim guessed. The swell was still high. *Sea Urchin* bobbed a quarter mile out. He could see the speck of Becky on the bridge.

Raymond looked back toward shore, then turned to Jim. 'Ann got knocked up by Cantrell when she was fifteen. I didn't know that until I read her journal. That trip to France? She never went to France. She went to upstate New York and had a dead baby. Told me later the scar was an appendectomy, and I believed her. Here we are twenty-four years later and she gets pregnant by him again. You wouldn't believe how bad we wanted that for ourselves. What am I supposed to think? I'll tell you what I came up with. I think God is a sour old bastard who plays tricks on us for his own entertainment.'

'How did you get to Goins?'

'No. I think Cantrell set that all up. Don't ask me how he found Goins when a whole police department couldn't. Don't ask me how he got him to write that note, then jump in a pool of boiling silver. Maybe someone convinced Goins he really did do it. Guy's a nut.'

Raymond looked down for a long while, then back toward shore.

354

Past his head, Jim could see the pale bluffs of Dana Point, the brooding spring sky. Two sea gulls hovered overhead, treading air without effort. To the north, Newport was nothing but an approximation, a gray idea somewhere at the edge of the land.

Ray dabbed at the drying blood on his head. 'We had some good times, didn't we?'

Jim didn't answer.

'I wish it could have ended better. What are you going to do?'

'What kind of choice do you leave me, Ray? I either use this gun in my hand to blow away my best friend, or I drag you back to rot in jail.'

Raymond ran his hand over the polished railing. 'I got to thinking lately about Francisco. I think his wife had a thing for Joaquin. That's why his men turned around at the last minute. They were on her side.'

'Maybe.'

Raymond ran his hand over his bare arms and shivered. 'Cold out here with no shirt on. What do you guess for water temp?'

'Low sixties.'

'How long would I last?'

'Two hours maybe. Half the time it would take you to make shore.'

'No chance at all?'

'None at all.'

'Let me take it?'

Weir looked at him. There was an odd little smile on Ray's face, the same expression he'd get when he brought a suspect out in handcuffs.

'We still friends, Jim?'

The idea hit Jim that the constants in life were the things you made for yourself. Everything else was just degrees of uncertainty. Faith bridges the gaps, but the gaps remain.

Raymond was smiling again now, a broader, less fettered smile.

A long minute passed as neither man spoke. Jim looked out at *Sea Urchin*, up to the gray moving clouds, back along the miniature coast to Newport. The big yacht swayed gently in the swell, and the minor sunlight brought warmth to her wood and decking. He was profoundly tired.

For a moment, he saw on Raymond's face an expression of absolute, unalloyed grief. In some strange way, it was what Jim had been wanting to see. Ray took a deep breath, and swallowed hard. 'Thanks.'

With that, he climbed onto the gunwale and jumped over.

Jim waited a moment, then went to the railing and looked down. Ray, true to Jim's prediction, had set off west, away from shore. His strokes were fast and short and the chop slapped hard against him. It was hard to tell how rough the sea was until a man was in it, trying to survive. It was an awful sight.

Jim watched for a long while. The swell kept Raymond pretty much in place, pulling him north a little and east a little, in spite of his determination to go the other way. Weir went back in and checked Cantrell. Shock had slowed his bleeding and his breath. Jim tore some fresh strips from Ray's shirt, did what he could with them, then wrapped two blankets around the man. He swung *Lady of the Bay* to starboard and brought her up along Raymond, then went back out on the bridge deck. Ray was on his back now, trying to conserve energy, his strokes already slowing. The sea was too rough to last in, too cold, too big. Becky had moved *Sea Urchin* on the other side of Raymond, and she looked to Jim with an uncomprehending expression. Jim signaled for her to stay in place.

Looking down at Raymond's struggle, Jim saw him instead at the age of sixteen, waiting for Ann to come downstairs for the prom. Oh, what a light in that boy's face.

Jim could see him standing beside Ann, facing the priest before them, saying 'I do.' Such conviction there, such belief.

Jim could see his skinny brown body riding the waves at Fifteenth Street; scurrying around the Eight Peso looking for dropped change; climbing into a fighting chair on one of Poon's charter boats, begging to go along for the day. What hunger, what life and promise.

When he couldn't take it any longer, he got out a life preserver and tossed it over. Ray took it and hung on, breathing hard. Becky pulled *Sea Urchin* up close, but Raymond just lay there, back heaving, looking up at Jim. Weir pulled the rope ladder from a deck well, hooked one end over the railing, and threw the rest down. It unfurled in the breeze and splashed down next to the ship.

Raymond was still looking up. 'Next time,' he said. Weir could hardly hear the words.

Then Raymond took a deep breath and dove under, vanishing immediately in the gray water. Five minutes later – minutes during which Jim understood not a single thing on earth except the passage of time itself – Raymond rose, back first, escorted by a scintillant halo of bubbles that broke on the surface and then disappeared, as if their duty had been completed.

Weir eased the ship closer, lowered a lifeboat, climbed down the ladder, and got Raymond into it.

Becky watched from the near-distance. Then she tied up to *Lady of the Bay* and spent the trip back trying to talk Dave Cantrell into not dying.

The Coast Guard cutter *Point Divide*, summoned by Becky, found them two miles from the harbor. They got Cantrell onto a stretcher and took him aboard. Nobody seemed sure what to do about Raymond except for Jim, who said he'd take Ray back to port.

33

It was evening by the time that Jim got back to the big house. Virginia was still gone. He showered, ignored the reporters on the phone, and walked down to Becky's.

Becky was wrapping up a phone interview when Jim walked in. She told the reporter that what had happened was far larger than the games of politics, that C. David Cantrell was a man who had suffered at the hands of someone enraged by disillusion and betrayal. She looked at Jim as she hung up. 'Enough,' she said. 'Let's go.'

They took *Sea Urchin* out into the harbor and anchored her on the lee side of Balboa Island. The breeze was strong enough to send the smell of the dead ocean past them. Becky had packed a dinner: good bread, a bottle of wine, cold steak for sandwiches, and some oranges. They sat on the deck and ate as the sun went down, finishing off the wine quickly. When the wind turned cool, they went belowdecks and squeezed into the little berth together. Jim dreamed that he was underwater and his eyes were closed forever, and no matter how hard he tried to open them, he couldn't. A big anchor was chained to his feet, and he wasn't struggling now, but simply descending with it, surrendered, giving himself over to a downward motion that promised nothing but its own irresistible velocity and the possibility that he might find someone he was looking for in this universe of water. It was nine o'clock before he woke up again. Becky was brushing the hair back from his sweating forehead, looking down on him in the near-darkness of the berth.

They watched the news in the big house. The local segments were all on Cantrell and Raymond: the DA's office had already acknowledged that the well-known developer was 'involved' with Lt Cruz's wife, Ann, and that the whole thing was possibly a 'love triangle that ended in tragedy.' The reports were little more than abject confusion and speculation. Weir was referred to as the 'grieving brother' of the dead woman. No one could explain the suicide of Horton Goins or the note he had left behind. Becky, her black dress still caked with the vermilion of Cantrell's blood, pushed her hand toward a camera and walked away saying, 'No comment.' Brian Dennison's glum face appeared next, saying that a full investigation was under way, focusing on Lt Cruz's activities of the last month. He announced with an almost-sullen reluctance that the suicide of Horton Goins was now being 'fully reevaluated. There are a lot things we still don't know.' Dennison looked like a man at the end of all conceivable tethers, but without the energy to care anymore. A spokeswoman for Hoag Hospital said that Cantrell was in intensive care but was expected to live.

An unrelated item from Newport Beach came in at quarter to ten: A man had been killed on the Back Bay at eight-thirty when his boat exploded on the water. Preliminary investigations indicated a fuel leak and an errant cigarette. Identity being withheld pending notification of relatives.

Jim heard the front door open, Virginia's voice, then footsteps in the entryway.

'Oh my God,' said Becky.

Jim turned. Virginia stepped into the living room, Joseph Goins beside her.

Weir stood and stared at the young man, who glanced only briefly back at Jim. Goins looked to him like a man who had long ago adjusted to the reduced dimensions of confinement. His eyes lowered and darted measuringly to either side; he put his weight on one leg, then smoothly shifted it to another; he seemed to be immediately aware of the objects around him and their distance from him. He struck Jim as less a presence than a kind of absence – receding as he stood there, threatening to vanish. He emoted an almost-palpable apartness, a discomfort in just being. His privacy, his remoteness, seemed huge. He held a small backpack in his right hand.

'Jim, Becky,' said Virginia. 'I'd like you to meet Joseph. He's going to talk to the DA tomorrow, get all this straightened out. After that, I don't know.'

She came to Jim, wrapped her arms around him, and hugged him longer and more tenderly than he could remember her ever doing

before in his life. 'It's going to be all right,' she whispered. 'It's
going to be okay.'

'Where have you been?'

'Sit down. Listen.'

Over the next hour, Virginia told of Ann's early pregnancy by
college-boy Cantrell, Virginia's belief that Annie – age fifteen –
would best be served by believing her child was stillborn rather than
alive, that Ann would never know what gender it was, that the boy
be placed far across the country, that Ann be forever encouraged to
forget the whole minor, ancient incident. Virginia had attended the
delivery, to make sure her deceptions were convincingly created. It
was only, Virginia said, when Jim showed her the photo of Horton
that her imagination was fueled, thus her visitations to Emmett
and Edith; the law firm in Los Angeles that had handled Joseph's
adoption; Lucy in Hardin County, who led her to Joseph's original
'family,' still operating the farm outside Dayton; and finally to a
big widow named Kate Hanf, who told her of the conversation she
had had with a California lawyer in an upstate New York hospital,
where he had said to her late on a September evening long ago the
simple words that Ann herself waited a lifetime and never heard:
You have a son.

Weir listened, speechless. He felt new and uncomprehending, as
if just born into a world that had been here for aeons, building up
secret upon secret, truth upon truth, without him.

Ann had a son.

When she was finished, she looked at Jim, then away. The
shadows of the room seemed to gather in the lines of her brow,
along the downturn of her mouth. It was the first time in his life
that he had ever seen Virginia register the emotion of shame. It
was also the first time she had ever looked at Jim with the need
for approval.

He thought for a long moment before speaking. 'You must get
tired sometimes, Mom, of trying to run the world.'

'I never meant to –'

'Nobody ever *means* to.'

'There was no other way to make things come out right.'

Jim shot a look at her and held it, but Virginia had already
turned away.

'As if,' she said quietly, 'this is right. God.'

'You should have said something. If I'd have known about Annie and Cantrell, maybe I could have kept it from going down this way. You should have just come out with it instead of sitting on everything.'

'I was trying to protect her from what people would think.'

'You were trying to protect yourself from what people would think.'

'Jim —'

Just admit it. That's the least you can do.'

Virginia's gnarled hands spread and closed upon her legs, looking for something to hold besides each other. 'Yes,' she said quietly. 'But also, I believed I was doing right. I consider the whole chapter the most . . . the great shame of my life. When I took away Ann's son, I had no idea I was taking away the only child she'd ever have, the only thing that might have prevented all this from happening. I thought it was best. I truly believed it was the right thing to do.'

In the quiet that followed, Jim listened to his mother's hesitant breathing, to the water lapping outside, to the steady, slow throbbing of his own heart.

Joseph, staring at his feet, then told about his correspondence courses in genealogy — taken while an inmate at the state hospital — his growing curiosities about his own beginnings, his fateful glance at his hospital file one afternoon while a disturbance took all the orderlies away for a few minutes, his final confirmation of what he had suspected all along — that he had never seen his actual parents. Then his burglary of the Los Angeles law offices referred to in his file, and later, his hours with library microfiche, finding out all he could about Virginia Weir and Blake Cantrell of Newport Beach — whose signatures were indelibly fixed in his mind from the law firm's adoption records of 1967. Joseph's voice changed as he told about first seeing Ann, playing with the toddlers at work. A strange urgency came into it, an edge that suggested unresolvable intensities. 'I'm still not sure why,' Joseph said. 'But I couldn't go up to her. I wasn't sure what to say, if she'd believe me, or if I might be doing something to hurt her by telling her who I was. So I followed her and watched her and took pictures. I talked to her only once. I asked her what time it was. She said quarter 'til ten. That was all we got to say to each other in twenty-four years. "What time is it?" "Quarter 'til ten." I was so nervous, I could feel my feet sweating in

361

my shoes. The next thing I knew, she was dead.' Joseph clutched the top of his backpack and looked down at his hands. He turned up his palms and looked at those, too. He said that there was something about the way she died that he 'understood.' It took him a few days to try to see his father. But Cantrell wasn't available by phone; his security guards wouldn't even let Joseph onto the floor where his offices were; and he had so many homes in the south county that Joseph could never figure out in which one he really lived. So he wrote the letter on Mrs Fostes's word processor and proposed the meeting in the cemetery.

Joseph said that Cantrell had showed up as planned, and offered him sanctuary in a big home overlooking the water in Laguna. A man named Dale was assigned to help him get what he needed, but Joseph had quickly surmised that Dale was more his keeper than his butler. 'Today about ten in the morning,' he said, 'Dale showed up without . . . without my father and said that he was arranging for me to see my grandmother – Virginia.'

Virginia leaned forward on the sofa. 'When I'd confirmed what I suspected about Joseph, it wasn't hard to figure he'd be in contact with Cantrell. David denied it, but I traced Joseph to one of his houses. But by the time I got there, Cantrell was gone and Blodgett wasn't exactly going to hand Joseph over,' she said. 'The situation was that Blodgett knew the toxic-spill investigation would lead to him sooner or later – Becky's press conference told him as much. He came right out and told me that he and Louis Braga were dumping in the ocean. I was to prevail upon Becky to drop that angle, and give Blodgett fifty thousand dollars in cash to bring Joseph to me. Otherwise, he'd kill him.' She shook her head at Blodgett's apparent stupidity.

'Well, what did you do?' asked Jim.

Virginia looked at him, then at Joseph, then back to Jim. 'I agreed to everything, left, and told Blodgett I had put the money out on one of the light beacons at the end of the jetty, so to hand over my grandson and I'd tell him which one. He said he didn't believe me, which is just what I thought he'd say. He took me along for the ride, which is just what I thought he'd do. Joseph was on the boat, too, of course – Blodgett guessed the cops would be all over Cantrell's properties sooner than later. Out in the middle of the bay, there was this accident that involved a gaff and the back of Dale Blodgett's idiot head. Later, some matches got mixed up with

362

the fuel. Joseph and I were lucky to get overboard and swim back to my car. We ditched our life jackets and sat with Mackie Ruff in his little ghetto while the police buzzed and the Harbor Patrol put out the fire. Mackie had some blankets and rum and a fire to dry our clothes. Mackie said he was a reserve cop now. By the time it was over, we just kind of drove away. That's the only time I'll tell that story – I'll never tell it again. I will answer no questions, entertain no discussion. It had to be done and I will talk about it no further. Joseph has the definitive version.'

Joseph studied his hands again, then turned his clear blue eyes to Jim. 'Your mother and I were . . . reunited by Mr Blodgett, down at the dock. He went to go get the money and his boat blew up. We swam out to help if we could – but we couldn't find him.'

'You forgot something,' said Virginia, in much the same tone with which she had drilled Jim on multiplication tables when he was ten.

'Later,' he said, 'we took a rental boat out of the Locker and got the money off the beacon.'

Jim had to admit it was a pretty tidy package. With all the other action for Dennison to cover, the whereabouts of Virginia Weir would be far down on the list. When Marge sang to the grand jury, Braga would be the only one left standing to take the fall – or, would he?

'So Blodgett was doing the dumping all along?'

'He was proud of it. It's been going on for years – way before he volunteered to be the one-man Toxic Waste patrol. He'd been doing 'personal security' work for Cantrell off and on for a decade. Cantrell was using plenty of TCE to paint all his new condos and houses. He was using Cheverton money to pay Blodgett and Braga to handle the disposal. That was just to keep PacifiCo out of the loop, in case someone like Becky or I wanted to make something of it – Cantrell could just say he handled his own waste. It was supposed to be by the book – permits and licenses, a thousand each for Dale and Braga to transport it to a Long Beach company every other month for disposal. Well, Dale and Braga just split the seven thousand that was supposed to go to the Long Beach people, and dumped the stuff ten miles out instead of transporting it to Long Beach. Everything was fine until Annie and I started finding trace. Things got bad when *Duty Free* threw a rod in the harbor and they either had to jettison the solvent or take it back to Cheverton. They panicked and dumped it.'

Weir tried to figure. 'Who were they scared of? If Blodgett was the Toxic Waste patrol, who was left to watch him?'

'Cantrell,' said Virginia. 'Annie had seen them loading drums at Cheverton, and she must have told him. Cantrell thought everything was legal. He never knew until Ann found out, then he landed on Blodgett and Braga.'

'Why did Blodgett tell you all this?'

'Because he was going to kill us after he got the money,' said Joseph. He looked down, blushing, and clasped his hands together. In a quiet voice, he added, 'I could tell by the way he was moving.'

'What about Dennison?' asked Becky. 'Can we sink him?'

'He didn't know what Blodgett was up to, either. He was too busy rising to the top to worry about what all his men were doing. And of course Dale was bringing him whatever Brian could use about what we were doing politically – and in the bay. When Dale told you he'd seen *Sea Urchin* that night, he'd already told Dennison, too. That's why Brian was so worried. He thought *we* were dumping to make a campaign issue out of it, but he couldn't prove it. I don't see how he can save his public face now – with one of his men confessed to murder and the other dumping toxins into the bay. By the time the press gets done with cover-up speculations and Marge Buzzard talks to the grand jury, Dennison will be finished. He knows that. I think he'll withdraw. Congratulations, Mayor Flynn.'

Becky sighed, shook her head, and sat back.

Virginia asked about Raymond. She had already pieced most of it together herself from what Cantrell and Joseph had told her. 'He listened to her phone calls, and read her mail and journal. The baby wasn't his, and he knew it,' said Jim.

Joseph looked down at the floor. Again, the great yawning absence of Ann had visited them – Ann, the very center of all this – Ann, departed like a guest of honor summoned to a more important engagement.

'What about your . . . suicide?' Becky asked.

Joseph explained that Cantrell's plan was to stage the suicide, close the case, let him disappear, and live with the fact that Ann's killer would remain free.

Weir couldn't figure it, until he remembered the old woman who'd spotted Joseph's car down by the Back Bay the night she

364

couldn't sleep. 'You knew it was Raymond, all along. You followed them down there that night. You'd been waiting around Cantrell's to see her, the same way Raymond was waiting to get her into the patrol car.'

For a moment, Joseph's eyes traced a pattern in the air, as if tracking an invisible fly. He looked down, pressed his fingers against his temples, then addressed his feet. 'I didn't think I could go to the police and tell them what I knew. And, well . . . the next day, when I read that Ann had died – I couldn't really remember what I'd done after I left the Back Bay. I . . . sometimes things aren't clear. I thought I should talk to Mr Can . . . well, my father.'

And, as Jim foresaw even as Joseph told it, Cantrell had been unwilling to go to the police for the scandal his affair with Ann would cause – not to mention his fatherhood of an illegitimate child, a committed sex offender. Cantrell's star witness was the one he couldn't call. Weir could hardly believe, though, that Cantrell was desperate enough to kill one young man and try to pass his body off as that of Horton Goins.

'No,' said Joseph. 'Dale arranged the body. He was a transient from a county morgue out in some desert town. No family, or friends. He was my size. Mr Cantrell – I mean, my father – said that we could depend on Chief Dennison to influence the coroner's findings. The handwriting was mine. I wrote the confession and signed it. I meant it, but not the way it was taken.'

Weir asked Joseph what was going to happen to him once he was officially dead.

'Montana,' said Joseph. 'He has property there, where I could start over with a new name and be a different person. I agreed to confess to Ann – it was my father I was saving from suspicion. And the more I thought about a new life as someone else, the better it sounded. He was going to come visit often. We were going to fish and hunt and ride horses. I think he likes me.'

Jim let the statement sink in, fully realizing for the first time that this young man in front of him had come two thousand miles, only to lose the mother he had never known. The strange part was that Joseph's expression now told him without question that he had been through things even more terrible than this.

Joseph looked at him directly. His eyes were windows to inner landscapes of immeasurable damage. Turning away, he seemed to know this.

Virginia stood and began unbuttoning her windbreaker. The shadows still hadn't left her face. 'My silence has been a lie. But I believed – I always believed – I was doing right.'

'Is that an apology or an excuse?' Jim asked.

'Both, son.'

'If you were a little weaker, you'd be pathetic.'

'What am I now?'

'Relentless. That's all I see.'

She looked at him, then turned and climbed the stairs.

Weir lay on his bed. Becky had gone home, saying she felt spent and unclean. Jim wondered again as he lay there whether Becky's statement had more to do with the blood on her hands earlier that day or the crushed expression on her face at the Wrecking Ball as she'd learned that George Percy was refusing to move forward against Cantrell. It was an expression confessing to Jim that she had offered more of herself to sway Percy than she could forgive, an expression that told him she had been bought for promises, then sold an hour or two later for nearly nothing. Becky, true to her spirit, had tried to dance it all away.

It was still before midnight. Jim could see a faint light coming from Ann's old room, where Joseph was supposed to be sleeping. He rose from the bed, went to Joseph's door, and knocked.

Joseph said to come in.

Weir stepped inside and shut the door quietly. Joseph was sitting in bed, fully clothed, with a leather-bound journal open on his lap. He was examining his fingers, which in the lamplight looked, to Jim, unremarkable. His electronic pillbox was on the nightstand beside him. His eyes shifted down, left, then right, as if Weir were a blinding light. He raised his knees. 'I'm not dangerous,' he said. It was almost a whisper.

'I wanted to look at you.'

Joseph colored deeply, still looking down. He waited. Jim had the feeling that Joseph was used to waiting.

'Is that her journal?'

He nodded, glanced quickly at Jim, then down again. 'I took it from her boat. I watched her rowing out there some nights when she came home from work. She wrote by candlelight. It was a beautiful light.'

Weir still hadn't seen what he was looking for. 'Read me something,' he said.

Joseph colored again, a tiny smile brushing across his face. 'There's a part in here that makes me feel better when I read it. It isn't for me, but I take it that way. It's the last thing she wrote.'

'Read it to me.'

Joseph gathered himself, centered the book before him, and quietly cleared his throat. 'May fifteenth,' he said. 'The night she died.

'"I have felt a sudden calmness come over me, maybe it's the eye of the tornado passing over. In these last few hours I've been sitting here on my boat, in my room, surrounded by the things that please me, and I've gotten a look down on myself from above, like God might have if he was watching. I love this time, these early evenings after Ray is gone and I have a few hours before work. And what I see is a life spent in earnest, in the relatively honest pursuit of what is good and fair and loving. I've made my mistakes. But when I look down on myself, I don't see a tangled web of betrayal and tragic surprise; I don't see a distant husband, a lover to whom I know I must say goodbye; I don't see a crazy, mixed-up woman huddled on an old boat out in the middle of some unimportant little harbor on the edge of the land. What I see is someone who gave love her best shot, who accepted what cards she was dealt without bitterness or envy, who always tried to keep an eye out for the reality of the world around her and not just on the little whirling storm she called her life. I see someone deserving of forgiveness. At any rate, I am settled."'

It was then that Weir saw just a hint of it, in Joseph's jawline – the form and shadow of Ann.

'"Tonight I am going to say my formal goodbye to David Cantrell, a man to whom I've been drawn, irresistibly, since I was little more than a girl. Now I see there was a reason for that – the reason is what I carry inside me. I believe in destiny. David begged me to come by one last time, and I will. I know it is not a goodbye in any final sense. He is your father, Dear One, and to him I will be forever connected, forever indebted. Have we loved? Yes. You were conceived in love. So will I crawl back to Raymond like a dog, curling and repentent? Never. I will walk on my own two feet back to him, one in front of the other, with my head held not high but level, and my eyes open to all the things that my life with him has given me, and all the things to come. I have a script to follow now, a deception to complete. Maybe it won't work. Maybe my child won't have enough of David Cantrell's dark good looks, and Raymond will leave me when he realizes the truth. Then again, maybe he'll see me in our child and that will be enough. But I will return to Raymond in spirit and body, offer myself to him again as a woman and a friend and a wife and a mother. What else can I do? I hope that I can find him again, waiting for me at the end of the great distance he has gone."'

As Joseph read, Weir stared at him in the lamplight. Joseph's downturned eyes looked like Ann's, too – the hint of sadness in them. If Jim let his eyes unfocus and his eyelids droop just a little, Joseph's fine blond hair became Ann's; Joseph's thin neck and broad shoulders became Ann's; Joseph's strong nose became Ann's. Even his voice had something of hers in it: a smoothness that comes from imposing a calm on oneself that isn't there to begin with. It was the calm of mind over the contending spirits of the heart. Ann could summon that calm; Joseph received it from a bottle.

'"Last night I had a dream. In the dream, I left David's house for the last time and Raymond was waiting on the street for me. He was dressed nicely and he had a bouquet of purple roses in his hand – just like the ones that David sent me. He said he forgave me and wanted me to know he loved me. He took my hand in his and we drove in his police car – how strange dreams are! – down to the Back Bay where David and I had been, and there he held me tight and kissed me gently and I could feel from the trembling in his arms how much he wanted me, how strong his love was. And in the dream I had a great surge of feeling – a feeling that was still with me when I woke up and is still with me now – that everything will be forgiven, that everything will turn out for the better, that all the pain of what has gone on was only there to make the joy of our new life all the stronger. He told me he forgave me. That word, it rang so beautifully in the dream, it seemed to come not just from Raymond but from the sky above, the water lapping at the shore around our feet, the wild tobacco plant that grew beside us. If I could pass along just one thing to my Dear One, it would be the capacity to forgive. I don't believe that life can go on without that.

But I realized in my dream that that word was waiting for something to complete it, that it was still not fully born yet – just like my child is not – that it needed something. It needed *me*. And I said it, first in my mind, then to myself, then to Raymond. I said I offer you my forgiveness, too. Please, my man, accept it. That, Dear One, is the word that I will live by. It will be my light . . ."'

When Weir, lost to inner visions, looked up at Joseph again, he realized that the boy was no longer reading, but reciting from memory. Joseph's eyes were closed tight, as if trying to keep certain things inside him and other things out. Jim let his focus fade, willing now to let Joseph speak for Ann, to let Ann speak through Joseph, to let Joseph be what Ann had intended him to be: her living flesh and blood, her most precious gift to the world.

'"From this moment on, I told myself in the dream, I will muster everything I can – forever and until I die – of sweet forgiveness. You must do that, too, Dear One, if only for me. You will never read this, never know these things. But I wonder, will you forgive me? And as I watched in the dream, Raymond reached into the pocket of his coat and removed something that he held in his hand for a moment before raising it up to my face. I stood there with my hands at my side, so ready for his touch, his blessing. He dabbed my eyes with his handkerchief, and then his own, then put it back in his pocket. And all the while that word still hovered around us in the night, hushed as a sigh from heaven.

'"*Forgiveness*."'

Jim knocked, then let himself into Virginia's room. She was sitting at her vanity, staring straight ahead into the mirror. She was in her robe and her yellow hair was unknotted and hung past her shoulders. She looked ancient. Jim saw her eyes move to his reflection.

'Are you okay?' he asked.

'Yes. Does that matter to you?'

'Sure it does.' He stood there for a moment, then went to the bed and sat. Her eyes followed him across the glass. He looked around the room, unchanged since the departure of Poon a decade ago. Ann's words rang in his head, but it took him a long time to speak. 'If it matters, I forgive you,' he said.

'Why?'

'It's the best thing I've got left.'

Virginia stared at him in the mirror. 'I will not accept that forgiveness in this house. I will not permit it.'

'It needed to be said.'

'What good do the words do?'

'Maybe they help. Maybe there's nowhere else to start. Maybe they're just for me.'

'Then you have to live without them, Jim. I choose to.'

Weir stood, then sat back down. Virginia's gaze followed him in the glass. 'How'd you get so hard, Mom? Did something happen . . . I mean, was it Jake, or Dad, or . . . what?'

She looked down at her hands, then back into the mirror at Jim. 'Twenty-four years ago, I looked at myself in this same mirror and I decided then that I would never forgive myself. This is my version of honor. It wasn't long after I'd given up my daughter's only child for adoption, after telling her it had been stillborn. Time doesn't diminish a thing like that – it only compounds it.'

'There must be a better way to live a life.'

She continued to stare at him. 'Do you know what Poon said to me when we found out Annie was pregnant and it was too late for an abortion? He said he thought that David and Ann should just get married like they wanted to. Or have the child and get married later. Or give them *Sweetheart Deal* and let all three of them sail around the world and be young and stupid together. "It doesn't matter what people think," he told me. "I know a lot of people," he said, "and there's not one whose opinion I care enough about to give a shit what they think. Fuck 'em all if they can't take a joke," he said – that was your dad's creed.'

Jim smiled to himself. Poon had had a way of getting to the nub of things. At heart, he was an outlaw. Does a man ever get over missing his father? 'I don't suppose that flew with Blake Cantrell very well.'

Virginia held his stare in the mirror. When she spoke next, her voice was taut with anger. 'Blake Cantrell said the same thing. So did his wife.'

Jim tried to figure it but couldn't. 'Why couldn't you just let it happen?'

'Because a person has convictions. They're there and you can't move them. Deep in my heart, I believed that it was wrong, that what he had done to Annie was wrong. I believed that no Cantrell was good enough for a Weir – especially not my only daughter. They were rich, corrupt people. I believed it was my duty to protect Annie above all else. I would have done anything for her. I would have gladly laid down my life. So I prevailed. I have always prevailed.'

Jim sat for a long while, watching the minutes march by on the digital bed-stand clock. Each one was portrayed in isolation: no future, no past, only the present. That is a lie, he thought – that is not the way time moves. Just look at her.

Slowly, Jim began to realize why his mother could never accept anybody's absolution. It was only partially to do with taking her daughter's baby and giving it away. That was something she had done according to the imperatives inside her. Rather, it had more to do with what Virginia herself understood about those imperatives. Virginia had known she was wrong. Even while she was making the arrangements in New York, she had known she was wrong. She had sacrificed her daughter's happiness – in the end, perhaps, her life – to principles she knew were less important than the needs of love and the living. To accept forgiveness – even her own – would be an admission she could never make, at least not with words. Instead, largely by her own design, she would acknowledge her guilt every day for the rest of her life in the eternally wounded form of Joseph Weir – a declaration without sound, the ultimate Weir confession.

Jim stood. 'I love you, Mom.'

'I can honestly say that I love you, too. More than you will ever know. And I'll try with all my might to learn to love him, too – Joseph. For Annie. But I won't accept your forgiveness. Don't ask me to do that. Give it to someone who deserves it.'

Weir turned off the light in his room and went downstairs. He stole quietly through the front door, locking it behind him.

The night was clear and the stars looked as if they were just a few inches above the rooftops. The bay was a black dance floor upon which the ferries waltzed and the houselights jitterbugged without sound. There was still, in all of this, the power to move him.

His stride lengthened on the sidewalk. At Becky's he stopped outside the hedge and peered toward the house. No lights were on. He went through the gate and shut it gently behind him, but the little brass bell chimed anyway, betraying Jim's presence in spite of himself. For a moment, he stood there, adopted by the oleander, a shadow part of larger shadows. My silence has been a lie. Jim yanked the bell string twice, hard, sending a pure and truthful sound into the night. Then his heart was beating fast and he was taking the stepping-stones across Becky's yard two at a time. The porch light came on and the screen door was opening.